THE
Velvet Rope
DIARIES

THE
Velvet Rope
DIARIES

DANIELLA BRODSKY

BERKLEY BOOKS, NEW YORK

THE BERKLEY PUBLISHING GROUP
Published by the Penguin Group
Penguin Group (USA) Inc.
375 Hudson Street, New York, New York 10014, USA

Penguin Group (Canada), 90 Eglinton Avenue East, Suite 700, Toronto, Ontario M4P 2Y3, Canada
(a division of Pearson Penguin Canada Inc.)
Penguin Books Ltd., 80 Strand, London WC2R 0RL, England
Penguin Group Ireland, 25 St. Stephen's Green, Dublin 2, Ireland (a division of Penguin Books Ltd.)
Penguin Group (Australia), 250 Camberwell Road, Camberwell, Victoria 3124, Australia
(a division of Pearson Australia Group Pty. Ltd.)
Penguin Books India Pvt. Ltd., 11 Community Centre, Panchsheel Park, New Delhi—110 017, India
Penguin Group (NZ), Cnr. Airborne and Rosedale Roads, Albany, Auckland 1310, New Zealand
(a division of Pearson New Zealand Ltd.)
Penguin Books (South Africa) (Pty.) Ltd., 24 Sturdee Avenue, Rosebank, Johannesburg 2196,
South Africa

Penguin Books Ltd., Registered Offices: 80 Strand, London WC2R 0RL, England

This book is an original publication of The Berkley Publishing Group.

This is a work of fiction. Names, characters, places, and incidents either are the product of the author's imagination or are used fictitiously, and any resemblance to actual persons, living or dead, business establishments, events, or locales is entirely coincidental. The publisher does not have any control over and does not assume any responsibility for author or third-party websites or their content.

First edition: October 2006

Library of Congress Cataloging-in-Publication Data

Brodsky, Daniella.
    The velvet rope diaries / Daniella Brodsky. — 1st ed.
        p. cm.
    ISBN 0-425-20782-X (trade pbk.)
    1. Chick lit.   I. Title.

PS3602.R635V45 2006
813'.6—dc22

                                                            2006021130

*For
Grandma Sylvia,
my kindred spirit*

"It takes a dedicated, committed, and courageous person to enter the blind, boiling darkness of a building on fire, to crawl through poisonous smoke, to confront the threat of the flames."
                                                                    —Dennis Smith

"my father moved through dooms of love
through sames of am through haves of give,
singing each morning out of each night
my father moved through depths of height"   —e.e. cummings

"One father is more than a hundred schoolmasters."
                                        —17th-century English proverb

"When a father gives his daughter an emotional visa to strike out on her own, he is always with her. Such a daughter has her encouraging, understanding daddy in her head, cheering her on—not simply as a woman but as a whole, unique human being with unlimited possibilities."
                                        —Victoria Secunda

"I asked, 'What happens, Father, when you die?'
He told where all the running water goes,
And dressed me gently in my little clothes."   —Robert Pack

"It no longer bothers me that I may be constantly searching for father figures; by this time, I have found several and dearly enjoyed knowing them all."
                                        —Alice Walker

"The pause between the errors and trials of the day and the hopes of the night." *(Defining the cocktail hour)*
                                        —Richard Norton Smith

ONE

On Your Mark, Get Set . . .

9:45 a.m., Tuesday, September 20

 Dear Therapy Journal that is supposed to change my life (but I'm not holding my breath just yet),

If you're like me, when you think about dying, you think about a sick person in the hospital with bags of fluids being dripped in and greasy, thinning hair, and an operation scheduled at 10 a.m. in the O.R. I happened to get that image from *Terms of Endearment*. But apparently there are other ways of dying that are a lot less visible. Like, "being numb to life emotionally." Or at least says my shrink, Dr. Fenwick.

That surprised me. Actually, it scared the crap out of me. I mean, I don't really want to die. I just . . . well, I wouldn't mind if I stopped thinking I could have saved my dad from that fire he died in twenty years ago, for just a couple of hours a day. This way I could free myself up to care about some other stuff besides blame, death, dying, cowardice, fire—a grim set of thoughts to say the least. Like for instance, if I saw a really great sunny spot on a bench open up, and I wanted to go for it, but then I saw another person—close to my age, not really old or anything—look at it just a second later, I would actually take the spot, instead of thinking I should give it to her, because what if I didn't, and then she sat somewhere else, and it was at that somewhere else that a car came flying up over the curb and right into that very spot on the park bench, and the girl about my age died because of it.

But unfortunately Dr. Fenwick doesn't do anything a little bit at a time, like allow me to just let the girl have the seat 70 percent of the time and then work my way down from there, asserting a little bit more and a little bit more, over a period of time such as twenty-five years. Dr. Fenwick wants me to jump right in. He calls it "behavior modification." He says I need to force myself to change my life, and eventually my obsessive emotions will catch up. We're starting with a new job and recording it all in this journal, so I don't make light of the "drastic changes" I've made. We'll see, I guess . . . technically I don't have to start modifying until Monday, so I'm sticking it out at my current job every last second until then.

Though I knew I'd be trying at least to quit soon, this fact didn't at all lessen the blow when my boss, Nasty, struck again. This time, I'd just relaxed into a fantastic article on harnessing the power of positive thinking through eating three Oreos a day (really, this is what it said, and it was quite intriguing . . . explaining about the importance of having such a simple ritual to help you meditate on the simple enjoyments of life). I was just thinking that would be a much better method than this crazy immersion thing of Dr. Fenwick's, and *much* easier, when I heard her voice like an ax chop, "An-*na*!" If this hadn't persuaded me to move my ass in two years, then I really don't think anything will.

And then the twister that was my micromanaging boss, Ms. Elizabeth Jackson, aka Miss Jackson if You're Nasty, aka Nasty, swished herself in her slim white pantsuit over to my unfortunately public cubicle.

Though I'd probably appear to be in the wrong place with my

halfhearted attempt at fashion, we're in the public relations department for the chic New York City daily paper, *New York, New York*, so I didn't need to act like I wasn't reading this article. In fact it's my job to read these kinds of articles and to know exactly what is trendy at every minute of every day, so that I can call up morning news show producers and print publications to pitch editors from our paper to come in and speak as experts on these very topics. For instance, last week, I had our gross, hygiene- and moral-deficient executive editor, Joseph James, on *Goodmorning City!* to expound on the latest trend of having nude portraits of yourself painted eating a fruit that symbolizes what kind of person you are (Madonna had one with a pineapple—spiked on the outside, but sweet in the middle; Paris Hilton's was just the opposite—a pomegranate, which is quite beautiful looking, but a real bitch to deal with). My roommate, Ray, thought very quietly, looking out our 87th Street, third-floor window, before he said he thought I might be an overripe banana.

"Why's that?" I'd asked him. I'd had my hair propped up in a loose bun, and I could feel it flop as I sat up higher on our sofa.

"If someone just looked at you, you'd seem okay, even with a couple of scrapes and spots . . . because you've got that protective peel . . . but if they could see inside, well there's all that bruised stuff that's deteriorating your base." His voice was tender and slow.

Boy did I wish I hadn't brought that up. That was the night we really started talking about the big *T*: Therapy. Before that I'd yessed him with no intention whatsoever of doing anything about it. I wasn't *that* kind of person. I didn't talk to myself or fear foods that started with the letter *P*. I was "fine." But that was just it, he said. "You could be so much more than fine." And that night I wanted to believe him so badly that I did.

So I didn't cover up the Oreo story on my screen when Nasty finally materialized, thinner than ever—scary thin, really—her unmanageable black hair curling wildly, the deadly corkscrews threatening to scratch away over my shoulder the way they did, oh, twenty times a day or so.

"AN-NA!" she screamed it just then. Her hands were on her hips, and she was standing over me, and all I could think was, that's it! I quit! Whatever it is she wants me to do, she'll tear it to shreds, say it would look worlds better in Georgia (the font, not the state), and if I switched everything around the opposite way, stood on my head, and whistled the theme to *The Gary Shandling Show*. And then she'd say, maybe she should just do it herself, since I'm so "incompe-sent" (she doesn't realize the word is incompetent). Only she wouldn't change a thing, but would take all the credit.

This would bother me more if I actually had aspirations toward any goal, but I'm more of what you might call apathetic. Sure, I'll invoke my mathletes bronze trophy from the second grade, but I won't do anything about it. I wasn't always this way, but let's just start this process by telling a little of the painful stuff at a time, okay?

"How can I help you, Miss Jackson?" I asked with as clean a slate as I could bring to the situation after two years. Sure, I could have left—thousands of times—if only I had the energy to . . . or the will. But I haven't found those two things easy to come by. Every time I feel an energy spike, think I might be on the verge of some activity, I think, but do you deserve it? Do girls like you—who allowed her very own father to burn to death—deserve to realize their dreams? I've been told it's ridiculous; it's ridiculous, but I can't believe it. Never have.

I should probably start eating Oreos tomorrow in hopes of gaining this type of inner strength and harmony, but I'm sure I won't. In a world of doers, I'm that one girl who mixed up the a.m./p.m. thing and overslept. I don't want to be this way, really I don't, but I haven't exactly found a way to be any other way. Although one day I know I will . . . all I need is the right opportunity. "Opportunities don't smack you in the face," my friend Nina is always saying.

"ANNA, DID YOU RECEIVE A CALL FROM DOCTOR FRIEDMAN ABOUT MY VACATION NEXT WEEK AND FORGET TO TELL ME ABOUT IT?"

Oh no. Not the vacations. Anything but the vacations. I'd take an assignment any day, over calling Doctor Friedman, the fourth plastic surgeon Nasty had mentioned this week . . . who was obviously avoiding her, because once again she wanted something else enhanced, nipped, tucked, or otherwise altered and wanted it now. I'd always assumed Nasty was more plastic than person. But no matter what I knew, she never let on. Nasty was a master publicist. And she made stellar attempts to cover up what she referred to as her "vacations."

"No, I haven't, Miss Jackson," I said, as if I were clueless. I blinked a lot and twirled a strand of hair in my fingers—for effect. I've found it always best to play dumb. She liked it that way.

"WELL, CAN YOU CALL HIM AND TELL HIM I WOULD LIKE TO KNOW WHETHER WE ARE GOING TO BE ABLE TO PROCEED IN PLANNING OUR VACATION?" Nasty screamed this, though she was standing so close her hair was scratching the front of my bare décolleté. She might have been hinting that my cowl-neck top was too low cut, which was probably true, although it was just because I couldn't get it to lay right, though it had looked fabulous on the girl at the store, who helped me into the same one, in a larger size. She was very nice, and so I started telling her too much about my life, until I realized I'd just let her know that I could lay for hours and hours, still, and rethink maybe if I'd not had my transistor going in my bedroom, I could have realized everything approximately 2.3 minutes quicker, and then I could have saved him. "I'll take two," I said and pulled the curtain quickly, so she'd remember that instead.

I pinched the shirt up a little higher, though it slipped right back down. *You are not her secretary! You are not her secretary! You are not her secretary!* I chanted it in my head, picturing the Oreos, trying to stand my ground . . .

That's another thing Nina's always saying: "Just stand your ground! Don't let her scratch you up with that grody hair!" Nina is a fabulous friend, the kind of friend who would fly halfway around the world to be with you, if she thought you needed it. The kind of friend that didn't ever ask, "Do you need me?" but instead just took it upon herself to be needed and didn't sweet talk around things in a way that would never help. She abhorred—on account of their "emptiness"—the words, *You'll be fine.*

Instead, she signed you up for "yogalates" and knocked on your door to accompany you there with a fresh bottle of Poland Springs. But Nina still didn't get that I just wasn't made that way. In my head, sure! I could say all sorts of things, such as, "It is very sad the way you are always trying to fix your outward appearance instead of working on whatever's going on inside," or "Rather than take your problems out on me, how about you get laid or something?" But they always came out as, "Sorry," or "Oh, you're right," or "Geez, I apologize for the error." Plus, I'm sure a lot of those things could be said about me.

Apparently I hadn't always been this way. My mom says that before my father died, I was always elbowing my cousins out of the way, so that I could dance in the middle of our holiday soiree musical reviews, stopping every once in a while to eat a green olive. She says I was fond of the words, *listen to me!* But I can't remember a bit of that. I'd give everything I own (which likely wouldn't be that much to most people), if I could remember even a shred of it. Again, I thought of the Oreos . . .

"Of course," I said, taking the pink Post-it with the telephone number printed on it in perfect handwriting from Nasty.

"Doctor Friedman's office," the chirpy voice on the other end of the line announced, as I crushed the balled-up Post-it in my palm. I avoided Nasty's eye, by staring instead at the mug next to my monitor. If you look too closely into her eyes, it'll scare the crap out of you. Her eyes are such a dark brown, you can barely see any distinction between the pupil and iris, and though I've heard them described as "elegantly deep," I think it's more of an *Exorcist* type of thing.

I focused so hard on the mug, it became fuzzy. But it didn't matter, because I could recognize it with my eyes closed. It used to be my father's mug. While we were sitting shiva, I'd climbed my mother's wobbly stepladder, reached up inside the cabinet to grab for the mug, and hid it under my loose velvet smock dress, while they all wailed, "So young, so young," devouring crumby rugelach and make-it-yourself corned beef sandwiches on pillowy rye in our living room. I've maintained an unhealthy attachment to the mug ever since. Fenwick says the mug is okay; Nina isn't so sure.

"Yes, ummm . . ." I found myself unsure of how to continue, given the fact that Nasty was standing right over me, and I wasn't supposed to know that Doctor Friedman was being called about a little matter known as cosmetic enhancement.

"Can I help you?" Chirpy prompted in a sweet, but remarkably efficient manner.

"Yes, er, I'm calling to see whether Doctor Friedman was able to schedule his vacation with Ms. Na— er, Elizabeth Jackson?" I could feel her breath on the side of my face, now that I'd swiveled my chair to face the screen and the mug. I gulped hard, praying this would work.

"Oh, ma'am, I apologize, but I think you've got it wrong. Doctor Friedman doesn't schedule *vacations*, he schedules cosmetic surgery procedures." Oh god. How was I going to get myself out of this one?

At this point, Nasty crouched down, so that her head was at the level of my own, her hands crossed over what would soon *not* be a concave chest, waiting for the outcome. This was definitely not in my job description!

I breathed deeply, feeling the tension and potentially explosive nature of the situation heavy on my own modest chest. "Yes," I tried to take on Chirpy's tone. "So, is he going to be able to schedule that very special vacation with Ms. Jackson, do you know?" Please get it! *Please* . . .

Nasty's face was turning, well, Nasty. And I knew I only had a certain amount of time before this got really ugly. How had I veered so far from my goals? I remember when I was young, I wanted to be a writer. Anna Walker, author. We had a calligrapher write that up all fancy at a town festival when I was a kid. The piece of parchment was still framed over my bedroom door. On the other side, my mother kept my room just as it had always been, with my yellow walls and my old quilt, mottled with spots of paint from my artistic days, and some posters of Duran Duran and Poison and all the books I'd worn the spines out on.

It had even crossed my mind, when I started working here, that I could eventually work my way over to the editorial side of things. I was intrigued by their quiet writing jags, by the grammar guides and the piles of magazines and books, by the intelligent-looking *New Yorker* cartoon clippings taped up haphazardly here and there. But things just hadn't turned out that way.

Chirpy was getting less sweet and more self-righteous. "I believe I already told you we do not schedule vacations, *special* or otherwise."

Just as I was ready to toss in the towel, give myself over to the idea that two years of crossing off torturous days as the assistant publicist was for naught, I heard a lot of paper shuffling on the other end, some low talking and then a big, *"Ohhh."*

Chirpy returned. "Ma'am yes, Doctor Friedman says he can

schedule the um, *vacation*, for a week from Friday, but that Ms. Jackson will only be able to enhance her *vacations* by half the size she originally had hoped she could fill them out to. Anything more would just add extra strain to her back."

The *vacation* episode turned out to be not all bad, after all. Nasty will get her new boobs, which might make her a nicer person, and as a bonus, it inspired me. I'd found a creative way to spend the afternoon *and* apply the new PowerPoint skills I learned at a boring three-day seminar the week before. It had been so mind-numbing, with its profoundly overexplained material, which covered possibilities I could never imagine being confronted with, such as, "when you need to program your computer to understand Mandarin Chinese," but sadly, it had been a whole lot better than my typical workday, which consistently proved even more mind-numbing with the addition of having to deal with the world's most infuriating boss.

Now I wouldn't forget the important points for lack of real work to do. Normally I waste the day, tossing paper clips into my dad's #1 DAD! Mug. If I get it in, he forgives me. If I don't . . . well, then I try again. It all has to do with the way he died, which I've already told you. But I'll add that when the fire started, I got so terrified that I ran out of the house without ever looking back. I tried to think of all the fire safety rules we'd learned in school, but all I could remember was, "There is an easy way to remember to change the batteries in your smoke alarm." I ran and ran until I was around the corner at Mrs. Sother's house, and she's the one who called the fire department when I finally breathed, "Dad in basement . . . there's fire." I can still remember exactly what I was wearing—Care Bear sneakers, with two Velcro straps and stretchy blue leggings and a striped,

long-sleeve, pink T-shirt that I'd dug a hole through the sleeve of—
I was always so painfully shy, it was just something I did. I had my
thick hair in two braids, which I hated because they hurt. My
mother always said that braids made me look pretty, so I wore them
every day, tugging the tops looser to no avail. She'd put them in just
before she left for the market.

I knew even before Mrs. Sother finished giving the address that
I'd killed him. It's never been easy to concentrate on anything since.
Amazingly, this paper clip game I play with myself works to make
me feel better for a few seconds at a time. And what seconds of bliss
they are! In the flashes of them I can see all the possibility, the beauty.
But always, it disappears again into guilt and regret.

Shrink Journal, if you've decided already that I am a terrible person, well I don't blame you one bit.

But today, Nasty's plastic surgery really inspired me, as I said. I
didn't look up from my computer for three whole hours, tossed no
more than a single paper clip (which did, in fact, go in), while I
compiled an animated PowerPoint presentation of the metamorpho-
sis Nasty's body had undergone in my two year employment period
with *New York, New York*.

Plastic makes perfect . . . or does it?

I even wrote in a game option I imagined licensing off to Mil-
ton Bradley: "Pin the Scalpel on the Plastic." I'd market it as a mil-
lennium update to "Pin the Tail on the Donkey," which, let's face
it, is pretty out-of-date. At first I was thinking I'd keep the tail,
even though I realized there was most likely no tail on Nasty,
though I couldn't be sure. I figured the hipsters who shopped at
Urban Outfitters would gravitate to a campy aspect like that. Plus,
Nasty looked funny up there on her screen with donkey tails hanging from her chest, calves, eyebrows, cheekbones, tummy, rear end,
ears, and chin. Really funny. I smiled for three hours straight.

I shut down carefully and met my roommate, Ray, for lunch. He's a trader at L.A.R.G.E. Bank and so he's got a great business sense.

"Pin the tail on the plastic just doesn't make sense, Anna," he said. He had his tie draped over his shoulder, though I've told him countless times how pompous that comes off. I've ceased pulling it down because no matter how many times I do it, he'll swing it right back. There are much better ways to pass an hour than warring with a man who's too good looking for his own good.

We were eating lunch at a sports bar near Ray's midtown office, which I make a point of lunching at once a week, under the idea that all of Ray's coworkers eat there, and they are all men, and so one day one of them will definitely talk to me. I'd once heard a wise writer say in a *Cosmo* article that if you want to meet a lot of men, then you'd better get yourself where there are a lot of men. It sounded like good enough advice to me. I chose to ignore the rest of the article's insights, which had something to do with the idea that surrounding yourself with a million men wouldn't help matters if you weren't ready on the inside. In the meanwhile, in my self-conscious way, I sit there and try to look pretty and not play with my hair or squeeze my brow up.

I met Ray at the University of Connecticut, when he'd "mistakenly" checked the "female" box on his housing questionnaire. He claimed female roommates were just better over all—neater, more thoughtful, caring. I happen to think he'd been thinking more along the lines of getting to steal some glances of a naked girl from time to time. Whatever the initial inspiration, we'd gone undetected four years (certain female Resident Advisers were actually onto us a couple of times, but Ray managed to diffuse the situations), and we've remained roommates ever since—just roommates and nothing else. It wasn't odd for me to be as candid with him as I was just then when I responded, "Yeah, well, fuck you."

In fact, Ray didn't even bat an eye. Instead he encouraged me. "Use that kind of fucking attitude at fucking work, and maybe you'd be fucking writing for that fucking paper instead of making up yet another fucking press campaign with a perfectly original angle that your stupid boss will take fucking credit for while treating you like you suck." After he said it, he took a boyishly huge bite of burger, dipped a fry in ketchup, and winked at a waitress at the neighboring table. She seemed intrigued, which in turn, made Ray bored with her, so he focused his attention back on me. So goes the plight of the good-looking trader. In my next life, that's what I'd like to come back as, I think . . . it appears a lot easier than guilt-ridden wallflower without a clear career path.

"Well said," I replied, snapping a garlic breadstick in half.

He smirked at me, and I shook my head. His womanizing ways always amazed me. It wasn't fair to everyone else for a guy to be that good looking. It threw off the curve, it upset the balance of things, it made all the nerdy guys have to wait years longer than they should have to, to finally get their chance. But as much as I could share things like mental illness, menstrual bloat, and overeating at Burger King with him—I could never imagine being romantic with someone who had such little respect for women.

"I won't be around for dinner, by the way," he said.

"Ruining another girl's life?" I teased.

"I'm on a strict 'a-girl-a-day' diet,' " he deadpanned.

He switched girls like I switched my lip gloss—which is quite a lot, since my other best friend, Nina, is a fledgling spa owner and rather obsessed with making me her guinea pig for just about any makeup and skin or body care procedure under the sun. She once cut my hair into a Christmas tree shape and called it a shag. I don't think

Ray ever laughed harder. The problem was my hair's thick as a lawn, and it was not attractive—for about five years or so. Nina decided she would remove hairstyling from the roster of services that would be offered at her spa. "It's better to specialize anyhow," she said, unpacking a new cream wax, which she was going to use on me I'm not quite sure where. In her defense, she did once help my anorexic eyelashes, which she described as looking "like God got called away before he could finish." She gave them a conditioning treatment and a clear mascara that made them look at least ten pounds heavier.

I glanced at my watch. I couldn't believe I'd still have at least three hours of work left. Surely, life was not supposed to be this meaningless.

"I would give anything not to go back to work right now," I said.

"Anything?" he raised an eyebrow, always the cad.

I rolled my eyes. However, I knew Ray was right—that the answer to all this would be to pursue my dream of writing for the paper instead of this thing I was doing because I was too . . . I don't know, lazy, scared, under-confident, undeserving to do anything about it. Even now, after I had been ordered to quit by my shrink— to save my life, no less—I was still pushing it off as long as possible. "Do you love your job?" I asked Ray. He never complained about anything, only said things like "Everything's great, what's up with you?" when you knew it couldn't possibly be great that often.

"Do I love my job? Hmmm." He sat back, stretched his legs, and clasped his hands behind his head. Three girls at a neighboring table smiled at him. He pretended not to notice. "It is what it is," he said. "But," he leaned in close, his chin resting in his palm. "You're different. You, Anna Walker, are all about emotion. You need to feel a certain way to be fulfilled. And you know what I think? You need to find an editorial position, quit your job, and tell that Nasty that she's just too nasty."

Either he knew nothing about me or he knew more than I, myself, did. This is another reason why I swore we'd never hook up—if he tossed me aside like all the other girls, then I'd lose our friendship, and I didn't think I could survive without that. I guess I must have been wondering too long without saying anything, because after a minute he blinked hugely, twice, like Elizabeth Montgomery in *Bewitched*.

"Sorry," I said, tossing my now-just-below-shoulder-length hair behind my shoulder. I am never, and I mean never, cutting it again. "I just don't think I'll ever be able to do it."

"Well, aren't you working on your project from Fenprick?" Ray never said anyone's name properly. Nina was *Meana*; his boss, Franklin, was *Stanklin*.

"Yeah. Of course."

"Then you'll be fine." He waved the idea of anything else away as an impossibility and asked, "Are you done?" I'd literally just swiped the last drop of ketchup off my plate with the last sliver of crisp French fry, leaving the whole plate gleaming white.

"I guess," I said. Thank god for friends, I was thinking. What would there be without them? I'd have been pretty lonely without them; it had been at least five months since I'd been on a date. I can't even remember how to kiss—how again, do you manage to get his lip between yours? And is it the top or the bottom you aim for? Really, these things can drive you nuts.

Before this I'd been sort of serial dating the one straight male publicist in print media—Jason Jones. But we were too opposite. He saw all the press events as temptation, rather than late nights with obnoxious, spoiled people who drank too much. We would argue about that and about his kissing girls in the V.I.P. when my back was turned. I would say, "Jason, you can at least wait until I go to the bathroom," but I didn't do anything about it. Ray said I was punishing myself and he wouldn't stand for it. If I didn't break up with Jason, he said, he would do it for me. It turned out neither of us had to do anything. Jason dumped me for the model Katrina Stina, which was an unbelievable thing, believe me. It actually boosted my ego that a boyfriend of mine would go with a beautiful model, though I hear she is under the misunderstanding that he is that caddish British actor who diddled his baby's nanny.

"I hope you're not thinking about that jerky Chase 'em Jones," Ray said, raised his finger for the check, gave his card to the waitress, and puckered his lips into a seductive stance.

"Of course not," I said. And the truth is, I don't miss him at all. The truth is, I'm sort of numb about what I want altogether. You know what I mean? It's like, I'm going through the motions—wake up, throw something on, go to work, hate it, do nothing about it; repeat.

"Or anyone else . . ." Ray hinted at my dad, but he wasn't going to bring it up. He's said about nine million times, "You know . . . you were just a little girl, and your dad wouldn't have wanted you risking your life through roaring flames and falling beams to save him." I just wish I could see it that way. Sometimes I wish at 11:11, like we used to do in high school, and sometimes I wish at the Alice in Wonderland fountain at Central Park, and I've wished in church at my cousin Rachel's wedding, and on Thanksgiving when I pulled the bigger part of the wishbone. But, despite that tiny part of your brain that wants to believe those kinds of miraculous things can happen, it never did.

And so Ray suggested a more practical route. He did some research, found the best person in the cognitive therapy for bereavement field, and set this whole thing up. As I said, I don't know what I'd do without friends.

My first meeting with Fenwick was terrifying. Not because of Fenwick himself, who is actually very gentle and looks a little like Albert Einstein . . . only his long hair is mostly black with just a little gray weaved through. He has some freckles sprinkled over his nose and cheeks that make him look way younger than he is—despite the gray.

"Hello," I said when he looked at me, half sitting on his dated green leather couch like I was ready to stand up and go at any second. I'd already said hello, but I didn't know what came next.

"Hello again." He smiled on one side.

We sat like that for a little while, and I wondered if he were perhaps doing some kind of outward evaluation. I played with the tassel on my purse and eyeballed the tissues on the table in front of me. *I should just go*, I thought. I should just run and forget all about this. I could see hours and hours of this stare down ahead of me, and it didn't look good.

We spoke at the same time.

"You know, I should just go—" I tried.

"Why don't you tell me why you're here—" Fenwick said.

This didn't exactly break the ice, but it chipped it a little.

"Well, I . . ." *Oh great*, I thought, as I reached for the Kleenex. Two words, and here I was blubbering so I couldn't even be understood. All this time trying (though failing) not to think of it, trying to get past it, and here I was digging the whole thing up with a bulldozer. But I looked up, and Fenwick seemed—unbelievably—to understand.

I found myself reciting the version of events I had on a circuit in my own mind. "I could see the fringes of my grandmother's afghan catching already, smoldering," I told him. "My mother was at the store. I couldn't recall one thing we were supposed to do during a fire. When I reached the basement door, just left of the sofa, I opened the door, and the flames burst out, the backdraft in action, and I saw my own shoelace had caught. I slammed the door shut, and I could smell it . . . rubbery, chemical. And all of a sudden the heat, the smoke . . . I was socked with it. And I tried to yell, *'Dad! Dad!'* But the words were too faint, I knew. I waited for him to chant back, 'Anna Banana!' Now the flames had come up through the door. Maybe he was gone, to the meeting place! I remembered suddenly this idea of the meeting place! I looked around, finally. The afghan gone, burned completely—the one my mother and I wrapped our-selves in to watch movies, no matter the season." I tried, I thought, like a skilled vacuum salesman to hype up the terror, the tangible ter-ror that would shed a rightful light on my fleeing the scene, the ver-sion of things I told people when I wanted them to like me, because I wanted Fenwick to like me and tell me I was fine, and why didn't I just go home and have an ice cream sundae? And so I continued, until I got to the part with Mrs. Sothers and the braids.

Fenwick sat back and crossed his right leg over his left— something I'd learn he always did when he was about to say some-thing important. "I am unbelievably sorry that happened to you. That is a hell of a thing to happen to a little girl."

I didn't know what else to say, so I stumbled on, "Thank you," which didn't seem exactly right. Though I sought it, I always hated when someone felt bad for me, as I didn't really deserve it. I squeezed the tissues in my palm and then released them over and over. One fell on the Oriental rug, and I bent over to pick it up.

"Okay, now tell me how you really feel about it," he said.

"That is it," I said.

"No it isn't," he insisted.

"No?" I turned bratty, indignant.

"No." he said, gentler now.

"Well, what is it then?" I asked, my head dancing like a charmed snake.

"How many times have you thought of this day? These few minutes?"

Twenty-five thousand, three hundred and fifty—approximately. "Once or twice," I said. I had memorized, certain portions from children's books that I'd checked out over and over and over, my name on the little mint green card all down the front. "The best advice in case of fire is this: Get out and stay out! If there is a fire in your home, follow the escape routes you have practiced. Don't stop to collect toys or other items."

"I see," he said. He continued on as if he knew exactly what was in my head, though I'd tried to shroud it. "Now, I am going to tell you this once, and then I am not going to say it again, because if I do, you'll keep coming back for me to reassure you about it, rather than learning to live with the doubt you have, the questions you will always have . . ." He leaned in close, his voice softend to just above a whisper, a tendril of his hair swung just above the surface of the table. "You did not kill your father." He let that hang there connecting us for a moment. "It is not your fault there was a fire. It is not your fault your father was in the basement. I am a father, and I have already taught my children their exit strategies in case of a fire, and if the situation should arise, the last thing I would want them to do is to go off of those paths to rescue me. You did the correct, natural thing for a child to do, and I am positive that if your father were here today he'd back me up on that."

I sniffed, but this did nothing to stop whatever was rolling out of me. This was exactly the kind of thing I craved unforgivingly, like a criminal, the kind of thing I would give anything to hear. And here, a professional was saying it like it might possibly be true, like the grizzly thoughts I'd had of myself all these years were nothing but a malfunction of thought.

The tissues were shredded, soaked, packed. There were more and more and more. I looked to Fenwick with unswerving attention. I drank up every single syllable he said, unabashedly. I was starving for this kind of thing. Still there were parts of me that didn't want to believe him. "But I was nine. That's old enough. I had babysat already by then." This was an automatic response for me. I had tons of them. I was the automat of blame—press button after button, and out they come. I knew how to cook. I walked to the bus stop by myself. I could count to five hundred. I was able to sign the word *hello*. But already I could tell these responses had been deflated, stripped of their power somewhat.

"Have you ever thought you have an obsessive-compulsive disorder?" he turned his head gently to the left, blinked softly.

I didn't say anything, just shook my head no.

"You think about this fire all the time, don't you?"

I shook my head, yes.

"You play it out and play it out, trying to think of it differently, trying to let that new view of it stick, so that you can stop thinking about it, feel good about yourself, and move on, don't you?"

I didn't say I'd almost missed this appointment because I couldn't get up off the park bench until I could accomplish that very thing. "Yes."

Fenwick shook his head, as if what I'd just said filled the profile of someone with my particular problem. This was somewhat comforting. I wanted him to be right. There was nothing in the world I wanted more than that. "It's going to take awhile until this all makes sense, before you can work all this out, but here's your strategy now. Never try to convince yourself of your innocence, because you'll never be able to do it, not for good, anyhow. Just try to live with the not knowing. Just try to do the best that you can to concentrate on now—on making breakfast or having a meeting at work—and ignore how you feel altogether. If you're gonna feel bad, feel bad . . . just let that hang out with you. Because the thing is, you just can't trust how you feel, Anna. You've been seeing things this way for so long, it's so embedded you'll have a very hard time trying to feel like you didn't kill your father, like you do deserve to care about yourself now. So let it hang out and eventually, the feelings will lighten up. Now, you tell me how many things in your life you've allowed to slip through the cracks because you didn't think you deserved to move on, or because you couldn't bring yourself to."

I looked to the intricate pattern of the rug, a twist and turn masterpiece and wondered whether one could ever find a way out of the paths we set out on.

2:00 p.m.

After lunch, Nasty was locked in her office, but every once in a while I heard her yell, "Chris!" Apparently Chris is her new boyfriend. He sends a lot of flowers with cards that I can't help peeking inside of. And she yells a lot. It's difficult to tell when Nasty is happier, but after two years, I recognize signs such as café latte rather than plain coffee and Chanel No. 5 instead of Joy. With her, you'll never get something as simple as a smile.

So I went back to the *Plastic Makes Perfect!* presentation. I wrote a script, taking an interactive route, imagining I'd ask participants, "Can you guess which body parts have gone on, ahem, *vacation*, ladies and gentlemen?" I couldn't help myself from coming up with yet another branding option: this one with an educational bent. I could sell the presentation to doctors to educate their clients on what might happen to them, should they go overboard on self-improvement. This would help the doctors' images and provide excellent opportunities for easy media coverage. Magazines and news programs love stories that come ready-made like that. I could imagine taking it one step further with the sale of publishing rights to a giant press like HarperCollins—and give them the option of a fun gift book, or a serious educational tome, whichever might fit into their upcoming catalog.

By the time I clicked on the "print" button, I was pretty satisfied with myself. It had been over a year since I'd gotten the opportunity to finish any project, and so it really felt good to do this. The day had flown by, I felt I'd accomplished something and used my brain, which I feared of late might atrophy.

Just then the telephone rang. It was Nina.

"Ohmigod, I got us appointments at Get Nailed, that sexy new nail spa everyone's talking about. We go Wednesday at five thirty. I can't believe I got these! I had to act like I was a French model." Nina was nuts for beauty. She wanted to research all the competition so that she'd know just what her spa should be like. We'd been doing this for as long as I've been working at *New York, New York*.

"Okay, now that's not nice. Why do you have to bring up the French model?" Of course, Nina didn't mean Katrina Stina . . . who wasn't even French. But that was our thing. We could unload things on each other in a way you couldn't do with others. Nina turned me on to this type of behavior. In fact, it was the reason I was attracted to her as a friend in the first place. It was back in college. We were hustled out of our dormitory during finals week because of a fire alarm, with no fire anyone could find, and she was standing next to me on the quad, tapping her foot like she meant business. I made the lucky move of turning my head in her direction and, she was off. "Can you believe the way they have us standing here with finals and everything? I can't believe how inefficient our dormitory staff is. Not that I mean anything negative to you, but everyone here is an idiot . . ." and on and on and on she went, until we were both laughing, and then we went out to the all-night diner, eating things that score double digits in the saturated fats department.

It's quite liberating to do this to each other. It's like yoga without the yucky sweat smell and all that darned energy. And it's our own little language that we don't share with anyone else. It's a bonding thing, you could say. "Get over yourself. You hated that Chase 'em

Jones, anyhow. You're too good for someone like him . . . and all the other stupid guys you always pick. Anyhow, we're going tomorrow, so don't waste money getting your nails done or anything."

As if I would ever have my nails done. With the money I get paid, I'm lucky I can afford to keep our apartment stocked with toilet paper . . . although I actually steal it from under the sink in the staff bathroom, because you really do need to cut corners, to be smart with your finances. The greatest part about all this research of Nina's was that I didn't have to pay for a thing, and I get to do all of these posh things that the people in *Harper's Bazaar* do. If I never had this experience, I would have lived my whole life thinking they made all of that stuff up. Because I'd never believe people would pay five hundred dollars for a haircut.

"Cool. Wanna come over for dinner after?" When I say *dinner*, I mean, the pub around the corner for burgers and waffle fries or a bowl of salad so big you could bathe in it. Ray and I basically live there. I once fell asleep in a booth, and they draped a tablecloth over me. This is New York City neighborhood life. At least for my group. We don't do the chichi spots like Bungalow 8 or Suite 16. We prefer darts and two-dollar beer.

"Sure."

"Oh shit! I gotta go!" I hung up and flung myself out of my roller chair, past the cubicle wall, and over to the printer. It had only been about twenty seconds since I heard the old printer stop buzzing its pages out, but I didn't want to take chances. If anyone got a glimpse of the plastic presentation I was out the door. My ass was grass. My career over and done with. I could forget defecting over to Editorial. Nasty would mop the floors with me. Though lots of authors made careers out of putting out romans à clef—airing their boss's dirty secrets for all the world to see, I did not have any wish to start my career that way.

I ran down the ten feet to turn the corner to where the printer was located, already relaxing into the idea that I'd be there in a second and that of course I had nothing to worry about. Who would see it? This printer was for the sole use of Nasty and myself, and Nasty refused to learn how to print her own documents, because that would mean she'd have to actually print her own documents. I once tried to show her the little printer icon, but she refused to get it. She said, "I don't see it. No, I don't," as if—rather than an image, clear as day—it were one of those optical illusions that look like a man's face at first, but if you really looked and looked, you would see the image of a woman's body embedded in it.

I was thinking that with a smile, watching my cute ankle-strap Mary Janes heel/toe, heel/toe their way to the printer. Which is how I wound up smashing directly into Joseph, of *Joe Says*—the senior editor who also happens to write the most-read gossip column in New York . . . the one who would live for this sort of thing. He grabbed a page off the printer.

But, huh?

What the heck was Joseph doing using our printer? Holy crap. Holy crap. Holy crap.

He held up the sheet in question, waving in his other hand what looked like a printout of his next column as he answered the questioning look on my face.

"My printer's broken. I.T. hooked me up to yours temporarily. They say you and *Nasty* are the only two using it."

Did he just say "Nasty"?

As if answering my subliminal question, he brought his little eyes right to mine. It was an unmistakable expression—yes, he'd seen the presentation about my boss. *Oh god, oh god, oh god, oh god.* Get ahold of yourself, get ahold of yourself. Surely, there's a way out of this. Surely there's a way to make sure that this does not go any further, and ensure that everything will be just fine! Of course there is.

I searched his face, hoping somewhere on its too-small, too-freckled surface, beneath the floppy red hair and between the big red ears, there might be a clue as to how I should attack this.

I noticed the corners of Joe's white lips curl up into a smile, his eyes crease at the corners, and slowly he asked a question nobody ever cared to hear the answer to, "So what are you guys working on these days?" This could not be good. Not at all. I had to say something and say it fast.

"Joe . . . listen. This is . . . a private . . . um, birthday thing for Nas—er, Miss Jackson. We were joking about it, and it doesn't mean anything at all. And it certainly should not be shared with anyone in the world. Ever." I must have been clenching my jaw up tight as I said that, because as soon as I was done, it started to pulse rapidly, like a heartbeat.

"Anna, Anna, Anna," he sang, shaking his head. "Certainly you don't think so low of me?" Could it be possible he knew how I felt about him? I'd never said anything to anyone at work. And I always made sure to smile with all my teeth showing whenever we spoke face-to-face. I'd even practiced that. Too much.

But it wasn't exactly a promise to keep the presentation a secret, was it? As if to place even more doubt, he lowered his lids, said nothing, flashed his eyes toward Nasty's door, and turned to walk back to his office at the opposite end of the hall.

I just knew he was going to ruin my life as he swished his butt from side to side under the glow of florescent lighting. He grew smaller and smaller, but not small enough to make me feel any better.

The first day I'd come to work here—which was as a temp, because Nasty couldn't keep an assistant to save her life—I remember thinking how glamorous it was. Everyone dressed really smart, with accessories and matching bags and everything. Sure, this is

Manhattan, and lots of people dress like that, I guess, but I never thought I'd know any of them.

And then what happened was that I didn't get to know any of them. They just didn't speak to me. It was like I had a sign taped to my head that said, "Don't speak to me." I tried too hard to dress better, employ accessories that would make me look more approachable. "Are you sure you want to wear two necklaces together?" Ray asked one morning as we walked to the subway. I took one off, but it didn't help any.

Even the receptionist would just sort of wrinkle her nose up in place of a hello. And that was really disappointing, because I thought, wow, this is the kind of place I'd like to be. The keyboards clicking, the stacks of magazines, messy everywhere, the messengers bringing and sending grand invitations in fancy envelopes or long tubes. The editorial area is an amazing place, let me tell you. They've got a mass of beauty product samples so enormous it nearly drove Nina to have a stroke when I brought her one night when everyone had gone off to a fashion show. They've got clothes and electronic gadgets and designer cleaning products and exotic coffees that smell up the whole floor.

But eventually, after I was hired, I got into my own little groove. There was Belinda, the secretary of the editor in chief, Ed. She was from California. Belinda stood tall—five-feet-ten-inches tall (a good five inches taller than me)—and she had this amazing blond hair that twirled down her back into a *V.* She called everyone "child" in her velvety voice. And I really liked that. I had something to bring to Ed, and she said, "Whatcha got there, child?" I wanted to hug her right then and there.

Sometimes she'll call me just to say, "Wanna go take a walk? I could really use a walk." And for an hour she'll chain-smoke Virginia Slims and tell me the most amazing stories about how she grew up thinking she had to be a movie star and wear jeweled glasses. You couldn't tell it from looking at her, but Belinda is quite a dreamer . . . though she doesn't allow herself much dreaming in these practical days.

My other friend is Judy, who works in advertising sales, which to hear her say it, is a crazy job. She has to go to dinner with potential ad buyers all the time, kissing their asses and agreeing to nutty things like, "Why yes, I love cleaning bathrooms, too!" if an ad buyer from SC Johnson Wax says they do. All the while she has to stick in little messages about how many readers we've got that make more than a hundred thousand dollars per year and how many stories about cleaning products we run throughout the year. Judy is a couple of years older than me at thirty-one and about to be married, so I've been helping her pick out dresses and throw-away cameras in silver and Jordan almonds in pink and engraved invitations that may or may not include her and Steven's middle names.

The thing is, I am really going to miss them. I know Dr. Fenwick said I'd have to get a new job, but I wasn't going to do it today! And I was really going to try to stay here! In fact, I thought maybe I could score an assistant editor position that I'd just seen posted on our employee bulletin board. I've never been big on change, and already I've had to make so many in a short time: seeing a shrink, using a lotion with preventative antiaging ingredients, I even ate Korean food the other day! There is a limit to how much a person can bear.

I packed my stuff up at five on the dot, walked into Nasty's office to go over our evening closing, and almost found myself thinking I'd miss her. I had promised myself that at some point I would find out why she was so hateful to everyone. Every once in a very long while I'd see her laugh at something I'd point out on my trend watch, and I'd catch a flicker of something warm in her eye. I thought, maybe, I'd know why I didn't see it more. You see, people like me have quite a tolerance for other people . . . we give them tons of leeway under the idea that everyone makes mistakes and hopefully someone will view me that way, too.

"That time already?" Nasty asked, swirling around in her chair to face me, sitting in her guest chair. I opened my evening project folder to a report and handed a copy to her. It was all a big joke, since she buttoned up all the deals after I put the legwork in. I could call *New York* magazine for ten weeks going, working them up about our holiday issue and why they should write about it, and then she'd see that in the report, say "I'll take that file now," and snag all the glory for herself when we got a three-page story placed.

Everything I said felt melancholy in its finality. Also, there was guilt. I didn't know whether her fragile ego could handle this kind of public humiliation. Boy did I feel for my replacement, at any rate. "Yes, I guess it's that time," I agreed, slowly, swallowing to open my throat.

"Okay, well, *Weight Watchers* magazine. That's a good market for us . . . all those overweight women love to sit at home and read, because they're too humiliated to go out looking like that. Could you imagine? It's disgusting, really. Put down that cream puff, I say."

I know, believe me I know it is an unbelievable thing that I could have been thinking at that moment how much I am going to miss her, how I am so sorry to have done this hurtful thing to someone like Nasty. But I never thought she really meant any of it. I didn't. I thought she suffered major esteem issues and projected it onto other people, because she didn't know what else to do. "That's what I thought. They've got three million readers, plus they are given out at three health club chains nationwide."

"Been speaking with them since May, huh? Okay, well, why don't you pass that over to me now?"

I already had the file for her. I had saved all my correspondence onto a CD, and I passed that over, too. Since it had been five months and they were ready to include us, I figured Nasty would want it now.

The rest of the meeting followed suit. Each sentence felt stuffed with meaning. Tomorrow she would hate me. She might even try to kill me. Again, it seemed my lapse in judgment would be my ruination. Maybe I should be seeing a brain surgeon rather than a shrink. Maybe he could implant some "judgment" where it's missing.

At the end of the meeting, Nasty tried to turn things into a failure, the way she always did. "Well, tomorrow's another day and maybe you'll do better then," she said.

Today I didn't get fired up at that and run off to drink two glasses of chardonnay over chicken fingers and salad with Nina. I simply said, "Goodnight, Miss Jackson." And I thought, as I pulled my fall jacket over my shoulders, how those words had a distinctly melancholy sound.

7:00 p.m.

Later, I explained to Nina how I thought of my time with Nasty now: a montage of memories, with Barbara Streisand crooning in the background. My head tossed back in slow-motion laughter, wiping tears of joy from my eyes. That scene fades into a smiling handshake, and finally a tête-à-tête over a pile of important papers and steaming coffees.

Nina said, "That wasn't you and Nasty. That was a young Tom Hanks and Peter Scolari—where the hell has he been?—in *Bosom Buddies.*"

"You're right. I know you're right." I could barely eat one ruffle of lettuce.

"And besides," Nina added, "why would he print anything about *her*? Although she ruins your life on a daily basis, nobody else in the world could give a crap about that frizzy-haired Barbie doll."

Wait a minute. Wait. That's true, isn't it? Joe's column is about celebrities! And Nasty is no celebrity! She's not the child or daughter of a celebrity, nor is she dating a celebrity. "You might have something there," I said. It was amazing how my heart could start beating so quickly, my breath could just stop, and the whole room could feel like it was crashing in, only for me to completely recuperate in a few moments.

"Good. Now, get some sleep because we've got our appointments tomorrow, and I read that they won't even think about taking you if they don't like the way you look. Wear something nice—not like I'm saying you don't normally—just maybe that cute little sundress we bought at that sample sale, you know? The one with the blue flowers?"

I was too tired to think whether I wasn't dressing nicely lately. I've never been great at knowing what goes with what. I used to follow the way they put it all on the mannequins at the store to take out the guesswork. Lately, though, I guess I've been too disinterested to do even that. On Monday, even Ray told me to go back and switch into the brown skirt.

Alone in the apartment later, I changed into pajamas I should have thrown in the garbage five years ago. I parked myself on the sofa for whatever Lifetime movie would appear on the television screen.

When Ray walked in, my brown hair was soaked with tears over Julia Roberts's heart-wrenching performance as a diabetic bride in *Steel Magnolias*, and the pigtails I'd scraped it into had generated quite a large amount of fuzz around the crown from shifting around on the cushions and getting soaked and matted from the tears; they must have looked more like horns than hair.

"Oh no, not horn hair and Lifetime Television for Women. Lord, tell me, please, why do I live with a chick who's not even fucking me? Why?" he begged of the ceiling, placing a plastic bag that could only be holding a Veniero's cannoli box down on the coffee table.

"How'd you know?" I asked him upon spying the much-needed pastry box, making the sort of sad little girl face I hoped would get me a hug.

"It was a conspiracy. *Meana* told me. Your mom told me. I read about it in the evening edition of *New York, New York.*"

"We don't have an evening edition," I barked. In his very unique way, Ray was so calm, soothing. He knew just what to say.

"Really? Cause I saw it there, plain as day: *Plastic Fantastic! Nasty's so fake that debate has begun on whether she can still be classified as human.*" He sat next to my feet, slowly untied his shiny shoes, and then leaned back on the sofa, letting his head drape back over the top of the pillows. He continued. "People were talking about it on the six train—oh my god, I've never seen so many people excited about one topic. Nasty—ooh, she's gonna be pissed. You'll be sacked for sure."

I kicked his thigh with my slouchy tie-dyed sock. He had almost convinced me by making light of the whole thing.

"Anna, with this getup, it's no wonder you don't have a boyfriend. And you better get one soon, because I'm not gonna let you stay here rent-free when you're out of a job, so you can forget that right now." He loosened his tie and lifted his feet up onto the coffee table, rubbing my pilled leggings soothingly with his left hand.

The very long, very dark night did have one beacon: The movie *Vision Quest*, featuring a young and really rather cute Matthew Modine, was playing on cable, and I caught it right from the opening credits (something I'd always considered a lucky sign in itself). And the film inspired me and made me promise myself that I would find a way to make my own dream come true. I promised my father, too, whom I remembered once saying to me, "Follow your dream, baby doll" (now, though, after so many years, I couldn't be sure he'd actually said it—although I thought I remembered the actual dream he'd been encouraging me to accomplish had been to meet Big Bird in person).

I knew about vision quests from Robert Frost's poems, and I knew a person had to come far from what they knew comfortably to accomplish life's greatest feats. And on that note, I woke to start the day.

TWO

Go!

At this point, I thought, as I crossed my way over Third Avenue to the Farlucks Coffee that I frequented, whatever was going to happen was going to happen. Now that I felt change was imminent, a strange calm settled over me. Without the worry, I was free to observe. The purposefulness of people who were sure of where they were going excited me. I let their wind rush over me, listened to snippets of their cell phone conversations, wondered about the "meeting" they were late for, or "that" which apparently, he did again. I watched them buy coffees and oversize muffins from street vendors in silver carts that always looked quilted to me.

I picked up a copy of *New York, New York* at the rack by the door. I held the paper rolled up . . . the newsprint dry on my fingers. But I didn't look yet. I knew if I looked at it *after* I ordered my shot of espresso, it would be luckier than if I looked at it right away. I faded out while I waited in line (there was always a line), really thinking of nothing in particular, until my favorite barister, Julio, called my attention to two shots of espresso—one for myself, and one for him.

I walked, as I did every day, toward him—today, completely ignorant of what I was about to encounter.

It was in slow motion that I caught sight of the words *Joe Says*, on an open paper lying at the nearest table. I shook my head, squeezed my eyes, prayed, Oh Lord, I'll do anything if it doesn't happen this way! I know I waited too long, I know, but not this way! I clinked tiny paper cups with Julio and said, "To the unknown."

He looked confused, but agreed all the same. It was his job. "Have a good day, Julio," I said on autopilot and snuggled into a corner table, my back to the open paper on the table a few feet away. I wanted to find this out on my own terms.

I turned to page five, where Joe's column is laid out each and every day. I breathed in and stared at the page straight on.

And there it was. The first page of the PowerPoint presentation was staring back under that now-sinister looking column name, Joe Says.

Just so you know, here's how the column beneath read:

Plastic Fantastic!

Word is, *New York, New York* exec **Elizabeth Jackson** has undergone more plastic surgery then even the eternally young Demi Moore. An inside source within Jackson's department was overheard saying "Nasty" Jackson is "extremely vain and constantly in search of the fountain of youth." Not only that, but a PowerPoint presentation created by said source approximates Jackson's body is currently at a 90:10 Plastic v. Human ratio (see inset)." But **Joe Says** he knows just why the plastic pressure has mounted as of late: It seems Jackson is secretly dating 24-year-old superstar hunk, **Christopher West**, the hottest, hippest, buffest man to ever be nominated for an academy award.

My heart beat double time in my throat. The shallow breath nearly choked me. That's why disgusting Joe cared about Nasty! The "Chris" she was dating was Christopher West! The idea was unbelievable. The flowers! The phone calls! He'd been promoting a new film with Julia Roberts a while back, and we put on an event for it! They must have met then. And if Joe had overheard that comment of mine, which I'd whispered to Ray on the phone over two months ago, then this setup had been a long time coming.

Okay, none of that mattered in the big scheme of things. The important thing was that a new life was starting now. Starting now. I'd put it off and put it off, but now it had caught up with me, and I just had to. I had to get up off this chair and go up and face Nasty. I could blame Joe or Nasty, but really, if I'd just faced my fears, forced myself to get a new job when I really should have, then none of this would have happened.

I stood, my fingers jittery, and pulled my purse over my shoulder. I saw a woman sipping an iced latte, and without warning my mouth opened and said something I often thought: "An iced frosty mocha latte is a dessert! Not a coffee!"

The woman's mouth formed a huge ring, but she couldn't get a word out, apparently from the shock. And didn't I know just how she felt?

"Bitch!" I finally heard her yell, as I stormed through the exit. And she was right. No matter how assertive I was now, it wouldn't change the past.

As I walked beneath that *New York, New York* **marquee for what** I knew for sure would be my last time, it occurred to me there was significant strength in desperation. As I passed the taxis, bicycles, Rollerbladers, I didn't worry whether they might smack into me. No, not today. Today I stepped off the curb, even though the palm light was already blinking red. I left five people waiting for the next WALK sign behind and made a taxi stop for *me*.

Now I had nothing to lose, I didn't have to concern myself with being, well, concerned. It would be clear to everyone that I was the only possible departmental source who could have leaked the goods on Nasty, considering I was the *only* departmental source other than Nasty. I could say what I'd wished all along, tell people what I really wanted to tell them. Pure, unadulterated freedom, is how I would describe it. At least I was free from Nasty and her petty ways and the meaningless position I'd held under her—a position I knew in my heart of hearts just then that I could have done something with, if I'd really tried, despite how difficult Nasty had made it. It was so clear now. I could have gone to Ed, the editor in chief. I could have gone to Human Resources. I could have asked for a departmental transfer. My whole life looked like a pile of "could have's" from this vantage point. And I'd never been angrier at myself. The regret just proved to make me angrier than I already was—anger at myself, at Joseph, at Nasty, it was all blending together into one giant cloud hovering over me. I must have looked like that donkey character, Eeyore.

It was with that very mind-set that I stomped my way to the cubicle-lined path to Joseph's office—the office of the mean-spirited, selfish jerk, who sold me down the river and probably got a million-dollar bonus for doing so! How could I have believed his printer had broken down at the exact moment I'd printed out those pages! He'd been spying on me for months, obviously, just waiting for me to say something or do something he could use to spill the beans on Christopher West's new squeeze!

"AARGH!" I screamed it, like a battle cry to that receptionist who'd never given me the time of day. I didn't even care that she laughed at me.

I stamped down the hallway, in my one good suit and a nice pair of brown sling-backs. I held my purse at my shoulder so tight my knuckles were white.

There he was. Joe was smugly reading over his column, legs draped up on a corner of his desk, stubby arms pulling the pages of the paper wide, midair before his eyes, like he hadn't a care in the world.

"How *dare* you?" The anger welled inside me, and that is what came out. I liked the way I sounded.

Joseph didn't look away from the paper, didn't give me a glance.

I glared at him for a couple of minutes and thought he must be the smuggest man in the entire world and what the heck is wrong with him and what kind of childhood must someone have suffered to be this much of an *asshole* and what *exactly* would happen to me if I smacked him across the face? And is he ever going to speak? EVER?

I thought of ripping the paper from his hands, but then thought better of it. I would let him come to me. I'd prefer it that way. Why give him the power? So, I crossed my arms, lowered my lashes to emphasize my disgust, and prepared myself to wait.

I'd show him. Just wait until he looked my way. Just wait.

Joseph wasn't moving.

Okay. Was he ever going to look my way? And what if I had to pee? Already I sort of did. My bladder would have to be strong; *I* would have to be strong.

Joseph wasn't moving.

Oh, I really had to pee now. I tried to will it to stay in place.

Joseph wasn't moving.

I squeezed my thigh muscles tight.

Joseph wasn't moving.

The paper was morphing into a swirl of colors and black print under my stare. When people said, "I'll stay here all day," did they really mean *all* day?

Joseph turned the page by bringing the two sides of the paper together, leafing with a finger, and then pulling the pages wide apart again.

I cleared my throat loudly.

Joseph smiled at something he read, as if I wasn't there.

I tried his name, "Joseph," concentrating hard not to call him Ray's name: *Gross*-eph.

He made a sucking sound with his mouth.

I said it louder this time. It was apparent he wasn't coming to me. "JOSEPH."

He allowed one side of the paper to sag, revealing half of his face. This gave me the unfortunate view of him picking something out of his tooth, briefly shifting his attention toward it, and then flicking it into the carpet. He then retained his former position.

I breathed deeply and felt an incredible strength build inside. Again, I didn't know what I was about to say.

Joseph again turned the page, recrossed his legs.

"What I said is, *How dare you*? And the reason I asked that is because, after ignoring my existence for two years, you used me like a tissue and threw me to the ground like, like—that piece of shit you just plucked from between your grody teeth! And even now, you sit here smugly, pleased with yourself, like an infant who's just made his first pee pee in the potty!" Whoa. Who the hell was thinking this stuff up? And where had she been all my life?

Joseph lowered the paper. Finally he turned his head to speak.

"Well, if you would have just come and ripped me a new one like that in the first place, Anna Walker, you'd have had your own column since day one."

A column? Really? That sounded so depressingly fabulous. Oh, it would have been so much better than working for Nasty! And rather than have to bend over backward for pain-in-the-ass journalists,

I could have *been* a pain-in-the-ass journalist! "You know what you are, Joseph? You are a royal pain in the a—!"

The suddenly chatty Joseph interrupted me.

"So does that mean you wouldn't be interested in your own column called 'Velvet Rope Diaries,' which the ed in chief has just demanded begin running Friday, opposite my column?"

I stopped, staring out through that open door—to the hallway that led to my cubicle and the evidence of my action, the slow death I was dying. Of all the things in that cubicle, I could think only of my dad's mug. He'd drunk his coffee from it every morning. He'd leave it outside on the stoop, where he'd sit with it and a sweet-smelling menthol cigarette. Mom would get mad each time she went out and found it staring up at her from that stoop. "Someone's going to crack their head open tripping over this!" she'd yell.

I liked that memory. It was real-life—the everyday reality of him. That's why I'd chosen it as my token. I could tell my mom liked to think of that, too, because sometimes—after he died—she'd go out there and sit the way he used to, though she'd never done that before. I'd taken that living symbol and killed it with my stagnancy, sitting dissatisfied with my life, holding it tight and grazing over its familiar chips until my palm had rubbed the lettering off the front.

"Why now?" I asked, my back still to him.

"Well, because it's time. I need a writer; you need a job. You've proven yourself creative enough. You've obviously got the paper's humor down pat."

I knew that presentation was good!

Well, here was my opportunity to move in some direction at least. To "save my life," as Fenwick put it—so bleakly. Okay, it wasn't ideal—with a shady boss, whose intentions I couldn't quite be sure of—but it was a chance, a really amazing chance to do something exciting, something that lots of people wanted to do, that I had often thought I wanted to do. And I was going to take it.

"I'll do it." And reconsidering the last few minutes, I went on, "And I didn't really mean your teeth are grody, so much as you know, just small, or whatever." That wasn't much nicer was it? I smiled, and he didn't, and I found myself bumbling on. "And you know, infants really *should* be proud when they pee pee in the potty. It's a pretty big accomplishment. Why just last week—"

"Anna," he cut me off—thank god—still picking at that grody (sorry, but it was) tooth. "You've got the job. Now pull up a chair, and let's go over the specifics."

It turns out—of all the things I am unqualified to do—the column is to detail the newest, hottest nightlife destinations in the city. The catch is, though, just as everything printed in *New York, New York*, it has to be an exclusive. Which means it can't appear anywhere before or at the same time as it is appearing in our paper. Which means—a lot of pressure! Salary, unfortunately, would remain the same. I tried to negotiate. It went something like this:

"So, I imagine I'll be getting a raise for taking on more responsibilities at *New York, New York*?"

"Absolutely not."

"Okay, then."

The portion of the meeting that left me the most harried, that gave me the shrillest ringing in the brain, which would require a minimum of four Extra Strength Tylenol to alleviate, was when I was given my due date for the first column.

"We'll need your piece tomorrow by five p.m. That's when pieces need to be passed on to the printer, to run in the following day, Friday's, paper," he deadpanned.

I wasn't even a night person. Often, Ray would wake me up at 8:45, when he found me asleep on the couch, and tell me to go to bed. "Or you'll be all stiff in the morning," he'd say.

Still, I probably wouldn't have been so freaked about the whole thing, if I was going in blindly. But I knew—as I'd been selectively granting them for the last two years—that getting an exclusive on anything was a tough deal in this city. There was a lot of competition between publications, and the likelihood of hearing about something before the select few who always seemed to get to information first, was not an easy task. I'd have to build relationships, I'd have to make telephone calls, I'd have to kiss ass, call in favors, plant myself at a few important lunch spots, get myself on information lists from all the publicists who handle restaurants and bars, get in nice with those guys and their door brigades, and beyond that, I'd have to meet some real Manhattan insiders who knew the people who owned these places. But first, I'd have to magically transform into someone who could actually do all those things.

Just as I thought that, I got a glimpse of what I'd have to deal with in a couple of seconds. Nasty had arrived. She hadn't seen me here in Joseph's office. I was half-hidden by the door and sort of around a corner where she couldn't see me. But I could see her throw my belongings, one by one, in a pile on the floor. There went papers, folders, a Statue of Liberty paperweight, a rubber-band ball, a shower of take-out menus, a Derek Jeter bobble head. She pulled my cardigan from the top of the cube wall and stamped on it and the entire pile. There was some crunching . . . and I thought, oh my god! The mug! My father! This time I was going to save him!

"I gotta go!" I yelled to Joseph and ran to the cubicle.

She disappeared into the farthest corner of the cubicle where I kept my mug, and I yelled, "No!" Nasty knew where that came from! Surely she couldn't be so mean!

I arrived and breathed a deep sigh when I saw it wasn't the mug she was after at all. It was a pair of scissors. She snip snipped it into the air, her eyes maniacal, the pupils indistinguishable as ever, her smile menacing. And then she picked up my cardigan and cut it into tiny black shards that fell around her on the gray carpeting. She cut off a particularly large piece and stared straight into my eyes. I had the mug safely in my hands. "Take your pathetic little mug, you pathetic little traitor. You think I give a shit about your problems?"

The funny thing was, despite it all, I thought she had. Even then, the fact that she hadn't crushed it into a thousand pieces proved that even more to me. I wanted to be angry at her for everything she'd done and for the way she was acting then, but I couldn't be. She'd just been publicly humiliated.

"Don't you have anything to say for yourself, you . . . you . . . insignificant, plain-haired bad-dresser?"

It was so obvious to me then that those were her own insecurities she was hurling at me, that I said, "I just want to say I'm sorry that this happened, Miss Jackson. It was childish for me to create that presentation in the first place, and so I have to take responsibility for the way things turned out, though I never meant for anyone to see it."

"I'll get you back," she said, taking a tall stack of papers from my in-basket and hurling them up, so they fell all around like autumn leaves. A small crowd had gathered around us by then. Some people were pointing at Nasty, and others were laughing. There were lots of hands cupped over mouths in shock. A guy I recognized from accounting whispered, "C-*rraackkkk!*" And my heart never went out to anyone more in my entire life than it did just then to Miss Jackson.

"I'm sorry, Miss Jackson. I wish you the best of luck," I said. And as I walked away from her, ignoring her cries—"*You* walk away from *me?*"—I realized that all of a sudden there wasn't much in my life that I recognized. At least, I thought, I knew those shoes scuttling me around in this new, crazy place. At least that was one thing I knew for sure.

THREE
Now What?

"Here you go, child!" Belinda escorted me to my new cubicle and passed me a box wrapped up in flowery paper, like something you'd have hanging on a bathroom wall. It was a pretty box full of fragrant loose tea.

"For your mug," she said, though she knew I never used it. "I know dear." She winked and walked away.

I'd have to think more about that. But for the time being, I placed my mug down in one corner of the cubicle, and then my purse. As far as I knew, I didn't have any other belongings left intact.

My new desk was in the features department, where everything was free samples and messenger deliveries, phones buzzing and keyboards tapping. When I thought of it before it was in slow motion and soft focus, everything gleaming and magical—too good to be true.

My computer was brand-new with a flat screen. I pulled a label off the corner of the monitor and played with it for a second, which turned into a minute, which turned into five minutes. What was I supposed to *do*?

All the blood drained from my face as I stared at my shadowy reflection in the dark, unused monitor and panicked. I didn't know the first thing about being chic. I didn't know the first thing about nightlife. Ray, Nina, and I have been going to the same pub every night for two years. At the events I've had to work that took place in fancy spots, I nearly always had trouble getting in. I'd see someone I recognized from the office and yell, "Hey Joan, it's me, Anna, from Publicity!" But she—like all the others—would squiggle up her features, toss her shoulders up, and continue on without me. I'd always get really insecure and want to turn around and go home. Instead, I'd spend the rest of the night letting in every poor schmuck I could. I'd lock my jaw and think, who made this whole system up, anyway? How could our society have come so far, and still we only choose the best looking and the most popular? When I said that to Nina she said, "Don't say that. That's what all the ugly, unpopular people say."

Then, sitting in the department that I'd wanted to sit in for two years, I looked around me, and rather than the soft focus, slow motion warmth in my heart, all I felt was a hollow, breathless occupation of terror. Why had I ignored that saying—be careful what you wish for? People were always saying that. But I couldn't just listen, could I? No. I had to go and create a creative (although mean), genius presentation that caught the eye of the most popular gossip columnist in the city and go and get myself one of the most sought-after jobs in the world. Who did I think I was? Candace Bushnell? She knew shoes like I knew . . . *nothing*. In college, I'd majored in English, and I still knew nothing whatsoever about that!

"So tell me about the English," Ray used to say when we'd have dinner in the cafeteria with the six or seven people from our dormitory floor that we hung around with. Everyone was fascinated with him, even then.

I threw my head down on the desk. I knew what I had to do. I had to run out and get some Oreos, take a second to meditate on what was important in life, and then I'd come back and be just fine . . . or something closer to it, anyway.

Pickles, I thought, walking the streets in an intense search. I knew about pickles. There were sweet ones and sour ones and half-sour ones. But then I realized there were probably so many new kinds of pickles I didn't know a thing about. I didn't even know everything about *pickles*. I walked on, feeling completely incompetent—a shapeless garment on a fifty-off rack that can't even get bought up as material for curtains. If I came across a garment like that, I would buy it. I really would.

Fires. I realized. I knew about fires. I knew all the terms: *backdraft* and *combustible* and *flashover*, but that didn't do me much good now.

This is the thing about New York. There are no supermarkets. All I wanted was a few simple Oreos, but the only signs I passed by said, "Gourmet Cheeses," "Italiano Cuisino," "Sushi," and "Soup, Soup, and More Soup." I tried the soup shop, thinking after a soup I always want something sweet. "Excuse me? Do you sell Oreos?" I asked. But the guy pointed up to the sign and asked, "You're kidding, right?"

I walked and walked. In my mind, I've somehow twisted up the Oreos and the success of my column, and I just couldn't seem to turn back. Finally, I stumbled upon a tiny superette that stocked cookies. I walked all the way to the end of the last aisle, and there— on the top shelf, were two dusty boxes of Oreos. I took them both. They cost ten bucks. The wan girl behind the counter rang them up quickly, her fingers dancing the foxtrot over the keys, and she didn't even glance in my direction. My "thanks" went unanswered, and I turned to go.

While I was walking back I passed a couple of carefree girls wearing cheap suits, and they were laughing on the steps of a church and eating sandwiches. Suddenly, my heart plunged, and I felt miserable that I had this incredible responsibility, that I now—today—had to prove that I deserved this thing I'd been pining for my whole life. But I couldn't even bring *myself* to believe I deserved it, so how was I going to convince the rest of the world? If only I could have put this off until I was *ready*.

All the way back to the office I thought of this one thing. In our original house, we had a wooden breakfast bar between the kitchen and the dining room, and my dad would sit at one of the stools and act like he'd come to my diner for breakfast.

"Whaddya want?" I'd ask.

"You got some bacon?" he'd say, looking funny.

"All outta bacon," I'd say.

"Eggs?" he'd ask.

"All outta eggs," I'd say.

"Toast?" he'd try.

"All outta toast, but I can make a mean donut," I'd offer.

"A donut sounds real nice," he'd say, shaking his head as if we hadn't had this exact conversation hundreds of times.

I'd walk over to my plastic range top and act like I was making a donut, plate it, and stretch my hand up onto the breakfast bar to serve it to him.

When I got back to the office, I called my mother and was depressed (though no offense against him) to find that she still lived with Roger—which obviously wouldn't be the case if my father were alive. I'm not nuts; it's just I wanted it to be possible really, really badly that this thing with my father never happened.

I bent my head over my desk as I explained my new position to my mom.

"Oh, Anna! I knew it, I knew it! Roger! Roger! Anna's got a column!"

This is my mother. For every good thing that's happened in my life, she had a premonition. She knew before everyone else that this would happen. She knew my tooth would fall out into the Italian hero at my cousin Suzy's tenth birthday. She knew my Cray-pas drawing would win the Earth Day contest for Nassau County.

"He wants to know what it's about dear," she said.

"It's about really chic bars. I have to review them . . . and stuff."

"And what kind of stuff?" she asked.

This was a fabulous question. I really didn't know. "Oh, write what I think of it all." Was that true? Did people really care what I thought? I mean, what did I know about bars?

"That sounds wonderful, Anna. I always knew you deserved this kind of thing. You are so talented, so . . . creative. When you were a little girl, you always used to write stories about the kids in the neighborhood. You put them together into a little magazine."

Did I? I don't remember that at all. That sounds like ambition, doesn't it? That sounds like something a person with goals and desires and motivation would say on an *E! True Hollywood Story*.

"Do you have that magazine mom?" I asked her, knowing she would. Though I found it difficult to be home, to deal with the memories there, she held on to me as tightly as if I were there every day.

"Of course. I have everything you ever made," she said. I really did have the best mother in the world. She was so good to me, even with me having killed her first husband and everything. You would think she'd be angrier, but she never was. My mom came to every event I ever had at school—all the lousy plays and the choral concerts and the science fairs—and she always had something fabulous to say about every miserable thing I underachieved at.

I can remember looking at her, trying to believe what she was saying, what Roger was nodding about, trying to think it was true that I was "a promising future scientist!" or "a terrific tenor!" But I didn't. I just chewed on my plush bunny until it grew a fungus and we had to throw it away.

I sat with five Oreos—ignoring the sell-by date, which was

slightly passed by a couple of months or so—and a big cup of water from the water cooler and tried to push the bad thoughts out and really meditate on the cookies. I took a bite of the top cookie and tried to describe it to myself. At first the familiar taste *was* kind of comforting. But in a matter of seconds I realized the cookie was stale. It was. It was lacking the . . . the crunch. And the cream part was kind of . . . well . . . wet. I forced the bite down my throat and tried to get it down with a huge gulp of water. But it was lodged there. I tried another sip, but my throat seemed to have grown narrow. I started to cough. Oh this was really embarrassing. *Help!* I tried to yell, but the word wouldn't come out. Nothing came out. Oh, I know I've said some horrible things in my darker moments, but I didn't want to die! No I didn't! I wanted to live! And I wanted to figure my way out of this and do a great job and make my mother proud—she was such a wonderful mother!

"Watch out!" I heard the voice from behind, but I didn't know who it belonged to. "I'm going to squeeze you really hard in the middle of your stomach!" It all happened so fast. I looked down and saw a couple of pretty rings interlocked on a pinky, and then all of a sudden a glob of Oreo flew out of my mouth and smashed right on the monitor. Oh my god, it was disgusting. Just disgusting. I couldn't bring myself to turn around.

"Are you okay? I'm Theresa, the style editor," the girl said, forcing me to face her.

"Hi, Anna Walker," I said, trying to cover the screen with my body.

"I tried that Oreo thing, too," she said. "Complete crap. Rooibos tea. You've got to drink Rooibos tea. It's the only thing."

"Really?" I asked, hating to be so transparent.

"Oh yeah. Put on some Sarah McLaughlin and drink a cup of that . . . you'll forget your own name."

Without asking or announcing even, Theresa pulled my suit jacket off and replaced it with a pink, satin, fitted jacket and then fastened a long dangling sword necklace around my neck. "Much better," she said. "Dear, you can't walk around dressed like you were when you are representing *New York, New York*. We've gotta have style. Period." Theresa had a cool, short haircut that was very blond with dark roots, like only a style person could pull off. She had one of those great rich leather bags with streamers hanging off one of the short handles. Her featherweight turquoise blouse was perfect and matched her patterned wool pants. She looked fabulous. I could never put that together. In my insecurity, I instinctively felt for my left sleeve.

She sat on my desk next to my computer, facing me. I resettled in my swivel chair. She chomped on a wad of gum and looked at me one way, and then the next. "I'll do your whole image," she said. "I live for this kind of thing."

"Oh . . . you don't—"

"Oh, but I do," she interrupted. "I do." I didn't get to tell her this wasn't necessary.

"Theresa," I tried, "Got any ideas about which exclusive new spot I should visit for my first column?"

"I'll get back to you on that," she said, hopped off the desk, and disappeared.

She never did.

Judy hurled herself toward my new desk the second she had a break. She brought me a potted ivy and placed it on the empty overhead bookshelf.

"Do you have any ideas for your first column?" Judy wanted to know.

"Sure," I lied.

"I'll make a few calls," she said anyway and darted back to her desk.

When she called me half an hour later, I was filled with hope. "What'd you find?" I asked.

"Nothing," she said. "Boy, that's a really difficult job, isn't it?"

"Yeah," I scowled.

I picked up the phone. "Ray . . ."

12:00 p.m.

I met Ray at Serafina. We both thought a place like that was likely to produce some good tips for where I'd need to go tonight. It was a hot place to eat if you were an editor. As a publicist, I had taken plenty of editors to lunch on lobster salad to pitch them. I was ready to go and do whatever I needed to do, to get the information—especially if it somehow included eating some twirly pasta tossed in pounds of cream. But as I started walking there, I realized I had absolutely no idea what to actually do to obtain the information—and already I was feeling bad about starting out a new career filling myself with carbohydrates. So, I asked Ray to join me.

When that didn't work, I begged.

When that didn't work, I pleaded.

Promised to wash his clothes.

Make those chocolate chip cookies he loves.

Yes, the Lord & Taylor recipe that everyone was e-mailing around a couple of years ago.

Okay, *and* watch *American Idol* with him.

The whole season—even the themed episodes with the guest judges who tell everyone they are awesome indiscriminately. And text in his vote.

"Just get here," I told him.

★   ★   ★

Twenty minutes later I was enjoying a glass of afternoon white wine, and Ray was drinking a Heineken. The garden was right beyond where we sat, and in the sunlight we could have been anywhere—a café in the South of France or a summer house on Nantucket (as if I would know what either of those looked like). But then a siren screamed, and bam! We were back in New York.

"Well, who could have known Nasty was dating Christopher West?" Ray was slurping up a stray length of linguine. The guy could eat carbohydrates—complex, simple, you name it—just like that. Well, he could also stick to a strict workout regimen—which helped. "You just go," he'd once told me to my utter puzzlement. *You just go, you just go.* I'd thought it over every which way. I'd never get it.

I stabbed at a piece of lobster, heart of palm, tomato—the ultimate bite of the ultimate summer salad. Still, that linguine looked good. "I'm sure she's miserable right now. I wish things hadn't turned out this way. I really do. Side note, though, I can't believe they used the exact same title you joked about last night!"

"What can I say? I would have been a great journalist. But honestly, you'd better watch out. She doesn't seem like the kind to let things go." He pushed his plate toward me. "Would you just have some? We'll do the switch. I ordered the cream sauce for you anyway."

With one lone linguini twirled across my plate and another plate barren, save for an empty lobster shell in front of Ray, he asked, "So, when are you gonna start doing your research? Let's see what a nightlife chronicler does. C'mon. Whaddya got?" He smiled encouragingly.

"Right! Okay. I'm in the right place, surrounded by the right people. Looking the part, with my chic Le Fontaine notebook!" I waved it in my hand frantically to emphasize the point . . . and to stall. I had absolutely no idea what to do. I've never been much for going up to strangers and asking questions.

"So show me your moves," Ray said, rolling out his hand like I was about to perform a magic trick, which is exactly what this would have been if I had accomplished something to help myself. The equation that would get me from this table to the stylish girls in the corner was beyond my comprehension.

Ray folded his hands under his chin, looked on in anticipation.

I knew just what he was doing. He was nudging me into it, putting me on the spot. He knew the sort of push I needed. Still, if I waited long enough, he normally caved and did the thing for me.

I smiled, scooted my chair in, sat up straight. Repeated the word *okay*, until it meant nothing.

"You have absolutely no idea what to do here, do you?"

"None whatsoever." Why was I here again? Was it really worth all this just to save my life? Should it be this hard? I could remember my mom saying that a lot. "Things shouldn't be this hard," she'd say—worry all over her features—when she'd pick me up late from the after-school center. I'd be sitting on the stoop with the principal . . . her stiff black bun coming loose after the long day. What made me think *I* could to do *this*?

He heaved a sigh of mock shame. It was his favorite sigh. It always went with a desperate head shake and dramatically fluttered lashes. And thankfully, it always preceded his caving in.

"Watch the pro. I'll bill you for this later—and I'm talking a lot more than cookies and *American Idol*."

Ray loosened his tie a bit and caught the eye of the blonde maître d' who'd been scuttling here and there during the course of the lunch, crouching by this one, bringing a complimentary dessert to that one. I had noticed each eagle-eyed recipient declare, "Oh I couldn't!" before diving in fork first, without asking anyone at their table if they'd like some. Ray tossed one big smile her way, and she was at our table.

"And how eez your lunch todee, seer?" she crooned.

"Oh, it was fabulous. But what I want to know, beautiful, is where does a guy go at night around here? Where are all the beauties like yourself going to be?" The gel holding his dark hair in place gleamed.

"Easy, breezy, beautiful" is the phrase that came to mind. He was that good.

"Oh, monsieur, you are too much. Where you need to go tonight is Stanton Social. Eez een zee Lower East Side. I weel be zere, for sure."

She batted lashes, repositioned hair, continued to otherwise make me feel completely inadequate by comparison, and then turned, revealing the longest torso and the most obnoxiously perfect butt ever seen without a pair of matching Victoria's Secret wings. I quickly attempted to catalog my strong points, came up with "I fall among the portion of the population who understands the brilliance of Larry David's *Curb Your Enthusiasm*," breathed, and remembered that the real point of this whole thing was that Ray should have his own column . . . not me! I could never have done that!

When Frenchie was out of earshot, Ray said, "And that's how it's done. Now you go over to those editors at that table over there."

Could I do that? "Just walk over to them . . ."

"Yes."

"To their table?"

"Yes."

I stood, and my chair shrieked loudly against the tile floor. People looked up clutching their ears . . . including the editors. There were three of them, and they were in head-to-toe black, all of them—pants, a skirt, and an Audrey Hepburn shift dress. They turned back around and didn't see me walk over. I looked over my shoulder right before I reached their table to see Ray's expression, check if he'd changed his mind and had a plan B, but he shook his head encouragingly. I smiled back as well as I could and turned forward. My heel caught between two tiles, and I went lurching right at one of the editors.

The three of them shifted their eyes back and forth as if they thought I was nuts. I was here, though, with nothing to lose. So I calmly slipped my foot back inside my shoe and said, "Hi ladies, I know you're super-chic editors. And I'm a brand-new editor—I've got a column at *New York, New York*."

"Really?" the oldest one asked, not very kindly.

"Yes, I do. It's a nightlife column. And as you know, *New York, New York* only does exclusives, which means I've got to get it first. So, I was wondering if any of you might know of a new spot I can write about."

"Why would we tell you?" another of them asked, pushing her green laminate glasses higher up on her nose.

"Well . . ." I didn't know. I just didn't know why.

"Yes, she's quite right. We're not going to give away proprietary information to someone we've never heard of."

They were drilling holes through my face with their eyes. I couldn't stand it another second. I'd put myself out there, which was no easy thing for me. And I didn't see the point of drawing it out any longer. "Okay then. Nice talking with you." I'm not quite sure why I saluted, but I imagine it had something to do with intimidation.

"Hey, you did a fabulous job," Ray said back at the table. "They're just nasty, sexually frustrated bitches." He said that loud enough for them to hear. And that made me feel a little better.

2:00 p.m.

Back at the office, I checked a trendy e-mail newsletter, *Shhh!*, and they reported that Stanton Social *was* in fact the place to be that evening—therefore rendering that tip useless for my purposes.

Great! Now what? How the heck was I supposed to figure this out? I followed up with Theresa and Judy, but neither of them had any ideas for me. "This is going to be, like, impossible," Theresa said.

3:00 p.m.

Despite myself, I wondered, if this didn't work out, would I get to keep the jacket?

Without a better plan, I braced myself and headed to Joseph's office to ask for advice. It killed me to ask, but surely he would expect me to need a bit of advice. Isn't that how people learn—by asking advice of people who've already succeeded? Sure! It even has a name! It's called *mentoring*. I'd even once been a mentor myself. We were in twelfth grade and were assigned incoming freshmen to mentor—teach them the ropes, advise them on social issues, provide the inside track information on different classes. My mentee was Coral Smithson. We met in the Cafetorium (that was a hybrid cafeteria slash auditorium) during first period, which I had free.

"I heard you're a loser," she said. I was stunned into silence. Here was this little pipsqueak in braces telling me this! Well I wasn't going to take it . . . that was for sure! But when I tried to say, "Go to hell, metal mouth," nothing came out except, "Kellmore High is a very diverse place," which was one of the suggested lines I'd memorized from the mentoring pamphlet.

"Do me a favor," Coral had said, "just turn around, walk away, and don't acknowledge me again. It's hard enough trying to make it through high school without being seen with someone like you." Webs of saliva had formed between her top and bottom lips at both corners.

The truth is, I wasn't that much of a loser. I had a couple of friends. And because of my dark past, I'd earned a sort of cult status, like Urban Decay makeup has—for being just a little mysterious and dark. It was just that this girl didn't get me. And explaining myself was never something I was great at.

Approaching Grosseph's office now, I thought maybe that was something I should have given some consideration to before getting into the writing business.

His door was closed, and I was just about to knock when I overheard a very loud voice come over the speaker phone.

"Joseph, is that you?" the soured voice wanted to know.

"Yes, Mom," he droned.

I had to clamp my hand over my mouth to keep the laugh in.

"It's not like I really need to ask," his mom went on. "You call me at the same time every single day. I let the phone ring and ring, but you don't let up . . . do you? You call too much. And you whine about everything. You never have any interest in my church group, book group, mah-jongg game. Or my gout."

Yuck! Now this was good stuff. How about an "Anna Says" column? But no . . . nobody's as sneaky as Joseph, are they?

"Sorry, Mom," he said miserably.

"What is it now, Joseph?" she chirped, "I'm ironing my favorite muumuu . . . you know, I would have thought Florida would be far enough to remove myself from your bullcrap. Life is short, Joseph . . . you know."

"Mommy, my editor cut my page in half to make room for a new column."

Mommy! This was priceless. But wait! That was my column he was probably talking about.

Mrs. James sighed deeply.

"Joseph, look, I'm not even in your business, and I know that these things are cyclic. It's like the stock market—it's about longevity; stick with it, and over time it all levels out. It's the advertisers—what they want. Don't take it personally, honey. You know all this. You are the one that told me the very same thing when you were talking about that guy who got pissed off at *you* when your column cut *his* in half!"

"But that was different," Joseph whined.

"How so? Ah, you know, there's nothing like a wrinkle-free, silent muumuu."

"Because this is *my column*!"

"Joseph! Grow up!"

"You just watch, Mommy. I'm going to get that Anna! You should see this girl I picked for the position! She's got no experience! And from what I've seen, she can get herself into trouble pretty easily. She won't last through tomorrow. The whole idea will be tossed. And I'll get my name back in twenty-five-point font in no time."

What?!?

"Whatever, Joseph. You're a lost cause. I've got mah-jongg now."

5:30 p.m.

Despite all the false starts, the attempts at my ruination, I don't know, something happened in my head. Though nothing was working out correctly, I was just in the midst of everything, just trying . . . and I don't know . . . I kind of went on autopilot. And now I felt like I had to get this done.

Unfortunately, determination does not exactly equal finding an exclusive nightclub to write about on a few hours' notice. I was spent. I couldn't think of a single concierge, publicist, cool boutique, or hair salon I hadn't already called to get a good tip from. *This month was slow. We already promised another publication. We aren't familiar with your work. We don't give exclusives. Anna Who? Why don't you call back when you're famous?*

"It's always difficult in the beginning," Theresa advised me. "They have to build up their trust. They have to see your column. And then you'll see . . . they'll start coming to you."

"Yeah, but how are they gonna see my column if I can't find a place to write about?"

"The funny thing with these wild research chases under deadline is that somehow, they always work out in the end. It's like the fairy godmother of deadlines swoops down to help, or something. It's kind of freaky."

I wanted to make a few more calls before I met Nina at Get Nailed. I figured the spa would be a much-needed break if I was going to have to blindly pound the pavement this evening. I'd come up with a script, after trial and error—a mixture of butt-kissing, "I'm-a-columnist" importance and a no-nonsense punch.

"Is this Charlotte Ronson's shop? Oh it is? Well, I'm Anna Walker, a brand-new columnist at *New York, New York*. What's that? You're reading it right now? That is *too* funny. Well, just goes to prove you're the right person for me to be calling! Yes, of course I want to talk to you. I thought, hey, I'm gonna go about this the right way, you know, call the really cool folks like yourself who really know what's going on in this city. Oh, Stanton Social tonight? Yeah, I'll be there."

I felt like a used car salesman. And not even a good one. Apparently this couldn't be accomplished in one day. Unfortunately, for me, it had to be.

6:30 p.m.

"Joseph said the dictum of the column is it's got to be never-before printed, to make me the authority on what's hot—'those are the sorts of standards that make *New York, New York* the hippest, hottest paper, and we will accept nothing less.' That's what he said." I was sipping an iced frosty mocha latte while I spoke—God! Why were those so good? Dessert disguised as coffee, it was genius really.

We were standing in line with twelve other women, waiting to be among the first to have a manicure and pedicure at Get Nailed. The spa was after that chicer than chic clientele. I wondered if they'd let me in. The front room was green—all green: green walls, green curtains, green plants that stretched up to the ceiling—cactus and palms and big spider leaves. There was a soundtrack of chirping birds and even a green parrot flying here and there, stopping on one plant, and then on the other. It had been trained to say, "Get nailed, get nailed."

Green candles of various sizes glowed here, there, and everywhere, and one regal, green velvet sofa with ornate gold detail held the two luckiest girls in the room, the ones who could rest their high-heeled feet. One of them was chatting away on a cell phone in that loud way that annoys just about everyone. Except of course, for the other people talking just as loudly on their own cell phones.

All of a sudden, a very large, very not-smiling Russian-looking woman rose up from her very tiny, in comparison, laptop computer/register, pushed her rolling chair away, sent it crashing against the wall, and walked right up to me.

"No food in here!" she said not two inches from my face, spitting a little.

I was frightened, but managed to find my voice, maybe from all the practice I'd had mustering up courage on the phone all day— saying anything to anyone, making mistakes and living through it, getting hung up on, laughed at.

"It's a drink," I tried, smiling sweetly.

"You not kiddink anyone mit dat—everyone know iced frosty mocha latte is a dessert disguised as coffee!" And in one fluid movement, she stole my drink/dessert from my hand, grabbed my arm, grabbed the girl on the cell phone—who didn't even look up—and closed the pair of us inside a treatment room. I looked back at Nina miserably. I needed to be with her then.

As I was yanked into Room 2, I wanted to be angry and upset, but it was just so fabulously soothing in that room. The room was all pink—like a fluff of cotton candy. Pink cashmere blankets draped over two pedicure/manicure beds, and pink mosquito netting, which made a luxurious cocoon around everything inside— including the television units hanging from the ceiling above each bed, the complete collection of Madonna films in a pink basket, each and every Madonna music video, that racy documentary she'd produced, and the MTV film about her European tour. The pedicure basins were pink Italian marble and rested at the foot of each bed.

Cell Phone barely noticed. She got naked, something I wasn't sure we were even supposed to do, gabbed away, and left her clothing in a heap on the floor. Immediately, Cell Phone was draped in a pink cashmere robe by two silent sets of arms, her clothing was gathered and hung on a pink satin hanger behind the door, and as she was led to her cotton-candy cocoon, the pink cashmere blanket was smoothed over her body.

As I was given my own opportunity to disrobe and wrap myself in cashmere, I couldn't quite relax and enjoy the bliss that surrounded me (bliss I knew Nina must have been paying a fortune for under the guise of "research," bliss I could never afford myself, especially if I lost my job). First there was the stress I'd come here with—no hotspot for the Velvet Rope Diaries column, which I now knew Joseph was trying to sabotage, never mind the crazy events surrounding Nasty. In the morning I'd have laughed at the idea of having my own column. It was amazing how much had changed so quickly. It was amazing how quickly I screwed it all up.

But beyond that, there was this woman—so rude!—making relaxation a remote possibility. How could these big burly women let her gab away like that, when they wouldn't even let me enjoy my harmless iced frosty mocha latte! When did an iced frosty mocha latte ever hurt anyone? Maybe an extra calorie or two thousand here or there, but that was it, really, and wasn't the enjoyment really more weighty than the few (thousand) calories? It's not like my drink/dessert was infringing upon the relaxation time that was supposed to calm me back into thinking straight and finding a solution!

Wait a minute.

Were those rose petals I smelled in that pedicure basin?

Was that ylang-ylang wafting through my olfactory system and chakras?

River stones I was rubbing my feet over?

And what exactly was in that eye mask they slipped over my head? It was cool and tingly and ooooohhhh . . .

Swirls of light passed under my lids. I could almost block out the whole world, including the still-chatting Cell Phone.

Wait. She was off! The woman was off the phone! Okay, now I could start relaxing. I could get down to business. Aahh. Life wasn't so bad. I could do this. Just a little refreshing first. That was all I needed. Life wasn't that difficult! And there was still the idea of the fairy godmother of deadlines.

"Sandy?"

"Oh no, I'm not Sand—" Too late, it became obvious that the woman was not talking to me, hadn't even noticed me, when she continued right on with her next cell phone conversation.

"You would not believe what my private shopper at Bergdorf got for me today! No. Guess. No. Seriously. No. Guess."

Even as a silent pair of hands slipped a bending straw in my mouth and the freshest lemonade passed my lips and filled me with lightness, I couldn't stop feeling agitated by Cell Phone. Why? Why would they allow this?

"No. Not the Marc Jacobs military jacket with the big flower. Nope. Not the Choos with the enormous green stones along the toe strap. Duh, I already *have* those. Nope. No. You HAVE TO guess."

River stones, river stones. There was nothing in the world to think of but river stones. I told myself this and really tried to believe it. I tried to believe that I didn't want to wring this woman's neck and tell her to go to hell and that she didn't own the entire world. I closed my lids and tried to concentrate on my third eye. This is a yoga technique that works quite well when you are trying to contort your body and want to stop yourself from thinking, *I'm going to fall flat on my face and break my nose and then blood will trail all over this cute yoga top with the symbols I don't understand printed up the arm that I just spent way too much money on . . . ohm . . .*

I concentrated so hard I felt one of the river stones take off. Of course I couldn't see where it had gone, with the eye mask on, but one of the aestheticians screamed, "Ouch! My god!" But then she composed herself and said, "Is okay dear. You missed me."

"Sorry," I offered pathetically. See this? This is just so typical of me. I'll wind up killing myself and the whole world before I can bring myself to simply ask the woman to end her conversation.

"YES! Can you believe it? Yes! The moss green Luella Bartley purse with the heart tag hanging from the shoulder strap! Yes! I'm wearing it right now! And you wouldn't believe where I am. This nail spa, *Get Nailed*, has the absolute cutest cashmere robes. Yes. I was going to ask about the availability? Do you want one, too? Oh it would be so much fun if we had matching robes for the Hamptons! Ooohhh!!!" She went on and on and on.

R-I-V-E-R S-T-O-N-E-S. River. Stones. The stones of a river. Like a rolling stone. Roll. Roll. Do river stones roll? Do they? Hmmmmmmmm. Ahhhhhhh. Oooohm. WHY CAN'T SHE JUST SHUT UP?!!!

Suddenly, I removed my eye mask in a way that meant business. Cell Phone didn't notice.

"I mean, it's no Cornelia Spa. But it's nice enough. Yeah. I mean, it's okay." She lifted her eye mask up like a headband, sat up, and reached for her chamomile tea. This was my chance. And I took it. I stood up and walked right over to her treatment table. This felt a lot like approaching the editors earlier, but I didn't have a heel to get stuck, plus I now had the knowledge that I could live through a scene like this, no matter how painful it was at the moment. "Excuse me," I said.

Cell Phone's mouth dropped into an oval, and she said into her cell phone, "I'll call you back." She snapped her phone closed and clutched it in her hand like she couldn't quite let go.

"Yes?" she asked me. I could see she was a little older than I had suspected. There were some lines sprouting from her eyes, and they made her more likeable now her phone was off. Her makeup had been wiped clean by the aesthetician so that her pores could absorb the essential oils and her skin looked fresh. Her blond, streaked hair had been pulled back into a tight bun.

"Do you think you could refrain from using your cell phone in here? It's kind of difficult to relax when someone is constantly talking." There, I got it out. So I was shaking a little bit.

Her face fell instantly into a wretched look, and I wanted to take it all back.

She said, "Oh you're right. I know you're right." She put her hand on mine, which surprised me, and even the two aestheticians rubbing her back seemed shocked. "I'm afraid I'll do anything to stop myself from being still enough to think myself into a depression."

This sounded familiar to me. That was just my motivation for tossing my stupid paper clips every day. I couldn't help but soften toward her. "Why? What happened to you?"

"A stupid divorce. Don't ever marry a man with a twenty-year-old secretary. Please do yourself a favor."

I couldn't help but let out a light laugh. She had a funny way. "I'm sorry. That is really terrible," I said. The aesthetician had pulled me back to work on my pedicure, but I sat up and Cell Phone had lain back down.

"Hey, what's your name?" the woman asked after a few moments.

I was very ticklish on my feet, so I fidgeted a bit when I answered, "Anna."

"Well, I'm Susan," she said. "So what do you do, Anna?"

"Funny you should ask," I said. And I don't know if it was her honesty, or the essential oils or the rubdown, or the desperation even, but I told her the whole story.

She listened on her back, without looking my way the whole time. But it felt good to share, at the very least. I was still sort of— in an off way—counting on the fairy godmother of deadlines. And when I thought of that, I repeated that, too.

"Oh, yes," Susan said. "I've heard of her." She didn't seem to be kidding.

"You have?" Maybe she was a little nutty. Or just pulling my chain. That whole notion was a metaphor, anyhow, wasn't it?

"I think she just visited you." Susan sat up.

"What do you mean?" I asked.

"Well, you're coming with me. I'm your deadline fairy godmother, I guess. I've definitely been called worse. My friend Columbus—a terrible two-timer himself—is opening a new spot tonight in the Maritime Hotel. It's called S."

"Just S?" I asked.

"Well, yeah. Everyone's saying it stands for secret, but *we* all know it's for the name of his skanky mistress, Samantha."

"I spoke to about a million people and not one of them knows about it," I said.

"That's because the press launch isn't until a month from now."

"Susan?"

"Yes, dear?"

"I think you're my new best friend."

FOUR

Barefoot in the Dark

"Who's your friend?" Ray asked, looking at me, never directly at David. He was always suspicious of the men I dated. And with my track record I really didn't blame him.

—Velvet Rope Diaries, New York, New York

9:30 p.m.

Nina, Ray, and I pulled up to S in a taxi.

"We're not gonna have to wait on that long line when we're on the list are we?" Ray asked when we got a glimpse of the line of glamorous people snaking around the corner.

"Of course not," Nina said. "You just go tell that big bald guy that you're on the list, honey." She looked very pretty in a sparkly camisole and expensive jeans and pumps. I should have worn something like that. But no, I'd been inspired by the Madonna films and tried to put together a cool pyramid jacket like the one from *Desperately Seeking Susan*. And now I had some hot glue permanently affixed to my index fingers. At least Ray had managed to pull them apart. "Always in something Anna," he said, amused somehow, looking at the window as he held my hand in a bowl of soapy water.

Why couldn't we just wait on that line? What was so wrong with waiting on a line? There were plenty of people waiting on it already, obviously. The best part, of course, would have been standing in the line rather than mustering up the courage to go talk to that scary bald guy who must have been seven foot, at the least.

"Okay," I mumbled, tightening my hand around the retro gold lunch box I had decided—stupidly, I saw now—to use for a purse.

When I agreed to go up to him, I was under a lot of pressure. I was supposed to be some hotshot nightlife columnist. Sure you and I know the truth. And Ray and Nina did, too. But it was clear that some part of us—all three of us—wanted me to get to the front of the line for once and get us inside so that *we* could be the most important, so that people wondered who *we* were, so that could prove that we really *could* realize an extraordinary dream in this town. It was an exciting idea, anyway.

"Do it quickly, please, because I think I see William from my office." Ray hated William, whom he said was always "throwing his dick around," telling stories about escapades no one wanted to hear about.

I, myself, despised William, whom I'd met many times with Ray after work or at lunch. The first time, I overheard him say to Ray, "Whoa! She's got some hot tits!" Ray looked like he might sock the guy right in the nose, except this guy also happened to be the guy Ray directly reported to. So I'm sure you see why I didn't care to spend the evening with him.

"Okay," I mumbled, terrified. I left Ray and Nina in their spot in line, which already had grown a good twenty people behind them. I walked past hundreds of people, and I looked only at their shoes, wondering what I was doing here. Did I really think making a fool of myself this way—trying to fit in at a place like this—would save my life, help me feel better about myself, more involved in life? I couldn't see a way in the world I could make this work. I didn't have the first clue what to write about this place; I couldn't even come up with the words to get us inside. I watched my own feet as they made their way, slowly, but surely to where they needed to be. At least I had the right shoes on. In fact I loved these shoes. They were the only shoes I owned that weren't a sensible knockoff of some designer pair that Nina picked out for me on 86th Street. They were real. They were Marc Jacobs. I loved the stiff bows at the toe. They seemed happy to me, hopeful. And that's what I loved most about them.

Walking, walking, walking, I tried to think more productively. I realized I could make excuses about any venture I tried out and find a way to fail. Why *shouldn't* I get in? What about *me* was so different than these people? I felt a little more relaxed when I thought those things. I kept moving toward the line's origin, at least. And I don't know why, but just before I got to the beginning, I thought of this funny thing my dad used to do just before we'd part ways—before school or when Mom and I would visit Grandma. He'd squeeze his cheeks in, making his lips pucker up like a fish and say, "Hi, I'm a guppy." As soon as he'd start talking, my mom and I would be in stitches, he looked so silly that way. Then he'd finish the skit, "Guppies can't smile, but I can . . . see." And then he'd smile and the squeezed lips in between the squished in cheeks looked just like a Cabbage Patch Kid. All throughout the ride my mom and I would keep going back to it, saying, "That is so funny." Or we'd just think of it and laugh contagiously.

I was nearly to the front of the line when I laughed, just thinking of what my dad looked like as a smiling guppy—enjoying the memory like that—when I finally looked up.

The line outside S was insane. And like any opening night—I'd learn later—poorly organized. There were people trying to break through the velvet ropes at all angles. People were talking too loudly, giddy with the excitement of going somewhere other people didn't know about. I thought that might be addictive—wanting to know first, laying claim to that. These girls were dressed impeccably. It was like looking at pages in fashion magazines—they wore the glittery diamond necklaces and the long, dangling earrings; they had on the shirts so low-cut their stomachs showed and fishnet stockings and special edition purses you didn't see anywhere. Despite the shoes, I looked like a moron. The jacket was a disaster. My skirt didn't match entirely. I knew that instantly. But there was nothing to be done about that now.

I'd been the girl holding the clipboard at the door, so I thought maybe that would help me handle this.

"Hi," I said to the door guy, who was currently standing stony, not looking at anyone or anything. He was much taller up close. He looked like a vaguely German evil villain from any of Bruce Willis's movies.

"Hi," he said without looking at me. It was the meanest "hi" I had ever heard. In fact, I didn't know how mean a "hi" could be until that moment. Okay, never mind! Going home! This is what I thought, but amazingly I didn't say it. Instead, I pressed on.

"I am Anna Walker. I'm on the list with—" I didn't get to finish, he cut me off directly.

"Oh, you're on the list, huh?" He looked at me for the first time—up and down and side to side, then on a diagonal. And then he twisted up his face like he'd just gargled Listerine (and not that sweet minty kind!) and karate chopped his arm to a stop right in front of my face.

"Just a minute," he said, his scowl turning to a smirk.

He looked at the sky, as people tend to do when they speak into headsets.

"We've got an LYMJ here." He pronounced each letter loudly, clearly, importantly.

Ooooh! Okay! Now I was getting somewhere! That sounded really official. We used to use code words for important people. Like
celebrities were GLITTER-1, or GLITTER-2—depending on if it
was Tom Cruise or that guy who played Doogie Howser. Maybe
Susan had really talked me up. Maybe I'd get VIP entrance and then
I would just find Ray and Nina and it would be champagne and
caviar, or whatever rich people eat nowadays, until morning. Really,
this wasn't so bad. See. All I had to do was have a little confidence. I
was really feeling proud of the way I'd just gone up to the front of
the line like that. The way I'd kept forging on even after I'd choked
on the Oreos, been laughed at, hit a million dead ends. This was
something, really it was.

Like a waterfall of pitch, sound rang through the area in a beautiful song. "LYMJ!" "LYMJ!" "LYMJ!" "LYMJ!" "LYMJ!" "LYMJ!"
"LYMJ!" Someone had a megaphone. "LYMJ!" Then they turned
on the siren function. Okay, that was kind of loud. The entire line
looked up, probably wondering if someone really cool like George
Clooney or Gisele Bundchen had shown up.

"Okay, you really don't have to put on all this fuss for me," I said.
"I'd rather just go grab my friends back there and go in quietly."

He didn't say a word. Didn't even budge a feature. The megaphone guy pressed the siren button once more. I winced. Baldy's
head started to shake left to right. His mouth was pursed.

What the heck was going on here, already? It was getting chilly,
and I didn't have any stockings on, and I was going to have to walk
all the way back to get Nina and Ray. Couldn't we move this along
a little?

"You're not going anywhere," he said, his body barricading me.

"No, really, I don't need this sort of fuss! It's only my first day, really!" Despite the embarrassment creeping into my cheeks in the
form of a crimson flush, secretly I was honored. I never thought I'd

like this kind of attention, but it was actually kind of cool. I couldn't see them, and didn't know if they could see me, but I waved to Ray and Nina just in case, so they would know everything was okay.

"No, really," he repeated. "You're not going anywhere. Not in those Last Year's Marc Jacobs!"

It took a dizzying minute to sink in. Huh? LYMJ? Last Year's Marc Jacobs?!? *My* last year's Marc Jacobs? I was being denied entry because my shoes were from last year? My favorite shoes, by the way? Could this really be true? The idea was ridiculous, and simultaneously, inexplicably mortifying. If this wasn't a sign to run and give up, beg for my job with Nasty back, and resume making excuses in place of having an actual life, then I really don't know what would have been.

"And don't EVER try coming back either. We don't want your kind here."

I wanted to say all sorts of things about Susan and her friend Columbus, and *New York, New York*, but of course—I *am* Anna Walker, after all, no matter what had happened today—and so a big, fat, pathetic nothing came out. People had started to laugh. And point. A couple of European-looking guys in colored pumas and too-tight girly jeans were even laughing at me. And those were the kinds of people that everyone else usually laughed at. I took off, walking at first, and then faster, faster, I ran.

"I'm a guppy." I tried to laugh about it then, keep my center. But I just couldn't.

9:45 p.m.

All I wanted to do was get away from those people, so rather than walk toward the back of the line, where Nina and Ray were waiting, I went the opposite way past the bald bully—around the corner. I could still faintly hear them yelling, "LYMJ!" like a battle cry.

I was humiliated. I just wanted to curl back into the fetal position and grab one of my ratty childhood stuffed animals and ask why I ever had to grow up, after all, I'd always been a Toys "R" Us kid.

I walked and walked around S. The building was gigantic—one of those old factory clubs like everyone went nuts for in the eighties and nineties. I'd been really excited about it. It had sort of seemed like Dr. Fenwick's idea was actually working. But who was I kidding? I was no nightlife reviewer. I was . . . well, I was a loser carrying around a lunch box as a purse and wearing unfashionable shoes.

After what felt like an eternity of walking, I found myself facing an unmarked door of S. It looked like some kind of service entrance. Should I just try it? I looked to my right and then left and then swiveled my head to check over my shoulder for anyone who might be watching. "Shh!" I yelled to my purse when it jingled loud against the brick wall.

I looked up to the sky and said, "Please, let this door open." I held my breath, slowly grabbed for the knob. It turned. I was so surprised that it turned, I barreled through the door without thinking. And then the door slammed, and I realized I was in complete blackness. This must have been some storage room or employee room. I could faintly hear the music coming from S through a far wall, but who knew what was between me and that wall?

"Hello?" I tried. My words echoed back, *"Hello, hello, hello,"* in a ghostly way that scared the crap out of me. Little by little, the danger of the situation was coming clear to me. I was in a dark room in Manhattan, with no idea of who else was in here with me. When that all hit me, I screamed like a child and dropped my lunch box, spewing the contents on the floor—which of course I could not see.

Open the door is what I was going to do. I'd just open the door, find my stuff, and get the hell out of there.

Okay, I had a plan. On my hands and knees—despite the likely possibility of mice and roaches—I felt around for my way back to the door. The floor was freezing—concrete—and it was rough on my bare knees. What had I been thinking to step inside a dark room in Manhattan, where anyone could be there just waiting to kill stupid girls like me? I was feeling around and feeling around, and so far I hadn't come upon anything at all. And just when I was starting to think nothing could get worse, I felt a quick flash of fur on my calf and heard the scurrying of feet.

"Aaaahhhh!!!" It was a mouse. At least I was hoping for that over a rat.

"I am not going to panic. I am not going to panic." Then it occurred to me that possibly, I'd never get out. What if I couldn't find the door and no one could find me and I was eaten alive by whatever that was . . . It could have been something bigger like a fox or a mountain lion that had gotten lost out in Westchester! Even if it wasn't, I could simply starve to death. I think you have something like two days until that happens. And I could never eat rats or anything like those people on *Survivor* do. I won't even eat a Tic Tac if it has some fuzz on it from my purse.

"River stones. I'm thinking of river stones. I'm rubbing my toes over those river stones, in fact. I'm lying in that pink cocoon next to Susan, and she's telling me how she's my deadline fairy godmother." I started crawling faster and faster, but I don't know, maybe I was going in circles, because I still hadn't touched anything that felt like a wall. I'd never had a great sense of direction. Back home, I always got lost in the mall trying to find my way from Ann Taylor Loft to Bath & Body Works!

"RIVER STONES!" I was screaming. And then all of a sudden I heard a noise, which scared me silent. I slapped my hand over my mouth so I wouldn't yell, so I could mask the loud breathing. Holy cow, it is terrifying when you cannot see. Absolutely terrifying.

And when I saw a triangle of light grow and then shrink, I realized it was the door. Fear held my tongue, though, and I didn't say anything until it was too late. The door had closed again! And now there was no doubt about it. I was definitely in there with someone. This could be a hideout for drug dealers. Or hit men, or car thieves, or it could be a place that rapists come to. Or people who sell people into slavery. I really should have paid more attention when Ray was watching that special on human slavery! It was just that I didn't want to think about that. It was so disturbing . . . I just wanted to look through my *Us Weekly* instead.

Suddenly, my mind went wild with all of the horrendous possibilities, and I had never wanted to live and achieve so much in my life. If I got out of there, I would appreciate every single breath that came into and left my body . . . every single one. I would take all of Fenwick's advice seriously and do the best I could to live my life!

"Who's there?" a male voice asked.

As soon as I heard it, my body went all tingly, like my worst nightmare was being realized. I just knew I wouldn't be able to move if I had to. I'd be frozen. I didn't have a survival instinct. I always thought that if it came right down to it, that I would. That I would be able to just let my natural intuition kick in and save me. But I could see now that wasn't going to happen. I was going to be murdered. And all anyone would say is, "How could anyone be so stupid as to actually close themselves inside a black room in the city?" And then it would come out that I was escaping a particularly hairy LYMJ experience, and everyone would then say, "Oh, I see." I hoped Marc Jacobs wouldn't feel too bad about it, as he always seemed very nice to me in those unflattering thick glasses.

I didn't even like to watch murder mystery movies, or those frightening serial killer films starring Jodi Foster that Ray was always glued to. Oh god. Oh god. I tried to remember where the light had just flickered and disappeared, but already it was difficult to place it. I didn't even know where *I* was.

The footsteps came closer, and I tried to be still. I had my hands balled up on either side of my head and my elbows were on the floor—frozen the way I'd been crawling. I didn't want to make any noise. But then I thought, if the person was walking, maybe I could move at the same time without him noticing. I crawled as silently as possible, quickly, quickly; trying not to make a noise. I choked back breath. Oh god. Oh god.

And that's when it hit me.

Or rather, *he* hit me. Not a smack, much more of a collision, actually. "Agh!" In my fear I ran in what I hoped was the opposite direction and kept going until . . . smack! I (painfully) found the wall. I was furiously feeling around for a door, for a corner to take me to the next wall that might have a door. And in spite of the fear and bloodcurdling scream, I could tell his cologne smelled *really* good. Like, *really* good. The kind of good you didn't get all the time. The kind of good that couldn't possibly be worn by a criminal . . . I hoped.

"Are you okay?" the man scared me once again out of the silence.

He seemed nice. But don't they always seem nice? Did this mean anything at all? Really, though, he did seem nice.

"I have a knife," I said.

"Noted," he said, not seeming in the least bit startled by the claim.

"And Mace!" I made the gesture of spraying it even though he obviously couldn't see it. "Shhh-shhh-shhh!" I faked the sound as an afterthought.

He chuckled. "Gotcha," he said.

"Hey it's a really big bottle—industrial size. And I also have a black belt in karate—*and* Tae Kwon Do!" I felt my hands form tight fists at my chest.

"So I gather you are fine, being you've got all of those defenses at hand."

"Exactly. I am perfect. Never been better or better equipped in my life." Even as I said it, I realized I'd used up all of my bravery. I was starting to come apart at the seams. I felt my chest tremble with the beginnings of it. When I tried to continue on, I knew the sobs were destroying my credibility. "I (sob) am (sob) perf—(sob, sob, sob)—ect. Sob, sob, sob, sob, sob, *sobbb*." Oh, I was just hysterical now.

"Oh, can I help?" the voice asked. And it *was* a nice voice. You could just tell. *Could* he help?

"Well, first, are you a murderer?" I sniffed, wiping my face with the back of a hand. I recognized the ridiculousness of the question as I asked it, but really, if you were in the situation, you'd see there weren't many other choices.

"Er, no. Not last I checked."

"Rapist?"

"Nope."

"Criminal of any sort?"

"Well"—he let the word drag out long and low, as if he were playing with the idea in his mind before continuing—"once when I was five years old, I was at the supermarket with my nanny, and I really wanted a Kit Kat. I loved those back then," he said and laughed.

I found myself smiling, wondering if he'd thrown his head back nonchalantly. What was I thinking? He could still be a murderer! I reminded myself of the severity of the situation. He had indicated he wasn't a murderer or a rapist, but still . . .

"My nanny said no, and so when I got to the register and she was piling all the boring adult food onto the register belt—I can see it now, broccoli bunches and stalks of asparagus, steaks and eggs—I took not one Kit Kat, but *two* right from the display and slid them up under my shirt."

I couldn't help myself. A laugh snuck through.

"Really," he said.

I thought, despite the whole situation, that he sounded really cute.

"It was so frightening. They kept sliding all over the place. I was sure they were going to fall right out through one of my pants legs—I was so lanky back then. I always tell people—if you're going to steal, just don't get greedy, because it gets way too complicated. One I would have been fine with. I'll stick to that until this day."

"Did you get caught?" I found myself asking, breathing easier as I lowered myself back onto the ground into a seated position.

He answered quickly. "Nope. She never realized. But I felt plenty guilty. Really, I was remorseful."

He may have been laying it on thick, but I wasn't sure. It sounded pretty adorable, soft. "So you didn't eat any of it?" I asked, removing the straps of my shoes, which were starting to pinch at the ankle.

"Oh, no I ate it. But I thought about it first. I'd say it was a good five minutes I thought over what I'd done."

"So it tasted bitter sliding down into your stomach like regret?" I asked, thinking of the times in my life that I'd tasted that very thing.

"Well, I'm not sure."

"What do you mean you're not sure? It either did or it didn't."

"I'm not sure what regret tastes like exactly. If it's a mixture of crunchy wafer, praline, and chocolate, well then, yes. That is exactly what it tasted like."

Admittedly, the faceless stranger had an easy, comfortable way about him. And his smell. It was getting stronger now.

It was silent for a moment while I thought really how good he smelled. There was sandalwood in there for sure and maybe something sweet, like . . . vanilla.

"So, can I ask how you came to be in this pitch-black room?" he asked.

I squeezed my shoes in my palms as I thought over what had

transpired not moments ago. I could still hear the shouts in my head, "LYMJ! LYMJ!" Now that it didn't seem I would be murdered, the hopelessness of that situation came back to me.

And so I told him. Before I knew it, he was sitting down next to me, and I'd told him everything.

"So you say this Susan Levy is your deadline fairy godmother?" he asked me.

It sounded really stupid coming from him like that. "Yeah, but it's not like I really believe in that . . . obviously," I reasoned.

"Yeah? Well, why not?"

"Well . . . because, it's dumb . . . isn't it?" I turned to him. I wished I could see him. It had been so long since I was this attracted to someone. I hated to get ahead of myself, but he seemed perfect. I mean, other than the fact that I had no idea what he looked like or who he was. "Ray said it was a little nutty."

"Who's Ray?"

Was I nuts or did he sound a little jealous?

"Is he your boyfriend or something?" he asked.

"Ray? No. He's my roommate." This wasn't the first time someone had assumed that we were a couple. Sometimes, in college, I could console myself with the fact that at least people *thought* I had a boyfriend . . . that I didn't just have those short-lived flings that invariably ended with me yelling mortifying things into my ceiling, like, "Who's going to take care of me now?"

"Good."

That was a fantastic response. Wasn't it? "Good?" I hoped I knew what he was getting at, but I wanted to be sure.

"Yeah. Good. Because I want to take you out on a date, Anna."

"Oh. Okay. That would be nice."

We were silent for a few seconds.

And then I asked, "Can I ask you a question?"

"Sure."

"How did *you* happen to come into this room?"

"Well, I guess you could say your deadline fairy godmother sent me."

2:00 p.m., Thursday, September 22

Velvet Rope Diaries
by Anna Walker

No. No. That is all wrong.

Velvet Rope Diaries
by Anna P. Walker

Much better. Infinitely. The truth is, I don't really have a middle name at all. I never did. That *P* got there because I was doing my homework way back in the fourth grade and I was eating dinner at the same time and somehow a green pea got smushed right in between my first and last names. Roger thought it was hysterical . . . and voila, the rest is history. But, I think it goes quite nicely.

Annabananasplit: So, what do you think of this for a start? S is rather large . . . in size. It is very big. So big that there are whole rooms that are not even used for anything. They have all sorts of drinks and food, too— little nibbly things. Also, each room is designed after a different decade, which is cool.

Rayishotbaby: Wow.

Annabananasplit: You like?

Rayishotbaby: Anna, that is the absolute worst thing I have ever read in my entire life. And aside from that, it sucks ☺

Annabananasplit: What are you trying to say, exactly? Really, you don't need to be shy . . .

Rayishotbaby: What I'm trying to say is . . . that isn't YOU. Just be yourself.

Annabananasplit: A girl who couldn't get in, was publicly humiliated, then got locked in a room and nearly murdered?

Rayishotbaby: Yup, that's the one . . .

Could he be right? Could anyone be interested in hearing about that?

Rayishotbaby: Yes . . . they want to hear it!

"Welcome to S, Anna Walker!" That's what I thought they'd say when I approached the door of the brand-new nightclub—named for a "secret" of proprietor, Columbus Bryson. But what I got was quite different. What I got was denied . . . and made fun of for wearing last year's shoes. Here, I had to write this column and they wouldn't even let me in the club! Not only that, but thousands of people were laughing at me, and there was even a foghorn sounded! This wasn't the start to the fabulous career I had envisioned!

It took getting lost, locked in a back room, and the adorable lawyer David Levy—who happens to be the brother of my deadline fairy godmother—to get in. But I did get in. And what a place! S is a series of labyrinthine rooms designed to span every decade—way back from the early 1900s to the seventies and eighties. Each room is authentically done up and features food and cocktails reminiscent of its particular time. During the day, the place will host field trips for elementary and high schools in the tri-state area, with curators from the Lower East Side Tenament Museum in conjunction with the National Historic Landmark Preservation society.

Though I only got to speak with the elusive Columbus for a few moments—"I have better people to talk to," he said to me, honestly!—he says s was a dream of his . . . that he loves watching the History Channel and learning about "old crap," reading books about old New York and all the weird "sh_t" the society people did. He says, "It's a celebration of the best city in the f'ing world." And I'd definitely agree with that.

David Levy happens to be very close with Columbus, although I can't see how, since David Levy seems to be a wonderful, generous man with manners—but that is neither here nor there. Anyway, that is how he happened to come into the same secret back entrance that I accidentally closed myself into. Apparently, there is a Clapper system installed to turn the lights on. After we'd sat in there for a while, David clapped twice, and the whole room was flooded with light.

"You knew about that the whole time, didn't you?" I asked.

He shrugged. "Yeah, I did."

"That's a cruel trick," I said, surprised to find myself not in the slightest bit angry.

"I know," he said, his voice softening—almost to a whisper. "But I'm holding your hand now, aren't I?"

I had to give it to him. He was holding my hand. And this was doing all sorts of strange things to my insides—squishing them here and there; shooting them about like so many atoms under pressure. Now I could see him, I could tell he was gorgeous on the outside, too. He had chestnut eyes dotted with spots of gold, and light brown lashes. His hair was short, slightly gelled. He was wearing a gray pinstripe suit that wasn't the slightest bit rumpled the way Ray's is when he doesn't hang up his pants. He had a strong forehead and a nice nose that had a wonderful imperfection, like maybe someone had broken it before along the bridge.

Finally, after long moments of us just holding hands and inspecting the planes of each others faces, he spoke. "Can I kiss you?"

I didn't answer. Just leaned in, felt his hand at the back of my head, at my neck. He found my mouth and pressed softly there, his hand at the back of my hair, gentle like it was considering me. He pulled back, breathed, then drew me in with the strength of his arms and this time he kissed me like his life depended on it. I could feel the weight of his teeth behind his lips, the substance of him.

I wasn't sure if that part was a bit much. In fact, I hadn't really considered that my mother would be reading this. Though it's not really an accurate assessment, I sound a little too experienced with that description, don't I? Like someone who chooses a different guy each night to go to bed with? I don't want to be seen like that, especially if I haven't been reaping any of the benefits of that reputation whatsoever. I decided I would come back to that part later. I tried to continue on, but my mind wandered, like the sick part of me wanted to destroy this whole effort, prove to me once and for all I couldn't get past this, couldn't move on to accomplish a thing . . .

"Fires can start in all sorts of ways. Some fires start with one simple action. For example, some people think that the Great Chicago Fire started when a cow knocked over a lantern in a barn."

I told myself to concentrate—that I would do this, even with these thoughts crouching in, I would do this thing now.

"Whoa," he said to me, with his lips on mine.

I felt it more than heard it. The vibrations tickled. We laughed. Then he stood me up, helped me gather the contents of my purse, and opened the door.

Now why did I keep writing this kind of thing about David? The whole morning I couldn't stop thinking about him at all. You know when you walk down the street and from far away it looks like every other guy could be him? Like that is the way his hair falls at his ear and that is the way his shoulders slouch slightly? I would speed up like a crazy stalker, create a diversion to get him to turn around—like drop my bag or cough or say "My, it *is* cold out," to absolutely no one—but it wouldn't be him, and it wouldn't be him.

I twirled my pen a few times and tried to think what the skin just beneath his chin felt like. When my eyes happened to fall on the clock, I nearly fell over. I only had an hour and a half left to hand this in! Okay, back to writing, back to writing . . .

He squeezed my hand until my fingers were crushing together. And he led me across the room, securely—like he'd make sure none of those people would ever make fun of me again. The light came flooding in. There was blinking. A lot of blinking. And everything that had been slow and dark was now too bold and bright and quick. I could see his look was commanding attention from the people there—the ones who'd snubbed me so blatantly.

People stepped out of the way for me, because he led me directly in their path. I'd never had a guy treat me like that before. Normally I got the unreturned phone calls, the "I'm just not ready for a relationship right now," "I'm not the kind of guy you need," "I was just holding that girl for my friend . . ."

I turned my head for a second, and when I turned it back, there was a glass of cabernet in my hand. It was an unimaginably intimate thing to be sipping that wine while he watched. There was music—that hip-hop song about "it's your birthday," which I'd always liked but couldn't quite get all the words to. I vaguely recognized the refrain as the room spilled into view. Despite myself, I relaxed and allowed my head to shake back and forth to the beat. "That's cute," David said, "the way you bop around." I felt shy because of this attention, since I wasn't used to it, and looked around—I was here to work, after all! This particular room was elegant, in that old New York way I loved—deep woods, regal reds, lots of detail work at moldings and on the furniture. Rich Moroccan lanterns and ottomans lent an eclectic feel.

There was someone waving to someone right in front of us. She was screaming, "Tammy! Tammy!" And this tiny detail made for a surprisingly cool moment between myself and David—we turned our heads to face each other, smiled, and rolled our eyes in her direction. It was as if we already had a connection . . . just the two of us. He slipped me in closer, with his hand around my waist, and easily, my body moved in toward the security of him.

And all of a sudden, there were my friends Ray and Nina. Ray looked so comfortable, like Hugh Hefner in his smoking jacket, you'd swear it was his party we were attending. I smiled at that. He popped up from a seat next to a fire-eating dancer. He waved away a flame as if it were merely smoke from a cigarette and grabbed for my hand.

"This is David," I said.

"Hi," Ray said.

"Hi," David said back, looking annoyed.

"I'm glad you're okay," Ray said. "We were worried. But we figured you just went straight to the VIP." Somehow, surprisingly, Ray hadn't heard about the LYMJ★★★ episode. I considered this a small miracle. Or a great big lie.

I would have introduced David to Nina, but she was making out with a drummer. I knew he was a drummer, because he had a pair of drumsticks poking up through his back jeans pocket. "That's Nina up there with the drummer," I said, pointing to where they were sitting up on the back of a banquette.

"Healthy lungs," David said. He looked at me with a soft smile, as if he adored me. What a wonderful, wonderful look that was.

Ray jerked my arm so hard he nearly pulled it out of the

socket. "You must meet Phil and Trace!" He evoked the names of our favorite TV characters. His breath smelled like the inside of a shot glass.

"We told you those are our character names! We are the actors, Jim and Nancy!" said Trace.

Ray barely noticed. I could tell he was drunk, because his eyelids were a little heavy, like each blink took tons of effort to accomplish.

I hadn't seen him like that since last New Year's, when I'd had to literally carry him into a taxi and hold him up the whole ride, finally dragging him up the steps to our apartment, while he sang the theme from Three's Company. "Come and knock on my dooorrr, take a step that is newww."

"Guys, do that thing for Anna, when you go 'no, I don't,' 'yes, you do.'" He swung an arm over my shoulder, despite the fact that David had a hand around my middle. We must have looked like a piece of performance art. I looked out from under Ray's arm, to Phil and Trace.

"No, I don't."

"Yes, you do."

"No, I don't."

"Yes, you do."

On cue, they both laughed at themselves. It was just as they did it on the show every week. Ray and I enact it all the time. Like I'll say, "You have to do the dishes!" and he'll say, "No I don't . . ." and the whole thing will go on and on and on.

I was still holding my shoes in my hand, when Phil and Trace left us for the 1960s. Apparently, they heard there was more nudity in there. I wasn't putting those shoes back on any time soon. Ray had started talking to a very blond girl in one of those adorable peasant skirts and a lacy tank top. I shook my head at that, and then thought, why did I just do that? So what if Ray hooks up with another girl? What do I care?

David called over a waiter, and within minutes we were at a high-backed, red velvet booth, with intricate wood carvings all along the border and arms. The waiter disappeared.

"Your feet must be freezing," David said.

"Well..." I didn't get to finish. The waiter was back with a shopping bag that said the most wonderful words in the world on the side: Sigerson Morrison. They were the hottest shoe designers, known for sexy heels. I turned to David, confused. "What's this?" I asked. I mean, I don't have the kind of life where men buy me $400 shoes on a whim because they felt—correctly—that I really wished I had another, better pair to wear.

"They're for you," he said, edging the bag toward me.

I tried to slow the growing, growing, growing smile on my face by pinning my lips down with my fingers. I didn't want to appear overzealous. In David's world, women probably got $400 gifts every day. I didn't want to seem like an outsider. I tried to look like I just got a Jaguar this morning. I don't think the look came out quite right, because David chuckled a little.

I turned the bag on its side, slid the box out, gulped. I looked at him. He pointed with his eyes toward the box. Inside were the most delicate, sexy shoes—a skinny heel and a cool, pointed toe that had a vintage curve to it.

"Allow me," he said.

Swiveling, I draped my leg over his lap. Oh! This was JUST like a really chic version of Cinderella! Let me tell you, I was never more turned on in my life. I smiled for all the times Nina had said, "You're never going to get Prince Charming to slip a high heel on your foot and take care of you forever!" I know I'm supposed to be thinking more independently now, and not looking for impossible fairy-tale endings, but there was no denying this! Just look at what was happening! He took the shoe from my hand gently. Where his fingers touched mine, there was a shadow of feeling that went hot and stayed that way. Slowly, he slipped one shoe on, and then the other. Then he took me over to see his sister at the VIP.

"Darling! So glad you made it! Sorry about the LYMJ fiasco! I should have warned you . . . David, dear . . . don't you break this girl's heart. She's my friend." And that's where me, my prince charming, and my deadline fairy godmother spent the rest of the evening.

***LYMJ = Last Year's Marc Jacobs—a horrible, mean thing to yell at a person trying to do her job.

FIVE

A Little Healthy Competition

Paris Daahling has the most wonderful pool table. The low lights, the red felt, the curved mahogany—it all makes for one intense game of eight ball.
—Velvet Rope Diaries, New York, New York

4:00 p.m.

I just finished typing and clicked on "Print." I pulled the documents from the printer my computer was hooked up to and looked around at all the different editors and really felt a part of something great. I mean, look at me! I'm a real journalist, struggling against deadlines, writing drafts, mining the depths of my soul to find the right words.

On the way back to my desk, I waved the papers at Theresa, but maybe she didn't see me or something, because she didn't wave back. To recover my dignity, I lifted my arm up really high to make it look like I was just stretching, and when I turned around to sit down I felt the papers pulled right from my hand.

"What the?"

JOSEPH! What is *up* with him?

"Time's up!" he sang, like a very, very mean game show host.

"What do you mean? I have an hour left!"

"Oh, well, I have to leave early—dentist appointment; you know my grody teeth and all . . ."

8:00 a.m., Friday, September 23

Dr. Fenwick looked over my notebook for a long while. I saw him snicker, though he tried to turn it into a cough both times. And he shook his head up and down a lot, which I took as a good sign. He also stopped, looked up to consider an idea, and smirked once.

It could be exhausting trying to translate the reactions of your shrink.

"So!" he said, swinging one leg over the other. His legs were on the long side. In fact, he was rather tall, Dr. Fenwick. His hair was even messier today—like he'd been caught in a wind tunnel and couldn't find the exit. For a long time. "You've had a busy week!"

"I sure have," I said.

"So how is the new job?" he asked. "I saw your column today, and it was really fantastic. My wife and I were saying it's a kind of soap opera in print. We're dying to see what happens with David. And I didn't realize, but it seems like Ray likes you, too. So we'll have to address that."

"Ray? That's just nuts. He doesn't like me! We're friends! He's just protective, because he doesn't want to have to deal with me watching Lifetime movies in those ugly pajamas! Believe me, it's not pretty."

Dr. Fenwick picked up his coffee mug and slid his fingers up and down the side. "Just consider the possibility, Anna. That's all I'm saying."

Hmmph. And what did he mean about "too?" Was I here to save my life or to debate whether or not Ray and I are in love with each other—a thing that people have been bothering us about for, I don't know . . . forever! I didn't really want to talk about it anymore . . . After all, I was paying serious cash for these forty-five minutes, and so I tried to relax my face.

"So how did it feel to face your fears? To do everything you were terrified to do . . . in such a short period of time?"

I considered this, thought of the very, very strange events of the past twenty-four hours, the number of times I'd made a fool of myself and lived to tell. "It's kind of like stepping inside your favorite movie, but not knowing any of the lines," I said. "If that makes any sense at all."

"Yes, yes," he agreed, but how was I to know if he really understood? All I had was the knowledge that I was putting myself out there. Beyond that, there are no guarantees. This, he explained to me as I wrote out my check and tried to rebalance my checkbook.

"Maybe stop trying to read the books, Anna. The books about the fires."

I left the office slowly, sluggishly, hesitant to face the day. The thing is, I know Fenwick said he and his wife enjoyed the column, but no one else had told me what they thought of it yet (not that positive feedback ever sinks in with me; it's always, "Well, she doesn't know," or "He's just being nice"). I slipped out before Ray would have the chance to catch me. I turned my phone off. I just wasn't sure I wanted to know what people thought. I'd had my run of living, and though it was far from perfect, I was sad to think that if I'd failed, I'd have to give it up.

9:00 a.m.

"Ed wants to see you, child," Belinda rang my extension first thing. I didn't know which way this would go, since I knew Joe was out to sabotage me. Plus I hadn't received any edits from the copy editors except, "Can we change this comma on line 17 to a colon?"

And I had my doubts that this could have been the only problem. As I saw it, there were two scenarios: Either it was so bad there was no point in trying to fix it, or it was so bad they'd gone ahead and rewritten the entire thing, and that one sentence on line seventeen was the only one of mine remaining, and therefore the only one that had a problem in it.

Really, why would I think that *anyone* would be interested in *me* and *my* stupid problems? People want someone glamorous, intriguing, someone they can be jealous of or be horrified by or obsessed with—a movie star type, a society girl, or a business tycoon—not a boring, mediocre-looking girl with bushy hair from Kellmore, Long Island, birthplace of the twelve-foot hero sandwich. Let's face it, I was on my way to my funeral, here.

I'd only been in Ed's office once, to take notes for a meeting he'd had with Nasty. I just remember him jabbing his finger a lot and saying, "Get us on *Entertainment Tonight*. I don't care if you have to sleep with every guy there . . . just do it!" and slamming his fist on the table over and over and over. I've heard stories . . . about people being so scared of Ed they never speak again, the one girl whose hair turned white around her face, the guy who passed out and nearly fell from the window out onto the street, the secretary who suffered a heart attack. But surely those were rumors— stupid rumors, too. Let's face it, nobody's hair turns white like that. Geez.

Right?

"Have you seen my little princess here?" He turned a silver photo frame around for me to see in place of a more traditional greeting, such as "hello," maybe. The picture was of a fish stick of a girl—probably around two years old. She was on a beach in one of those adorable ruffle-waisted swimsuits printed with hippos doing the backstroke. It looked like she was about to eat a pile of sand from a plastic pink shovel. Her hair was a fluff of gold.

"Oh, she is too cute!" I said. I bet Ed was a fabulous father. He didn't seem so scary to me.

"Yeah, takes after her dad," he said, winking. "Here's the follow-up photo," he said, chuckling roughly. In this picture she *had* actually eaten the sand. The shovel was slumped down over her knee, and she was hollering her head off—you could see clear back to her tonsils, face red as a beet.

"Now, I want to talk about your column," he said, folding his hands in the middle of his desk, which was completely organized— just a couple of clearly labeled folders on one corner, marked, "Joseph James, disciplinary," and "Joseph James, disciplinary 2." Now *those* were interesting! I'd have to ask Belinda about them for sure.

He sat there quiet for a moment, chewing on the inside of his cheek. Then he lifted one eyebrow. He smiled huge and said, "Anna, by some crazy, fucked up miracle, the advertisers loved it. The focus group loved it."

He was kidding, right? This was a joke . . . pretty mean spirited, but . . . a joke. Right?

He continued. "*I*, on the other hand, freaking *hated* it. I thought it was complete crap! I mean who the hell cares about you and that stupid guy you live with who's obviously in love with you and vice versa—and that poor old chap you've brought into the ridiculous, deranged triangle. It's like . . . a soap opera for newspapers—like we need another medium for those, right?"

He looked at me like I was supposed to answer this. And of course, like a moron, I did. "Right." When he didn't say anything, I rolled my eyes for effect.

"Still, it's a more powerful reaction than I've seen in a long time. Believe me, I would have thought that 'Wear Someone Else's Clothes for a Week' column would have been critically acclaimed. I really did. But who knows anymore what's going to make those damn advertisers happy. It's like bloodsucking! They're sucking our blood!"

He seemed to have gone off on some deranged tangent, his arms heavenward, his head in on it—shaking wildly—and I clawed my nails into the chair arms, fearing the validity of the aforementioned rumors.

Suddenly, he appeared to have snapped out of it. "I wouldn't have expected this sort of thing. I was just envisioning a straight review—maybe with a couple of snarky comments, some full-of-it conflated verbiage in the style of the *New York Times*, you know . . ."

"Right," I said again. It was just that was the only word I could find.

"But you just went and crapped all over that. You turned it upside down, poked holes in it, transformed it into something genuinely unreadable, as far as I'm concerned."

I knew it. I just knew it couldn't work. I tried! See, I tried and I put myself out there, and Joseph didn't even let me fix it! Maybe if I fixed it . . . then it would have been better and I'd still . . .

"The thing is, though, it doesn't matter a piece of crap what I think, does it?"

"Um, no?" My nail cracked excruciatingly from the pressure of digging it into the chair, but I didn't let it show, didn't acknowledge the pain, although it broke way down the nail bed and pulled my skin away.

"Bingo!" Ed did his pointing move and collapsed back in his chair dramatically. "It's . . . all about the damn advertisers. No integrity anymore. None! But, hey, if the advertisers want it and those blasted 'readers' like it, well then I have no choice but to bring it on as a permanent column for the paper. Velvet Rope Diaries," he said it dreamy, motioned like he was seeing the words in print.

Then he pulled out the paper, which read just that. It was the first time I'd let myself look at it. I didn't realize it, but I must have been tearing up now that the roller coaster had come to an abrupt stop at

Amazingville, because Ed handed me a tissue and said, "Hey, hey, hey, there's no crying in journalism . . . though technically I don't know if I'd call you an actual journalist, but still, you get the picture."

Then the phone rang, bringing our meeting to an end. Belinda buzzed in, and he pressed the intercom speaker. "Rima on line one." His face fell instantly, flushed. And then he said, "I'll have to take this now. You know the way out."

Outside the office I asked Belinda, "Who's Rima?"

She leaned in and whispered in my ear, "Ed's psychic."

"No, really," I said.

"Really," she deadpanned.

As I returned to my desk, I realized I forgot to ask about Joseph's disciplinary folders. Maybe it was better I didn't know.

Afterward, Theresa and I lunched for *free* at this totally cool steak house that is members-only for journalists.

"He tells all of us that," Theresa told me. "The old 'I don't know if I'd call you an actual journalist' comment; please. He needs to get some new material."

I had a perfectly cooked New York strip, and Theresa said we wouldn't have to pay for a thing. The thing is, journalists get to do all these things for free, because everyone wants them to try everything so they write about it.

"Believe me, they are saving money by letting us eat here! The money they'll make off the publicity is better than any ad you can buy," she said. Theresa wasn't going to leave a tip. "They don't expect you to," she said.

I told myself I wasn't going to do anything to piss her off, but at the door I acted like I had to pee and ran back with twenty bucks for the waiter. There went dinner.

Next, Theresa took me to the "staff salon" for a new haircut. This place gave out free hairstyling cards to everyone on the *New York, New York* editorial staff.

"Please get a perm! Please!" Theresa said everyone was getting "the new perm," and that it would give my hair so much body. I kept thinking 1988 and poodle curls. And really, didn't my hair have too much body already—like it was a whole other body on top of my body? But Theresa can be bossy as hell. And a little scary.

So I did it. And whoa, she was right. These weren't poodle curls at all. They were beautiful flowing waves that looked like I'd put hot rollers in. And though it had more movement and shape, it didn't look like a Christmas tree at all. The effect was rather striking, actually. Richard at Mumble & Mumble was a magician, apparently.

"Oh, you know what, though?" he asked.

"She needs highlights," Theresa answered.

"Yes exactly, Miss Smartie Pants."

Richard (that's pronounced *Ree-shard*) doled out double kisses that didn't even come close to touching either cheek they hovered over and a French accent that sometimes turned Brooklyn when you were least expecting it. *Ree-shard* would not be "performing" the coloring services. However, he would bring Christi-*a*-na up to "consultate" with me before she applied "zee color."

Christi-*a*-na was tall. And beautiful. Really beautiful. Normally you wouldn't want to have your hair colored by someone that beautiful, because what might happen is that when she was done and spun you around to check yourself out in the mirror, she very possibly might look a trillion times better than you did.

But that day, it didn't matter to me. I felt happy for Christi-*a*-na that she was so pretty. She had great ideas, and I felt I could trust her and knew that she would not make a disastrous decision.

Ree-shard watched as Christi-*a*-na applied some "caramel" here, a bit of "honey" there, rubbed some ice cold "flash" over my hair to "bring all the tones together into harmony." She applied a handful of foamy styling product and smushed my hair around, and then blow-dried it so she could see what it looked like.

"Oh, that color is divine!" Christi-*a*-na exclaimed.

Really, it wasn't such a drastic difference in style. It was just more movement, a slightly lighter hue. But it made a huge difference. My cheekbones jutted out dramatically, the shorter layers brought attention right to my eyes. The overall effect was the way I had always wished I could look.

I was glad to look great. Probably, after years of not looking great, this was my proper due. I was even more thrilled when, back at the office, Theresa took me to the sample closet. She pulled out skirts, blouses, jackets, cardigans, vests, calf-height boots. I tried everything on right there in the closet—my lifeless chest on display—and she told me what should go with what, hung each outfit into zipped bags, and added long necklaces, dangling earrings, and cuff bracelets to each before she pushed me out the door. "You're really great at this Theresa," I said.

"I know," she said, smiling. "It's my job. Just like you're great at what you do."

I was never good at accepting compliments, so I barely heard it at all. Instead I settled back to neurosis, where I always felt most comfortable. "But are you sure I can just *have* all of this?" Already in my hands, this was more clothing than I had in my closet at home from a whole entire lifetime . . . never mind how much nicer. It didn't seem very . . . what's that word? I have no idea what that word is . . . wait . . . I might know it somewhere deep down, oh I think it's coming . . . oh yeah . . . *me*. None of this seemed very much like me.

1:30 p.m., Wednesday, September 28

"One *matzoh ball* and a *tuna* on *rye*!" the little man behind the counter called off my lunch order like a newsboy hocking papers on a street corner.

"A corned beef on *kaiser* with a *big pickle*!"

Belinda swirled her eyes around and said to me, "Oh, I better go grab my big pickle."

We brought our plastic orange trays to a seat in the back, under a deteriorating ivy plant. I was facing the wall.

"So what's up?" I asked. Her hair looked like it had just been set, the rolled back waves of blond stood nearly a half-foot off the top of her head. The sides had been pulled back loosely with two combs. Her unique brand of beauty always struck me. There was a melancholy to it, as if she'd had her heart broken and now wore it stuffed somewhere inside of her hairdo. Her lipstick was a little too bright, her blush unblended, like two pink polka dot stickers.

"Ah, you know," she said, biting into the generous corned beef sandwich half. A few poppy seeds hailed onto her paper plate.

"Yeah," I said. I tried the soup. It was a little too hot, so I stirred it, watched the skinny noodles swish around the big matzoh ball. "So what's wrong?" I could tell there was something off with Belinda today. She had a chipped nail, no necklace or earrings on, and that just wasn't her. She did herself up every day, in case she wound up in the hospital. "If one of those cute doctors sees me, I really want to look my best," is how she put it.

She breathed big, took a sip of cream soda. Some of it foamed back up through the straw. "Gerry's having 'anxiety attacks.'" She made the quotes with her fingers like this was a ridiculous thing. "A man . . . can you imagine?"

Me? As a matter of fact, I could imagine. Anxiety was something I didn't have a problem imagining at all. "That's pretty common, Belinda," I said. I chipped off a bit of matzoh ball with my plastic spoon and placed it in my mouth.

"Is it? I mean, there's nothing wrong, and he's sitting there and worrying about the most ridiculous things—called in sick to work, didn't eat dinner last night, woke up at two in the morning . . ."

"Did he go see a therapist yet? They can give him some medication."

"Yeah, he did that . . . but it's taking a while to get the right dosage. It's just I want to shake him and say, just stop being a moron!"

"That's difficult, isn't it? When you can't empathize with someone because you can't understand how they are feeling?"

She shook her head vigorously as she chewed a bite of corned beef. "That's it exactly. I can't understand it at all."

"You know what I've always found when I'm feeling really out of it—if people are just *there* for me. I don't expect them to understand how I feel, because very few people have this 'problem' of mine, but if I know the person loves me and wants me to know that, well that is all they can do. You can't fix it Belinda. You can't go over to him and yell, 'Snap out of it!' It just doesn't work that way."

"You're probably right." She considered this, bit off some pickle, chewed. "Hey, that's what I'm going to do. I'm going to stop trying to fix it, to make him feel warm and safe and cozy and better. I'm just going to support him. He's a good man, Gerry." Belinda smiled far beyond where we sat. She smiled at some funny thing Gerry did that made her love him, that made her want to do the right thing now . . . when it was most difficult.

And seeing her like that made me feel good, too.

5:30 p.m.

"Why don't we talk about the big day a little bit?" Fenwick said.

Was it worth it? Bringing this up over and over, giving it a second life this way?

"Go on," he said, fingering the hair over his ear. "Why don't you tell me more detail, about when you first noticed the fire, what you think you did. Don't worry so much over the accuracy, just what you think happened."

I wouldn't cry now. I knew that. This was a legend, an unbelievable thing now that hovered somewhere between truth and non-truth. "Well, I'd been drawing. Sitting there, drawing. I had my old transistor on, the one my mother had put on my bedside table. I was singing, singing—a popular song was on, and I knew the words. I was drawing jelly beans, because I had a little paper bag filled with them, from the tobacco shop. We'd gone there the day before, and I'd scooped a rainbow of them into that waxy paper bag. The man behind the counter weighed it, folded it neatly over once at the top, and handed it down to me. My father paid seventy-five cents. He hadn't even had to look at the change. He'd felt around in his pocket for it and he knew, passed it over like it was nothing. For me, these trips with my father to the tobacco store were something to look forward to. The way he held me up to scoop the candies, the way he half smiled, his tobacco sweet smell all around.

"I was getting the jelly bean right. I mean, I was getting the shine and the shadow and the plumpness of it. I loved to draw, but it had to be right.

"I smelled it—the smoke, I mean. And I did all the wrong things. I forgot all the things from school, from that fireman who'd come to the cafeteria with the coarse facial hair and the big arm muscles and put on his turnout for us, waved around the ax, while we all jerked back. I forgot to stop, drop, and roll, and I just stood at the top of the staircase trying to remember what to do and thinking only, *'There's an easy way to remember to change the batteries in your smoke alarm.'* It was getting very hot and very dark, and I barely recognized our house, its pretty beach scene paintings and my mother's afghans hung over the backs of all the chairs. I didn't know if I should stay put or go up to the attic or downstairs. I couldn't remember who was home with me. Finally, a thought hit me and I yelled, 'Daddy! Daddy!' I remembered he was working on that window seat, the one for our family room for reading in the sun. He was putting the polyurethane coat on it that day and the next weekend, when he wasn't working, he was going to hammer it into the area under the bay window.

"I ran and I ran, but he hadn't answered, and then I reached the door down to the basement and didn't think to feel the door with my palm, to open it slightly, quickly, to make sure there weren't flames. Instead I opened it right up and let in all that oxygen, and the fire came lashing out at me, catching, miraculously, only my shoelace—the pretty one with the rainbows and fluffy clouds—and I closed the door and ran. I screamed the whole way, 'Daddy! Daddy!' but nothing would come out, there was no air, like one of those terrible dreams, and mucous was running down all over my face. My tiny shoe fire had grown a little.

"Mrs. Sothers removed the shoe right away, stamped it out on her lawn, and called the fire department over, pulling me away from the window, not wanting me to see it all, the cracked glass and the heavy smoke and the men crawling all through my house like it was a jungle gym."

Fenwick fiddled a little too long at an itch under his eye, his Adam's apple rose and fell. He puckered in his lips and then let them out again. "Did you ever think, Anna, that people like you, people who've gone through these unbelievable things, that maybe they have a more intuitive perspective than the rest of us? That maybe you can use that to help people in some way?"

Me? Help someone? I thought Fenwick must be confused. It was the one thing I hadn't been able to do, it was the very thing I'd failed at. What in the world could *I* ever do to help someone?

7:30 p.m., Thursday, September 29

Tonight was Nina's birthday party. Ray and I found the best
photo of her, at this pie-eating competition we held at our holiday party two years ago, and we had it blown up to poster size and
plastered the entire room with the posters. In it, she's got blueberry
pie all over her mouth and a bit on her nose and above her left eye.
We bought her a gift certificate to this really hot spa, Perfect, which
claims to make you look five years younger in one afternoon. She's
been talking about the place nonstop for two months, so it was
pretty obvious that's what she wanted. I think the real tip-off was
when she said, "Get me a gift certificate to Perfect for my birthday."

I decided to wear this outfit Theresa gave me—with deep blue
velvet pants and a matching silk blouse with a huge gold necklace
that hangs all the way down to my waist. I wore the shoes David
gave me, because he was coming.

"I don't think those shoes match," Ray said. We were standing
in the kitchen mixing up a pitcher of frozen margaritas.

"What do you mean?" I thought they looked awesome. In fact,
I knew they did, because Theresa suggested I wear them with that
outfit, and she knew her fashion.

"I just mean, I think they're a little tacky. Like they are trying too
hard to be perfect, to be someone they think you need."

"Oh," I said. It was a little awkward, because it was pretty clear
he wasn't talking about the shoes. I didn't want him to hate David.
I didn't think there was much substance to Dr. Fenwick's allega-
tions, especially in light of the fact that Ray was bringing another
girl to the party—someone he'd met at happy hour yesterday—but
it was still a touchy thing to have strain between Ray and David.
What did he mean—"trying to be someone they think I need?"

Thank god, I was saved by the bell. The first person to arrive was

Belinda. Her boyfriend, Gerry, was different than what I expected. He was severely straight-laced. He was medium height—only a couple of inches taller than Belinda—with blue, but not beautiful eyes, and he wore a checked button-down collar shirt, with khakis and a brown belt with brown shoes. One was untied. Next to him, Belinda looked even wilder, and I saw why they worked. I felt my warmth toward her swell. My familiarity with her look, her swoops of blond, and her daring neck and hemlines were just then an overwhelmingly wonderful thing.

"Belinda!" I hugged her as if it were my own birthday. "And this must be the handsome Gerry." Gerry grimaced, like he knew he was anything but, and this made me like him immensely. I hoped they would get through their rough patch.

David showed with a gift for Nina, wrapped in pretty Chinese paper. One by one lots of my friends arrived—Judy from advertising, Theresa showed in some gorgeous baby doll dress in white lace. I had a habit of getting close to friends very quickly. And when I saw her now, it was like meeting an old friend, a person that completed you in some essential way. It was irresistible to me—the urge to bring them and share them with my other friends and pile up our good times to look back at when I needed to. "Theresa, have you met Gerry and David?"

They shook hands. "So this is the dashing David . . ." Theresa said.

"And where exactly am I dashing off to?" David asked.

"To get me a drink?" Theresa said, her gold evening bag turning and turning in her hands.

"What would you like?" he asked.

"A martini?" she offered.

David winked, and I escorted him to the bar. "You're a fabulous host," I said, feeling flirty beyond belief. He was in jeans—dark, dark denim—and a striped black and white and blue shirt, and he looked unbelievable in it.

"Anna! Emergency in the kitchen!" Ray pulled me from my fantasy, past the crowd, into our tiny galley kitchen.

"What? What is it?" Nothing looked off-kilter to me.

He opened the freezer and pulled out the cocktail franks. "I don't know how to do these," he said, grimacing with a metal tray in one hand and the two boxes of franks in the other.

"Oookayyy," I said, annoyed. He leaned over me as I placed each one on the tray, and when I turned around, he didn't move back. "Did you really need me?" I started to ask, but the words stuck in my throat. We were very close, and I think he was wearing a different cologne or something, because it took me off guard.

"I did," he said, his nose nearly touching my forehead.

"Are you okay, Ray? You're acting kind of strange."

"Me? I'm fine," he said straightening up, smoothing down his shirt.

I laughed nervously, unlatched his hand from the countertop to pop the hors d'oeuvres in the oven, and walked straight out of the kitchen without looking back. I had no idea what had just happened in there, and I wasn't going to figure it out just then.

David scooped his hand around my waist, and there it stayed the rest of the evening.

Eventually, Nina arrived, and she brought a troupe of three girls from her office. The guy she'd met at S—Bernard—was possibly joining her later. "Either way," she said, as if she couldn't care less. But she did. I knew she did. Nina wanted to meet the right man and get married so badly it was frightening. I sometimes felt bad for men she met, because they wouldn't know what was about to hit them. They'd have no idea how she'd picked out her caterer, florist, two-piece string ensemble, and wedding dress, and that her guest address list was updated quarterly. Still, I couldn't blame her for her overzealousness.

It was her mother's fault, really. She was that very outspoken sort of mother who liked to say, "I know it's not my place, but . . ." and continue on with the most outrageous things. "I know it's not my place, Nina, but I bought you this minimizing bra, because whatever you've been wearing doesn't seem to be lifting you up and pulling you in enough." This, over lunch at Saks Fifth Avenue, mind you. Her mom always took us to lunch there. She thought it was proper. One day at our proper lunch, over chicken salad scoops with rye toast on the side, Mrs. Schwartz said, "Nina, you know if you don't get married by next year, you'll never have a child before thirty."

Nina had said she had to go to the bathroom, and Mrs. Schwartz tried to figure out my equation, working it out on her fingers, until I excused myself and found Nina crying on a torn leather chair. "I don't want to care. I don't want to care." She just said that over and over, and I said, "I know, I know." And then she stopped herself and reapplied some under-eye concealer and powder, and we returned to Mrs. Schwartz, who said my magic year was this one. Thank heavens for my relaxed mom, I didn't care one bit. At least I had the one normal spike. I figured everyone was entitled to at least one . . .

At the party, we all ate cocktail franks and pizzas on bite-size bagels and mozzarella balls with tiny grape tomatoes and basil confetti until there was nothing left. Then we blindfolded everyone in turn to take a swing at the cheerleader piñata we had filled with chocolate candies and individually wrapped licorice ropes. Whenever someone missed and took out say a lightbulb or a kitchen chair serving as extra guest seating, we laughed like crazy. Partially, the alcohol made it so funny. In the end, it was Belinda's Gerry who cracked the cheerleader right in half across her stomach and sent the candy raining toward the floor. Belinda glowed with delight. I liked him even more.

At one thirty in the morning, it was just Nina, Ray, his date—Cherry or Cheery or Cheesy—and me and David. We were on the couch, drunk enough that we all looked like hell. Within seconds

Nina's Bernard called. He agreed to come and meet us at the apartment.

"Hey," Nina said to me, "Why don't you get us in at one of your super swanky places now?"

This sounded like a crazy person's question to me. "I'm not cool enough to pull something like that off," I said.

"What are you talking about? Ray . . . tell her she could definitely do that."

"I don't think she's cool enough," he deadpanned.

"Yeah, me either," Cheesy Cherry said.

We all looked at her like she was a moldy piece of cheese.

Ray said, "I was kidding," to his date.

"About what?" she asked.

Nina and I looked at each other, and I don't know what exactly it was that made me do it, but I called this club promoter that I'd spoken with a couple of times earlier that day and asked if he could get six people into this hot place, Blossom. And he said he could do better than that. He could get us into the not-yet-opened, exclusive to me for *New York, New York* spot, Paris Daahling, a wine bar. "But why?" I asked. "Because I like you," he said. "You're honest. And I've got a hunch I'll get thanked for it by the owner one day."

Half an hour later, the six of us were at Paris Daahling with some people who were working on the interior design, the construction, and one of the owners—a down-to-earth guy named Pete—who'd always owned pubs but got the idea for this kind of froufrou place when he and his friends were playing pool loaded. And he kept joking about it until he realized it was "a damn good idea."

They had a pool table there—a beautiful red one, with fancy carved legs and net pockets for the balls. "Wanna play?" David asked me. His casual attire was inviting, a fragrant laundry vent on a winter night . . . He was such a strong, tall guy, and I just wanted to snuggle in at his chest. It was difficult not to. We hadn't slept together yet, and the fact of it pulsated around us.

Before I could answer, Ray cut in and said, "Let's play teams. Me and Cherry versus you and Anna."

David stood and chalked his stick in a way that said he meant business. He chalked a slightly shorter one for me, too. He stood against a wall on one end of the table, tipping his head back every once and again to allow some beer to slip down his throat. His other hand, I was very aware, was around my waist. I was sitting on a high stool next to him.

"Let's flip for the break," Ray said. He pulled out a coin.

"Heads," David called before he was asked.

When Ray flipped the coin in the air, caught it, and slapped it onto the back of his palm, it was in our favor. I was drunk, but could still perceive the stress this result produced.

Without speaking, David stood over the table, pushed the cue back and forth a few times for aim, and then smacked the cue ball expertly into the triangle of pool balls. They scattered in all directions, and three striped balls went in. "Nice break," I said, though I could feel the tension thicken and overtake our passion. The words sort of faded out in the fog of it.

He sank three more balls, and when he missed one, David took it in stride. Parentally, he cheered me on for my turn. "Ah, you'll win the game for us, baby." I liked the way he called me *baby*, or maybe I didn't. I wasn't sure. And yet until then I'd said to Nina, to Ray, over and over again, "I just want someone to take care of me, someone who'll call me baby."

Ray was horrible at pool. It was one of his traits I liked best. He stood, serious, trying to line up his shot. I knew his technique. He stared at the ball, not at the stick, and he thought there was some magic to that tactic that allowed him to make the shot perfectly. But it didn't always work. That was because he wound up moving the stick over to the right or left at the last second, and as a result, he wouldn't hit the ball where he'd meant to. But he didn't like to hear that.

Cherry was standing off to his side a little, and at that point I downright hated her. Everything she did bothered me—the way she adjusted her shirt as she walked over to the table, the way she kissed Ray in between each turn—like she was some kind of magic luck talisman instead of a one-night stand. She was just dumb, and she didn't try to get to know any of us, just sucked up to Ray, like that might make him love her. You could tell she'd be the kind of girl-friend to break up a group, to say something like, "Your friends are mean to me, and I don't want you to hang out with them." I wished she'd just go home.

"Shit!" Ray yelled, when the six ball he was going for rolled slowly into the nearest bumper and then stopped.

"Hey, that was a good try!" I offered—a cross between a cheer-leader and a den mother—a role I didn't recognize, a tone I hadn't noticed before.

"Your turn, hustler," David said. He *was* funny. I couldn't take this rivalry with Ray too seriously. Ray never felt *anyone* was good enough for me. And, wasn't I doing the same thing with Cherry? It was all in good fun, wasn't it?

"You want some help?" he offered when I walked up to the table. The truth was I was pretty bad at pool and some help was just what I wanted.

"Sure," I said, smiling. I wanted to kiss him right there and then. Instead I just leaned in close and pulled him by the hand over to the table.

"Here, why don't you go for the three ball, over at the end. You can get that right in if you stand here." He moved me gently by my hips, positioned my stick just at the right angle, stood back, and nod-ded his head for me to shoot.

Smack! I got it right in. I couldn't help smiling. It felt great when you did something like that. I could see Ray pouting in the corner. He was against that kind of hands-on help. I knew that he preferred people to do things themselves. "Otherwise you never learn!" he was known to say.

There must have been some truth to that, because right away I went for the four ball, and I missed it by a mile.

"Hey it was a great try," David said sweetly, dishonestly.

Ray just looked me right in the eye while he stood back to allow Cherry to screw up her own shot.

six

And the Stakes Are Raised . . .

The signature drink at Comfort, the "Comfort Cocktail," is made with Southern Comfort mixed with Dr. Pepper and a twist of lime. It's the perfect blend of sweet and bitter—goes down smooth and follows with a slight burn—like the good parts of life itself, I guess. It is served in an enormous mug, so that you feel it goes on and on and on . . . with no end in sight.

—Velvet Rope Diaries, *New York, New York*

9:00 p.m., Tuesday, October 11

"Are you sure this is the right block?" David asked, with good reason. We'd just circled it three times looking for the entrance to Cream and Sugar—a super-exclusive password-only spot down on the Lower East Side.

"The guy said to look for a homeless guy wearing a flannel shirt . . . and we did pass that guy," I pointed out and then craned my neck to look out the back window for something I might have missed.

"True," David agreed. "But is it possible he's not the only homeless guy in the city wearing a flannel shirt?"

This *had* crossed my mind, but I wasn't sure what else to do. I went over the other details I'd scribbled in the Le Fontaine. "There's a streetlight right in front of the door. The sign says, 'piano tuner,' and a small mailbox shaped like a squirrel is to the right of the door."

"I remember when you could just duck into whatever bar was on the corner," David said.

This struck a chord with me. I'd been thinking that I wanted to show him my local place—somewhere that was part of my world. "Would you like to go somewhere like that after we're done with this place?" I said, just as I spied the squirrel, stopped the cab, and pulled David to the door.

"That sounds perfect," he said. "But what do we do, now that we're here?"

The guy who owned the spot had been kind of obtuse about the directions. They didn't have a publicist, and he seemed pretty sinister in his view of the media. "Well, now we have to give the password," I said.

"So what is it?" he asked, pulling me in around the waist against the slight chill.

"He gave me a riddle. It's—"

David cut me off. "How many licks does it take to get to the center of a Tootsie Roll Pop?"

I smiled and delivered a friendly jab to the ribs. "Well, what's the answer to that?" I asked.

"Seventy-six," he answered seriously.

"Let me guess . . . you stole a couple?"

"No. Just one."

"Okay, let's concentrate here." I pulled out the paper I'd written the riddle on. "What have you made if you mix cream, sugar, hazelnut, and semisweet chocolates?"

"Dessert?" David offered. "Let's see if it works." He walked right up to the mailbox and yelled, *"Dessert!"*

I couldn't help but laugh. "Who are you talking to?" I asked.

"The squirrel."

"And what made you think that's how you do it?"

"It seemed pretty obvious. You see a squirrel at a secret door next to a bum in a flannel shirt, below a piano tuner sign. I mean, come on. Don't tell me you've never done this before?"

"Of course I have," I said. "But I normally use the buzzer right here." I walked over to the hidden buzzer below the squirrel that I had spied seconds earlier, with my journalistic instinct, and pressed it.

"Yes?" a voice came over an intercom along with lots of static.

"DESSERT!" I yelled.

"Nope." The voice came back self-righteously.

"Hmm," David said. "What could it be?"

"Chocolate hazelnut cookies!" I guessed.

"Nope. Not much of a baker, huh?" the voice said.

"Hey, she's a wonderful baker," David defended me.

"What makes you say that?" I asked, turning to him, smiling.

"You've got the cute little nose and nice, fluffy hair of one."

I leaned in a little closer. "Why, I'm flattered," I said.

"That's what I was hoping for," he said, his breath warm on my lips, his mouth centimeters away from mine.

"You've succeeded," I whispered before we kissed—a tingly, soft, long, we-haven't-yet-had-sex-but-have-danced-around-it-for-long-enough sort of kiss.

"HEY! Do you mind?" the voice over the intercom interrupted us.

"We don't know the answer," I said.

"Geez, doesn't anyone know anything anymore? It's truffles! TRUFFLES!" He buzzed us in.

David and I exchanged shrugs, and he pushed the door open for me to walk through. The place was dark and narrow, not much bigger than my own apartment's living room. There was a high tin ceiling and hammered copper tables snuggled inside circular, cushy, leather booths.

"You're not the typical hoity-toity media type are you?" the owner, Carl, said, offering his hand first to me and then to David. He was a bit shorter than David, and just as nicely built—wearing an Adidas T-shirt and dark denim with Puma sneakers that seemed to compliment his looks in an inviting way.

"Sorry, no," I answered.

"David Levy," David introduced himself.

"Oh, yes . . . your sister's the one going through that messy divorce with real estate giant Lawrence Scrimp, right?"

"Yeah, she is." I could see sadness in David's eyes. I knew he felt bad for Susan. In fact it was he himself handling the divorce, and I knew it was occupying the lion's share of his time—depressing him all day long. I squeezed his hand. It was there—an intimacy between the two of us—and it was tangible there in the elegant little bar, with just one other couple seated at the very back table. David squeezed back. Some protective coating around my heart peeled away. Here was someone who didn't seem to be running anywhere just when I was beginning to feel safe.

"You should bring her in sometime. Or better yet, why don't you give her my number? She's hot. Plus, I like that plucky attitude of hers."

"She'd like that," I answered for David, for Susan. Just that morning she'd called me from Eli's, singing, "Please, hook me up with someone. Anyone!" She'd hung up right after that, saying, "There's a cute guy slicing up lox over there."

"It was more original than a boring old good-bye," I explained to David after our drinks arrived—a raspberry mojito for me and a vodka martini for David.

"She's really had it hard. Susan fell in love with Lawrence back in high school, and she really never knew any other life. Now she just doesn't seem to know who she is." David could shock me with his intuition, his patience for people's idiosyncrasies. I could see him standing over all of us, directing us like in a video game: "Go left! Turn right! Yes, ask that guy to go for a drink!" I think I was doomed to be one of the little, hopeless players, never listening, always making mistakes, losing bonus lives.

We finished our drinks and a couple of complimentary truffles and cabbed it up to Sampson's.

"Anna!" Richard said from behind the bar as we grabbed two barstools. "I'll get you some fresh cabernet. You know we leave these open bottles up here for a month before we start using them for salad dressing. What'll the guy have?"

I glanced at David with a questioning look.

"I'll have a Heffeweisen," he said. To me he noted with pure, childlike pride, "It's the best beer." He smiled, toothily. My hand instinctively went to his back.

"No Hefe-whatever," Richard smiled—breaking our moment.

"Okay, then, a Sierra Nevada."

"Nope."

"Harpoon?"

Richard shook his head apologetically.

Out of nowhere, I heard Ray's voice. "David! Slumming?" He was obviously a little drunk.

"I'll have a Miller," Ray said to Richard, before David could answer, his eyes boring holes through David, more than a little mockingly.

"Make it two," I said gesturing toward David, trying to ease the tension. I felt for David's hand. Why was Ray acting like this? He'd been hard on guys I dated before, but never outright rude. I hated to have stress between us, but here it was, clear as day.

"What happened, David? All the fancy, rich places went out of business?" Ray asked after a long sip of his pint.

"Ray, stop—" I tried, but David cut me off.

"Funny you should say that. I was wondering why *you* were here? All the skanky girls away on vacation?"

My face burned. My emotions were oscillating back and forth, and I looked to Ray sympathetically. Though deserved, I could see David's jab had wounded.

"Nah. I got one right over there," he said, returning my look, challenging it.

I thought he was searching for me to say something, show something, like I understood why he did that and I should defend it. But I didn't know why, and I didn't know how to defend it. I wanted to, desperately. I realized then that I probably *should* know . . . after all, look how well he knew me.

After a moment, he defended himself . . . puzzlingly, like that riddle from the bar earlier.

"Things don't come so easy to all of us, I guess," Ray said. He took a long sip, grabbed a redhead in a tiny dress from near the door, and left without looking back.

After a second David spoke sincerely, softly. "I don't get why you stay friends with him, Anna. Honestly, he's such an asshole. He doesn't want anyone to get close to you, and that's no way to treat a friend." He looked genuinely shook up.

No, it *is* no way to treat a friend, I thought. Could Fenwick and Ed be right? *Could* Ray have feelings for me?

That was one scary thought. And even scarier was the way my heart had dropped onto the sticky floor when Ray grabbed that girl's hand. If there's one thing I hate, it's when my heart gets all sticky like that. It's just what I'd been trying to avoid all along.

I'd already had my head all screwed up with those obsessive

thoughts about my dad, and now I've gone and screwed up another organ. At this rate, I didn't know how long I'd last. But who knows—they do say things have to get worse before they get better . . . right?

8:30 p.m., Wednesday, October 25

"All righty!" Susan popped into the back of the town car looking about one thousand times more chipper than she had sounded on the phone earlier. It was a breath of fresh air for David and I, we'd been awkward when Ray called me twice on my cell phone earlier.

"You can answer it," he'd said politely.

"No, no," I said even more politely; neither of us being ourselves.

"Change of heart?" I asked, as Susan kissed me bi-cheekly and then did the same to David. We were on the way to meet Carl.

"Oh, that old bout of paralyzing depression? Pu-lease! I took a couple Xanax, thought about what a great opportunity this is—a good-looking man already endorsed by the two of you—and then I realized something amazing. I hate men, right? So, now I can just use them for sex, the same way Lawrence did with that skanky secretary, although he's acting like he's going to marry her, which I'm sure he isn't."

David and I were quiet for an awkward moment. "Congratulations?" I said. It was all I could think of.

We met Carl in the lobby of Comfort, where he seemed quite comfortable.

When he saw Susan, his whole face lit up, and I felt badly, because I knew she was just planning on using him for sex.

"Carl, this is Susan," I said.

"Why Susan, it's . . . well, it's unbelievable to meet you."

"Of course it is, darling."

David squeezed my hand, and the host led us to a fabulous grouping of a chair and a half and a chaise arranged over an oriental rug. "You wouldn't believe we had to kick someone out of this VIP table for you," the host turned his head to share this with us. "This skinny woman and some weird guy with grody teeth snuck in here, and we had to literally have them escorted out of your seat."

I swallowed back a gasp. But of course that wasn't Nasty and Joseph! I was just being paranoid.

Dreamy impressionist paintings and botanical prints lined the walls above. The place definitely lived up to its name. Within ten minutes, Susan and Carl were pawing each other on the chair and a half, while David I relaxed on the chaise, my head against his chest, and his long legs next to my smaller ones. My red heel was dangling from my right toes. It finally fell to the ground, and David reached down to get it before I had a chance to.

Susan and Carl were really getting inappropriate. To be honest, they were making Comfort quite *un*comfortable. But as it stood, David and I were already uncomfortable, quiet, and awkward in the wake of what had happened with Ray at Sampson's. Every time David reached for my hand, I was startled. When he started to speak, I inevitably spoke over him at the same moment. We were out of tune, our melody one big *American Idol* audition gone terribly wrong.

By ten p.m., we'd had enough of trying to come up with pathetic things to say, like, "Oh, I really can't believe how big a drink is when it comes in a mug."

"I'm tired out from all this chitchat," he said. "Maybe we should grab a taxi and leave the car for Susan." He looked so adorable, sensitive, and wonderful when he said that, that I leaned over and kissed him. I was two centimeters from his cheek, when he caught me in a question.

"Hey, are we all right?" he asked, his breath at my lips.

"Yeah," I replied too quickly, my voice faltering. I needed to convince him. I needed to convince myself. I wanted this. And this Ray thing was merely a thorn in my side. He was just being jealous, immature and jealous. Nothing more. It was a passing phase and therefore would, by definition, pass. I was sure I hadn't convinced him. I hadn't convinced myself.

"David—" and "Anna—" we said at the same second. He looked at me sympathetically, like all he wanted was to be with me. And maybe it wasn't just Ray. Maybe I hadn't really let him in all they way. But now I would. I would try. I wasn't going to risk things because I was going through some life transition. Here, everything seemed right for once, and why would I go and wreck it all?

I picked up my mug of wine carefully, with both hands, as a gesture that we should try a bit longer. I opened my mouth to speak, to tell him . . . a bit of the pain, of the history of my father's death, to let him in. I started, "David, you know I've been wanting to tell you about all this stuff with my dad."

But he stopped me with a finger to my lips. "Shh," he said. "You don't need to go backward into the bad stuff, Anna. Just be here with me and let me make you happy." He said this, and I didn't continue.

Unable to stumble upon common ground in conversation, we retreated into silence until a scream so piercing, so bone-chilling invaded the air around us that we had to cup our palms over our ears.

"Annnaaa!" It was Nasty. She was angry as hell, tossing her head back and forth, as the police officers dragged her away from the VIP lounge. Her inky eyes were as threatening as I had ever seen them.

The maître d' raced over apologizing profusely. "She snuck back in. I don't know how she did it! Got a busboy's uniform and a false moustache! I'm so sorry. We've called the police, and as you can see they are removing her."

This was not going to be good.

She continued to scream until she was out of earshot. "I am going to ruin you! Ruin—"

I'd been so horrified I hadn't even noticed David's arms squeezing me like he was making Anna-ade. "Are you okay?" he asked, kissing me at the crook of my neck.

In light of everything, I decided to have the taxi drop David off first, though he protested greatly. I didn't like the way I'd huddled into David for protection during the nasty Nasty incident. It made me feel pathetic and vulnerable. Now, I wanted to test my own strength, test what it would be like to go back to this life without David and go back to depending on no one but myself . . . something that had scared the breath from my lungs before Fenwick and David and all of this. It seemed an important thing to do.

Three blocks from my apartment, my heart started beating like crazy, I felt panic set in. I was alone. In grave danger. Anything could happen, and who would help me? David was a wonderful, beautiful person. And he loved me. And I could, I thought, very likely fall in love with him and enjoy a comfortable, safe existence. Whatever thoughts hedged in on the periphery of that one, I ignored them for the time being.

12:30 p.m., Thursday, October 27

I sat in my cubicle, deep in thought. The thing was, I didn't know how I felt. On the one hand, here I was with this amazing guy, in this amazing place, and two days ago it seemed like everything I wanted. But now Ray had gone and needled around with my thoughts and I couldn't help but feel curious.

Always, in my life, there'd been Ray. On a cold winter night, when the wind blew, I turned my head and saw the back of a man who I just knew was my father . . . alive and well as I'd wished him into being thousands of times . . . when I'd followed him all the way to 37th Street and 1st Avenue, where he turned around and said to me, "What are you, some kind of a freak?" there was Ray to come and get me from the customer service desk at the A&P, where a kind, Dominican produce manager had taken me, after we crossed paths on his cigarette break. Ray would say again and again, "It wasn't your fault, Anna. It wasn't your fault," until the sun came up behind our television set in the window.

If there were romantic feelings between us now and we followed through with them, what would become of us if it didn't work out? Where would I be then? I wouldn't let the door open for that happen. I just couldn't. With my relationship track record, it would be too great a risk. I'd stay friends with Ray and nothing more.

2:45 p.m.

I'd been watching my back all day. Wracked with terror, her voice still ringing in my ear, I didn't know what Nasty might do next. Every time the phone rang, I jumped like a jack-in-the-box. I received two threatening e-mails that I guess she meant to be anonymous.

> TO: annawalker@newyorknewyork.com
> FR: elizabethjackson@newyorknewyork.com
> RE: Anonymous threatening e-mail
>
> Little Miss Anna,
> You'd better watch yourself, because someone is going to
> get you.

TO: annawalker@newyorknewyork.com
FR: elizabethjackson@newyorknewyork.com
RE: Anonymous threatening e-mail

Little Miss Anna,
Your days are numbered here.

Though it was kind of funny that she didn't understand that I could tell it was from her, now I was scared.

I escorted Belinda out on her cigarette break to show her the e-mails.

"What should I do?" I asked, baring my teeth. I hadn't remembered to bring my coat down, since I was distracted thinking maybe this was all happening to me as my punishment for killing my father, and maybe Fenwick was just crazy and making all of this up about me just *thinking* I had done something to make my father die, and that it really *was* my fault, and soon he'd be found out for impersonating a shrink (very elaborately, with the photos and the office and the diplomas), and I would have to face the truth and possibly a death sentence, like those two kind of nice killers in the *Capote* film. I was freezing.

"Well, you can't exactly go to the police with something like that, can you?"

I didn't really want to go to the police. I pushed off instinctive feelings that police involvement would only speed up my martial punishment and tried to do what Fenwick suggested and just laugh at them. "Ha ha ha."

That worked out nicely, because Belinda thought she'd been funny, and she likes to be funny. With just letting those fears "hang out" and thinking beyond them to rational, real things, I didn't want to involve police or anything like that, because I just wanted to work this out. I said as much to Belinda. I left out the part about also feeling like maybe I deserved all this because of what I'd done with the presentation. I don't know why I still did that, because I always try to treat people as you (I, in this case) would like to be treated. My mother told me that incessantly as a kid—though she didn't need to, because I was always obsessively careful not to hurt anyone's feelings—because she had always been bullied for being heavy, although she is so beautiful, I can't believe anyone noticed.

"You're going to just walk right up to her, say you're sorry, and can we end this once and for all?" Belinda indulged in a giant inhale, considered this, and then let the smoke out with her head shaking in agreement. "It's so crazy it just might work. But, child, she said one smart thing—you'd *better* watch yourself. I know you are thinking you deserve this for some reason or another, and I'm not going to let you sabotage this for yourself. You know what? Let's go together." There was something about Belinda that I just knew she would be a wonderful mother. Unfortunately, she couldn't have any children. She'd had one that was born dead, and after that they found out the problem she has, which has something to do with her ovaries malfunctioning.

Belinda stubbed her cigarette out in the pretty pedestal ashtray, and she grabbed my hand, and we made our way through the double doors, across the lobby, and up the elevator. We walked with confidence, our heads high. Around the time we reached the second conference room, I started to lose my nerve. I pulled her into an empty, dark office with an open door.

"Do you really think we should do this? Now I'm thinking maybe this wasn't such a great idea. I mean, didn't I already apologize? If that was going to work, wouldn't it have already? Maybe we should just leave her alone. You know, I was thinking—" Belinda cupped her palm over my mouth and dragged me around to the other entrance to the conference room. The door had been left just the slightest bit open, just enough so that we could hear voices.

"We've got to set her up. We've got to find something incriminating on her and *ruin her*. DO YOU HEAR ME, YOU GRODY-TOOTHED PIPSQUEAK?"

Belinda and I were crouched by the door in a tiny alcove, with dozens of sleeves of paper drinking cups standing up on either side of us, where people only came to hang their coats in the morning, so no one could see our mouths and eyes stretch into giant Os as Nasty and Joseph revealed more of their plans.

"We are going to stick with her like oil to water, and—"

"But I thought that oil and water don't mix," Joseph tried.

Belinda and I were glad for the comedic break, no matter how short. Belinda smacked her forehead with her palm, but didn't let it make the noise. She's good at this spying stuff and maybe should join the FBI or something like that.

"Are you going to argue with *me*?" Nasty asked. Boy did that bring back memories, and for a second made me realize I was crazy to think *I* was the evil one, but of course that faded quickly as always. What a bully, though! Only now, I couldn't imagine why I ever listened to her. The only thing I hated more than having my instincts be wrong is having my heart get all sticky, and I've had both things happen to me in a matter of days, and now it looked like things were about to go from bad to worse with some sort of conspiracy against me, like the Warren Commission had against President Kennedy.

"I'm sorry, Miss Jackson," he moaned.

"You'd better be. Now listen to me. We are going to dig up some dirt on her and capture it and ruin this whole Miss Perfect Everybody Loves Me crap she's got going on. Now get out of here. Your teeth are making me sick."

Belinda and I kept our posts until we saw the pair make their way back to their offices. I spoke first. Or maybe it was more of a gasp with some words mixed in. "What am I going to do?"

"Well, I guess we're going to have to move to Plan B," Belinda said.

"What's Plan B?" I asked, doing my best to let my terror stand here with us among the paper cups and the fancy raincoats—and just let it be. Whatever happens, I will just be here, I will just be here, I will just be here.

"Margaritas," Belinda deadpanned.

I'd never heard a more pleasing word in my life.

SEVEN

You Better Watch Yourself

All U serves 350 "mind erasers" on a typical evening, explains barkeep Jon Templeton. The layered concoction—a mix of vodka, kahlua, and tonic water—helps men approach women, gets girls swaying their hips all sexy . . . "You know, sometimes I think it's good to forget everything you know and look at the world in a completely different way," Templeton said, quite poetically.

Ray got real quiet afterward and said "Yeah. Bring on the mind eraser, Jon Templeton. In fact, make it a double."

—Velvet Rope Diaries, *New York, New York*

1:00 p.m., Friday, October 28

Judy, Belinda, and I went to a crazy Mexican spot for lunch. Cantina Mexicano is hung with streamers all over the place. There are bright pink rugs and chili pepper lights are strung over the eaves.

I was inspecting a bottle of "Kick Your Butt Hot Sauce" and enjoying a frozen strawberry Plan B. I was letting everything just hang out with me; I was a killer, and that was fine, even if I felt I didn't deserve this nacho chip and this zippy salsa verde, because there is no such thing as deserving, Fenwick says (hopefully he is not a fake). Plus I was drinking this drink and trying to find a way to protect my column, and I was letting the possibility that the column might be the absolute worst piece of trash just hang out with us here, and this wasn't going to change the fact that I should be defending myself and working toward something I wanted, like success and fulfillment, and to keep my job.

Belinda crunched a nacho chip with a mound of salsa verde piled on it haphazardly. "I have to tell you something," she said to me.

"Oh no," Judy and I said in unison. Everyone knew that when Belinda said, "I have to tell you something," that it was never good. Never. And considering the bad news we were already there to talk about, it would have to be pretty bad to require an "I have to tell you something."

I sipped at my frozen strawberry margarita for strength. "Is this about Joseph?" I'd felt the content of his conversation with his mother hovering around me like a haze for so long it had almost fizzled into a clear day. Today brought on a surprise storm, coupled with a severe thunderbolt (named Nasty), and now it looked like hail was on the way.

"Child, in all the meetings I've been in with Ed and Joe in the past couple of weeks, all Joe has said is that your column 'sucks,' that it is 'self-concerned crap' that has no place in the paper, that no one is interested in it."

I'd been operating under the impression that Ed and I were the only ones who thought that (though I didn't really think it, my brain misfired and made me think I think it, Fenwick says, so I don't ignore this, since this doesn't work, I just let it hang out and eventually we will coexist to such an extent that I will laugh at this kind of thought that I think I think). And I'd managed to convince myself that Ed was crazy, and so it didn't matter what he thought. Now all my circuits were switching on to paranoia mode. Every cell in my body was flashing "YOU SUCK, YOU SUCK" in green neon. "Don't hold back, Belinda," I said, because I didn't know what else to say.

"Oh, see now that's why I didn't want to tell you! *I* don't think that, and I think it's been growing on Ed now. It's that moronic duo—Nasty and Joe—making all the problems now! Listen, I wasn't going to tell you, but after what we just witnessed, I figured you better have all the information. You know it's not true what he says about the column; he's just pissed because his column is shrinking."

I did know that. I'd heard his mom rake him out over it. "But what do you think I should do?" I asked them both. They were silent, and the waiter came balancing our three plates on a round tray on his head. I love this place. I wish I could write about this place. I really do. You don't get talent like that every day.

We inspected our rolled up flour tortillas, smothered with cheese and variously colored sauces, each filled with something smushy and accompanied by Spanish rice.

Since we were bringing all our cards to the table, I brought up those folders I'd seen in Ed's office. "Belinda, do you know anything about those folders Ed has in his office labeled Joesph James Disciplinary 1 and 2?"

She lifted a fork full of rice into her mouth, and when she'd only half finished chewing she answered, "Oh god. Those are good—top-secret info I'm passing on here by the way," she said and leaned in farther.

Judy and I met her halfway across the table, our mouths open to flies, anything.

"Ed came in not once, but twice in the morning to find Joseph fishing around in his Rolodex. He was going to fire him right on the spot the first time, but Joseph started crying! And Ed felt so bad that he said he'd give Joseph another chance."

"So why didn't he fire him the next time?" I asked.

"I don't know. I asked him that, and it looked like he was about to tell me, but then all of a sudden he stopped himself midsentence and said, 'That's none of your business, Belinda. If you want to keep *your* job you'll keep your nose out of it, too.'"

"Whoa! I wonder what it was," I said. I wouldn't put it past Joseph to have dug for some dirt on Ed so that he could blackmail him or something. I said as much.

"I don't know, but now that I think of it, I have an overwhelming feeling that if we find out, we'll know exactly what they are up to."

We quietly ate hunks of our burritos for a few minutes.

Judy spoke first. "I know what we should do with Joseph."

"Oh yeah? What?" I leaned in over my plate. A grain of rice stuck to my blouse.

"We should poison him," she said and sawed a hunk off her enchilada.

"Cheers to that," Belinda said. We held up our glasses and sucked up some frozen margarita.

"Wouldn't that be great, though, if we really could?" Judy said.

"You're scaring me," I said, forking rice into my mouth haphazardly.

"Why are people always saying that to me?" she said, smiling.

"What you need is a defense plan," Belinda said, waving her fork around with authority. "So that you can defend yourself from the unknown."

"That's true," I said. But what? What defense did I have? All I had was my column, and I didn't even know if it was good or not. I said that out loud after I thought it.

"That is so sad," Judy said.

"What?" I asked.

"That you don't have confidence in yourself. That you let some loser like Joseph and some freakazoid like Ed dictate your point of view."

I had a propensity toward this sort of behavior. If there were two points of view, I'd always go with the worst one. Despite everything, I guess I still felt . . . undeserving. "You can't trust how you feel," Fenwick always said. So I switched onto automaton and forged on. Then I lied. "I do have confidence," I said to my burrito. I took a bite, and all the stuffing plopped out onto the plate.

"Well, you are a terrible liar, but thankfully, there are other people who have confidence in you," said Judy. "Other people like Kate McCarty from Skiffer instant floor cleaners."

"Huh?" Belinda and I asked in unison.

"A potential advertiser . . . Kate McCarty from Skiffer *loves* your column. She asked if I could bring you to a dinner meeting this week. If we can get her to insist on an exclusive advertising plan for *your* column only, then we make you an invaluable asset impenetrable to the evil doings of the moronic duo . . . and I make advertising history and a huge commission."

"Oh that's good," Belinda said. Her hair was half up today, which always lent her style extra height. She smacked her hand on the table, "You are too good, child," she said, winking at me like everything would be okay.

Boy, did I want to believe her.

When we got back to the office, Judy flew off to make a phone call, and I stood outside with Belinda, while she smoked a cigarette. "Been doing what you advised about Gerry," she said and took a long drag. The ash burned red hot, and then she flicked it off.

"How's that going?" I asked, readjusting my purse on my shoulder, looking around nervously for god knows what.

"Well, he hasn't gotten much better yet, but he told me the other night that I've been such a great support system for him, that it means the world to him to have me there by his side. I said, 'Yeah, yeah, yeah, you are the world too, child,' because I hate all that mushy stuff, but he knew I liked the sound of it. He knows me." She smiled, but tried to squeeze her lips out of it immediately, took two last, quick drags, and stubbed her cigarette out in the pedestal ashtray, and we went back to work. "Now don't tell anyone I've got this soft side, or I'll kick your skinny little ass, so Joe and Nasty won't have to," she said to me sternly, without a trace of a smile.

7:00 p.m., Monday, November 14

Judy and I arrived at Odeon to meet Kate McCarty a couple of minutes early.

"Now listen to me, Anna. This is going to work. We are going to get your column to bring in the money Ed is looking for, which will protect your column and in turn give Joseph a sticking where it hurts. Now, this is how it's going to work. I like to get the table all set, pick the power seat, rearrange the salt and pepper shakers, so the client will have to ask, 'Can you pass me the pepper?' . . . that kind of thing," Judy said as we walked over to the table. She had three folders and placed one in front of each chair.

I inspected the one in front of me. Inside there were stats on my column. My head shot was there—fresh after the perm—and a couple of quotes pulled out from the columns.

"Darling! So glad you made it! Sorry about the LYMJ fiasco! I should have warned you . . . David, dear . . . don't you break this girl's heart. She's my friend."

—at S

Nina looked to Bernard like none of us mattered, like it was the two of them and then everyone else. It was beautiful really.

—at All U

They sounded kind of smart like that . . . didn't they? Like something I might want to read. The stats covered readership and demographics. Apparently, I appealed to stay-at-home moms in the thirty-to-forty-five age range, with a disposable annual income of two hundred thousand-plus. I tried to picture this woman, shoveling orange mush into her baby girl's mouth, while she read about David giving me a pair of heels. "C'mon, little Cassie! Be a good girl and eat it all up!" she'd say, missing, smearing orange all over her daughter's cheek, nose, ear, her own eyes on the paper.

"Now, just shake your head yes a lot, and whatever I say, agree and expand. Agree . . . and expand. Yes?" she asked, smiling wide, as Kate walked toward our table, carrying two long Skiffer poles with boxes around the cleaning end.

"Yes," I shook my head, though I wasn't exactly sure what I'd agreed to.

"Hello, Kate!" Judy said in a happy voice I'd never heard her use before. She embraced Kate, knocking the tall poles of the Skiffers into each other so they were slipping a bit from Kate's grasp.

"Hello!" Kate said, pulling her shoulders in high next to her cheeks, smiling huge. "Is this . . . ?" She darted her eyes toward me.

I squirmed a little, standing behind my chair, my cheeks firing up. Don't worry about how you feel, I told myself. Don't worry about being a phony, a nobody acting like a somebody. Just act the part.

"It sure is!" Happy Judy exclaimed, squeezing my shoulder.

"Yes! I'm Anna Walker. It is such a pleasure to meet you, Kate," I said, using a stiff line from some "Intro to Business Meetings" book and shaking her hand.

We sat down when Judy said, "Sit ladies! Take a load off!" She was truly in command. Now *there* was someone good at her job.

"Anna! I can't believe I'm sitting here at the same table as you! I don't know if Judy told you, but at my yogasize class at our gym in Plainview, Long Island, we talk about your column every single day! In fact, my friend Brie thinks David is all wrong for you. She says she knows he's really nice and caring and everything, but she doesn't think that's what you need. She keeps talking about the possibility of you and your friend Ray getting together. You remember that night at All U, when you wrote that he 'got real quiet' after Jon Templeton said that thing about looking at the world in a new way? Well, she thinks that was a sign. She thinks he's waiting for the right moment to tell you."

I was so taken with what Kate had said, with her interpretation of Ray and David, and with how much she knew and what dedicated fans she and her friends were that it took me a second to process it all.

"Well, we'll have to see, won't we," Judy directed my answer, raised her brows for me to *agree* and *expand*.

"Yes, we'll have to. You know, Kate, your friend Brie isn't the first person to say that. Sometimes it seems like everyone knows you better than you know yourself, doesn't it?"

"Oh, I totally think that. It's unbelievable the take my friends can have on a situation. I barely do anything without running it by them first." Kate appeared to think about what she'd said for a moment and then added, "Maybe they should change the column, Anna, so that you could solicit advice from readers on your situation . . . and in exchange, they could ask for your advice with their problems. It's just like you said—sometimes others know you better than you know yourself."

That was sort of genius, wasn't it? I thought of those choose-your-own-ending books I used to read as a kid. God, did I enjoy the power of that—the power of getting to decide on fate, even if it wasn't my own.

"That is a wonderful idea, Kate. You should be an editor over there." Judy bore through me with her eyes.

"Yes, it's a great idea. I think people like to be involved. And you know, I've often wondered whether there was some reason for some of the things that have happened in my life, as I'm sure everyone does. If I could somehow help people because of the troubles I've suffered, that could mean something, maybe."

Judy beamed.

"You are right about that." Kate said. "People who've experienced suffering are the best advisers on the planet. For instance, my friend Stephanie—she totally wore the wrong hairdo on her wedding day, and so when I went for my wedding style, she went with me and nixed all the ones that would have been a disaster." She seemed reflective for a moment, probably thinking of swoops and swirls of her chestnut hair beneath a veil. "You don't know, Anna. You're a real celebrity where I live. Everyone's talking about you. My friend Serena asked me to ask you if you remember a guy named Thomas Peterson? He says he knows you from Kellmore."

Thomas Peterson. He has been my Thanksgiving hookup for at least seven years. We were on again/off again—commiserates in misery and self-deception—back in high school. He was dark and brooding, the type who looked like a musician but didn't play an instrument.

"Yes, I do know him . . . but I wouldn't want to give the whole story away," I said, winking.

Kate squealed, thrilled with that nugget of information.

"Now," Judy said to Kate. "Order the most expensive thing on the menu, let me pay for it, and then let's sign this exclusive advertising contract for six months opposite the Velvet Rope Diaries."

"Deal," Kate said.

My eyes popped to three times their normal size.

Kate scanned the menu, said, "I'll have the surf and turf," closed it again and turned to me with her hands at her chestnut bob. "Now . . . about that Ray," she said, moony. "Tell me; how do you really feel about him?"

10:00 p.m.

That Kate asked a good question.

"So how'd it go?" David called, as I approached the subway station on my way home.

"Good," I said, uncomfortable at the question I'd been dwelling on all night long. "So what's going on with you?" I tried to change the subject.

"Oh, let's see . . . Susan, Susan, Susan. I don't think we'll ever settle this thing. Every time he agrees to another amount, she ups it. Hey, I don't want to talk about that. I want to talk about you . . . coming over now."

I wanted to. I really did. But I felt dishonest doing it. I didn't want a replay of the other night. I wanted to take one night, at least, to be alone with my thoughts. To talk to Ray and assure myself once and for all that we are friends going through a mutually rough patch and nothing more.

I was disappointed when I opened our door to find Ray wasn't home. Had he always been away this often? I couldn't recall it bothering me this much before, if he had been. There was no question the episode with David at Sampson's had put a strain on our relationship. I wanted to talk to him, find out where that had come from. Why then? What was so bad about David? And finally, what did he hope to gain by ruining things between David and me? But mostly, I just wanted to talk to him. He was my most insightful, kindred friend, and it was starting to seem like my greatest fear was about to be realized: Our friendship looked, quite obviously, to be at great risk.

3:00 a.m.

"Anna, Anna," Ray woke me with a whisper.

I guess I'd fallen asleep on the couch after an episode of *Emotional Eating* on the Food Network. They'd made "Are You and David Going to Make It Meatloaf" accompanied by "Why Was Ray Acting Like This Potatoes," or something like that.

I'd been dreaming of having sex with David, something we'd come close to, but hadn't actually done yet—mainly because David, unlike Ray, was a gentleman of the first order. So I was shocked when I realized it was Ray, and not David, waking me from my dream.

"Whoa! What were you dreaming about? You're unbelievably red," Ray teased, the back of his hand pressed to my cheek.

I swatted him away, surprising myself with an incredible rage. Here he was getting in the middle of things again! I couldn't hold back any longer. "Ray! What is going on with us here?"

He smiled, like I was amusing and endearing. I hate when he does that, because it swipes away all my anger and replaces it with the warm fuzzies, which really pisses me off. "Well, it's kind of complicated, but let me try to explain it to you. I just got home from a night of—well, you don't want to know what kind of night it was—and I found you here, snoring on the sofa with an episode of *Emotional Eating* on (so predictable by the way)." He shook his head in playful disapproval before continuing. "So I woke you up so that you could get into your bed. Hope that clears things up," he said, kissed me on the cheek, started loosening his tie, and made his way to his bedroom. "Goodnight, love," he said, and closed himself behind the door.

AAARRRGGGHHH!!!

3:00 p.m., Friday, November 18

"Anna Walker," I answered the phone in my cubicle.

"Anna Walker," a female voice chirped back.

"Who's this?" I asked.

"Who's this?" she mocked.

"No, really," I huffed.

"No, really. All right, fine! It's Susan! Remember me?"

"Susan!" We hadn't spoken since we left her getting funky with Carl at Comfort.

"Don't you want to know about what happened with me and Carl?"

I wasn't sure. I mean, no. I really didn't want to know. Susan can be very graphic in her descriptions. Plus, here they had probably done it six ways to Sunday, and David and I haven't even gotten past third base. Why am I always so caught up in *thinking* about everything? Why can't I just go and *do* it, like Susan?

"Hello! Okay, here's the story. Carl is, by the way, the most amazing kisser in the entire world. He's got this amazingly sexy chip on his shoulder. Like, he acts like he just doesn't give a shit about anything in the world. Don't you find that hot?"

"No?" I said.

"Oh, but darling it is. It's very hot. Don't you watch soap operas? I mean, what do you do all day long . . . There's nothing else on the television . . . Anyway, he just looked right at me, through me basically, and when he would kiss me, he would moan like crazy, which really, really turned me on."

I held the phone away for a minute. I'd had enough. Why was

I not getting this kind of action? I'd been the passionate dark one! That was *my* M.O. she was describing here! David and I had met in an extraordinary way. In fact, I'd say it was even *more* passionate than what Susan was talking about. So what happened?

I replaced the receiver to my ear.

"And then we just did it, like animals, for hours really."

"Does he know your plan to be with as many men as possible and use them all for sex?"

"Yes. He does. He said that was a major turn-on. Although I did have a hard time kicking him out in the morning."

"Occupational hazard, I guess," I said.

"So, I'm calling to invite you for a girl's night on Monday. You know I'm recently divorced, poor lonely leftovers, and I need my friends more than ever."

You had to hand it to Susan. There was no one in the world like her. Not one person. And I really loved that about her. And given my current state, a night without men sounded fabulous. "What's the plan?"

"Well, I wanted to see if you wanted to bring your friend Nina over for a fab evening."

"That sounds great, Susan. I'll just ask Nina. What do you want to do?" I pictured take out, *Ten Things I Hate About You*, chocolate.

"Oh, don't you worry. I've got it covered."

I called Nina after I hung up with Susan. "Wanna go to Susan's apartment on Monday night for a girl's night?" I asked.

"Whatever," she barked.

This could not be good. "What's wrong?" I asked. Suddenly, I had become a shrink.

"Oh, you know. It's the same stuff," Nina said. She got down like this every once in a while when she thought this spa idea was never going to happen, or that she'd never get married—so I knew it had to be one or the other.

"Having a problem with the spa?" I guessed.

"Anna, I just don't know. It feels like it's never going to take off. I can't get a backer. I can't get a loan. I can't get it going." I felt like a jerk. Here I was realizing my own dream right in her face. It just kind of fell in my lap while Nina went nuts arranging meetings, writing letters, reading books, attending seminars called "Own Your Own Spa," spending thousands of dollars on research. It had to feel particularly unfair now.

"I'm sorry," I said. "Maybe you can bring your stuff to her place, and we can all see if we can think of some kind of new angle to get you there. You know Susan's dad owns about a million businesses. She must have some great perspective."

"That's true," Nina said. "Yeah, she might have an idea or two for me. I'm not getting my hopes up, though."

My phone just didn't stop that afternoon. About five minutes after I hung up with Nina, it rang again.

"Anna, dear?" It was my mom. I could tell by the mixture of delicacy and pity in her voice. What could I say? I'd really made my mom earn her title over the years—killing her husband, mini-breakdowns, clinging to her like a baby panda, and now, pushing her off so that I wouldn't have to be faced with all that hurt. Through it all, unselfishly, like a Civil War nurse always on duty, whom someone forgot to tell the war had ended, she's remained the most caring, wonderful mother.

"Hi, Mom!" I tried to overcompensate for the lack of visits with an enthusiastic tone.

"So-*oooo*, what's the big writer doing now?"

"Not too much, really. Just finished up a column about this new bar called Comfort."

"Oh, now that's a lovely name, isn't it?"

"I guess so. We should—" I was going to say that we should go sometime, but I stopped myself. See, I've been down this road before. I make plans, thinking it's a long way off, and I'll be fine once the time rolls around, thinking I won't freak out or get consumed by guilt that I ruined my mother's life, and then make up an excuse as to why I can't do it.

But I always cancel. I cancel and just make things worse. And she knows why, and so she doesn't do anything, because she loves me and knows I'm hurting. This is a vicious cycle, and it's truly ruined our relationship. We love each other . . . through a thick, blinding fog, where you're helplessly screaming out things the other person can't hear, where you can't see the other person, though they're right there six inches in front of your face, unfortunately. "—talk later. I've got a meeting," I excused myself, not exactly lying. There was a staff meeting. It just happened to be scheduled for Monday.

The day was nearly done when Belinda came running over to my desk. She was so frantic that her entire bouffant had separated in half and looked like two hills with a valley running through the middle. It was a rare thing to see inside the hair. I felt, in the funniest way, that it brought us closer. "Child," she kneeled down next to my chair and whisper-screamed. "I am so sorry about the e-mail that is about to—"

She was cut off by the e-mail jingle . . . a great echo of jingles, actually. We both turned our attention to the computer monitor.

TO: All Staff
FR: Belinda Lewis for Ed Richards
SUBJ: White after Labor Day

I only had to look down at my snowy white self to know this was not good.

It has been brought to our attention that one of our
employees, namely, Anna Walker, has been wearing white
after Labor Day. Since it is our mission to be a high-
fashion, trend-setting newspaper, we are obliged to dress
accordingly. You'd all do best to follow this advice if you'd
like to keep your jobs.

   Now have a very, very nice day,
   Ed the Ed (isn't that cute?)

"I'm so sorry. I didn't have a choice but to type it up. Ed doesn't
know how to type." She looked miserable, tormented. "He stood
over me the whole time."

"Hey, Belinda, I don't blame you at all. No you keep doing your
job. First of all, you need it, and second of all, I'm gonna need you
to keep trying to find out what the heck they are up to. If we don't
have you there, we will really be in the dark."

"You're not angry at me, child?"

"I could never be angry with you, Belinda. You're the best."

"All right, well, now that's out of the way, I'll tell you how this
came about." She leaned in closer and cupped her hands around her
mouth. "Nasty came in about half an hour ago. I kept calling you,
but your line was busy."

Shit. See that. All those phone calls.

"And ten minutes later, she came out of the office, and Ed
handed me a tape dictating this e-mail."

I tossed my head back in the seat. "This is too hard, Belinda. I
think maybe I should just give up. Maybe some people are meant to
be happy, satisfied, and some people just aren't. Maybe what I should
do is go ask for my old job back and rectify this discord I've created
in the universe, trying to be happy when really all along, that's not
what I was destined for."

Belinda stood up, hovered above me, jabbed her finger at me, and said, "Now you listen to me. I don't ever want to hear you talk like that again. *Ever.* People like you—who've come this far—make it possible for the rest of us to believe we can, too. And without that, we've all got nothing. And I just won't *have* that. I just won't." Then she kissed me lightly on the cheek, pinched it, and walked away, her imposing, womanly silhouette so convincingly impenetrable, just as she liked it.

After a couple of years of trying to stay home as many days out out of the school year as possible, I moved on to convincing myself that I was a brave person, who, if given the chance, would do whatever she could to prove that.

I started out small. If I found our Tropicana OJ was a couple of days past its expiration date, I would drink it anyhow. I'd fill glass after glass, until it was all gone. I'd wiggle the empty container and throw it into the trash, sure for a few minutes that I was brave, that I would, given the chance, do whatever I could to prove that. But then, that wasn't enough. I needed something bigger. Didn't I realize that anyone could drink OJ a couple of days past its expiration date?

I graduated to pop rocks and soda. I'd hold it and hold it, my mouth stretched to capacity. I wouldn't jump or spit it out at the first terrifying crackle bursting on my tongue. I tried participating in dodge ball. Before, I'd made up excuses about "girl problems" and sat safely on the side picking at my cuticles. But then, I stood there. If a ball came booming toward me, which it always did, since the other kids knew I didn't like to play, I stood there and let it smack me right in the face. I once received, as a reward, a bloody nose. I said to myself, hey, look, you stood there and got a bloody nose! But after a while I couldn't remember the way it had all played out; it became like a dream, and I couldn't use it as my touchstone any longer.

Later, older, it would only be worse—higher stakes, more dangerous consequences: the possibility of STDs and allowing a drunk senior to drive me home, holding on to the dash without a seat belt, like I was a superhero, a fearless superhero.

Eventually, my thoughts turned to another tack, they needed to be sure, positive, that I hadn't done anything wrong. This became more important, somehow, than being brave. I had to know. Over and over I had to place myself in the Care Bear sneakers and the uncomfortable braids until I was sure. Soon, soon, I would feel confident and move on with everything I'd had on hold in the meanwhile.

Was I going to allow myself to have come this far from that wretched place, only to give up?

EIGHT

Testing the Waters . . .

Fashionable is a new lounge on Seventh Avenue, where people can "finally go after the fashion shows." I hadn't realized this was an existing problem. I ran it past Theresa, and she shrieked, "Oh totally! I once wound up in a TGIF after a Benjamin Cho show! It was mortifying! I drank some kind of an Oreo shake, and all I saw around me were poorly dressed tourists!"

—Velvet Rope Diaries, *New York, New York*

Monday, November 21

When the time rolled around, I took a seat in the second conference room, the one where Belinda and I had overheard Nasty and Joseph nearly a month ago. Judy plopped down on my right, and Theresa filed in and took the seat opposite. I was feeling awfully nervous to see Nasty and Joseph, because who knew how far they would take this whole thing?

Belinda must have been busy, because she came in last, a few minutes after Ed took his place at the head of the huge oval table.

Ed started to talk to the entire staff. "All right, *New York, New Yorkers*. What in Sam's Hell is going on here?"

Nobody batted an eye, because this was the way he started every meeting.

"It's been brought to my attention that page 4 is lacking the most in terms of quality, style, and content."

My page!

Every eye turned my way.

"Our publicity department, Nasty over here . . ."

Everyone chuckled at Ed's joke.

I sank down a foot or so, before Judy pulled me up by the back of my hair.

". . . says it's the only page she can't get a bite on from any of the media outlets."

This couldn't possibly be so! I knew it couldn't be! I remember those girls telling me, "If you ever do get over to editorial, we'll cover you. You have my word on that!" How many times had we talked about it? Dozens!

I wanted to say it! I had to say it! I couldn't just sit there, while thirty pairs of eyes bore holes through my face!

But I did.

"Are you sure you don't have Anna's page confused with *Joe Says,* which is on page 5? I've been hearing a lot of negative things about that page. Like, 'It sucks,' and stuff like that," Judy said. "Right, Anna?"

Again, the holes boring. All I could muster was, "Errm, huh . . ."

Ed took the stage again. "I don't doubt that either," said Ed. "Let's move on, people. I've gotta get home in time for *Everyone Loves Raymond.*"

"Midget Dating column, yes or no?" he continued.

But my mind was somewhere else.

5:30 p.m.

Dr. Fenwick's office was between *New York, New York* **headquar**-ters and Susan's place. I ducked out of work a couple of minutes early. This never seemed to matter anymore. With Nasty, it was "be here for the sake of being here." She'd actually said that out loud once when I'd asked to go down and get a coffee. So I didn't go down to the coffee shop on the first floor, which would have taken all of three minutes. Ten minutes later, she buzzed my line and said, "Go down and get me a coffee."

This system, I thought, worked out a lot better. I liked writing the column. It was a fantastic job—I got to go to all these great places, and just look at the change in my hair and wardrobe. Still, I could definitely use a pay increase, and maybe even some more work to do. Now I didn't have to research the bars, there was really just the visit part and the writing part. I was almost always done five days early.

Speak of the devil, on my way out, I saw Nasty waiting in front of the elevator. Now, normally I would hide in the coat room until she was gone and then ride the elevator safely down alone. But something inside of me said, Anna, just go and do it. What was the worst that could happen? Whatever it was, it had probably happened already. We *had to be* even now, didn't we? It was funny, seeing her there, after all that scary threatening, it wasn't as frightening as I'd built it up. More than anything, the fear had turned to anger. If she could fight, couldn't I fight *back*? Of course I could. It never would have occurred to the old Anna, but this new one was just pulling her boxing gloves on, and her adrenaline was starting to flow like crazy. I wasn't going to sit with my face covered any longer.

I tied the waist of my coat slowly, carefully, slightly wishing that maybe she would just happen to get in the elevator and sail down before I made it through our glass *New York, New York* doors and out to the elevator bank. I still didn't have my hat and gloves, so that was the last thing I could do to waste time. I adjusted my faux fur coat lapels and positioned my chin high. My eyes focused not on her shoes, like I normally did, but on her scary, too-dark eyes. I hadn't seen her assistant around lately and figured the rumors of her quitting were probably true. She might have been going down to get her own coffee, which would put her in a terrible mood. She hated to do anything for herself.

There was about ten feet between us, and Nasty hadn't noticed me yet. She moved toward the buttons and pressed incessantly, clucked her tongue in annoyance, and teetered on one stiletto point until her toe was up off the ground. She was in a brown and white printed blouse and a pink and mocha pinstripe pantsuit that looked immaculate.

I don't know what came over me, but I sailed through the doors toward the elevator, and as soon as her head turned in my direction, I said, "Hello, Miss Jackson."

I took her completely off guard. It was obvious from the backward jerk of her head.

Before she could think, she responded, "Hello, Anna."

The elevator opened with a ding, she walked in first, and I followed. We stood side by side, looking at the door. She didn't say a word more, and neither did I.

As the doors began to open, my mouth did, too, and the most genius thing came out. "You could try and make me throw in the towel, give up on everything. But I'll tell you this, Miss Jackson, I'm not giving up. I will *never* give up."

Her head was slightly pulled back on her rail neck, and she looked genuinely shocked.

"Good day, Miss Jackson," I said and trotted in my seasonally inappropriate suit far off ahead of her, through the doors, and on with life.

I felt odd being so joyful, but there definitely was something to this facing life head on. I had tossed that idea of forgiveness from Nasty aside, consequently come to the conclusion that there just wasn't a shred of goodness in her, and I was free to move on. Now I realize why I'd been so obsessed with her forgiveness in the first place.

I'd dreamed of forgiveness for so long, I'd dreamed of my father coming down from Heaven, wearing those faded black jeans he always wore and a dated, horizontally striped red, yellow, and navy tank top with his armpit hair puffing out. He'd say just the things I thought would cure me of my guilt. "Anna, you silly girl! How could you think my death was your fault? I was trying to get out of the basement to save you, and I couldn't do it. I am so happy that you made it out. There was no way both of us could have." You could say I craved forgiveness like some people crave that bittersweet narcotics high—like a pathetic, dirty trick of feeling good that I played on myself.

I walked to Dr. Fenwick's with my hands in my pockets, those thoughts in my head, and pressed the buzzer at the front door and walked down the hallway to his office. He was wearing a bright orange cabled sweater. His hair was sticking out in spots, with static, and it looked like a halo.

I told him about Nasty and the strange feeling I had now.

"Listen, Anna, I know it feels good when people forgive you, give you that thing it is you think you're looking for, but if you continue on that path, eventually it won't feel good. Eventually you'll start thinking there's no logical reason your boss's forgiveness, or anyone else's would have anything to do with your father's. Or you'll get the forgiveness, feel good about it, and then lose that good feeling and imagine that now he's taken his forgiveness back. This time, you nearly lost everything not sticking up for yourself against Nasty. Whether or not you feel like you deserve to fight back, you must act like you do. You have to just ignore the feelings and move on. Otherwise, you'll get sucked back in . . . every time."

I knew Fenwick was right, but who wanted to hear it? I was feeling good and didn't want to think about all the missed opportunities right then. I imagined myself sucked into a vortex in space somewhere, spinning and spinning for eternity. *He forgives me, he doesn't, he forgives me, he doesn't.*

"But isn't it good that I confronted her, at least?"

"Yes, yes," Fenwick said. "But saying something and doing something are two very different things, aren't they, Anna?"

"Yes?" I didn't know if I liked where this was going.

"Look, you know . . . she *may* have a good side. You may be right about that. *Still* acting in defense of yourself, pointing out her deceitful, unprofessional behavior, or thwarting her efforts is not going to kill her."

I wanted to believe him. He is a kind man. A father! He is as warm and gentle a shrink as a girl could ask for. "But what if she gets fired? And spirals into a great depression and swallows a bunch of sleeping pills? In the end, it would be me who started the whole thing with the presentation!"

"Maybe you did start it. But *Joseph* is the one who printed it! And you apologized. You did everything in your control to show her you were sorry. There *is* nothing else within your control that can be done—good or bad. Anything that she does is *her* responsibility. The blame rests on her. Now, listen to me very closely here— if you protect yourself, you are *not* going to kill her. Okay?"

I mopped my face up with a couple of tissues, willed my breathing to come more evenly, and wrote out a check for a hundred fifty dollars. I guess you *could* put a price on your health.

There was a new lamp in his office. This one had a huge brushed steel base, and tiny tassels fringed from the white shade.

"Nice lamp," I said curtly, as I pulled my coat on and let myself out. I don't know why I said it, maybe testing the waters, maybe because I didn't want to face the things he urged me to.

I sat on a bench in Central Park afterward. The plan was to e-mail Nasty. I began by watching a couple of sporty guys fix a flat bicycle tire. Next I watched a stoplight across the way switch from red to green to yellow and through the whole pattern again. I found an old bubblegum wrapper in my pocket and folded that, origami-like, until it couldn't go any smaller. I wasted some minutes scrolling around my cell phone features to reach the e-mail functions, and then soldiered on.

> **Dear Ed,**
>
> I am writing to tell you that I did some research further into the comments Miss Jackson shared about my page at today's meeting. In fact, Miss Jackson never pitched me or my column to any of the media contacts she mentioned. I phoned each of them and now have five interviews for next week.
>
> I share this with you in the interest of *New York, New York*. I would like to ensure it is receiving the media attention it deserves and needs to thrive in today's competitive marketplace.
>
> **Best,**
>
> **Anna Walker**

I pressed "send" before I could change my mind.

I spent some minutes investigating whether I could retrieve something I already sent, and then I sat back realizing that I'd done this thing and couldn't take it back.

I went into shock—I felt freezing, shaky.

"Hello?" I called Ray. I hadn't even thought of what I was doing. I just phoned him.

"Ray, I just sent an e-mail to Ed, ratting out Nasty's lie."

"And now you're freaking out that she'll get fired and you'll have that hanging over your head, and you'll never be able to do anything again for the guilt."

"Sort of."

"By 'sort of' do you mean 'exactly'?"

"Yes."

"Listen, Anna, either you're going to stick up for yourself or you're going to get fired. Those are your two choices. You have to choose to protect yourself over protecting Nasty. It's the only logical thing." I noticed his instinct to help was not hampered in any way by what had happened with David the other night. This part of us seemed okay, whatever this part was.

"You're right. Okay. Thanks. What are you doing tonight?"

"Ah, you know, this and that. I might call it quits early, though. I'm beat."

I hated that he didn't ask what I was doing. Was Ray playing one of his games with *me*? Trying to act aloof?

I gathered myself against the growing wind and crossed the street to Susan's place.

I arrived first. Her apartment was on the second floor of the famed Dakota. It had a grand entryway with an antique pianoforte and a window that looked over the courtyard to Yoko Ono's windows.

Before I went to the building gate, I waited a couple of seconds, to see if Nina would come by. The guard came out and told me, "You're not allowed to stand here. Move it along please."

I almost did just keep moving along, my cheeks burning, my teeth scraping each other, until I realized I had a right to be here. "I'm visiting a resident," I said.

"Oh yeah, who?" he asked. "And what is your name?"

"Anna Walker and I'm visiting Susan Levy-Scrump," I said, pulling the lapels of my coat together. This sticking up for yourself stuff was not easy.

"Oh, well then, let me escort you to the office to see if that's so," he said.

Again stones in the path. It shouldn't be this difficult to visit your friend. It shouldn't be this difficult to stick up for yourself. "Fine," I said, my ego sorely hurt. I was already growing wretched from the ups and downs of the afternoon: the feeling mortified, angry, good, like crap, numb to the tempting thrill of forgiveness—correctly (according to Fenwick)—but unsatisfyingly numb, and now pissed again.

"Ms. Levy-Scrump, I've got an *Anna Walker* here, says she's your friend." He handled my name as he might a particularly embarrassing venereal disease, and he looked down at me with a smirk, as if I were about to be undone.

"Oh! Anna!" I could hear her through the phone shrieking.

The guard turned green. "Through the gate, make a left, up the elevator to the second floor," he said and turned from me to the security screens behind his desk.

"Nina—our other friend—will be coming soon. And you might want to think about treating people with more respect," I said with enormous effort, as I turned to go.

It felt like I could be in another country, another decade inside the hallway of the Dakota. And surrounded by dark-wood paneling and low lighting and lots and lots of molding—enough molding to do ten houses—I felt very out of place, and not just because the security guard had pointed that out. I rode the elevator to the second floor in complete awe, sliding my hand up and down my purse strap.

Susan was waiting in the open doorway with foam separators

between her freshly painted toes. "Hello!" she screeched and pulled me in for a hug.

"Hi, Susan," I said. She didn't look good. There were enormous puffs of purple green under her eyes. There was a dry flakiness to her nose, like she'd been crying, despite the sexual healing. Divorce had to suck. You think you have found the person to share your life with and then one day they say, "Nah! Never mind! Just kidding!" and there you are . . . out on the street, or in the Dakota . . . with a flaky nose, addressing too familiarly, someone you barely know and using sexy bar owners for their bodies.

"Where's your friend Nana?" she asked, getting her name wrong.

"She'll be here in a minute," I said. I handed over a bottle of wine. It was a good one we'd gotten in the editorial department. It had a French name and an etching of an estate on the label.

"Oooooh," Susan said and called over her maid. "Risa! Uncork the Chateau St. Francais, please!" Susan smiled and winked at me.

Risa appeared—a miniature woman with a tiny spray of black hair cropped at her ears. "Madam," she said.

"I told you! It's Mademoiselle, now," Susan said unhappily.

Nina arrived momentarily, and Susan took us both into the living room, where she'd had an entire mobile spa unit set up, care of Fab! Spa. "It's beautiful," Nina said, her face screwing up and springing tears. "Just beautiful."

"Oh darling, Nana, what is it?" Susan asked. I rubbed Nina's back. Often it was the only thing I could think to do.

"Susan, it's stupid. It really is."

Susan took Nina's coat, dumped it onto an empty couch and led her to a fabulous Louis the XIV chair standing behind a basin of rose petals floating on bubbly water. Susan and I took the other two seats, though Susan had no basin—she'd had her pedicure already, obviously. "There's no such thing as stupid! What's stupid is me being single again, with only one friend . . . who is really the worst, most selfish friend in the world!" We didn't know what to say to that, as we always had each other. So my hand started up again, rubbing Susan's back this time.

"Well, if you really want to know," Nina said, "I have always wanted to open a spa—"

Susan didn't even wait for Nina to get the rest out. "Let's do it!" she said. "I love spas! I hate my husband! I need SOMETHING TO DO!!! I NEED SOMETHING TO SPEND HIS MONEY ON!!! You wanna call it Susan and Nana's?"

Nina was crying again. But this time, she was smiling. "You mean, you want to back it?" she asked, obviously trying to make sense of what she'd just heard.

"Why not? I'm a freaking billionaire." She thought for a second, and then said, "But I don't want to do any—what do you call it?— oh yes, work." She made a face like she'd tasted a sour lime, and we all laughed . . . though Susan looked like she didn't know exactly what was funny.

"To Susan and Nana's," I said, raising my expensive wine in my expensive wineglass, a woman scrubbing my feet with a big wooden brush, Yoko Ono's big glasses or something else I wished into being them reflecting light across the way.

Nina hesitated before raising her glass. "Maybe we should call it Susan and *Nina's*," she said in her best attempt at subtlety.

"Why in heaven would we do that?" Susan asked, oblivious.

"Because that's my name," Nina said.

"Well, you should have told us if you went and changed your name like that, silly!"

"I'll drink to that!" I said, clinking glasses with what I imagined to be—if unconventional—an excellent business duo.

★ ★ ★

"So you dissed me for my sister?" David said. I was on my cell phone on the way to his apartment. Without gloves, a hat, or scarf, I was frigid. I kept squeezing my hands into fists to keep them from going stiff. His voice was a length of sturdy cord, pulling me somewhere safe, warmer than this . . . exposed fingers and neck and ears. A part of me warmed at the sound of it, tried to ignore the way I'd felt at Ray's breath on my lips, though I could feel it again, terrifyingly, when I thought of it.

His building was as intimidating as his sister's was; both had that otherness that lent itself to creating outsiders—marble lobby, buttoned-up doorman.

"Can I help you, miss?" he asked down the bridge of his nose. "17 D," I said, gulping, even as a chic nightlife chronicler, a chronicler of nightlife chic who'd been so bold earlier.

"Mr. Levy, there's a—"

"Anna," I said. I'd had it with doormen, with exclusionists and fighting the people who wanted to keep me on the outside—Joseph and Nasty and sometimes even myself, the lot of them. I'd already been to David's apartment twice before, and this guy had been there on both occasions.

"Anna," he repeated into the mouthpiece of the intercom. I watched his reflection in the mirror behind. I saw myself in there, too. I was glowing a little from the facial and the wine and the cold. And I knew I was better than this. I'd come far, but there was farther to go, louder to yell, more territory in my heart to reclaim.

"I don't know any Anna," David said into the phone. He said it loud enough so I could hear the vibrated, tone-deaf transmission of it. He was kidding, a sing-song to his voice, but the doorman didn't catch it—and by way of this result, the joke of it turned sour. Was this the truth? Did he not understand me? Did he not "know" me?

"Says he doesn't know you," the doorman announced it thus, his chin higher, his eyes sinister, the champion of distance, separation, prohibition.

"All right then, I guess I'll just go home." I also said this loud enough so that David would hear, and maybe to test what it would feel like if I retreated from it all and resolved to be defeated. I was reminded instantly of that night at S and David's easy way. Why now did it truly feel like I did want to go home? Why did the thought of sitting on the couch with Ray—playing Super Mario Cart and munching corn chips—sound so appealing? It was all a joke, I knew that. But something in it stung. I guessed I'd just had enough for the day and tried to chalk up my layers and layers of re-action, of interpretation, to that.

"Just kidding! Just kidding! Send her up," I heard David say.

The doorman didn't say a thing. What *could* he have said? He just pressed the buzzer, and I pushed myself through the door, trying to tell myself, impotently, see, you can make it, as I was whisked up the elevator and then made my way to David's apartment.

"Who is it?" David asked through the door.

I covered the peephole with my palm. "It's your dream come true, baby."

"A huge ice cream cake with crunchies delivered right to my doorstep?" He swung the door open and tried to look disheartened.

"You don't look anything like an ice cream cake with crunchies," he said dejectedly.

Now I saw him, his fluff of barely thinning hair up top, his sophisticated eyes and expensive loungewear, I knew he was none of the things I'd felt in the lobby, on the way up. Those were my own issues I was projecting onto him. He kissed me expertly at the threshold.

"If I had a quarter for every time I heard that," I said. He struck a familiar chord now, when I saw him—like finding your own long-lost coat in a friend's closet. He was a good person, a wonderful person.

He leaned in and kissed me again after he took my things, and then he squeezed me like he really meant it, like he'd missed me in the two days since we'd eaten Ethiopian food and gone to see that horror film about a misguided Victorian troll—trying to smooth over the bits that had grown lumpy between us. I missed him, too. At least through my exhaustion, I think I did.

"Wanna watch anything on TV?" David asked, inching closer to me on the sofa.

"Sure!" I said, overzealously, because I was feeling kind of queer.

I flipped and flipped through the channels, while David rubbed my shoulder. He was such a great, caring guy. I tried really hard to concentrate on that. I should be honored to have someone this great be this interested in me. Especially since I haven't been in an actual relationship since college. I was never good at playing it slow, at taking care of myself. Quickly, too quickly I'd fall into the patterns— wait for them to walk me home, slip their arm over me to protect me while I slept—and then I wouldn't be able to do anything the way I had before—alone. How could I wash my clothes alone? Study all by myself? Walk to the bookstore . . . alone?

And then they wouldn't want to, and they wouldn't want to. They wouldn't call back or drop by to say "Hey, let's get a drink or something." And I'd know; I'd know what I did wrong—the smothering and the neediness—but I'd do it again and again, because I didn't know another way than to look for someone to take care of me, to fill that hole where my dad hadn't been for so long.

However, now . . . now was different. Here I was sitting with David, a real, worldly man who saw something special in me, and I knew I could have stayed over and he'd hold me with a hand sweeping the nubs of my spine, and still I kept one foot on the floor like I didn't want to get too comfortable.

"Reality television is ruining entertainment," I said meaninglessly, turning to him.

"It's the downfall of society," he said, with no passion, no pitch, like we were filling space with words that had nothing to do with what was happening here, which we were.

He slipped the remote from my hand and placed it soundlessly onto the coffee table, next to a book about famous photographs. I fell easily into the way his lips tugged at mine, the way his tongue teased and then pulled back, the way his eyes looked desirous of me, saying what our words hadn't.

It was too easy to lose myself in the rhythm of him, and so I allowed us to go farther through buttons and zippers and elastic waist bands than we had before . . . way, way beyond our sort of casual beginnings . . . all the way. And all the while, I tried earnestly to ignore the tides turning in my heart, the rumblings of confusion they were stirring up as they churned and churned me toward darker, deeper, more daunting waters of Ray, of what was undeniably growing there in the weeds, where one could easily get a foot caught and drown.

At eleven thirty, David pushed my hair off my face, and I pulled the blankets up like a strapless gown over my chest. I had the distinct knife-sharp pang that I'd done the wrong thing. After I'd done the wrong thing for a few hours, I'd fallen asleep briefly, and now David was gently running his fingers through my hair, just as I'd dreamed someone would do so many, many times. I shocked myself by deciding to leave the cocoon of this behind and saying, "I'm so tired David, I think I'm going to catch a cab home."

Outside, in medallion slippers and striped sleep pants, David waited for me to hail one down, in fact he hailed it for me—a gentleman of the highest order—and he handed ten bucks to the driver and said through the plastic divider, "Eighty-sixth Street, sir!" and he smiled, his lips tugging into a soft curve, though he probably didn't feel like it.

Inside the heat blasted in my eyes, drying them, and I wondered whether it was a sign that we caught all the green lights. Every single one.

I didn't recognize this snaky, lurking me, half stirring up trouble, halfheartedly quelling it, like someone laughing, smiling, coughing at their smoking habit while saying, "I know, I should really quit." My breath caught in my throat as I pushed open my apartment door.

"Watcha watching?" I asked Ray as I plopped down on the sofa in my coat, the heat overwhelming in there. I could see that he had the window propped open with a copy of *Webster's* dictionary, but the breeze was insignificant—a dainty swirl of cold that didn't quite make it as far as we were sitting across the room.

"*Motorcycle Guys,*" he said. It was a documentary type of show about a couple of guys who make highly detailed bikes and argue a lot. "The dad just threw a major fit." Those were Ray's favorite parts, but he didn't smile.

"About the budget?" The dad was always yelling about the budget.

Ray didn't answer. My question hung there . . . fading away as that bit of cold air did—helpless, not saying enough or doing enough.

He turned to me, and with us sitting shoulder to shoulder like that, when I turned toward him, we were close, too close.

I felt a tiny rush of air as his lips parted, and it looked like he was going to kiss me, and I felt two ways at once: like I would throw everything away for this crazy, improbable, dangerous thing that felt exactly like love, and that I would never risk that kind of thing in a million years. My chest heaved. I was ashamed, because I knew this was precisely what I'd come home for.

The commercial ended, and Ray turned back to the television without a word. We sat like that for another fifteen minutes, during which I didn't watch anything but the replayed scene of Ray and I nearly kissing, and then I poured a glass of water for myself and went to bed.

"Good night," I said.

And this time he said, "Night," but he didn't look at me, and he didn't smile, and there was something, a boulder or a Mack truck standing in the space between what we meant and what we said, and I closed my door, but not all the way, and lay down to sleep.

9:00 a.m., Tuesday, November 22

This morning the company received another e-mail.

> TO: NYNYStaff
> FR: Belinda for Ed
> RE: Fashion Regulations
>
> It has been brought to my attention that it is completely unfashionable to have yellow "grody" teeth, Joseph, and that anorexia is extremely last year, Miss Jackson. Please correct these transgressions at once.
> In future all company fashion advice must be cleared through Theresa Jet, our fashion director.

Ed is already calling the success of the column, now in its third month, a "freaking ridiculous phenomenon."

"People just love an underdog," he said. I didn't take it as a compliment. I don't think he meant it as one.

"Don't get all pissy about it," Ed said. "It's a good thing. It means you're flawed, likeable. You don't see people liking perfect people, do you?"

In fact, I had seen that. In fact, I'd spent a large portion of my life hating those people, because they were so well liked. But maybe it was people like me that liked those screwed up people better. Could it be that there were other people like me out there? That was a frightening thought.

"Skiffer bought six months of pages—exclusively across from

your column. Poor Joseph's page is now cut in half again, but, hey!
Money's money! My father built this magazine from scratch—
printed it in his own apartment! And he didn't do that by caring
about people, you know what I mean?"

This was not a kind man.

I nodded and stood to go as quickly as I could.

"Hey, hey, hey. Wait a minute," Ed said, my back already to
him. I didn't want to know about my e-mail. I didn't want to hear
anything good or bad. I didn't know which things would be good
or bad.

"What's that?" I asked. But I didn't need to. I saw her righteous
figure approaching through his glass door.

"I've called Nasty, great name by the way, to meet us and clear up
this whole business you e-mailed me about."

What was he going to ask? What would I say?

She swooshed in shaking her head back self-importantly. She
said, "Ed," ignoring me purposely.

This had the opposite effect on me than she probably assumed.
"Elizabeth," I said, surprising myself. I paid for it with a rapid heartbeat.

She crossed her legs. Recrossed them. She looked uncomfortable; a college friend at a work friend's party. She rubbed down the
bridge of her nose nervously.

"Ladies," Ed said, smiley, as if he were enjoying himself too
much.

I set my lips into a firm line.

"Can't we all just get along?" he said, laughing immensely at his
own joke.

"Anna here says you made that up about her page."

"Lies!" She stood and yelled.

I clasped the arms of my chair.

"Anna?"

I looked at Ed long and hard. I thought of what Fenwick said. I remembered my conversation with Ray. She didn't deserve all of this thought! I had to protect myself. This was ridiculous. She was not my father. She was not my responsibility. No matter how I hopscotched around life, I would hurt people, and that was a risk I had to face.

I stood. I'd never realized before how much shorter she was than me. I stood over her now, close—the way she used to do, scratching me with her hair. "Elizabeth, I phoned all the publicity contacts you claimed to have pitched me to, and they all denied that ever happened. And they all booked me for appearances on the spot. That's black-and-white evidence you are lying, not doing your job, and this is no good for the company, and I think we all know that."

She stared at me with those vacuous eyes, never blinking.

"Okay, sorry," she said, finally.

"Now maybe, Nasty, you can stop trying to live up to your name there and just do your job, okay?" Ed laughed at his joke.

Something about it all felt so right. Except, of course, for my left hand vibrating like an old car engine.

8:00 p.m., Wednesday, November 22

The owner of Fashionable was affiliated with Selvin Krein—a fashion legend. And all the waitresses wore elegant lamé dresses designed by Krein himself. At the private viewing they'd had me in for, they gifted me with one, too. You got gifts at all these things—my cubicle was full of them now, bigger and better trinkets to replace all the tokens Nasty had destroyed; there were fourteen-karat gold desk calendars and crystal paperweights and expensive candles and cashmere mouse pads.

I took David to the viewing, and he wouldn't let me out of his sight the whole time.

"I was thinking of you all day. I was reading a thirty-two-page brief, and there you were; I ordered a chicken Caesar wrap for lunch, and there you were," he said when his town car picked me up at my office.

"I was in your chicken Caesar wrap?" I teased.

"You were . . . and you look just as I imagined you."

"You mean, with lettuce and tomato squished in all around me?"

"Exactly," he said. He looked seriously at me, through the jokes, and I felt sleazy and see-through, felt that he could see right through me, right to where I was trying and failing to pump the Ray thoughts out. My eye began to twitch.

I was about to confess when finally he broke the silence. "Your shirt's on inside out," he said, fingering the tag at my neck.

I giggled, a little too giddy, at the realization that he wasn't thinking anything serious after all, and then fixed myself up. Town cars—among their other benefits, offer ample privacy, so that you can lift your shirt off and put it back on the proper way.

"Wait," David said, once I had my blouse up over my face. If I let him, he could really get me tingling . . . that was pretty obvious when he kissed me right at the base of my bra strap. I felt surprisingly comfortable with him—for being half-naked in the back of a town car and possibly falling in love with my roommate.

"Let me do that," he said, when I started the buttons again. And by the time we stopped in front of Fashionable, I looked kind of like Courtney Love—glamorous but rumpled, and with some of my gloss rubbed off. There was this thing about David—he knew how to make me feel safe as anything. He offered chivalrous gestures—guided me out of a car, took my coat, called to see if I had arrived home safely. I'd always dreamed of that. Nina had always said, "That's ridiculous. No guy is like that. Plus it's kind of sick . . . you want to date . . . well, you want to date your father or something." That wasn't exactly delicate, but in a way, I guess I did want that—

not in an Electra complex kind of way, but someone that could fill up that emptiness where the paternal safety net was torn. I had to admit, it was wonderful having it now.

The cool thing about Fashionable is that you come in through a real, genuine catwalk. They actually bought the catwalk from a production company that puts on the fashion shows in New York City and Los Angeles.

"Of course, nobody takes those Los Angeles fashion shows seriously, right?" the owner, Thomasto Severino, said, winking at me.

"Of course," I said, though I had no idea whether this was true.

David had his arm around me and said, "It's a travesty—those Angelenos dreaming they can be fashionable!"

Thomasto missed his sarcasm altogether. "I know. I mean, thanks to them, it's jeans and zip-up hoodies all over the place! People barely wear black anymore!"

"Horrible." David shook his head affecting misery.

"What can we do, right?" Thomasto said.

"Everyone must do their part," David said, tightening his hand into a passionate fist.

When Thomasto left us at the table I whispered into David's ear, "LYMJ, LYMJ," because I couldn't help but be reminded of it then. We shared a laugh over that. "Hey, if that never happened, we might have never met," he said. "I'd like to encase that shoe in glass and put it on display for all the world to see. It's a very special shoe. Very special." His fingertips slightly pulled me in at the shoulder, a basketball grip, on a place that was now his, that he knew—and this felt good. He kissed my lips gently, a precise, soft touch. He wore hungry eyes and I know that I wanted this, though it made me uncomfortable to be wanted that way. My hand flew to my hair, toward the safety of that.

Because I couldn't be serious, I joked. I said, "Whoa." It was clear this moment is what people hope for, this vantage point, where you can see front-loading washing machine/dryer duos and custom kitchen cabinetry in your shared futures.

We didn't separate the entire evening. Even when I went to the bathroom, he waited right outside the door for me. I could hear him whispering right at the tiny space between the door plank and the doorway, "I don't know what it is tonight, but I am just crazy over you. Honestly, I don't know if I'll be able to turn around now with . . . umm . . . whatever's going on down below. You might have to stay in there for a while."

I switched into the gold lamé dress, mainly so I could tease David through the doorway saying, "Now I'm taking off my shirt," and "Now I'm unzipping my skirt." I liked the way he kept saying, "Oh my god, you have to stop that. Please if you have any mercy on me, you'll stop."

I shoved my own clothing into the gift bag, reapplied lip gloss, and tousled my waves a little bit. This was fun, and it occurred to me to fully give in to that, to forget this nonexistent idea of a Ray connection and stay in the secure bird's nest of this.

I opened the door a crack, so that I saw half of one eye and his beautiful scarred nose. The bit of mouth I saw was the bow of his top lip, and when his gaze traveled down to see me in the low-cut lamé, I could see that bow curl devilishly.

"Oh god," he said. "We are really in trouble now. Hand over that bag so I can cover myself with it."

"Poor lovesick boy," I hadn't meant to say the *L* word, but it had slipped out, my mind's Freudian attempt to save me, set me onto this course. Reflexively, I scanned for his reaction.

"You don't know the half of it," he said, seriously, slowly, wonderfully terrifying. He pushed the door open gently, relieved me of the shopping bag, arranged it and me so that he wouldn't be charged with indecency, and we walked back so lusty with the possibilities of us that neither of us could manage a word. It was all deep breathing and chests heaving.

We were just finished with a delicious array of hors d'oeuvres, and drinking a boutique French white with great oak undertones, and, clandestinely, David nodded to the manager, his neck slightly shifting in the charcoal gray of his collar.

"What are you up to?" I asked.

He didn't say anything, just widened his gaze.

I shifted my toes inside my shoes.

The lights went dark, and David and the manager started to sing, "Happy three month anniversary of your column to you. Happy three month anniversary of your column to you . . ."

This was it, wasn't it? The road to forever?

The waiter began to slice my cake into pieces, and my cell phone rang the conga song by Gloria Estafan, to a few laughs.

Only to me, that song never signaled greater terror. It was a distinctive ring that belonged to Ray and no one else. We had picked it out together at that little coffee shop where the *Godfather* scenes were purportedly shot, over in the Village, drinking dainty espressos, remembering how frightened we'd been when we first moved to New York and came to that café nearly every night, only because we knew the way.

I wanted to ignore it, I really did. But my voice came belting out, too loud across the cake, "Excuse me, I have to take this."

I ran, breathy, a little wildly, outside of Fashionable, where it was frosty and windy. My voice came hushed, "Hello?"

"Anna," he said.

"Hey Ray," I tried to sound casual, like a girl who'd just cut her three-month anniversary cake with another—PERFECT—man should. But there wasn't any point in trying. I was reacting to him now.

"Where are you?" he asked.

"A new bar off Sixth Avenue," I said, already knowing I would leave, run away like a thankless, sick, very sick girl if he asked.

"Cool," he said.

"Where are you?" I asked.

"Ehhh, you know," he said. But I didn't. I didn't know, and I hadn't thought about it, but now I would, torturously, I would.

In the seconds of silence, I thought of a million things to ask: Why are you calling? Who are you with? Are you thinking what I'm thinking? But nothing came out, and then he said the inevitable.

"All right, so see you."

"See you," I said. Nothing had happened and yet everything had. One thing was clear: There was no turning back. And this is precisely what I'd been terrified of all along.

"Who was that?" David asked.

"Work," I lied uncomfortably, my hair my only protection.

When I arrived home, distracted and terrified, prepared to tell all, Ray wasn't home. I fell asleep in my coat on the sofa.

3:00 p.m., Wednesday, November 23

I had to file my column about Fashionable, the place where everything had seemed perfect until Ray called.

Later I was going to meet Nina for a drink and some "big news" before going home for Thanksgiving. I was thinking I didn't feel up to going there. My fingers were poised over the keyboard, ready to write an excuse. "Dear Mom, I'm no longer celebrating Thanksgiving. I'm moving to Bolivia where there aren't many things to be thankful for."

I wrote the words, but I knew I would erase them. I was under

Fenwick's strict orders. I'd turned down a trip to St. Martin with David just to be at the scene of the crime where everything seems fresh, and normalcy becomes an overwhelming goal. Also, I was a little worried because my mom was so overexcited about the success of the column that she'd gone and invited everyone she ran into to come to our house for Thanksgiving dinner. We had a big dining room, which opened onto a giant family room that Roger had built a few years back, so we could fit everyone, no problem. But it wasn't the room that had me worried, it was the giant smile I'd have to wear, the plastic, ecstatic grin, though I'd long to torture myself— descend the basement stairs and replay the fire, searching for the alternate ending that never came.

The cool thing about my mom is that she is so thoughtful she drives to the city to pick me up. She has Roger drive me home. They've always split it up this way. I hope I am such a generous mother one day. Mom was picking me up at nine at night, so she could avoid the traffic and zip us back to Long Island in under a half hour.

But first I had to meet Nina.

NINE
Home Is Where the Heart Is

There is something about an exchange at a bar that hits so much deeper. Probably it is because of the alcohol.

—Velvet Rope Diaries, *New York, New York*

"Hey!" Nina was at a corner table at my local bar. I hadn't been there for a while. It seemed a little different now. I didn't know what it was exactly—a change in lighting? A re-arrangement of furniture?—but it disoriented me as I slipped my jacket off and hung it over the chair back.

"Hey!" I called back and hugged her. She was dressed in a smart charcoal pencil skirt and a white blazer. Nina had to look like that for the law firm she worked for as a paralegal. She had the manuscript of tomorrow's column I'd e-mailed to her on the table.

"This column is great. It really is."

When Nina was polite, I worried.

"What?" I asked.

She gathered in her lips to a tiny squiggle.

"Jesus! What?"

"Well, is everything okay?" she asked.

"Of course!" I lied.

"Is everything okay with David?"

"He's perfect!" I said too loud, listing things that proved this on paper, though not necessarily to me. "He's a gentleman, gorgeous, rich, generous. Perfect!" This was a third-grade book report, not a person, and I knew it.

"I'm not gonna push if you don't want to talk about it," Nina said.

I changed the topic. "Now what's your news?"

She took a sip of water and said, clear as day, "I told Bernard I'm obsessed with getting married."

"What?" I asked.

"I blurt out, 'I'm sitting here, and I'm trying to smile with my top teeth only, like my mom told me I look best,'—I really said that—and then I said, 'I'm wondering if I'm wasting my time *again*? Because I can't do this for another freaking second.'"

"What do you mean you told Bernard that you are obsessed with getting married?" I couldn't believe it! I thought you were supposed to bury your fears deep, deep down and only ever retrieve them when they were killing you or something.

"Anna, I don't know. We had just come back from dinner at that cheap Italian place down in the East Village, and it had been such a great night. I ate something called 'Priest Stranglers,' and we couldn't stop laughing over that—that I was the kind of girl who'd order the 'Priest Stranglers.'"

She laughed now when she remembered it, like a giddy teenager. "But inside I felt all this crazy pressure. I couldn't even enjoy myself. I just kept thinking, when is it going to happen? When? When? When? I was thinking, well if it's not going to happen, then what is the point of this right now? And why should I enjoy this joke so much and start to see the characteristics of his that he didn't show right away? And why am I sitting here trying to act interested in the Jets or Giants or whichever basketball team it is he likes? And why am I letting myself like him so much that I hover my finger over the first digit of his phone number for five minutes? And am I going to have to do this all over again in a month or so?"

"Those are football teams, and five minutes is a long time to hover over a phone number," I said, stupidly . . . because I really didn't know what to say. Then I realized what the normal response would have been and continued on. "Whoa. That is nuts. So what happened?"

"He was surprised at first. Of course he was surprised, I'd never said a thing, and then all of a sudden I tell him I can't take it if I don't know if he's going to marry me, and that I have all this stuff on my computer, and the guest list and the dress is ready to be ordered, all I have to do is press 'send' on my e-mail. At first he didn't say anything. He just blinked a lot." Nina stopped to order herself a cobb salad and a coke rather calmly.

I asked for the same, minus egg. And then she continued. "Then he started to smile. And then he started cracking up. And I was getting mad and getting ready to chuck him out and call you to go get ice cream at that place with the pink awning, you know. But he took my hands and he said, 'Hey, everyone's got quirks.' " It was nice to see that glint in her eye, that smirky smile of contentment, as if she didn't feel ill at ease and judged, but *at* ease and free to judge others.

I was stunned into silence.

"Whoa," I finally said.

"I know. Anna I was just as shocked as you. He kissed me, and then we . . . well . . . we had awesome sex."

"Okay, too much information," I said, covering my ears.

She steamrolled on. "And after, he told me that he hopes he can make all my dreams come true."

I nearly spit my coke out. "I'll have a martini please!" I yelled to the waitress.

Nina smiled big. "Partially, I owe this to you. If you hadn't tried to overcome your guilt about your dad, face your fears, be honest with yourself . . ."

I rolled my eyes, the world's worst compliment taker.

"No, really. I don't think I'd have had the courage to come clean, to make the effort."

"All right, all right, I get the picture. You owe me your firstborn." I cut her off, maybe because I wasn't sure this was true of me at the moment.

"Are you sure you're okay?"

I smiled toothily, unconvincingly, and lied. "Perfect."

She was quiet for a second and then scrunched her brows into angry caterpillars. "I just want to tell you, it's a whole different thing being in a relationship with someone who really knows you."

"I have to go now," I said before I could fall apart. I calmly threw a twenty on the table, kissed her good-bye, and said, "Happy Thanksgiving. I love you, and I'm very happy for you."

If I stayed another second I'd break apart into a thousand Humpty Dumpty pieces, and I didn't have the luxury of that right now. My mom would be arriving shortly.

9:00 p.m.

My apartment was kind of messy. Ray had left for his parents' house directly after work, and around the apartment lay clues of his rushed packing job. He'd left a blue plastic travel soap box on the sink. There were a couple of pairs of sneakers he'd decided against next to the hall closet. And unfortunately, his toothbrush was wrapped in tinfoil, but left on the coffee table. I picked up his UCONN sweatshirt and held it, thoughtful.

"I bet you have tartar," I said into the phone, sitting on his vacant bed, wishing Ray a happy holiday. Somehow, it was easier to communicate now we were in different states; I got the sense this should all be much easier.

"Oh, you know I love it when you talk dirty to me, Anna," he joked, obviously feeling the same. Then I was struck with a sudden idea: Maybe he'd had a change of heart. It hit me with equal parts terror and relief.

"You left your toothbrush, you know," I said this, though it was probably obvious.

Ray's parents lived in New Jersey, in a beautiful little house, with his sister who'd just moved back in from her own house down the block, which she'd left to her husband in the divorce. I could hear them yelling in the background.

"I don't know what I'll do." He sniffled like he was crying, but it wasn't a convincing joke.

"Ready for the old high school reunion?" Though we grew up in different places, there was the same Thanksgiving tradition: Go out with all the people you say you hated all of the other 364 days of the year and get really drunk and say stuff like, "Why did we ever lose touch?"

"Can't wait," he said.

"Ditto," I replied. "I'm famous now, so it should be pleasantly ego conflating." What I was really thinking was that I could drink myself into a stupor and then pass out so I wouldn't have to think about my dad all night in place of sleeping.

"Hey, just be strong, okay? You're doing great. You really have a lot to be thankful for this year—*Fenprick* and all of that."

"Thanks, Hallmark," I said, wondering if this return to our normal ground was temporary, or if maybe we'd finally found our footing—along which path I couldn't say.

★ ★ ★

My mom liked to listen to Christmas music from October through January, and it was on inside her SUV when I sluggishly opened the door.

"Anna!" She was always thrilled to see me. Her bangle bracelets jingled familiarly as she hugged me too tightly across the front seat.

"An angel laughing," she always told me was responsible for the sound. I was a dreamy child and tried to focus on that; it affected me still.

"Mom!" I used my best effort to show her the excitement I knew she stayed up nights worrying over.

She kissed my cheek, squeezing my head, and I felt my eyes burn. I hated that I'd let the guilt stand in the way of our relationship. I hated the look on my mother's face. I tried to gaze right into it, rather than convince myself it was all okay. My chest went numb.

She made sure I buckled up, and then we were headed for the Midtown Tunnel. My mother drove like a race car champion in Manhattan. She edged taxis out of the way like it was nothing, crossed three lanes in one fell swoop . . . her right hand at the bottom of the wheel and her left resting on her leg.

Already my hands were folded up in tight balls. We lost the music in the tunnel, and my mother asked, "So, when do we get to meet this David, huh?"

One problem with writing about your personal life in a newspaper is that your mother knows too much about it.

I wondered if my mother would like David. He was very "Manhattan." He grew up there, and he only knew Manhattan people and international people. Not one person he knew used the word *mint* as an adjective in high school. He didn't eat fast food or macaroni and cheese from a box. He was spending Thanksgiving in St. Martin, with Susan and their parents and a couple of cousins. He had asked me to go, nearly begged me. In fact, he surprised me with a ticket and said, "I'm taking you to St. Martin for Thanksgiving."

Normally I was the one waving everyone off on their trips, wondering when it would be my turn. So I went back and forth in worry over it, but I knew I needed to go home. For one thing, it meant the world to my mom, and for another thing, Fenwick insisted. Facing my fears was the heart and soul of this type of therapy, he said. And it was imperative to my well-being that I go . . . especially now, when everything was so good. "You've got to get past *this* velvet rope," he said in our last session. Probably, he would have been a better writer than me.

The funny thing was, I'd expressed to David how important it was for me to be at home for Thanksgiving way before he gave me the tickets. But when he gave them to me, he said, "It would be good for you to get away," as if he hadn't paid any heed to what I'd said about going home—as if he knew what was best for me, and that was that. Still, saying no was one of the hardest things I'd ever done. All I had to do was compare the idea of fresh lobster and pink cocktails and ninety-two-degree weather and snorkeling, to a night at McSullivan's with the Kellmore class of '94, and I was nearly in tears.

He had bought me a very thoughtful Thanksgiving Day gift—a long, delicate gold chain with three antique-looking keys looped through it. I hadn't even known about the "Thanksgiving Day gift." I was wearing it right now. I showed it to my mom.

"That is so beautiful!" she said. "Wow. I've never seen anything like it. It's sort of antique-y and yet very modern. He has good taste. You didn't say that in the column . . . about the taste."

I wouldn't dare mention the St. Martin thing to my mom. If I did, she wouldn't like him. Period. People stayed home for holidays in her mind. She'd said that plenty of times. "Yes, he has wonderful taste," I said instead and looked over to a bunch of orange construction cones blocking off the left lane.

* * *

There is a distinct smell inside my childhood house. It's probably just a cleanser my mother uses, but to me it triggers such complex emotions that every time it smacks me in the face at the front door, I have to breathe extra big to keep from choking. So far, I'd made it through therapy improving and improving, but this—here—this was different. It was easier to avoid this when I didn't have to breathe in that smell or eat those cookies, all the things we'd done here—where all the hurt had lingered.

They rebuilt the house entirely after the fire. My mother and I lived in a little trailer in the backyard where we shared a springy bed and cooked lots of grilled cheese sandwiches with tomato fried up on the miniature gas range. We missed my father so much. We kept saying stuff like, "He hated tomato," and "Dad loved the theme song to *Three's Company*." We hadn't one picture of him that wasn't burned in the fire.

It was early fall and still warm, and after school I'd sit with a couple of cookies and a glass of ice-cold milk and watch the men demolish the blackened bits of our house with loud crashes and lots of banging. And then, as the weather grew colder, I watched them build it back up again like magic. When we first returned to our new house, I missed the trailer, the same way I'd missed our original house when we moved to the trailer. It would be a couple of years still until I realized the full extent of what I'd done.

Roger was one of the construction workers who rebuilt our house. He'd sit with me sometimes and watch the same way I did. He didn't say that much, mainly he was just there, twisting a twig around and around in his fingers. That's just how it was to this day.

My mother nudged him to say things, sometimes. "Roger, why don't you tell Anna about that friend of hers you saw in the supermarket?" But I understood Roger's silent affections. Still, we indulged my mother, because she liked to feel like she'd helped, done something to make everything better—such as mend a broken family.

At dinner, which, the night before Thanksgiving, was always from a Chinese restaurant around the block, I was slurping up a lo mein noodle, when my mother said, "Roger, why don't you tell Anna what you said about her column?"

Roger turned purple. Sometimes I thought it crazy that I really wasn't his daughter, we were so alike. He positioned his lips into a small, straight line and then said, "It's real good."

I started to say, "thanks," but his word economy, his face, it got me laughing, and this got Roger laughing and then my mom, too. And then things loosened up some.

It was difficult, being there. But I tried something Fenwick had advised. I tried to imagine my worst anxieties were 100 percent true, that I had killed my father, that I didn't deserve any of this happiness I was receiving. But the most important thing to do was to keep doing whatever I was doing anyway, to ignore my feelings altogether and just continue on. This procedure left me in a fuzzy haze, a little numb, but functioning—able to put fork to mouth, ask for some iced tea, clear the dishes—rather than sitting in my room convincing myself I deserved to be here, stuck in the loop of that impossible feat. Now I was freed up to enjoy the grainy iced tea, the sweet taste of duck sauce over oily lo mein.

After dinner, I helped my mom prepare the cornbread stuffing. We mixed dry ingredients and then the eggs and butter and some molasses. We toasted two trays of bread. She seemed amazed I hadn't spent the time in my room. She tried to talk about everything we hadn't been able to before.

"Do you think you'll stay at this job? Is this your ultimate goal?" she asked, really wanting to know me—what made me tick, me— this woman, her daughter.

She looked years younger, her pretty brown eyes alive, her bracelets tinkling vitally. We talked of ordinary things . . . an extraordinary thing for us. We spoke of Nina and Ray, and what we might want for Christmas—though we'd never really get each other the mirror she spoke of or the CD I had mentioned. We gave what we wanted to, my mother and I. We exchanged what *we* thought the other person should have—what *we* wanted for them. They were big, enormous gifts really, to take the place of the things we really wanted but could never have.

"Mom?" I asked, shaky with the fear of bringing it up, "Did Dad like Christmas, too? I mean, he was Jewish, after all."

She was at the sink, facing the window. Her hand stopped scrubbing. Her head lifted. I could see her back expand with a great breath. "You know," she said her back still to me. She turned and smiled meaningfully. "He *loved* it. Said Chanukah was boring, and he wanted you to have a tree every year. 'None of that Chanukah bush crap,' he said." She tread carefully, as she continued into this uncharted territory. "He would have gotten a kick out of us all observing his shiva like that . . ."

At eleven, I got ready to go to McSullivan's. I wore one of the cool outfits from Theresa and arranged my hair the way they'd taught me at Mumble & Mumble. I was me, but stylish.

Karen picked me up at eleven thirty in a pretty BMW.

"Holy moly! I didn't know you won the lottery!" I was impressed. I didn't know anyone, besides David, who owned a nice car.

"I did. His name's Jonathon Silverman. And he's a lawyer." She smirked and then turned to look at me for the first time. Karen and Jonathon were marrying in the summer. They'd been going out for a couple of years. Jonathon was a dork back in high school, but all of that changes when you stay in the same town as adults. When you leave, people remember you as you were. You don't get a chance to show you've changed.

In high school, I was so consumed that I never put in enough energy to make *A*s or cheerleader or the most popular circle. Amazingly though, I still had a few friends, and as I mentioned earlier, my aloofness actually gave me a reputation of being sage and wise, and often at parties, people would come to me sloppily baring secrets and lifting weights off their chests.

Karen rarely came into Manhattan. We were Kellmore friends and only got together when I was in town. Tonight, it was the greatest relief to see her and not only to escape my problems with David and Ray, but also to get a break from all the effort to keep it together at my mom's.

Amelia was sitting on the curb outside of her parents' house smoking a cigarette. She lived in northern California now. "Bitches," she addressed us, stubbing her cigarette out and sliding into the backseat.

"And a happy Thanksgiving to you," I said.

"It's freaking freezing," she complained.

"Yeah," Karen said. "So, what's new?"

"Oh . . . only . . . THIS!" She slammed her hand over the front seat, and I turned around to see a huge diamond engagement ring.

"Oh my god! Congratulations!" Karen and I yelled in unison, like paid extras in a bad movie. Was *everyone* getting married? Had everyone figured their lives out a long time ago and left me behind? What happened to the torment that used to bind us all?

"We're getting married in five months—right on the vineyard." Her fiancé, Keith, made wines. His entire family did. It sounded like a dreamy thing the way she described it—something that just might save you.

McSullivan's was just exactly as I remembered it—smelly pint glasses of watered-down beer, a sticky floor, torn Killian's Red posters tacked onto the walls. Every person in there was familiar, or vaguely so.

"Hey, Anna," Thomas Peterson called as I approached the bar. I'd crushed on him hardcore from sixth to eighth, and then we'd dated on and off through ninth and tenth. We hooked up every Thanksgiving. I was sort of hoping, in the same way I always do, that I'd see him. He still had longish hair—to his shoulders—and too much facial hair. He was still nicely built and smelled like a mixture of pot and oranges.

"Thomas." I kissed him on the cheek.

"Annaby," he said, his name for me. "I saw you looking for me." He was the only person I knew who said exactly what they thought.

"Ah, well, you know."

"What are you drinking, Miss Velvet Rope Swinger?" he asked.

"Stella," I said. You didn't order anything but beer at this bar. Everything else tasted like crap—literally.

"Karen, Amelia," he addressed them as they approached with their own pint glasses.

"Oh no, you guys aren't going to hook up again, are you?" Karen said.

"Hopefully." Thomas raised his eyebrows twice. I elbowed him, though I was excited. I told myself I'd never do anything, I wasn't interested in Thomas, in the way we'd escaped through each other many, many times. I was beyond that now, and in a proper, decent, adult relationship, where both people felt good about the time they spent together, not as if they sought to blame the other for all their problems, said "fuck you," a lot, and wound up half-unbottoned and not having used protection in a damp basement bedroom.

Abruptly, I was struck with the unwelcome idea then that I hadn't been against the idea because of David himself. I realized then that I didn't exactly miss David. I tried to concentrate on the way he looked, tried to feel sad at not sharing the holiday with him, tried to picture that I wished it was him sitting here palming at my thigh and not Thomas. He was perfect. And I should miss him. I thought, sort of longingly of his slightly thinning "Jack Nicholsons" as he called his balding spots, and tried to feel better.

Thomas settled in closer on my side of a booth and brought up old times, trying to rile me up. Maybe I did want to punish myself more. Maybe the idea of that would always be irresistible. "Anna, don't try to deny it. You and I both know. We've got nothing. Holidays fucking suck." He rested his head against the torn upholstery and considered the ceiling fan, swirling cigarette smoke around the room. "Nearly thirty, and what have we got?" He left without an answer and came back with two tequila shots. "Nothing," he said, wiping his mouth with the back of his hand.

At two in the morning, I was drunk. Thomas was drunk. Karen and Amelia were drunk. And so we had no way home. The four of us decided to walk the five blocks to the diner.

"Whose fucking idea was this?" Thomas asked over and over along the way.

"Aaayyy!" A table of our fellow class of '94 grads must have had the same idea.

The hostess sat us at the opposite end of the dining room. I ordered a plate of French fries and two cokes. I knew they put too much ice in the drinks, and that I'd drink the first one down in a matter of seconds.

"This is so much fun!" Amelia exclaimed. "We should do this more often. Why don't we do this more often?" This is the same thing we say every year.

"We don't do it more often because that would be pathetic," I said.

"Cheers," Karen said, lifting her mai tai, which she'd ordered from the paper placemat drink menu.

Thomas was quiet next to me and seemed to be turning more

morose. "You *should* do this more," he said, missing the joke. He moved his body in a little closer to mine, and I could feel my heart speed up. It would be so easy to slide in and crook my arm and be safe, safely away. I tried to think, David, David, David. Inexplicably, I couldn't remember what he looked like. I tried to think whether his eyes were brown or blue, or maybe green? I tried to remember that pulsing in my skirt when we were in the town car. Three months before all this, I would have given my life for someone like David. And now I seemed to be on the verge of carelessly snubbing him. What exactly was going on here?

We called a local car service to take us home after the diner and smoked a couple of cigarettes while we waited outside, freezing. Karen was falling asleep in surprised jerks on my left shoulder, and Amelia was doing an old cheerleader routine at the bottom of the steps. "Give me an *A*," she yelled.

Thomas and I moaned back pathetically, "*A*."

A car drove by, and someone yelled, "Shut up!"

Our laughs were hard, catapulting out disappointment, and then they faded to moans and died in the cold as sighs.

Amelia kept on, and Thomas asked, "Annaby, are you coming back to my place?" He kissed behind my ear, his lips slightly weather-beaten, after he whispered it. He was sad and beautiful as ever, his left eye crinkling with thought. How many times had I held on to him—liquored tears wetting his flannel pillow?

"That's the best offer I've heard all night," I said, "but I've got to help my mom start the turkey at like six in the morning." *And I've got a boyfriend*, I thought. But I didn't say it. He took my hand, and our eyes locked, and for some reason, I just didn't say it. I escaped by the skin of my teeth. I knew two minutes more and his hand would have been desperately searching for something beneath my shirt, under the wire of my bra, in all the painfully comforting places we'd traveled before. Still, action, I tried to convince myself, spoke louder than words.

4:30 a.m., Thursday, November 24

The funny thing is, whenever I'd come home I'd always think of Thomas. I'd think, well I'll have to deal with that basement torment, that instant-death replay, but then he could save me from it all. I'd try to lose myself in his smell and his thick eyelashes, his dark Roger Waters music, and the way he whispered, "Annaby," like I was the tragic heroine to his hero. I knew what the inside of his basement bedroom looked like well enough. I knew the way he bit his bottom lip and slowly let it slide away. I knew the relief of being in there rather than in my own home.

But tonight I hadn't run away.

Now I stumbled up the stairs to my bedroom with a huge glass of water and tried to step out of my clothing and into one of the huge nightshirts I wore at home. This was always the scariest part— being alone here when everyone was asleep. I checked my phone, and there were no messages from David. I didn't know if they were on a different time zone there, so I didn't blame him. Plus, I hadn't called him, either. I wasn't sure what was going on with me, but I didn't think now was the time for figuring it out, what with the way I couldn't stand up without holding on to something for support.

I took a tour of my room and stopped at something new. My mother had framed in curly-cue wire, a picture of Ray and myself from our college graduation. Ray looked so much younger there! He was still muscular, but much thinner. And I wouldn't tell him this, but it looked like he had more hair than he does now. Still, I'd know that face anywhere. And that shirt! I remember he wore that shirt all the time. It was just a black collared shirt, but he thought he looked so good in it. For a while, he was wearing it every Friday night to parties, at the bars, around school. With a heavy ache that traveled from my knees to my heart, I missed him now. It was the only thing I'd been sure of the whole night.

I looked at my phone for a couple of seconds before calling. I was pretty sure he'd be awake, too.

His cell phone rang once, twice.

"Anna!" I had to hold the phone away from my ear, he spoke so loudly. I could hear a couple of guys reciting Bruce Springsteen in the background. "What's up?"

"Ah, you know," I said.

"Have a good night?" He wanted to know.

"Yeah, I did," I said, realizing it was true, mostly. "Went to McSullivan's, got loaded, ate fries, nearly hooked up with Thomas Peterson . . ." I turned off the light and curled up under the covers, still talking to him.

"You *didn't* hook up with Thomas Peterson? Isn't that a Thanksgiving tradition? It's like stuffing or sweet potato pie."

"You might remember someone named David Levy . . ."

"Never liked him."

"Ray, you never like anyone."

"I like *you*," he said—in a funny way. I didn't understand my own reaction to it, either—a mixture of gratitude and excitement and anger—and so I didn't know how to respond. It occurred to me, embarrassingly, that I might have been secretly enjoying this jealousy Ray had been displaying toward David. That would make me a bad, bad person. Finally, I said the worst thing I probably could have, despite the obvious—that it was wrong, dead wrong. "No, you *love* me," I said.

He was quiet. And it was the strangest silence. We may or may not have bypassed joking, and headed straight into screw up your safety and friendship-ville.

"Ray?" I asked after a second.

"Yes, beautiful?" I thought I heard him exhale a cigarette. The funny image of the way he never really inhaled brought me momentarily back to more familiar footing.

"My mom framed a graduation picture of us, and I just keep thinking about that black shirt you wore all the time."

"Wish I still had that shirt. I was hot in that shirt." He was quiet for a second, coughed once, and then continued. "How come we never got together?" he asked.

"The friendship," I said instinctively, without knowing for sure if it were true.

"Right, the friendship," he agreed.

"Ray?" I said.

"Yeah?" he asked.

"I'm gonna go to sleep now," I said, too tired for any more of this right now.

"I just want to tell you something, Anna," he slurred a little, sniffled. "I'm really proud of how you're handling yourself. You're . . . well, you're becoming the person you were always meant to be, I think."

"Why, thank you," I said quickly. "You're not so bad yourself."

"Can I tell you something, Anna?" he asked in that funny tone, sending me back onto shaky ground.

"Of course, anything," I said.

"I don't think David's the right guy for you," he said.

And just because I didn't know what else to do, I said, "Good night," and I hung up. Thankfully, I passed out immediately.

6:00 a.m., Thanksgiving Day

Unfortunately, I woke up with a papery, dry mouth that required water. I tried to ignore this urge and will myself back to sleep. But I lay there, wide awake and terrified, and finally I gave in. I descended the stairs quietly. Roger's snores were audible even down in the kitchen . . . a slow creak of a horror movie, it sounded like to me.

My limbs numb and misbehaving from the drinking and smoking, I struggled to pull a glass out of the cabinet and filled it with water from a pitcher in the refrigerator. I refilled it after a long draught and meant to go right up the stairs, but turned left instead, down toward the basement.

I didn't turn the light on. I don't think I could have borne to do that. Instead I walked down one-two-three-four steps and then sat, my glass slippery in my hands, pinched between my bare knees. I knew I wasn't supposed to do this, to go through it until I was sure this was the way things played out, but I imagined him anyway. I placed him over in the far left corner, where his tools were hung neatly, symmetrically, on white pegboard. I had him listening to the radio, something mildly fatherly, such as Al Green. The flames, as I saw them came quick, like wildfire, or a marathon runner, toward him, engulfing him as he made his way in it, through it, to the staircase, to me. I tried to hear the scream, always my name, always, "Anna! Anna! Save me, Anna!" And always, cowardly me, with my too-tight braids and my novelty sneakers running, endlessly running away. I tried, always, but I could never change the ending. And though I knew better now, though I'd been taught not to try, I found the urge irresistible.

It was a setback, but I told myself, as I pulled the thready quilt up to my chin, that tomorrow was another day.

11:00 a.m., Thanksgiving Day

"Anna, darling! You look like hell!" My mom was chipper beyond belief. Harry Connick Jr. was singing "My Heart Finds Christmas" through hidden speakers.

"Love you, too, Mom," I said and hugged her. I looked out the window to the very spot where I'd sat, watching Roger rebuild our house, and I felt the tears coming. I was hungover, even more confounded about David and Ray, and sitting at Ground Zero of my emotional problems, and I knew this type of depressing indulgence didn't help. My mom pulled my head away to look at me when she felt my body shaking.

"Honey, oh, honey," she wiped some tears away and swallowed back some of her own. I knew she hated me having this legacy. I knew it hurt her more than it hurt me. I was all she had, and she wanted me to enjoy life. She'd indulged me that first year, let me play sick with a thermometer held under the lightbulb so I could stay home and plant bulbs or bake apple crisp with her, just be the two of us here in the house, pretending that Dad would come walking in at the end of the day.

But she didn't do that now. "Mom," I said. "We've got a lot of cooking to do." I smiled big and said, "Are you gonna make me some coffee or what?"

She stood for a second, probably shocked that I wasn't going to run upstairs and hide away until dinner, that I was going to be with her and do this. She blinked twice, and then she started to tear up, breathed it away, and said, "Well, Miss Fancy Velvet Rope girl, Roger got something special for you this year." She reached up into a cabinet and pulled out a cappuccino machine. "Now all we have to do is learn how to use it."

We laughed, and at the same time called around to the den, "Roger!"

9:30 p.m., Friday, November 25

"So, how'd you like that party?" Roger asked, as we approached the tunnel. He hadn't spoken up until then. The party was funny, what with sort of familiar people such as the mailman, the customer service woman from Waldbaum's, the high school nurse, and others stopping by to congratulate me on my column and my success.

"It was . . . well, it was very Mom." I smiled and turned to see his reaction to that.

"It sure was. You know what, though . . . you are a celebrity over there. Those people all asked your mom about you. Not the other way around. People like to have a celebrity they can relate to." I'd never heard Roger say so many things all at one sitting.

He drove me to my door, parked, hefted my bags out of the back, all the leftovers tucked into freezer-ready Tupperware containers, and the things my mother bought for me every winter—socks and throw blankets and slippers and pajamas with feet on them—and brought them right up to my apartment.

At the door, he said, "I'm real proud of you, Anna. You're doing really well." It was nice to hear Roger say that, to think of the way he'd met me and the way we'd sat on that log so many days watching my house rise up . . . and to be here now.

"You're a real good dad, Roger," I said. I'd never called him that before. He flamed purple and ran down the stairs before I could see how much it meant to him. Despite the setback, I considered myself very thankful this year.

TEN

The World in Your Hands . . .

"The theme at World is that they carry beers, wines, and liquors from all over the world, including lots that you won't find elsewhere in the city. To me, it's that unique quality, that thing you can't get anywhere else that really makes something desirable," Jimmy James, rancher-turned-nightlife impresario, said.

—Velvet Rope Diaries, *New York, New York*

Monday, November 28

When I came home from Thanksgiving, David was still in St. Martin, but Ray was home already. We both greeted each other with a lot of "What's up?" and "Nothing, what's up with you?" and "Nothing, what's up with you?" and somehow managed to act like nothing had been said on the phone the other night, though it was obvious to everyone involved that something—something HUGE—*had* been.

For two days and three nights we relied heavily on television movies and short, simple phrases such as, "Can you pass the stuffed crust pizza?" This allowed us to put off making any moves or decisions—after all, we'd known each other eight years now, why rush things? When he'd brush by me, or nudge me, I'd find myself blushing. Eventually, it seemed we'd nearly succeeded in sweeping the entire thing under the carpet, where we could more comfortably catapult ourselves over the huge bump it created. And in this state, we met after work on Monday to check out World.

You might recognize Jimmy James, World's owner, from Candle, Fire, and Tambourine. He's got the world's best publicist working for him, and she just happens to be a fan of mine. So I got my exclusive.

This was a very soft launch, with no press whatsoever, except for me. There was no line, and when Ray and I arrived we were escorted around by Jimmy James himself on a guided tour of World.

The place wasn't 100 percent finished, so there were still lots of places where we had to use our imaginations to envision the finished product.

"This here," Jimmy James waved a hand with a cigarette in a V-hold, sprinkling ashes along the way, "is going to be the California reds section." At a flick of his finger, the bar and surrounding lounge chairs were bathed in light. "This here's sunshine," he said.

"Isn't it a little hot under those lights?" Ray asked, looking up at the blinding spotlights above. We were ridiculously giggly.

"Yeah. We didn't think of that before." Jimmy James shrugged, and then he moved right on. "And so, you see, we've got a sandy area here, to signify the beaches of California, and then there's that Hollywood sign up there." He gestured above, and Ray and I were blinded as we strained to catch a glimpse.

Behind Jimmy James's back, Ray and I blinked like mad, covering up laughs with a cough here and there. It felt good to be so light. We bonded by being on the outside of someone else's crazy problems, rather than dealing with our own.

We turned a corner, and Jimmy James said, "We're going to fix that sign right there, because you can probably see that we spelled Hollywood with just one *l*."

"This here's gonna be Disneyworld . . . you know in Florida," Jimmy James said. We were following along, and something had been left behind as a residue of the laughter. There was a glow of it around Ray and me. I couldn't help but think about our Thanksgiving call.

Now, I felt that frisson again, and I looked at Ray, and I tried to see something clear in it, something that said, yes! Okay! He feels the same, so you can proceed! All I got was the murky green of his eye, a nonsmile that could have meant anything really. He looked at my hand, and I followed his gaze as he swooped in and took hold of it, a shock of current flowing between us, lodged, finally in a huge knot at my throat.

Jimmy James led us around, and we held hands still, two jerky teenagers, unsure but searching, trying this on for size.

"And this is Italy. That Prada sign is actually being remade, because they spelled it Preda," Jimmy James said.

We'd gone from California to Italy, and inside it felt as if we'd taken an equally long journey—or started one, at least, after an eternal warmup act.

Ray stroked the inside of my palm with his thumb up and down, up and down, and my throat went dry, so I could barely breathe.

In Spain we stopped to admire a bullfighter rendered in plaster, and Ray squeezed my hand real tight and looked at me, biting his bottom lip. There was something so thick between us I could almost grab a handful.

With David, I'd been flattered, attracted, and I always enjoyed his company. But it wasn't like this. It was never like this. And now that I think of the history Ray and I share, of our memories and friendship, of the way we know each other . . . how could it have ever been like this with David?

The tour seemed to go on forever. "I feel like we've been around the world," Ray joked in the Chilean hot springs of the Big North. I said, "We have," and how different Ray looked with that determined look in his eye, with that bit of fear that accompanied it—as if, for once, he'd let his own guard down, and part of his well-being was in my hand.

Jimmy James went on for a while, and I aha'd him when I thought it was appropriate.

"I'm sorry, so you *don't* understand that I can't take you through the Washington State area, because there is no floor yet?" he asked when I'd misspoken out of inattention.

"Oh, of course I do," I corrected myself.

Jimmy James turned around and looked at me and Ray kind of funny. "Boy, you guys are really in love, aren't you?" he said. "I wish I had something like that for myself."

We'd reached the VIP room, dedicated to the New York State wines, which I thought was a nice touch.

"This is where I'm going to leave you," Jimmy James said. "You enjoy your meal and international beverages and write us up a fabulous review."

We thanked him and sat down in a booth that had a nice view of the Empire State Building (with a broken needle at the top) and the Statue of Liberty (with a cracked torch) rendered in paper mache. The release says it took two hundred pounds of newspaper to make that.

Jimmy James left us. Ray and I were Doris Day and Cary Grant. We laughed for no reason at all and then became serious just as quickly. We were having an old-fashioned romance with plenty of star crossing, but there was the risk, too. I watched him hold my hand, fan the fingers up and then, spidery, down again—the silent movie of our beginning. Despite the way no one else seemed present, the way time ticked along more slowly then, I knew there was enormous risk and that everything should be done correctly to minimize it. If I could do things right, maybe this just might work out for me, I thought, like a child stepping over cracks in the sidewalk, in hopes of altering her fate. He sat on the same side as I did, our hands an intricate, timeless weave.

A waitress brought us a tray of five glasses half-filled with New York wines to try. Ray passed the first one to me, and it tasted a little bitter, I thought. And then I passed it to him, and I saw that his lips were just where mine had been, and I thought of kissing him.

In that second I knew that I had to break things off with David because though he was just the sort of man I thought I always wanted—a wonderful man to take care of me—I was not in love with him, I was not this other thing I was now. And I knew that I would feel terrible over hurting him. But something had happened, and I didn't need a man to save me anymore. I'd saved myself, and now I wanted an equal, a partner, and more than that, I realized that equal, that partner had been there all along. The strange thing was, though, David was the one who stirred all of these feelings up between Ray and me. If I hadn't met him, if I hadn't had a relationship with him, Ray and I might never have gotten here.

I was going to do things right. I was going to wait. I owed David at least that.

"Ha!" Ray and I heard the shrill voice like an evacuation siren, and we jumped. The red wine spilled a little over Ray and onto my shirt. I yelped. There were lots of napkins, and then I looked up, and there was Miss Jackson.

"Gotcha," she smirked, childlike.

"What do you mean, Miss Jackson?"

"Don't you mean *Nasty*?" she threw her head to one side. I could see Christopher approaching. He was a beautiful man, but was he worth turning yourself into *that*? "I saw the two of you fooling around there. And don't you think I'm not going to use that piece of information!"

Christopher approached. "Oh, sweetheart, there you are," she said, her voice shifting drastically. "Meet my friends here, Anna Walker of Velvet Rope Diaries, you remember her, don't you, the one who humiliated me, dear? And this is, I don't know, who *are* you, darling?" she asked Ray.

"I'm Ray," he said. "And we weren't doing anything. I don't know what you think you saw, Miss Jackson."

"Oh, don't you worry about a thing," she said. She stormed away, and Christopher lingered at the edge of our table for a second.

"I'm sorry, guys," he said, his thumbs hooked through his jeans belt loop. "That article about her being plastic really hurt her, you know. She used to be really fat when she was young, and she has this . . . this hang-up about looks now. Though I know it's difficult to see it, she does have a good side. I just thought you should know that," he said, like a true gentleman, like an old-fashioned knight clearing a maiden's name.

"Whoa," I said when he'd walked out of the place.

"Can you believe that?" Ray asked.

"You know, I always thought it! I did!"

"But, Anna, don't let this change anything. You tried to apologize. You did everything you could, and she's still out for revenge."

"I know. I still need to protect myself." I thought of Fenwick. I knew it was true. Though this added a complicated layer to my already existing neuroses, I couldn't change course, or she'd fry me up for breakfast.

"So what are you going to do?"

"I'm going to be careful to tell the truth in my column, so that David gets the respect he deserves."

Though he winced at the name, Ray nodded gravely. "It's the right thing to do."

11:45 a.m., Wednesday, November 30

"I love the intrigue—the admission of guilt, Anna, love it!" Ed said.

I couldn't believe my own ears. He actually *liked* the column this week?

"You do realize Miss Jackson was trying to ruin my life, right?"

"Oh, yes. Definitely. Very grave. Very grave indeed. But *excellent* journalism! Stellar."

I crossed my arms and grimaced.

"Okay, okay, you're hurting. Here's what I'm gonna do. I'm gonna tell that wanker, Joseph, to give you a mention on the cover this week." As deputy editor, Joseph normally had free reign over those decisions. I had a feeling he wasn't going to like this, although in a way it was partially his fault I'd wound up here. Despite all those terrible things he'd been up to, I still felt bad that his pages had been cut in half to make room for mine . . . and even worse when his page had lost a little of the top, too . . . to make room for my overflow. Now, I wasn't worrying about hurting feelings. Okay, maybe I was, but I "let the worries hang out," to use a Fenwick line, and continued on with what needed to be done.

"You're a saint," I said.

"Aren't you Jewish?" he asked.

"Half!" I replied and turned to go.

I was about three feet from his door, when Ed called me back, "Good job, Anna, fooling around behind your boyfriend's back. I almost forgot, we are going to run the little 'Seen At' bit about you sucking face with your roommate in Joe Says, right alongside your 'I'm a little innocent' column. It'll be a sort of double feature, if you will." He laughed wickedly, and I thought maybe my own hair turned white. "Excellent journalism. Honestly—you might have what it takes, after all."

"I *am* innocent," I barked. My chest went cold. This was just treacherous. I knew I hadn't done anything wrong. I'd purposely waited so that my relationship with Ray wouldn't start off on the wrong foot, so that I wouldn't hurt David, who hadn't done anything wrong—who'd wound up being the person who made me realize I loved Ray in the first place! I'd tried to do the right thing. *You didn't do anything wrong. You didn't do anything wrong.* I repeated it, but that didn't make me feel any better as I walked to break the news to David Levy before the column came out.

2:00 p.m.

We met at Googie's—a sort of diner spot on Third Avenue. David was very tan.

This would be the first time in my life that I ever broke up with someone, rather than the other way round. You'd think it might feel empowering, but it was just the opposite. The second I saw him, I turned into a piece of paper, flapping around frantically in a windstorm, catching on branches and beneath shoes, swirling endlessly, helpless to hold my own. *Had* I missed him? Had I somehow misunderstood myself?

He kissed me right at my hairline—half on my forehead and half on my bangs—as he always did by way of greeting. I felt like an impossible phony, playing the roles we had before, when obviously nothing was as it had been. He led me to the seat, and I felt my stomach churn and churn. I knew that no matter what I did, it was going to hurt him, and there was nothing I could do about that. The old Anna would have told herself never mind, you do whatever you have to not to hurt this boy. Don't think so much of yourself. I reminded myself my life was still at stake here, and that I could slip back into that sort of behavior very easily.

"I'll have a Coke," he said. "And she'll take an unsweetened iced tea with lemon, please." It wasn't right that he should care to know that kind of thing about me when I was about to hurt him. I was overcome with hesitation. I longed to pull the pages from the printing press and yell, "Wait!" What if I'd made a terrible decision? What if this thing with Ray didn't work out? What if his feelings were really just jealousy that I'd finally found someone who was wonderful? Once I broke it off with David, would Ray lose interest and revert back to his old ways? Here was someone who knew how I took my iced tea and I was going to toss him to the wayside. Suddenly everything was stuffed with significance.

We looked the menus over in silence. "Oooh, there's mushroom barley soup today," he said.

"Nice," I said, though I myself had never understood the allure of mushroom barley. Now I wondered if that were a sign.

Eventually I ordered the chicken salad on wheat, and he asked for the BLT club. Just then, to me, those seemed the saddest lunches on earth.

"Wow!" I said, attempting to smile.

"Wow," he mimicked. "What's up, beautiful?"

I wasn't beautiful! I was a mean, horrible girl who caught you up in my web of confusion, in my inadequacies as a fatherless child with a mother lode of guilt. I was a moron who was probably passing up the very best thing that ever happened to her . . . for something I had zero reason to believe would work out!

"David!" I offered weakly.

"Anna!" he returned. "What's going on?"

I must have seemed awkward, my knee bopping and my hands touching my fringy hair compulsively.

"I have to tell you something."

"I don't like the sound of that *something*." He smiled at first, like maybe I was going to say I had to get back to work quicker than I'd expected, or I'd forgotten to apply deodorant this morning. But then my face fell, his followed, and his joke died halfway out.

Now David fiddled—with his straw wrapper—twisting and twisting it, as if it was the one thing he could think to do.

A worn-out truck tutt-tutted by. I thought of the way we'd met in the dark, the fantastic moment when he'd clapped the lights into action, the mystery and excitement that had led to our first kiss. From the second I'd realized he wasn't a murderer or rapist, I'd felt exceptionally safe with David on hand. He had a presence that told you everything was going to be okay. And now I recognized that this was what I had mistaken for love—this safety, this illusion of safety that David had represented for me. He'd saved me that first night, and I'd never stopped looking at him in that light. It was a fantastic, rare thing we had, but it wasn't what *I* needed, though it seemed easiest and safest.

"David, I can't tell you how wonderful these three months have been for me."

His jaw dropped, and right away I could see that he knew where this was going.

"Anna," he grabbed for my hand. "Don't break up with me. Please don't break up with me. You are the most real girl I've ever dated. Even my sister loves you. And my sister doesn't love anyone. No screw that. I don't care about my sister. *I* love you. I want to care for you and love you and . . ." He didn't finish the sentence, but he'd made himself painfully clear.

I just wanted to say, "Okay, forget it. Just kidding! Hang that strong, safe arm around me! Do you mind if I have your pickle?" But I didn't. I swallowed back the round of tears I felt heating up my face and eyes. It was my turn to speak, and I had to find the words somewhere. I wanted the words to be the truth, because

David deserved that. "David, it's just that I've been discovering a lot about myself lately. And, along with that, I guess, I have discovered that I've loved someone who's been in my life all along."

"Oh, please don't tell me it's Ray! Please not him! Anyone but him!" A few people turned around to stare.

I didn't have to say anything.

"It is. I knew it. I freaking knew it. How can you trust him? You yourself told me time and again how many girls he's screwed over." He sat back and looked up at the ceiling, blinking a lot. He was angry, hurt, and he was right. It sounded even more terrifying coming from someone else, as if the evidence was more real, the fear more deeply founded. His lip flopped around like a fish out of water and then he bit it down, hard.

"I'm so sorry, David. You are wonderful. The most wonderful person I've ever had a relationship with. And you are so caring and warm." I was so bad at this. I always knew I would be. I didn't know how to put my feelings into words. Nothing fit. I tried not to cry, though I felt my face heat in preparation for it. I wanted to put my hand on his arm, which was squirming madly. But I knew that would only be worse. He didn't want pity. He wanted to be with me and take care of me, and terrifyingly, I was turning this away for the unknown, insecure chance to be with Ray.

"Please don't. Just don't say anything else, Anna. I know you're not mean and you're doing the right thing if you're in love with that moron—God help you, by the way—but I just can't take another word of it."

David stood.

I had to tell him, though. I had to tell him the worst part. "And David, the gossip column is going to print something about it. I just wanted you to know I didn't cheat on you. I never did the things they are going to say."

"Oh, well in that case, everything's just peachy, isn't it?" he said, acidic, given over wholly to bitterness now. Then David left, his coat over his arm, the hem dragging along on the floor. And I was sitting in the booth alone when the waiter came with the big plate and asked, "BLT club?" like I was supposed to have an answer to that.

The walk back to the office was dreadful. I felt exposed and alone as I always had been without a father. At every corner, I half expected to be mugged or hit by a taxi.

Yesterday, Fenwick had leaned back with his own daughter safely on his desk, in contrast to my own tetherlessness, and said, "The truth is, we're all vulnerable—even people who have fathers. As scary as that might seem to you, if you make peace with that, you'll stop looking for safety in places that are merely illusions. And you'll realize you can and *do* take care of *yourself*."

I straightened myself against the wind and tried to believe I hadn't just made the second biggest mistake of my life.

2:45 p.m.

"Stay low to the ground if you are caught in a fire. Crawl out on your hands and knees."

3:30 p.m.

I meandered slowly back to work, circling blocks and stopping at a bench to catch my breath for a few moments. I found myself walking right into Nasty's office, where Joseph was perched like a pigeon in need of dental attention on her guest chair. "You've hurt me now," I said. "There. Done. Are you happy now? Are you done now?"

"Oh yes. Yes, we are completely done now," Nasty said. "You don't have to worry about us. We're even Steven."

I left wanting to believe that with all my heart.

4:15 p.m.

I called Ray's work number: "Hi, this is Ray Right from Trading. If you're not buying something, I'm not going to call you back."

Because I didn't know what else to say, I said, "I'm not buying something." I reddened, gathered my things, and made my way toward the door.

"Good night," the receptionist said . . . proof that things had changed. Trouble was a whole new set of problems had set in.

7:00 p.m.

"Would you like violet with apricot kernel or cocoa with shea butter?" my aesthetician Martha wanted to know.

"You better ask my boss over there," I replied, nodding to Nina, whose massage table was right next to mine. Nina and Susan had just signed the mortgage on the spa space, and they already had an interior designer and an architect putting together the look of it. These were unbelievably dynamic times for all of us. There wasn't a thing going along unchanged. I always knew Nina would accomplish her dream someday, but it seemed her struggle toward it had become part of our lives.

"She'll have the apricot," Nina said. Now *there* was a woman who knew what she wanted, not someone like me who was sure they wanted one thing, then realized they were in love with their roommate, let that first thing go, and now worried she might have ruined everything.

"So you broke things off with one of the wealthiest men I've ever met for regular old Ray."

"You know, you're not really helping the situation."

She shook her head, but it was obvious she approved. "You must really love him," she said. "All these years. I can't believe it took you two so long."

"Well, we're not really 'together,' " I said. I felt panicky. I mean, I just broke up with my boyfriend, and Ray and I hadn't discussed one thing! Given his track record, this could be very, very bad.

"I wouldn't worry about the technicalities. It's pretty clear he's been in love with you forever. I remember one party back during sophomore year, homecoming. He was so drunk, and you were talking with that dorky Sam whoever-his-pants was from the math department . . ."

"Sam Slessinger. He was the only guy I hooked up with my first two years in college." He'd been a horrific dork, but I liked that about him. I liked that maybe I saw something in him that other people couldn't.

"Yeah, well, Ray was almost crying. And I was like, 'Ray, you hooked up with a different girl every night this week.' And he was like, 'Well, I'm just wasting time until she's ready.' "

I couldn't believe my ears. Could this really be true?

Forty-five minutes into our massages, Nina said, "Oh yeah, and I just got engaged this morning."

I sat right up, exposing my entire front. "What!?"

"Bernard asked me to marry him. And I said yes. You'll be wearing salmon in April. But you already knew that."

7:00 p.m., Thursday, December 1

Dr. Fenwick was wearing salmon. The color didn't look very good on him. I watched as he read my journal, my words at his lips, his eyes dipping and skipping, jumping, sidestepping like a Western dance.

"You've been busy."

"I have," I said. I was unabashedly proud of myself, despite the pain. Here I was, living—feeling the ups and even the downs of it all, like an actual real person. I couldn't wait for him to tell me to get out and never come back.

"Tell me about being home," he said and rearranged his legs. It looked, from the group shot at the ski slope behind him, as if his family were happy. Could this be me one day? Smiling through an adrenaline rush—pink cheeked and so alive?

"Definitely, it was difficult. But I did what you said. I lived with that worst case scenario. And I didn't try to feel better. I just did . . . whatever it was—helping my mom cook, or being out at the bar with Thomas and Kelly. I had a setback on the first night I was there. I went downstairs, and I fell into my pattern, playing out my version of what must have happened to my dad, trying to get right the burning smell and the pain and the length of time, but I bounced back from it. And eventually, I hardly thought about it. I mean, I never got to the point where I felt, Lord! I'm cured! I don't feel guilty at all! Of course none of this was my fault! Nothing like that. It was just that numbness, just the ability to be present and participate in whatever trivial thing was expected."

"Well, I wouldn't expect you to feel perfect. You've been thinking you've killed your father for twenty-two years. It's going to take a while until you truly realize the irrationality of that . . . until it really sinks in. And you're correct about the setbacks. There will be setbacks, but the important thing is to accept them and move on. Don't dwell on them and say 'I knew I couldn't do this.' But you should know that, overall, you are doing fabulously. You're standing up for yourself, going for the things you want, not letting your fears stand in the way of that."

"So I'm done?"

"Anna. Do you really think that's where we're at?"

I had. I really had. I wanted to achieve this, to look at it, like a diploma on my wall and say, "I did that. It was hard, but I succeeded." Right then, with Nasty and Joseph out to sabotage me, the safety of David gone for good, and the question marks around Ray and me bolder than ever, I just wanted to button this one thing up neatly.

But the way he phrased that, obviously that had been the wrong answer. "No?" I asked, wanting to crack up into a trillion pieces, looking past him to those photos again, those far-off photos of a life I always wanted for myself. I was pretty sure no one wanted to talk about this more than was absolutely necessary. His daughter had nice, thick ponytails. It looked like maybe she had inherited Dr. Fenwick's hair genes. It was impossible not to envy daughters with fathers, no matter how much you didn't want to. It was impossible not to dissect them and notice where security lent a gleam to her eye, a confidence to her manner of dress, that you could never have.

"So what else is going on?"

"Well, Nasty is definitely up to something, I know that."

"So, why don't you just report her?"

"I couldn't do that," I said.

"Why not?"

"Well, she's not done anything too bad."

"You mean that sabotaging your career isn't bad?"

"I mean, I don't know, I've done bad things, too."

"Like kill your father."

"Yes." There, I said it. I tried to sink into the sofa, tried to sink into a tiny ball that didn't have to put itself through something like this.

"So you think you don't deserve things?"

"Right." I looked at the tabletop. It seemed he could definitely afford a nicer table than that. I inspected the Oriental rug— anything to not look at Fenwick, who was looking deep down inside of me.

"And who decides who deserves what in this world?"

"I guess society," I said. Ten minutes left. Nine minutes fifty-eight seconds. Nine minutes . . .

"And society said you are a murderer who doesn't deserve things?"

"No."

"Then who did say that?"

I knew where this was going. I knew what I rationally, logically had to say. But, strange as it was, I couldn't yet fit comfortably into being happy. All the way home from Thanksgiving, all the days after, I searched for that something that was missing, that backroom gory torture I was so used to. It was the relationship I'd made with my father. "Me." Always the tears here, always the things I held together so intricately, delicately, my emotional house of cards, always it crashed down in here.

I sat quiet for a minute wanting to hate Fenwick for messing it all up, disturbing the rhythm of everything, for taking me so far outside the lines.

"Let's talk about Ray."

"What about him?" I wanted to be mean to Fenwick, to resist him and disagree with him and his efficient techniques that could have saved me so many years, if only I'd known. I didn't think it fair that all those years had gone by and gone by and suddenly, he came over and said, "Oh this is the simplest thing to fix." All the college tests papers that seemed printed only with the words "I heard his voice, and I ran down the stairs. The smoke worse than the flames. My shoelace on fire. The basement door gone, completely gone now, and the red licks coming up at my face hot, hotter than anything before. And I could have gone down, gone down into that, but I didn't." The low marks and the questions: Anna, it seems like you didn't even read the test. Are you concentrating? Maybe it's too difficult for you. And it wasn't, but then it was. Running a brush through my hair was too difficult, and saying "The library is right over that hill there and to the left," and "No, I don't like asparagus very much."

"I want you to realize that you have changed quite a bit, quite rapidly. And now you've reclaimed so much of yourself, you may be surprised at the kinds of complications these sort of assertive actions have. Of course, they are never as bad as the complications of inaction, but they will arise, and you'll have to be on guard. Be prepared."

"You don't think it will work out with us?" This was all I needed to hear! Another doubter . . . especially with Ray completely missing since yesterday afternoon when I broke things off with David. The whole thing was quite obviously doomed. Why did people keep giving me choices when all I seemed to do was screw them up?

"No, I'm not saying that. All I'm saying is that you need to be prepared for anything."

"Okay," I said, rolling my eyes like a bratty teenager, all the while convincing myself that Fenwick just didn't know *us*. "I'll take the train out to Queens to purchase an emergency kit at Target."

Fenwick frowned. "Anna, I know it doesn't feel good right now. But trust me. Eventually it will. You just keep working at everything. Don't look to feel good."

People like me don't deserve to feel good. I couldn't help thinking it.

I went home and waited up for Ray as long as I could, busying myself counting fire engine sirens, my blanket tugged up to my chin, until my eyes started to droop. It had been a long day. It was a busy night for fires. Twenty-seven. He must have arrived after I fell asleep.

9:00 a.m., Friday, December 2

The wet towel Ray left hanging on the back of the bathroom door—the only evidence I had that he'd been there at all—was salmon colored. Were we all just a bunch of fish, swimming around aimlessly until we possibly might bump into something good?

Belinda, Judy, and I met up at Farluck's for an emergency meeting. Juan, the barrister, and I shot our espressos, and then I sat with the girls and a latte.

"Okay, so remember those Joseph disciplinary folders?" Belinda asked.

"How could I forget?" I asked.

"I thought we were past all of that crap! Anna made the front page today," Judy said.

I didn't want to look at it. I didn't want to think about it.

"You little tart!" Judy teased.

I slivered my eyes. Unbelievably, Judy eased up.

"Can we get back to the point, ladies?" Belinda asked.

"Of course, sorry," we both apologized, as Belinda was exceedingly serious.

She leaned in. "Well, remember I said the second time around that Ed was very strange about the reasons why he let Joseph slide?"

We leaned all the way in and asked in unison, "Yes?"

"You're not going to believe this. Or maybe you will, I'm not sure. Hmmm."

I cleared my throat.

"Oh, sorry. Joseph was looking for Ed's psychic's card."

I searched around in the far corners of my mind, but I couldn't make any sense of it. "What does this mean?"

"This means that Joseph is trying to see Ed's psychic, Rima."

"Is that bad?" Judy asked, mimicking my own thoughts.

"Well, Ed listens to every word Rima says. Every word."

"How did you find out?"

"I put the pieces of the puzzle together. This morning, Ed called me in early, frantic. He said Rima's card was missing from his file, and did I know anything about it?"

"No!"

"Yes! And so I reminded him of the situation with Joseph, and he called Rima, and she said that no, Joseph hadn't called. She said he should keep Joseph on at *New York, New York*, that his own future depended on it, and that he should come in to meet with her in two days. That she had vital information about the future of the newspaper. She refused to say anything more, except that he knows better than to call her between appointments, and that he should mail her a check for two hundred fifty dollars for an unscheduled appointment."

"That sounds very shady!" Judy said.

"I bet Joseph went there and paid her to say that!" I exclaimed. "I've got to go there and find out for myself."

Belinda reached deep into her cleavage and pulled out a pink note card. "Great minds think alike," she said. "I'm coming with."

"But what if Ed finds out, and you get fired?" I said.

"Then I get fired," she said, though I knew she was terrified of the possibility.

When I finally settled at my computer, the day only got worse. My Instant Messenger popped up, and Ray was already logged on.

> **Rayishotbaby:** Just wanted to let you know I'm leaving for DC for a few days for work.
> **Annabananasplit:** Oh?
> **Rayishotbaby:** Yeah.
> **Annabananasplit:** Did you see the column?
> **Rayishotbaby:** Yup. Good job. Gotta go. See you on Thursday.

Thursday? Could this really be happening? I knew it! I knew he would grow bored of me as soon as he could have me! Had I not predicted this exact thing? With nothing more to stand in my way, I unrolled my copy of *New York, New York* and looked over the damage.

On the cover was a picture of Ray and me in that booth holding hands. And it looked bad. It really did.

Anna Walker's Bizarre Love Triangle: Exposed!

Inside was my column. It was the truth, and I knew it, but it still looked terrible, with the pictures they'd used to accompany it—a closeup of our hooked fingers as we followed Jimmy James, a far-off shot framed in a heart.

On the other side of the spread was Joe Says.

> Joe says *New York, New York*'s own Anna Walker needs to learn a thing or two about honesty and respect. She was spied at the opening of World, canoodling with none other than her roommate, Ray Right, despite the fact that she has been exclusively dating David Levy, brother of bitter divorcée Susan Levy-Scrimp. Well, that's two dumped, two-timed siblings, apparently. Word is Anna connected Levy-Scrimp with friend Nana Patterson in a business deal to open a spa called Susan & Nana's, which will celebrate its grand opening after the new year.

The room spun as I considered this. Had I really just read that horrible, horrible trash? I read through it again. Wait a minute! Wait a *minute*! The only person who calls Nina 'Nana' is Susan!

I dialed her number frantically.

"Hello dear! Did you see our fabulous publicity in Joe Says today?"

"Ummm, yes."

"Great isn't it? Well, except for the 'bitter divorcée' part."

"Yes, that. I, well, I . . ."

"Honey, please don't apologize. I know you didn't want that smut printed. David knows that, too. I just got off the phone with him, and he felt really bad for you. He said you were a good person and didn't deserve this type of thing, when all you were doing was being true to yourself. But I'm dating this yogi, Shakti, or something like that, and what he always says is that you have to turn a negative into a positive, and so that is why I took the chance to publicize the spa dear . . ."

I wasn't so sure publicity is what Shakti had in mind, but she went on and on about it anyhow. I was so relieved to hear what she'd said about David, I barely know what she said. Thank god for little miracles. I got the weirdest feeling thinking that. That's something my dad used to say all the time. Thank god for little miracles, I got the car working, it's a sunny day, Anna Banana remembered to bring home all her books today.

"Is this Rima Vimley?" I whispered into my cell phone. I was hiding behind a tree in Central Park, from whom, I'm not quite sure; Belinda had her ear shoved in next to mine.

"Who vants to k-now?" She pronounced the hard *k* awkwardly.

"Well, my name is Anna Walker, I'm—"

She didn't let me finish. "Ah yes, Anna. I figured I'd be hearing from you. You come in Monday. Bring fifty dollars cash."

She hung up, and Belinda and I stared at each other, wide-eyed. "What the hell have we gotten ourselves into, child?" Belinda asked, her head shaking dismally.

ELEVEN

Will You Lose Everything?

Downtown Club was going to be strictly membership only. But the cool thing about it was that anyone could get the memberships. They would stop at 200, and that would be that. "We want to capture the real downtown—all kinds of people coming together. Not just celebrities or just socialites," Jose Martin, one of the owners, told me. I liked the idea of that. Why didn't our society care more about the everyman? To me, that was where the fascination lay. Every single person I ever met could amaze me.

—Velvet Rope Diaries, *New York, New York*

5:00 p.m., Friday

"**Will you come with me to look at my wedding dress?**" Nina wanted to know when she called a little later. She didn't waste one second. We were on the phone, but I knew her binder was all tabbed up and organized. She'd had her finger hovering over the print button for so long you wouldn't believe it.

Maryann's Wedding Gowns was just off of 3rd Avenue on 79th Street, upstairs in an old brownstone.

Though I was miserable, I tried my best to be a good sport as

Nina and I sat on an ornate, upholstered bench, sipping champagne, and Maryann herself went through four gigantic closets that lined each wall of the room, pushing through the dresses, pulling out the ones she thought fit our criteria. She also pulled out the ones *she* thought would look good on Nina. "Sometimes those are two different dresses," she informed us.

Nina had her heart set on a specific dress with a scooped out neckline and those delicate lacy cap sleeves—by some Italian designer. She'd added it to her dream years ago, when she found it in a magazine, and that was just what she wanted. Period. She tried to act like she'd just thought of it recently, but I think Maryann could read a bride. That was just the kind of impression she gave.

"Why don't we just *try on* some other ones anyway . . . just for the heck of it? After all . . . you're already here. And you only get to do this once."

We shrugged and nodded her along.

Trying too hard to be a good sport, I wore a maniac's smile and nodded whenever I could.

When Maryann had one to show that *she* liked, she said, "Aha???" with big eyes. When she had one that fit *our* qualifications, she said, "Is this what you meant?" She was neatly dressed in head-to-toe taupe. Even her hair looked taupe.

Maybe marriage and married people and happy endings are boring, I told myself. Maybe in the end, it would turn out I was the lucky one, having murdered my father, given up a wonderful man for a runaway, and losing one of the most coveted jobs in the world to a grody-toothed jerk and his plastic accomplice.

I doubt that was true, because looking at the dresses made me downhearted for all of it. An end and a beginning side by side. It seemed the whole thing had been reduced to one part of an equation. I employed Fenwick's technique. I played out the scenarios my guilt took the form of all the way out to the extremes. I could live with the possibility that I hurt David so badly that he wouldn't be able to concentrate at work, he'd get fired, lose everything, get depressed, walk outside, and get hit by a taxi.

I thought these things while Maryann asked, "Aha???" and Nina said, "Ooooohhh, look at that em*broi*dery!" I felt I was living a double life. The champagne helped to fuse them together.

Once inside the dressing room, I sat on a slipper chair, striped in gold and taupe, and Nina shimmied inside a crinoline and was strapped into a bustier. She looked adorable—like a little shepardess.

"Oh, get my digital camera out, Anna. It's in my purse."

A camera. Crap. I should have thought of that myself. I am the maid of honor. I should have realized Nina would want to document every second of this. But no. I was too busy thinking of myself, feeling sorry for myself, trying to stop thinking I was a murderer, but not trying to feel good about it. I was a pathetic, horrible friend. I promised myself I'd think of something great to do to make up for it, like paste the pictures into a scrapbook and use all of those adorable, overpriced embellishments you can buy these days.

I looked at her in that little screen, and she was so happy. Nina in her old-fashioned undergarments, so exposed and open, and yet happier than she'd ever been.

"Smile for the camera, daaahling," I said. "Now hold up your champagne." We got really into it, and then Maryann came in with the dresses.

"Get in there, Maryann," I said, because I knew that was something that Nina would do. She hesitated, but scooched in stiffly. And by the time I said, "Lay sunatics!" and they said, "What?" and I said, "I mean, 'say lunatics,'" Maryann cracked a smile.

The second Nina put her dress on, you just knew it was her dress. Unfortunately it was one of the "Aha???" dresses, which neither of us wanted to have work out. The dress had a tiny bodice, like a china doll's, and then went out into a fancy princess skirt, with a long train that swooped around like a giant's ping pong paddle. There were crystals all around the waist.

Maryann yelled, "Let me get the veil!" She left the two of us in there, and Nina swished back and forth in the big dress watching the tiny stones glimmer in the lights. She was glowing with happiness and looked better than ever. I, behind her, looked half dead, despite what I'd been trying to accomplish here. Maybe I just needed to believe that things got worse before they got better. Maybe I just needed a better blush.

"Oh, Nina!" I pulled out the camera and snapped her several times, at this angle and that, with her train held up in the crook of her arm, from the front and the back, so she could send the pictures to her mother to criticize. "Hold your head up straight, Nina," I said as I maneuvered the various buttons and levers questioningly. "Or who knows . . . maybe you'll miss your magic number year!" We laughed and laughed, because now it was over it could be funny.

I put Nina in the first taxi, her binder now stuffed with a receipt and a guarantee her dress would be in by February sixth. She was going over to Bernard's, which was downtown . . . and just then it felt she was off to a different country of happiness and contentment that I wasn't sure I'd ever explore. I smiled and tried not to be jealous. On the way home, my heel cracked right off my shoe, and I had to clip-clop unsteadily home, while snobby girls pointed and laughed.

"Come in, I fix the shoe, shine it up. Maybe you smile," a man standing alongside an easel beckoned me inside his cobbler shop. I stayed too long, enjoying the careful, graceful way he fixed my shoe, the light conversation. "You have big plans tonight? Such a pretty girl, surely the men are lining up!"

He shined my shoes while I sat up on a high wooden seat, and for a little while I was just there in that worn place and nowhere else, nowhere grisly or shameful—only half listening to the scratchy foreign talk radio, picking out the few French words I could recall from high school. *Aujourd'hui* and *lendemain* and *le garcon*.

I counted my change out slowly, left him a tip, though I didn't know if that was customary, and walked home. The weekend stretched out long ahead of me. I didn't know what I'd do with myself. Nina was meeting Bernard's parents up in Westchester. Ray was in D.C.—supposedly on business. I tried Belinda. "Sorry, child," she said. "I never come back to the city once I get home. If you want to come out to Queens, I'd love to spend some time together." I couldn't muster the energy to navigate new trains, check the stop names, hold on tightly to my purse.

I thought of my mother, how much she'd love to come and spend the night with me. I wanted to call her. I held the phone with every intention of doing so. But I couldn't. I felt myself slipping back, ready to give up and reclaim the pathetic but relatively easy life I'd led before, the comfort of having nothing to push for.

On a whim, I tried Susan. "Oh, let me take you out to dinner. I've got all this alimony to spend, and I just can't get through it, no matter what I do. Have you ever done the Strip House?" She asked.

Oh god, where was she going? "Oh, Susan, I don't think I'm up for exotic dancing."

"Heavens no! I would never do that *before* dinner. You work up such an appetite stripping! This is a steak house, down on Twelfth Street."

"Okay," I said. That sounded nice. A nice dinner with a very entertaining girlfriend. I pictured us laughing and laughing like diners did in movies. Just a nice dinner between two friends.

9:00 p.m.

My train stopped dead in a tunnel for twenty minutes. There were no lights, no announcements. Two little girls who'd been wearing matching green sweatshirts cried and cried, and their voices carried in the frightened silence a long way. Finally, the lights returned, the train moved and we continued without a hitch to Union Square. Once I reached the block, I walked past the restaurant twice. The sign was small, and my mind was elsewhere. Where did one go from here? I tried Ray's cell phone after I'd missed the restaurant the second time.

"Hello, you've reached 917-555-1212."

He didn't invite messages, he'd once told me. I hung up, turned around, and passed the restaurant again. When I reached the corner of University Place, I tried the number again.

"Hello, you've reached 917-555-1212."

"Ray, I just found out I might be undone by Joseph, spent two hours in a wedding dress salon, got stuck in a train for twenty minutes, and passed the restaurant I was supposed to be at a half hour ago for the second time. And why am I telling you this? Why? Because I'm standing here wondering, *Why did I trust you?* Why have I been wondering where you've been for days and days—conveniently starting right when I broke up with David—and now feeling like a complete idiot for trusting you?"

I listened when I was through, hoping there'd be a re-record option. But there wasn't.

I found the sign, descended the staircase, and pushed into the cocoon of a restaurant, soft jazz playing in the background. A couple of regular looking patrons at a small lounge in front turned around possessively when the door opened.

"Can I help you, mademoiselle?" the host asked warmly.

I resisted the urge to cry on his perfectly dry-cleaned shoulder and said, "Susan Scrimp-Levy's party, please."

"Ah, yes, ma'am. He leaned down to pencil in a note on his reservation sheet and then raised his head again. "Excuse me for asking, but are you . . . Anna Walker? From Velvet Rope Diaries?"

It was the oddest sensation, to be recognized. "Yes, I am," I said, trying not to fidget. At least I am for the moment, until the truth is revealed: Anna Walker is unqualified to hold opinions about stylish places. She hasn't got the taste for it. She doesn't deserve it anyway (though deserving is a ridiculous concept, and she knows she isn't supposed to care about it).

"Right this way," he said, grinning, leading me with a stiff arm toward the rear dining room.

Everyone seemed to be having a great time, finding something funny, worthy of a throaty laugh or a high laugh or a tinkly one. I watched the walls as we walked, turned completely to the side, like someone who doesn't want to face things. On the walls were framed calendar girls—curvy, well-proportioned women, with huge rolls of hair and pointed chests. Along the way I fell into old ways and wished I were that one and that one or the one with the Carmen Miranda hat on.

"Anna!" Susan yelled, facing me on one side of a booth, a scraggly man in nylon to her right: Ostensibly this was Shakti, though he looked more like a Norman.

As I approached, I realized there were two other people facing opposite—a woman with wiry maroon hair and a man whose slightly thinning, delightfully puffy hair I'd recognize anywhere. It was David. I fought the urge to hold my purse up over my face, spin around, and run for my life. "Hello, everyone," I said instead, an over-enthusiastic kindergarten teacher. "I didn't realize we were such a big party!"

There was a chair for me—one empty chair at the end of the table adjacent to David. I looked at Susan, and she hoisted up her shoulders as if to say she couldn't help herself.

I avoided David's eyes for as long as possible, fiddling with my coat and then my purse and eventually the positioning of my chair. When it was inevitable, I turned, recognized the knowing gaze of someone who you once knew, who still held various facts about you lumped in their mind, possibly in their heart. I tried not to, but probably looked on him similarly.

"Anna," he said, and leaned in to press his mouth at my cheek.

"I'm Romaneta," the woman next to him said, pushy, annoyed, too blinky. "From Ukraine, you know?"

"Of course," I nodded slowly, though I had no idea what significance this might have.

I had worn a light blouse, and suddenly felt a chill, as if someone had opened the door. Involuntarily, I shuddered.

"Here, take my jacket," David insisted, standing, removing his navy pinstripe and snuggling it over my shoulders, smoothing it down with his palms.

I looked up at him, swallowing back the emotions I felt on the rise. I would not cry. I had done this to myself. But did he have to look so inviting sitting there?

The menu had too many choices, so when the waiter arrived to ask what I'd like I randomly zeroed in on one and said, "Steak frites."

After the entrees were picked over, scavenged, I excused myself for the ladies' room. Romaneta wanted to join me.

"Don't you think he izzz so cute?" she said. "And very rich."

I wanted to tune her out, forget her, ignore it all, hunched against the tile wall in the stall. Finally, thankfully, she flushed the toilet, didn't wash her hands, and left.

I closed my eyes, tried to steel myself against this situation. I would not be tempted by the shelter of David. I would not use myself and him so poorly. But if I could, wouldn't it be wonderful? Wonderful to laugh like those raspy, tinkly, high laughers and fall asleep with the kidney shaped shadow across his bureau?

There was no answer, so I straightened out, flushed the toilet, though I hadn't used it, washed my hands, found my face drawn and sickly looking in the mirror, tried to blame the lighting, found it very soft and innocent, and pushed my way into the tiny hallway, off the side of the restaurant.

David was waiting right there.

"Hey," I said.

"Let's get a drink after," he started to say, grabbed my hand—a gesture that squeezed tears from my eyes.

I quickly wiped them, tried to cover my face with my bangs.

"Hey, hey," he soothed, his hand wiping my back up and down, up and down, his eyelashes tickling my cheek.

A few blocks down along Fifth Avenue, there was a beautiful restaurant with windows all across the front and elegant white lights, and we went in there and sat at the bar. He leaned one elbow on the smooth mahogany and faced me, smiling.

I crossed my legs and told him I was very sorry, that it was very nice to see him now, civilly. I didn't know where these polite, adult words came from, words that didn't allow me to give into the out-of-control spin I'd taken off on, a child's top gone wild, threatening to spin right down off the balcony, plummet twenty stories to the ground.

"Anna, you know, it's not too late to change your mind," he said with his hand at my shoulder, as I pulled my coat belt too tight.

I looked long and hard into his eyes so I would remember, finally, what I'd risked for love.

I slept off and on with my neighbor Mrs. Olstead's cat whining at the door, long, haunting meows. I knew she'd been left. I could recognize the sound of it.

1:30 a.m.

"Hello, you've reached 917-555-1212."

2:45 a.m.

"Hello, you've reached 917-555-1212."

7:00 p.m., Sunday, December 4

I walked around all day, watching people, mannequins, anything and everything that looked more fortunate than myself. It would be so easy to do the wrong thing, but once I'd suffered through the first night of perseverance, I wasn't about to waste it. Everyone knows the first night is the worst.

When it was dark and too cold, I looked for a taxi, with my arm shoved up limply, half heartedly. But none came by, so I decided to walk over to Second Avenue. It was freezing. Why didn't I have on gloves or a hat or a scarf like everyone else did? Had I always lived my life so haphazardly? I made a note to get those things tomorrow. I could get a nice set—maybe at Bloomingdale's. My mind had wandered a bit, considering shades of blue—navy or royal—when out of the corner of my eye, I saw a man as haphazard as myself, stepping off the curb, into the street, without realizing a taxi was barreling toward him.

"Sir!" I screamed at the top of my lungs. But he didn't notice. I started to run, fast, faster. There were several feet between us, and the distance was growing as he came farther from the curb. I could see the taxi approaching even quicker. It seemed to take forever, but finally, I reached the man, grabbed him by the collar, and finally he realized what was happening, and we both landed back on the curb exactly when the taxi would have killed us both.

"What an asshole!" He yelled, punching the air in the direction of the taxi.

I wasn't about to point out that the taxi had the right-of-way and that he was walking into the street without paying attention. I was too blown away by what had just happened. "You saved my life," he said. "You saved my life."

I looked in the man's eyes very deeply, all the way, I think, because this seemed to hold unbelievable meaning to me. The girl who'd killed her father had just saved someone's life. Surely someone was trying to tell me something. "I'm just glad you're okay," I said the words I'd dreamed as the alternate ending to our fire so many, many times, waking to a cold sweat, my sheets needing to be changed.

And as I turned to go home after a long, long weekend, I realized what this sign was trying to tell me. The person whose life I'd nearly forgotten about saving was my own. And though I may have faltered, I wasn't going to give up now.

8:00 a.m., Monday, December 5

Belinda and I met at Farlucks to discuss strategy.

"I think we should go after work. Just go through the whole day, act like everything's fine, and then we take the train over to Astoria. This way you can go straight home from there." I'd always been afraid of psychics, afraid of sitting down with one and she recognizes right away there is something not quite right about me. She wouldn't know exactly what it was at first, but eventually her bushy eyebrows would jolt, and she would see it there. I wasn't sure of the kind of responsibility psychics had to report murderers to the police—but I didn't want to chance it. I don't think I could live in prison. All those criminals.

"Okay. Yeah, that's a good plan. I just hope we can wipe this whole thing out quickly and move on," Belinda said.

Boy, did I ever agree with that.

"Belinda, do you believe in psychics?" I asked.

"Absolutely not." I could tell she was lying.

"Me neither," I said, not sure, really.

5:00 p.m.

We took the N train, and when the doors opened, we mean-dered around looking for 31st Avenue. At the doorway of a tiny liquor store, there stood an easel sign that read, "Psychic: The Famous Rima," in curly, handpainted letters.

"*Cccchow* can I *healp* you?" she wanted to know once we made our way through the incense cloud, sat on the two folding chairs across the card table that—along with a dusty tapestry hanging behind her—made up her office.

She looked at Belinda first. "Oh, you want to know about *jour* boyfriend—is he going to be okay?"

We wanted to be furious here, but how could you be mad when someone dangled the knowledge of the one thing you were dying to know right in front of your face? Belinda looked at me, questioningly. I nodded for her to let Rima continue. As long as we were here.

"Yes," she said.

"Do you have the fifty dollars?" Rima asked, the quintessential businesswoman.

Belinda looked to me again.

"Well," I answered for us. "We are actually here to ask if someone came to see you . . . someone named Joseph James?"

Her fleshy hand went to her forehead. She closed her eyes and swallowed immensely.

"You speak the name of evil," she said.

"Yup, that's him," Belinda said.

"*Isss* tiny pipsqueak with grody teeth?" she verified.

"Yes, aha." I shook my head excitedly. I felt we were onto something, but I didn't know exactly what.

She was silent.

"So, he was here?"

"You have fifty dollars?"

I looked at Belinda, and between the two of us, we scrounged up $49.50.

"I give you half session for that price."

"But that's only fifty cents less than you asked for," I said.

"You want *nothink* then?" she said.

"No, no, please continue," I said, feeling desperate, though unsure why.

"First, your boyfriend," she turned to Belinda. "He *eees* going to be fine. You give him *dees*." She pulled out a small poultice tied with a pretty ribbon. "You put in tea, and he drink. No more panicky."

"Second, Joseph . . ." She shivered as she delivered the name. "He was here with scratchy hair plastic woman, and they want to know about you." She pointed at me. My eyes went unfocused.

"What did you tell them?"

"Not too much to tell. You Goody Two-shoes. Always do the right thing. They say, so make something up and tell it to Ed, tell him whole paper will go out of business if he keep Anna on."

"You aren't going to do that, are you?"

She was silent.

"Well, *are* you?" I pressed.

"Depend." She leaned across the table, her swingy sleeves sliding down around her elbows, revealing cushiony arms.

"On what?" Belinda asked.

"Your offer," she said, recrossing her arms over her chest. "You think about it, but I tell you meanwhile, Miss Anna, I am getting a strong sense of someone trying to contact you from beyond, someone trying to say, he love you, he not mad at you, he so proud of you."

I tried with everything I was not to concentrate on this, not to dwell too hard on it—I knew the danger of trying to believe this, lock into the idea of it, only to have it float just out of reach forever and ever, me straining impossibly to grab hold and getting nothing but water in my fingers—but the sound was one of the most brilliant I'd ever heard. Still, I couldn't help but feel it was worth it maybe that I'd come here, that I'd been placed in this predicament, that I might even lose my job—to hear this. Everything in me wanted to believe it could be.

"Oh, Anna, here, take a Puffs Plus," Belinda said.

"That's not a nice trick!" Belinda yelled at Rima. "You don't mess with someone's life like that!"

"I don't make this up! Also, Mr. R man in your life—he love you, just mixed up! I don't make up! And you thinking about that advice column . . . it's perfect. You should do it!"

"Sure you don't make it up, except for when Joseph and Miss Jackson pay the right price!" Belinda yelled, probably angry at the possibility that her own advice could have been false, that the poultice in her hand would not work.

"It's not that. It's . . . well, they—" She didn't finish. She looked up to the bare bulb overhead and folded her lips in so we couldn't see them anymore.

"What? What did they do?" I encouraged her along.

She looked straight at us, her eyes unwavering. "They threatened to have me deported. I'm illegal alien. They said if I don't do this to you, I will get sent back to Russia. And my little girls, too."

The news hit dull, heavy, and I realized it was hopeless.

I didn't want her to be deported.

★　★　★

We all slumped against our chair backs. Despite it all, we were just three women, trying to make our way. I noticed some brown water leaking through a ceiling tile, making its way through, somehow—moving along no matter where or how.

"I got it!" Rima said, punching the air. Maybe Rima, too, had seen the water.

"What?" Belinda and I chorused.

"We put a spell on Joseph and Nasty, and they want to do the right thing."

I exchanged a disbelieving glance with Belinda. Sure it would be wonderful to believe this might work, the way I could sometimes dissect my horoscope so that the outlook of my day would appear glorious, but to place all of your hope on it? I wasn't so sure.

"What other choice have we got?" Belinda asked.

6:00 p.m.

Rima sent us out all over Astoria searching for crazy ingredients like lodestone and dragon's blood resin. We had instructions to ask for specific people at the shops to help us: Boris and Trovsky and Zora. We ran, our feet aching in our heels, avoiding sidewalk cracks and children in roller skate sneakers, frantically seeking out the solution. After two hours of this, I pulled Belinda onto a bench at a bus stop.

"What are we doing?" I asked her.

"Looking for a horse's butt hair," she said, looking at the list Rima had scribbled.

I shook my head.

"Do you really believe all this?" I asked, skeptical.

She rumpled her lips, then straightened up, turned to face me. "Listen to me, Anna. I need to believe there is some magic in this world. I'm a freaking secretary. I work in a cubicle. I live with a geeky computer programmer who has an anxiety condition. I'll never have a child or own a home or get to see the pyramids. The only way I can shake things up is to wear my hair too big. I need to believe there is something more . . . so get up and let's find that damned horse's butt hair and get you back on fantasy track before I lose my hope altogether."

Some people had turned and listened. Two ladies waiting on the next bench applauded. "Get that butt hair!" someone yelled.

In the end, we found all the items, each wrapped in old-fashioned butcher paper and tied with bakery string—big and small—and watched Rima boil them in a misshapen pot, over a rusted hot plate, yelling profanities and long flowery Russian words we didn't understand.

We, all three of us, wanted to believe in the possibility of this, this easy, magical way out of all of life's problems. We wanted to leave and be free of it all, a trio of careless girls in pigtails, free to live the way we had before fires or stillborn children or terrible lives we didn't want to be deported back to.

Belinda squeezed my hand, her long, shapely nails pinching, and I squeezed my boyish nails into her palm. No matter what happens, I thought, here was the magic, right here at my fingers.

10:30 p.m.

"Hello, you've reached 917-555-1212."

10:45 p.m.

"Hello, you've reached 917-555-1212."

11:00 p.m.

I stayed up real late waiting for Ray to call, worried sick about tomorrow. On *Emotional Eating*, they cooked "Blinded by Love Linguine" and "Do You Believe in Magic Pie." When I fell asleep twisted on the sofa, no one woke me to go to bed.

10:00 a.m., Wednesday, December 7

Ed called me into his office to go over the column. I was shak-ing like the last crackly ochre leaf of fall, holding on, holding on, but knowing all the while there were larger factors at play here, and that all the strength in the world may not save me after all. I didn't really believe the spell would work, would help me to maintain my hold, but I wanted to like heck.

The meeting started out relatively well.

"I hate to say this, but it's starting to grow on me . . . like a mole." He laughed at his own joke.

He was impressed, but I couldn't enjoy it with all I knew to be coming. The amazing thing though, is that despite all the pain, the possibility of having lost everything with Ray, having made a monstrous mess of everything . . . I could still live my life. I could go on. That was the strength Fenwick and I had found in me. It was empty as hell, the prospect of this life, but I moved around in it all the same, putting pen to paper and fork to mouth.

"I'm glad," I said. "You think I could get that raise now?"

"Good one!" he hooted.

Was I home free? I sat there for a second while he pat his desk in hysterics. "I got something for you," he said. He leaned down, picked up a bulging shopping bag from behind his desk. He handed it over.

I reached inside and pulled out a handful of envelopes. They all seemed to be addressed to me. I looked up questioningly.

"Your fans," he said.

Dear Anna,

Maybe Ray is just freaked out because he doesn't want to ruin your friendship in case things don't work out.

All the best,
Cindy Gummel

Dear Anna,
    I think it was really brave the way you broke things off with
David right away like that. I have such a hard time doing things
like that. In fact, I've got a similar quandary and wondered if you've
got any advice as to how I could break up with someone gently, how
I can face the possibility that I might be alone afterward?
Sincerely,
Caroline James

Dear Anna,
    I just wanted you to know that in my book club, nobody believes
you were fooling around with Ray while you were still going out
with David. However, we do want to tell you that we all think that
Nasty and Joseph might do something really, really bad to you. We
are worried! Please be careful! Also, I'm trying to figure out if the
guy I'm with is the right one. We've been together so long it has
become a routine, and I can't even figure out how I actually feel
anymore. Any advice?
A big fan,
Louisa Santos

I thought of what Rima had said about the advice column. It
seemed coincidental that I would receive these letters now. Maybe
this *would* all work out? I wanted to believe, and I wanted to believe.
Maybe if I wanted to so badly it would just work.

I don't know what made me think of this, but I put down the
huge bag of letters immediately and walked the hallway to Nasty's
office. There was a new assistant there, and I recognized that look of
manic confusion in her eye. When I first started there, I was always

reeling because I didn't know what I was doing, and every time I handed something in to Nasty, she yelled and yelled at me.

I walked behind her cubicle, because I didn't want her to see me. I stood for a couple of minutes outside of Nasty's office, not sure what I was going to do. Just at that moment, the secretary noticed me standing there.

"Can I help you?" she asked. She was extremely well put together. She wore matching earrings and a necklace . . . even a belt. I felt like a mess, although I was wearing one of those outfits from Theresa. I crossed my hands over my chest. Old habits die hard. I said, "Umm."

"Hey, I know you. You're that Anna Walker! You used to have my job!"

I turned her around to her cubicle, because I didn't want Nasty to hear us.

"What's the deal with her?" the girl asked, her eyes wild.

I sighed. "She's really a good person." I shocked myself when it came out. Deep down, I guess I still believed this, despite the fact that any day I'd be fired, by her own doing. "She's just insecure."

"You're shitting me. Right?" The girl had her hands at her hips. "Yesterday, she made me go to Victoria's Secret to try to exchange a thong she had for three years. I almost threw up."

She had a point, but so did I. "I'm gonna tell you something, and don't take it the wrong way," I said. "You can get another job. If you stay here and you don't like it, it's not her fault. It's yours." It felt wonderful to have the wisdom of experience, to be able to share it with someone, see them benefit from it.

"It's true, you *are* a bitch," she said, turned her back to me, and sat down in her chair.

I left the office, another column in, my job still—amazingly— intact. I wondered, had the magic actually worked?

"Hello, you've reached 917-555-1212."
"Hello, you've reached 917-555-1212."
"Hello, you've reached 917-555-1212."
I didn't know if Ray and I would ever talk again.

5:30 p.m., Thursday, December 8

Still no word about my being fired. I hated to believe it, but it appeared, maybe, just maybe, the spell had actually worked. Each morning, squeezing paste onto my toothbrush, I'd steeled myself to the possibility of being let go, and each evening I huffed up the four flights to my apartment with relief.

Tonight, I left the office early so that I could head off Ray, since he'd be back from D.C. I was going to make him come out with me tonight no matter what. He'd been ignoring me for over a week now, and if I was to take it one more second, I was afraid I'd lose something of myself I'd never be able to retrieve.

I ran to the six train and down the stairs and in between the doors, and when they closed, I stood against them so I could be the first one off. Now I ran up Third Avenue and around the corner and up the three flights of steps. He was just outside, twisting the top lock tight when I opened the door.

He was surprised when he turned and I was there. He started to step around me.

I grabbed onto his jacket sleeve. "Hey," I said.

He blinked too much. "What?" he asked, guilt all over his stiff features.

"What the hell are you doing?"

"Going out," he said. "It's happy hour. I'm ecstatic. Can't you tell?" He bit at the inside of his cheek.

He was standing closer to me, now that I'd pulled him there, and neither of us spoke. My cheeks heated up, and I could feel the heat coming from him, too. Our chests expanded and sank, expanded and sank. We were angry, so angry. The fluorescent-lit hallway dimmed slightly and then brightened back to normal.

"What the hell is going on here?" I stumbled on the words.

"What are you talking about?" he jabbed, but while he did, he pulled my head close and closer, my hair all tangled in his fingers, and looked at me like that while my stomach plummeted toward my soles.

"You know what I mean," I breathed, his face so near it blurred now. "You know I called and called." I thought I'd cry, but only felt anger, desperation.

"I know. I saw it. I saw each call and fought myself not to pick it up."

"What? Why?" I was yelling.

"I didn't want to rush you, Anna. I wanted you to take your time and be sure."

"Don't you think I can figure that out for myself?"

He looked to me like he knew me—knew me better than I knew myself.

"I didn't want you to decide rashly and then feel that since you told the whole world in your column that you just *had* to stick by that. I didn't want to have you and then lose you because of that."

I didn't know what to say. My anger was disassembling, breaking up into tiny pieces, transmogrifying into something altogether different.

"But you leave me no choice now. I knew I couldn't be this close to you. I fucking knew it."

And he looked at me, swallowed me with his look, tore off large bites of me with his pointed irises, steady, so steady, and then placed his lips on the tip of my nose and then my cheek, and then he pulled my chin up, and we kissed with the hostage passion we both had hammering out all over the place in shaky jerks and irregular breaths. It was deep and soft and angry and had been misunderstood too long. I was backed against one side of the doorway, and he was against me, and I could feel him at my groin. I tore his jacket off from the collar, and he pulled at my sleeve. My purse fell against the radiator beneath the hallway window with a jingle and a thump.

I heard the paint-on-paint scrape of the door opening at the apartment across the way and then a gasp as Mrs. Olstead caught us—our lips and arms joined.

"I'll have you reported!" she yelled.

We pulled apart, gasping for breath. My hands shook—an old, tired engine being pushed, pushed beyond capacity.

Ray picked me and my things up and carried us into his bed. We didn't bother to remove our clothing; there didn't seem to be time. If we did, would this all change? Would we be back where we began? It was impossible all the while not to think each move, each fingertip press, each tiny hair snagged accidentally, each toe that tickled, wouldn't signal the end of it all. The odds were against us. We might not make it, the intimidating odds said, careless as to our individual merits. When it was done, underpants and belts half off and half on, we started again, with a single finger along my thigh.

"All this time you had the bigger room!" I said afterward, looking at him with my cards all showing, with no way to bluff. My eyes, I'm sure, gave me away, carelessly. A tender grin looked me over, down to my legs—dangling feathery, weightless. We lay, an intricate human knot beneath the damp blankets.

At ten o'clock we showered only slightly awkwardly together, and Ray sang, "No More Tears!" in his best Ozzy Osbourne, while he so gently rinsed the shampoo from my hair, kissing me on the ear every now and then, soapy and loud. I think we were delirious. He had very long legs I kept noticing, looking down at him, wet and naked like that. Ray had very long legs, and I hoped he wouldn't use them to run away from me.

We laughed at everything like we'd just discovered it—his underwear on the back of the desk chair now, my smooshed-in bra cups, our foggy vanity mirror. We were familiarly unfamiliar.

"Now you've really got something to write about," he joked. We were in the back of a taxi—clean and shiny—heading all the way through the East Side, to the edge of the city, at a distance where the whole place seemed unreal, like something you could store in a box over the winter. A new waterfront bar was waiting for us. Ray's arm looped around my waist, the other hand tickling at my stockings. We couldn't stop kissing, just feeling each other's mouths, communicating like that, getting to know each other—reinventing the way it had always been in this new, unbelievable way.

You could believe you were in St. Martin at this bar, named Orient Baie, for the most celebrated beach on the French side of that island. Everything was bamboo and bright, elegant teakwood and plants, huge flowers with unbelievable pistils. I'd finally made it to St. Martin.

"You never saw pistils like this before," I said to Ray.

"Hey, you don't know anything about my pistils," he said.

"But I do," I tried on a sexy line—it was how I felt, bold and better than myself. Ray and I watched the water, the few barges floating past.

"I want something that arrives on a barge," I said.

"Oh yeah—everyone should have at least one thing that arrives on a barge," he said.

We drank pink drinks, and I thought how interesting life could be, how it could surprise you and restore your faith in it without explanation . . . just like that. How one thing might begin as another might end.

"Can I have your pineapple?" he asked, removing the giant wheel from the rim of my glass.

"Oh, you know I love it when you talk like that," I said. Our tablecloth was a clean white waffle weave. A big palm curved over us like a giant hand protecting us.

We breathed heavy. We looked seriously, very seriously into the depths of each other's eyes. We ate giant shrimps sprinkled with coconut shreds, and Ray danced them around the plate, their wiry antennae swaying this way and that—a 1950s musical starring shellfish. We tried each other's desserts—pineapple upside-down cake and coconut cream pie—and danced to steel drum music from the band. Everything was unsubtle foreplay.

12:30 a.m.

"Ray?" I asked as we were calming to sleep, in his bed, down the hall from my own.

"What is it?" he whispered, his hand unbelievable, smoothing my hair from my forehead.

"I didn't know you had such long legs," I said, not sure why I was mesmerized by this one detail.

"And I didn't know you had such beautiful breasts," he replied, touching one like it was his now.

And we fell asleep, my legs clamped between his, the sirens fading up Third Avenue, and the heat blowing so high it whistled.

5:30 p.m., Wednesday, December 14

I told Fenwick first about Rima, about the horse's butt hair and how I couldn't help but want to believe it could work, that maybe it was working.

"Look, Anna, I'm not saying magic isn't possible. That isn't my field, but there are two ways this could work out, and . . ."

"I shouldn't try to convince myself that it will go the way that I want, because I have to live with the possibility that it might not, and go on."

He smirked. "Very good. By George, I think she's got it."

I told him I was always afraid of psychics because of the way they are supposed to be able to read minds and the possibility of going to jail. I was almost getting used to talking about all the insane things that go on inside my head. Fenwick never stood up and said, "Oh, that is just off the wall; we'll have to commit you," the way I always half expected. Now it became a sort of strength test—can I go on putting myself through this manner of humiliation each and every week? Can I get up and leave after saying the most inane things, as if I were like everyone else running to cross the street before the light turned?

"And Ray and I are finally . . . well . . . we are, I guess . . . a couple."

"Anna, that is so wonderful. I am very happy to hear it."

"But don't convince myself it will be perfect, that we'll be happy, that I deserve it. Don't try to enjoy myself or have a good time. Right?" I don't know where the hostility came from, but it was there, and I was giving it to Fenwick—good.

"Do you think maybe you're still looking to clean your slate, so to speak? To have me say, 'You are totally innocent,' each and every time you are here, the way I did for you in our first session? Tie it up neatly so you're free to enjoy all of this exciting stuff?"

"I don't think I am," I lied. I was always doing that to Fenwick. Whatever he said, I didn't want it to be true.

"Why don't you think so?" Fenwick asked. He looked very gentle and nice as he always did. And whenever I noticed that, I started to back down slightly.

"I don't know," I said, lamely, fidgeting at the sofa arm, already feeling guilty about treating Fenwick poorly, too.

3:30 p.m., Friday, December 16

"Hi, Ed. How are you?" I asked.

"Good, good," he said, "but how are *you*?"

I wasn't sure what he meant. He followed up quickly with another question.

"I mean, how is your hair? Is it thinning at all? Has it lost some of its sheen?"

Had Ed officially lost his mind and someone forgot to tell me? My hair? Could he be serious?

"I, well, it's always a little thinner in the winter."

"Oh dear," he said, shaking his head.

Oh no. I'd said the wrong thing. "Well, but not so much as last year, I guess. It's definitely thicker than last year at this time." What? What could this possibly be about? Was I not looking the part again?

He glanced down at a paper on his desk and then looked up, full of concentration and asked, "What about your skin? Have you been breaking out at all?" I had that pimple on my cheek, but surely it wasn't that bad! In fact, I was now thinking it was only hives.

"I . . . well . . ." I didn't know what to make of this. Did I have to answer this? I should have used cover-up that morning, it was true. But this was really mortifying. Was this really the problem? I mean, I really thought I was looking much better now.

"Spit it out! How's your skin?"

"It's fine," I said, panicking.

"But isn't that a pimple I see on your cheek there?"

Instinctively, I cupped my palm over my cheek.

"Did you just pick out a dress for your friend's wedding? Nina or whoever?"

This was too much. It really was. My heart was racing. I didn't know if this was a nightmare or what. It seemed like it had to be. It was too surreal—these questions, this inappropriateness, Ed's wild-eyed demeanor. "I did, but what does this—" I didn't get to finish.

"That'll be all," he said.

11:30 a.m., Saturday, December 17

The office of photographer Glenn Dubin was in a nice loft down in TriBeCa. It was all white, with some white curtains separating areas off here and there. One corner was set up with a roll of screens you could pull down for different backgrounds. Currently, there was a farm scene, with a swirling yellow road and a red log fence and a couple of solid looking cows standing in front of a silo.

"Kids." He shrugged when we looked in the direction of the farm scene.

We shook our heads like we completely understood.

Nina had her binder, and she pulled it out, turning to a checklist of questions. "How many people on your crew? How many pictures do you take total? Will they be available on a website? Do you give any credits toward prints?"

Now *she* could be a journalist. We both looked through some of Glenn's albums and oohed and ahhed over what could be done with digital effects these days. It was all quite impressive. I hated to be so selfish, but my mind was elsewhere—it was in splendor one minute and terror the next—but I tried to be there, too, caring about how much digital alteration Glenn Dubin gave to the photo of a couple dancing, whether in that particular picture the sister's blue dress had been too distracting, if it had been worth it to remove her completely, change the truth to make things better. I tried not to think how simple a solution that could be for me, if possible.

I was flipping through Gregory and Tamara's wedding, smiling at the pictures of the ladies getting their hair set in giant rollers, a cat pawing at a table piled high with dyed shoes (wondering, before digital retouching, had that cat really been pawing at something else, say poop?), a little girl sticking her toe into a river in a huge frothy dress, her shoes off to the side (wondering, well, had that river even been there, or was she just dancing the hokey pokey?). And then I came upon a photo of a father dancing with his daughter, her head resting on his shoulder in an official last dance of childhood . . . There were a few tears glossing his eyes up to a high shine. This picture, I was sure hadn't been altered. It couldn't have been. The things we want most, the things we mythologize, can never be explained away as easy as that.

"Anna? Anna . . ." Nina was talking to me, but I didn't realize. I was transfixed. It was at that moment I realized I'd been so busy feeling guilty, testing myself, always testing and searching for the truth, the truth that would finally, ultimately shed light on my innocence, that I hadn't been able to *miss* my dad at all.

But now, at this second, I did. Horribly, I did. I thought of all the things we'd missed doing together and how I didn't know how to play any sports well, how I didn't understand a thing about football games. I was always asking Ray, "What's that guy doing?" "Why's that guy running in the other direction now? Is his butt really that big, or are those pads?" I could have asked Roger, sure. But I hadn't. And he hadn't. We were too polite. We were too worried about boundaries and respect and emotional breakdowns (him for me).

I thought of the Thanksgivings and Christmases and my school plays and my mother with Roger, her hand curled up in his. Had this "bothered me? It all came flooding at me, and I thought I might drown.

"Anna!" I must have looked crazy for Nina to use that tone.

"Sorry, I'm fine," I said. But I wasn't fine, didn't even know if I could be digitally altered to look fine.

★ ★ ★

We didn't go with Glenn Dubin.

"He's too . . . cutesy," Nina said—a flimsy excuse.

"C'mon, I've got a surprise for you . . . a pick-me-up," she said, smiling, her arm on my shoulder.

"TAXI!" she called. We climbed in, and she said, "Twentieth between Broadway and Fifth, please."

"Where we going?" I asked, trying to show her I was interested, that I didn't require pick-me-ups during her wedding planning, which was supposed to be about her.

"You'll see." And then she turned to face me. "Hey," she said. "You don't have to be perfect just because I'm getting married. I don't want perfect. I want you. It's hard for you. I know it is. And that's okay. I can't even imagine how hard this would all be if I didn't have a father. It means a lot that you are doing all of this with me despite that."

I shook my head, swallowed gigantically. I felt wet alongside my nose, cold, a little refreshing.

She hugged me tight, and then we got out of the taxi and she pulled a key ring out of her purse.

"Oh my god! The spa!"

Three floors up, it was all beams and dust, but you could just see how great it was going to be. The potential was all there. Some places you just walk into, and you can tell that. And I thought, if Nina had come this far, well then I would, too. I'd face my father once and for all; I'd fight for those memories, and for this life. After all, in between dark stages, I had sometimes felt that same flicker of possibility that I felt in Nina's spa—felt that I could be something great, too.

Ray and I spent the evening inappropriately groping each other in public at Sampson's. I enjoyed myself immensely. Everything felt right. Like it was falling into place once and for all.

5:30 a.m., Wednesday, December 21

James was a tiny, new spot in the East Village, which served beautiful free-range chicken, with dramatic sprigs of rosemary, and pot roast with big, rustic carrot chunks. The wine list was exclusively Parisian, but only boutique labels. I'd taken Nina in place of Ray because she begged me. She said she wouldn't become chopped liver because Ray and I became a couple. But she complained the whole time that she didn't like small places with small tables that served food still on the bone. She only had negative things to say of rosemary.

"Why would I want to eat a Christmas tree?" she demanded.

She complained so much, I was waiting for her head to pop off. I couldn't imagine what was making her so ornery.

"I don't know if I love Bernard," she blurted out after declaring the carrot cake far too creamy.

"Nina," I whispered. I didn't know what to say.

"I don't know if it's Bernard or actually getting married. I think I'm completely screwed up. Now I'm actually having a wedding, I keep getting disappointed, thinking . . . isn't this supposed to be so much more monumental than this? Isn't the linen supposed to be crisper, the invitation weightier? Where are the chubby singing cherubs and the little animated chipmunks that talk?" She cleared her throat, as she'd gotten loud.

I waved away her apprehension.

I remembered something that Fenwick had said.

"You know what, Nina? There's no such thing as perfect."

Too quickly she responded, "I know *that*."

I gave it a second to sink in, as I knew this was one of those things you could know without actually grasping its full meaning. And then I said again, "There's no such thing as perfect."

When a waterfall sprouted from Nina's eyes, I figured she got it. I handed her my cloth napkin and offered some advice. If I was considering doing this for a living, I might as well try some advice out.

"In the meanwhile, why don't you set up a little test and do more things without Bernard. This will help you to see how you really feel about him. It will make you miss him."

She was quiet for a moment; she hiccuped. "That is a very good idea, Anna. So, what are *you* doing later?"

"Anything you want," I said, glad to be there for her, finally.

I was ready to leave, and then Nina said, "Hey, why don't we ask for a little more of that carrot cake?"

"You mean the one that's too creamy?" I joked.

"Yeah. That's the one."

Afterward, we went to Sampson's and got loaded off the sweet college drinks we used to love—cranberry juice and vodka. Pete indulged us in some obvious flattery, and we spent twenty bucks on the jukebox playing old Led Zeppelin songs and imagining ourselves having epiphanies left and right. After all the swanky places I'd been, I would have thought I'd outgrown our local dive. But that hadn't happened at all. Instead, I'd been far and wide and come back with a new perspective: Everything I've ever wanted was always right here. I just had to figure out how to get it, was all.

Thursday, December 22

Most people were giddy with the idea of being off for four days—more so in the case of those staying out until the new year. I'd already eaten so much caramel and cheese popcorn from a gigantic tin with Santa on it that I had to unbutton my pants. I sat back in my chair, pulling my blouse hem down a little farther to cover up the open button.

★ ★ ★

Later I handed in the article to Ed. He handed me another bag of mail.

> *Dear Anna,*
>   *I wanted to wish you good luck visiting your father's gravesite. I* *lost my mother a few years back, and I know how difficult it can be.* *Merry Christmas,*
> *Stacy Miller*

I looked at the letter and started a new document. I called it "advice column." A half hour later, the phone rang.

"Hello," I said, breaking away from the screen.

"Anna, Ed wants to see you." It was Belinda, and she had a strange tone to her voice.

"Oh no." I knew already. "It didn't work, did it?"

"No." She sounded as deflated as I felt. All the adrenaline, all the hope, like a snapped elevator, now it screamed down into the moldy basement of loss.

As I made my way to Belinda, the office was quiet. Minutes ago, I'd been happy for that, enjoying the rush of an inspired writing jag, creating something I was actually proud of. But now it seemed to say something different—everyone had gone and left me behind.

People had taped printer paper banners across their cubicle openings that read, "Gone to get drunk," or "Happy Freaking New Year." These were creative people, and their kinds of jokes. I wouldn't have ever thought of those things. I should have recognized this as a sign.

"Hi," the receptionist said with her own brand of bland friendliness, passing by me on her way back to her perch.

After all this time, it hadn't been quite as rewarding as I imagined it—her acknowledging me. I watched her ponytail swish rhythmically to and fro, keeping time, perfect time, though for me, it had stopped dead.

"Are you okay?" I whispered when I approached Belinda's desk. She looked smaller, less vibrant somehow. Her hair was crushed in on one side. "It's not your fault, Belinda. We did everything we could. We did." But I knew it was more than that that had her this way. "This isn't the end, you know," I said, though I'd felt it, too, the screeching of the brakes, the burning smell of it.

Belinda just shook her head, her lips pursed and walked me to Ed's door. She squeezed my arm, just below the elbow and held it a second or two. She knocked twice, opened the door, and shuttled me inside, closing herself outside the door.

"He's ready for you," was all she said, as if anything else would break her. She looked miserable, chewing on her pink lip.

I made my way to the empty armchair, somehow, but I didn't know what to do with my hands. They kept making their way to my sleeves.

Ed had his elbows on his desk. All the times I'd been in there before, he'd sung my name like a doorbell, "An-na!" But now he just jerked his head in slight acknowledgment.

He waited a moment before he spoke. "The good news, as you know, is that your column was a hit. For some reason, people are interested in your life, Anna. They want to know what you're going to do with Rick or whoever, and they want to see you happy, angry, whatever."

Was. Such a short little innocent-sounding word.

"*I* even started to enjoy it by the end. But, I never in a million years would have thought it would be so popular. Honestly, you don't know a thing about journalism. Your writing . . . needs work . . . to say the least." He shook his head and let out a stab of a laugh. "You couldn't get fewer facts about the bars in there if you tried . . ."

I shook my head in agreement. "Aha."

"Despite these problems, sometimes phenomena occur. You have a voice, an instinct that just works. People respond."

"The thing is, Anna, despite all the times Joe begged me to get rid of your column, I was dead set on keeping it. Shit, you got us tons of advertising, as you know."

Finally, something rose in me, and I yelled, "Ed, what *is* it already?"

His eyes flickered, expanded. "You don't have to *yell*," he said, his chin dropping.

"Sorry," I said. "You're just dragging this out way longer than is necessary."

"Okay, well, then here it is. I have it from a trusted source that your streak is coming to an end. If I keep you on, it will mean the end of *New York, New York*. So, you understand. I have to let you go. You fit the profile of the person my, um, source said I had to ax—the pimples, the thinning hair, the bridesmaid thing . . . so you're out. Happy New Year. Can you send Belinda in here on your way out?"

But I hadn't come this far to give up like that. "You're kidding, right? Surely you aren't firing me with a successful column that is bringing in tons of money for you." I wouldn't say anything about Rima. I wouldn't hurt her that way, but I could give myself one last shot.

"I know, it sounds nuts. But I always listen to this, um, source, in these matters. She told me to do everything I've done along the way, and it has worked perfectly. I'm just not going to go and change things now."

"Ed. Please, tell me what I can do. Maybe I can go to your source, and they can verify that I am not the person she was seeing.

It could be someone else. It could be . . . Joseph, even! He has some pimples, and certainly his hair is thinner than last year! I wouldn't be surprised if he was trying on bridesmaid's dresses!" Not my proudest moment exactly.

"No. No. It's you. I'm sorry. She said it was a woman . . . although with Joseph, who knows . . . but it *was* you. She also said the person steals toilet paper from the ladies room, and everyone knows you do that. And *nobody* sees Rim—um, my source, you see—but me. Nobody. Now pack your stuff up, Anna. Oh, and have a happy New Year!"

I don't know how I did it, but I got up. I walked myself to the door. And then I turned around and said, "Thanks a lot!" I slammed the door as hard as I could as if that might say something I hadn't.

The few people left stood up to gawk. Belinda pulled her coat around my shoulders and said, "Let's go take a walk, child." Just then, all I wanted to be was a child.

It was freezing outside, but Belinda didn't seem to mind, in her flimsy blouse. "Listen, he's nuts. Everyone knows that. You knew that. And he's right about the toilet paper—we all know. What do you want that sandpaper crap for anyway, dear?"

"Enough with the toilet paper. I'm sorry! I don't know what I did that for! But it was crazy! The way he started asking about my pimples . . . which aren't even there anymore! It was just one, really, anyway. And it might have even been hives. I ate a strawberry. It could have been that."

Belinda looked at me sympathetically. She turned very serious and then said, "That was no hive."

"How could you fire someone right before Christmas?" I asked to the building tops, the cloud of my breath. We were at the back of the building now, walking fast. Everyone seemed to be going the opposite way, so that we had to cut through the stream of them.

"Lunacy waits for no man," Belinda said, lighting a cigarette.

3:30 p.m.

I sat at my desk and stared at my computer screen for a good while before attempting to pack anything. Nobody was around. It was just me. When the receptionist left, she showed me how to lock the door behind me. She showed me how to punch in the code outside the door, and then she said, "Hey, I'm real sorry about your column," she said. "I really enjoyed it."

Imagine that.

I put some music on—a mix CD I'd gotten at World—and started backing up all of my contacts and files. I told Ray what happened while I watched the file icons fly on the screen over to my CD. I waited for him to offer to come and help me with it, but I knew he wouldn't. It was something I should do on my own, and I knew he would see it that way, too.

I grabbed a couple of boxes from the mail room, taped them up with signs for keeping and saving, and like I heard you should on an organization program, I started from the bottom up. On the bottom, there was a lot of dust. All the pairs of shoes I stored down there were covered with a layer of gray that started to rise all around me when I picked them up. There was the sensible pair that I never wear, and next to them, there was the nonsensible, beautiful pair that David had bought for me after the LYMJ fiasco.

I sat there, with my legs crossed beneath me, and this pair of shoes brought me back to that first night. I'd been so scared and insecure about the column, about my qualifications for writing it, for being the kind of person who could actually do something like this.

But I hadn't been right. I had done a great job. No matter what Ed said, I'd entertained people. Those people had felt so connected to the content that they'd written me letters about it. They'd invested thousands of dollars in advertising pages. They wanted to see what my bridesmaid dress looked like, and it meant something to them that Ray and I actually make it. It seemed unbelievable that something like that had landed in my lap. And it seemed unbelievable that something like that had been yanked away just as easily.

I tucked my shoes into the box—heel to toe—though I didn't think I would wear them. They were part of the past. They were beautiful, fabulous, and something I would always think of in my heart with warmth, with the idea that I wouldn't have gotten to this point I'm at with Ray without them.

There was a huge mailbag under my desk, and I dug my hand inside to pull out a few letters.

Dear Anna,

I know what you mean about Christmas being hard. I think the holidays can be pretty difficult. In fact, I kind of dread it. You see, I don't have a family, and I always wind up walking around feeling useless on Christmas. I'd like to handle it differently next year. Do you have any ideas on where a person might go on Christmas by themselves?

Sincerely,

Erin K.

Right then and there, I put down my packing and pulled out a sheet of paper and wrote back to Erin K.

Dear Erin,

I am beyond sorry to hear you feel that way at the holidays. I, too, have a very difficult time around Christmas . . . in fact, every single time I go home. You see, my father died in a fire when I was eight years old, and I always blamed myself for not rushing down to the basement through the flames to rescue him. I hated to go home and face all this, and so I took myself out of the life game and avoided everything as best I could. But then I realized you have to

make things happen for yourself. You have to just forge forward, put the bad stuff aside, and make good things come into your life. If I were you, next year I would tell one of my friends that I'd like to spend Christmas with them. Really get into it and enjoy yourself. You'll see . . . you'll snowball from there. The next year, maybe you'll throw your own holiday party. On Christmas Eve, I always like to go to (don't tell anyone this, because it is so not New York, New York) Benihana. It is a great show, and you sit with a whole bunch of people, and so you won't feel lonely.
Best regards,
Anna
    P.S.: E-mail me anytime at anna@supermail.com

I sealed the letter inside an envelope and dropped it down the mail chute before I could take it back. It felt wonderful to help that girl. Really wonderful . . . much better than trying to fit in at some swanky bar that didn't want me in the first place. I got the sense that maybe all the pain had a purpose after all.

Into my "keeping" box, I plunked fun trinkets from the different bar giftbags—key chains and notepads and funky pens that light up in waves of fiber optic color. And then there was my mug. There were no words left on it at all, as if I had nothing left to learn from it, as if it had been somehow more powerful than just a token I'd kept. I threw everything from inside of it out into the garbage, and I planned to bring it home and use it for drinking—bring it into my everyday life and face it that way.

I went and got a coke from the machine and shifted over to the desk chair to empty my drawers. I laughed at a funny picture of Nina and me from last Halloween. We were Rocky and Adrian. I had a pair of boxing gloves hanging around my neck and one of those uncomfortable plastic mouth guards over my teeth.

Nobody recognized Nina's costume. She had on a dark wig and

unfashionable glasses. Ray went as Drago. He wouldn't pose for any pictures. He kept saying, "No photos, no photos," as if this were part of his disguise. I saw a portion of his hand in this photo, and I was overwhelmed. I wanted to see him now.

At 11 o'clock, I frantically stuffed the rest of my belongings into the box and a couple of shopping bags, arranged them in my arms, draped the mailbag over my shoulder, and said good-bye to *New York, New York*. For the second . . . and final time.

11:15 p.m.

I tried Ray once more on his cell phone before I reached our apartment via taxicab. I couldn't get him. I snapped the phone shut and squeezed it tight. I tipped the taxi driver a couple extra bucks, because I was feeling symbolic.

Once I was in our hallway, I realized I was going to need to take two trips to get all this stuff upstairs. I left one of the boxes and grabbed the other and the mailbag and huffed up the three flights.

I struggled as one of the box sides seemed to give way and finally tossed it in front of the door. I knocked to see if he was home, but there was no answer. "Jesus!" I yelled to no one, to the empty hall and all of my belongings and my firing and my insane ex-boss. I stamped my way back down the hallway toward the staircase like a child. Mrs. Olstead came out. "I should have known!" she yelled. "I'll have you thrown out."

I turned around and blamed all of my problems on her. "Good!" I yelled back so strong my whole body jerked with the force of the words. "Then I won't have to live across from you anymore!" She was that bad, and so—obviously—was Nasty. And I wasn't going to give everyone a million chances anymore.

You could hear a pin drop then as I stood at the top of the staircase. It was so quiet. And then, just as I stepped down the top stair, I heard a chuckle. And if I wasn't nuts, it sounded like it was coming right out from behind my own apartment door. Olstead and I looked at each other, and then I stamped over there, fished in my coat pocket for my keys, and shimmied the lock open. And then the other lock, and the other lock, and finally the last one.

The door pushed open slightly, and then I undid the chain latch. The light streaming out through that tiny sliver was flickering, like the moon on a lake.

"What the?" I pushed the door all the way open, and there were candles—hundreds of them.

"Well, what *is* it?" Olstead asked, unable to see obviously, from where she was standing. The tiny tea lights were on the dining table and on the breakfast bar and the coffee table and the unused fireplace mantle. And right there on the couch, in his torn Knicks T-shirt and old college basketball shorts was Ray. It was the most welcoming sight then—like coming home, finally, after a long, hard journey. And he was smiling gingerly, as if he hoped that were the right reaction. He was so adorable, with his green eyes so nervous and his perfect features, which I never would have dreamed I'd fall for. The thing was that his imperfections were on the inside. There were things about him that only I could appreciate, and that made him infinitely loveable to me, for me.

"Welcome home to the rest of your life," he said.

Mrs. Olstead poked her head through the doorway. She was smiling, there it was—something she'd held private all this time, and then she yelled, "That's a fire hazard, you know!" and she slammed the door shut.

"Olstead." I shrugged.

"Olstead," he said. "Hey, Anna—"

I cut him off. "Shhhh," I said and leaned in, kissed him, amazed by him this way. With that honesty and those eyes and the fumbling, stumbling for the right words—a Ray I had never known before.

Ray helped me up with the rest of my things. And then I watched this mysterious Ray cook, trying and failing to toss mushrooms in the air. Then we ate filet mignon with one mushroom each (the two that had not wound up on the floor) and string beans. We drank martinis with six olives apiece. And then we were in his bed, the old plaid sheets and the worn comforter. And we lay, two people who've known each other for a very long time and were now discovering a funny scar that looks like the state of New Mexico and a freckle that could be mistaken for Mickey Mouse on each other's bodies.

"Ray, hey, I don't want to ruin the moment or anything."

"Oh no, here it goes. I'll wash the dishes tomorrow morning. I promise." He pressed his hands together in prayer, willing me not to push him on this now.

"It's not the dishes," I said, smiling. I knew he'd never do them in the morning. "It's just, I was wondering. What is it exactly that you see in me?"

His smile inverted. He looked at my face through drooping eyelids. I thought he must be searching for something, because it would be pretty bad to come up with no answer to that question. His chin quivered the slightest bit, like an old woman's hand might, and then stopped. "You don't know. Do you? You've shown me how to love. I don't know if you realized it before, but I have gone through quite a lot of women, and I've used them pretty poorly. Each one, every single one, I hoped—maybe this one! Maybe this one I can love! But never, and nothing. Each one a miserable failure. I thought it was them, but then it became impossible, ridiculous. It was me. It was always me. I couldn't open up. I couldn't say the simplest thing. I couldn't say—no, I didn't have a nice weekend; my grandmother died. I wanted to, but I didn't know how, and I just . . . I just couldn't. It sounds dumb to someone like you, so in touch with their feelings, I know, but for me . . . it's, I don't know, it was impos-

sible. Don't you ever wonder why I never had any other close
friends besides you? They just don't stick around. They don't stick
around, because they don't know me. And how could they?

"But you—you reached down into the worst parts of you, and
you brought me into that, and you let me help you. It was, it was a
wonderful thing to feel that with you and for you, to watch you
grow and to know I'd been a part of it. We've always had that
something—you and me. And this, this way you've opened me, it
just brought me over the top for you."

1:00 a.m.

Later, we were warm in each other's arms, in blankets. I finally
brought it up. I said, "I can't believe my editor is a lunatic and makes
all his business decisions based on the advice of a psychic named
Rima, who said he needed to fire me because I had a hive and my
hair was thinning."

"That was no hive," Ray said.

I smothered him with a pillow and roared with laughter. The
dirty martinis had dulled the anger.

"Shit," Ray said, more serious, the pillow tucked under his arm.

"I'll drink to that," I said.

"I bet you Fenprick would say this is a great test for you, though,"
Ray said. And that's why he's so perfect for me. It really is.

10:00 a.m., Friday, December 23

"Anna, Anna, Anna, Anna." Fenprick looked over my journal and
ran his palm over his thick, thick hair. He blinked three times, bit
the side of his bottom lip, and then said, "Shit, you've had a bad
week."

I didn't know what to say to that. Surprisingly, I wanted to smile, as if I'd been recognized for outstanding achievement. Yes it is true! I had a horrible time! Now I am free to go home and fall into a deep depression, or revert back to that avoidance thing that I found so easy, so much easier than this failure I feel now. Whatever the reason for my termination, I had only one equation in mind: Bad writing + no talent = failure. I'd doodled that at least four times on the last page I'd entered into the journal.

"So," he continued, taking his regular stance, ankle over knee, hands folded over it. "I guess you think you should have never taken the chance and that you failed because you have no talent and you write badly. I guess you should just try to get your old job back."

Sadly, I had thought that exact thing that morning. It seemed my replacement was no longer around, and I thought Nasty and I might be even now. It would be like coming full circle; it had a certain poetic appeal. Maybe I could do wan assistant. "Of course not," I said.

"Good!" He smiled. "In fact, you've come so far . . . this is just the kind of obstacle you need to show you that you can overcome anything, that no matter what type of bad luck seems to land in your lap that you're never going to let that ruin your life again! This might sound crazy, but I'm *glad* you lost your job."

"Thanks?" I screwed my face up.

"Now get yourself out there and find an even better way to use your talents. You said yourself you didn't really like going to all these bars."

Sure, it had been okay to say this then—when I was afraid I didn't fit in and that everyone thought I was lame. But now that I wasn't going to get free outfits and dinners and be treated like Lindsay Lohan all the time, I did miss it. Plus, trying something that I really wanted would leave me excuseless in the case that it didn't work out. But I couldn't say that.

"Don't forget," he said. "You're going to your father's grave this weekend."

How, ever, could I forget that?

TWELVE
You Live for the Now . . .

Fittingly, this week's bar is called CHRISTMAS. At first I thought it was a great idea—Christmas all year round, that majesty and charm, the spindly leaves of mistletoe. I walked in and spent some time by the hearth, next to the twelve-foot Christmas tree, done up in the traditional style—ribbons and balls in red and gold. A giant angel watching over the top. But after an hour it was too much. We'd just had Christmas, and now I was thinking maybe there's a reason we only have it once a year.

—Velvet Rope Diaries, *New York, New York*

9:30 p.m., December 23

"I'm outside," my mom said into the cell phone.

Ray and I were sitting on the couch. We'd been kissing. He'd been feeling inside my waistband. "I love you, Anna," he whispered. It was the first time he'd said it.

This might sound insane, but he was the first guy to say that to me for real. It sounded funny, since I'd only ever heard it from my mother before. And that's why I laughed, though that wasn't any reflection at all of my feelings.

"Oh my god, I'm sorry," I said. But I didn't say it back. The words just didn't come, though I wished them to. I knew what it was. I recognized this barrier, this tight rubber that bounced all the good things back—off where they'd come from, away, far away from me. How many people must I have hurt this way, not meaning to, but hurting all the same?

His nose squiggled, but he quickly steeled himself.

"I'll get the bags," he said and walked out the door in front of me with two shopping bags loaded with presents and our overnight bags, too. He looked so hurt in his big, tall body, his stiff hair gel no match for such hurt.

I did love Ray. But it scared the shit out of me!

"Ray!" My mother insisted he sit in the front seat.

I stuffed myself into the back and craned around to kiss her and then crouched in the seat behind Ray. I could slightly see his face in the side-view mirror.

"How's work?" my mother asked him. She had on a red turtle-neck and a snowflake pin. Her hair had been set, I could see.

"We've been working with a new tech stock that's pretty hot. The guys are going nuts for it," he said. My mother loved this shoptalk. For a short time she was a secretary at a firm and worked entering orders for the traders. She reminded him of this now, though she'd said it before.

"You know I used to work down on Wall Street. I was every-one's favorite inputter. I really loved it. So exciting." She'd quit be-cause I was having so many problems in school that she wanted to be right there in Long Island if I needed her, if they called her to say, "Mrs. Walker, Anna is crumpled up in the corner of the girl's bath-room and she won't get up."

My mother would never say that, though Ray already knew it. He knew it and loved me anyway.

"I just hated the commute," she said, though I remember her

saying it was such a great time to relax, read the paper, do some knitting.

All I want for Christmas is to stop hurting people, I thought. It was unbelievable, my capacity for this.

"Don't you two make a beautiful couple," she said, looking at me in the rearview and then over at Ray. She took his hand, and I could see a couple of tears in her eyes. I wove my hand through the space between Ray's door and the seat and found his other hand and squeezed it myself. I squeezed it three times to the rhythm of "I. Love. You." And he smiled—a little distorted in the rearview. He knew me.

My old bedroom still scared the crap out of me . . . but a little less so. The stuffed pig appeared a little friendlier. The porcelain toad—nearly sympathetic. There were all the high school pictures still. We'd go out and see those guys later. We'd wonder what the hell had happened back on Thanksgiving, laugh over the things we couldn't remember. Thomas would sulk in a corner and hook up with another girl in front of me. Ray wouldn't like him, but he'd say he did. And on the long, freezing walk home, I would turn to Ray and say, "I love you, too." We'd walk home in silence, have sex, giggling wildly in my room and yelling, "Sshhh!!!" while we cupped each other's mouths to drown out the laughter. There would be a plush rabbit that tickled Ray's butt.

"Ray, you'll be staying in the spare bedroom," Roger said now, trying to look gruff.

Ray looked at the flowered bedspread, the quilt framed on the far wall and chortled, "Manly, isn't it?"

Roger laughed and shrugged like there was nothing he could do.

★ ★ ★

The four of us went to dinner at Benihana. We sat at a huge hibachi table with a younger family of four. There was a young girl and boy—both somewhere between five and seven years old. "Dad! When is the guy going to throw the shrimp in the air?" the boy kept asking.

"Soon," the dad said, wise in his knowing this thing.

We all ordered some kind of stir-fry, and our waiter, "Steven," stepped up to the sizzling hot grill and slathered on some hot oil with the back of his spatula.

"Oooooh," the little boy and girl called when it started to bubble up. Steven juggled the spatula and a ginsu knife like a carnival clown.

"Oh my," my mother said, her hand at her heart. "That really is outrageous, isn't it?" She loved Benihana. I could tell she was getting excited, by the way she kept touching her hair with her fingertips.

"When's the guy going to throw the shrimp in the air?" the boy yelled.

Steven looked at him and smiled big.

The boy beamed and then looked into his Coke. I didn't allow myself to wish I were him. Instead I appreciated his view of this, his experience of this, and gathered it into my life bundle, folded it up to pack in the middle of it all.

Steven had sliced an onion into generous rings and piled them into a volcano. He placed some butter on the grill, moved the volcano over it, and out came a steaming butter eruption.

We all clapped at the feat.

"Did I hear someone say shrimp?" Steven asked.

The boy looked gingerly to his dad—suddenly shy—to check that this was all right. His dad nodded.

The boy raised his hand and meekly uttered, "*I did?*"

Steven pulled a silvery shrimp from a platter with his spatula and tossed it up in the air, spun around, caught it behind his back and then flipped it onto the hibachi. Within seconds, he flipped it over, chopped off the tail, scooped up the tail with the spatula, and sent it sailing way up high only to nonchalantly lean back, hold his breast pocket open with a thumb and catch the shrimp tail inside of it.

The boy was mesmerized. Steven was good.

"Now who ordered the steak?"

"Me!" I called, relaxed somewhat from the sweet plum wine, thinking there had to be hope if simple pleasures like this one still existed.

6:00 p.m., Saturday, December 24

The next day, Christmas Eve, was going to be the culmination of it all. It was going to be a face-to-face. Me. The cemetery. The attempt to accomplish this thing, this impossible thing I had sat at the window and tried to work out, peeling paint off the sill, half hoping morbidly it contained lead, nature's method of revenge—this color hat and that scent of rose, those tears and who'd been looking at me how, thinking she should have and if only she had. Later, there'd be a honey glazed ham, mashed potatoes with white gravy, fresh asparagus spears, and homemade rolls that mom and I had prepared, our fingers through the lumpy, just-wet dough, while Ray and Roger laughed over a football game and unflattering photos from my formative years.

Ray drove the SUV along the Southern State to the cemetery, and we didn't say much. There were abandoned roadwork projects here and there—a few crushed cones and lots of dirt dusting everything. I wasn't going to leave my own projects that way, unfinished and unusable, vacant and helpless. Inside, my chest was a drinking cup with no drink, waiting, hoping to see what would come and fill it. My hand curled around a bunch of amaryllis like a life preserver.

Santa baby, hurry down the chimney tonight.

I hated that I didn't remember this exit and the main street name and the plot number. I had to go into the little office that smelled like frankincense and ask, "Can you tell me where plot number C32 is?" I hated that I didn't say "my father's plot," because I was ashamed that I didn't know where it was.

"Why, of course I can," the man said in a gentle voice. He was young, I thought, to be working at a cemetery. He wore a pinstriped suit and a somber navy tie. He removed a photocopied map from a pile on a table and uncorked a yellow highlighter. On the sheet he traced the path to my father's grave. While he did, I realized what a silly thing I'd thought—there was no appropriate age for death. There was just the randomness of it and the struggle to pick up the pieces.

"There is something almost alive about a fire. It needs food, it reacts to heat and cold, and it takes in oxygen. And when you're trying to put it out, a fire even seems to have a mind of its own. In order to stop a fire, firefighters need to know exactly what keeps it alive."

When I returned to the car, Ray looked uncomfortable, but he tried to cover it up. "Okay, so where we goin'?" he asked, attempting a little too hard to be cheerful.

I showed him the map and said, "I think you just go straight and then make the last right." While we drove, the Christmas music continued, completely oblivious to where it was.

I'm dreaming of a white Christmas . . .

Bits were coming back now. I thought I remembered that twisted tree. I thought I could feel myself standing with my mother, not exactly sure of where we were and why we were there. I nearly remembered hearing them say his name, Martin Walker, and understanding that he was in there in that black box and now lower and lower and then the dirt—thump! But I couldn't be sure. I didn't need to be, Dr. Fenwick had said. I didn't need to be sure. After all of those years of painstakingly attempting to figure it all out exactly, I shouldn't even try. I should just go and be there now, whether it had been white roses or red, whether there'd been a lot of tears, or silent numbness, whether my shoelace had charred slightly or caught into flame.

I liked that Ray didn't ask, that he just came with me. Because if he'd asked, I probably would have said, "No, you can stay in the car," without having meant it at all. We walked slowly from the car and carried on an unnecessary discussion over whether we should lock the doors. "You never know," I said, just wasting one more second, just holding on to the car door as long as I could.

"Come," Ray said. He had my hand in his, and I looked at him now. He looked scared, too. *Everyone hates cemeteries*, I thought. Inappropriately, I remembered a stupid joke I once heard. *This corpse walks into a bar . . .* It didn't seem very funny now, though I'd laughed terribly; I'd laughed like a murderer might.

"When you open an oven door to remove fresh baked cookies, that oven is heated to about 350 Fahrenheit. A fire burns almost three times hotter."

At the grave, the grass was a little wet, probably from the dusting of snow we'd had overnight. Even now, it surprised me to see my last name up there on a headstone. "Martin Walker—loved by all, 1953–1983," it read.

I wasn't sure what to do. I fiddled with the plastic sheet around the flowers for a minute or so and then lay them down, and then leaned over and pushed them over a little to the left. I stood and looked at the stone waiting for something to happen. I tried to think of a time before he'd died—something we'd done together. But the only thing I could think then was him on the step with that cup of coffee, with that mug, which lay on my desk at work, all that time collecting dust and paper clips and the odd scrap of paper— and now was at home. It was really all I had; everything else I'd trampled over, destroyed with my *could I*'s? and *should I*'s? With a start, I erupted like Steven's volcano—all those losses I had blanketed over with guilt were coming to light in little domino reactions now. Here was my father lying under there. Here was the five minutes I'd tethered myself to all these years. Here—could I leave it?

Ray was wet-eyed, his freshly buzzed eyebrows jumpy. Inside his Wall Street wool coat, which I'd once considered to be smug, he now pulled me—the silky lining cool and warm at the same time. Everything, up and down simultaneously. Good with bad. *I love you.* One day I would believe it. And he held me there as long as I stood, and when I looked up there was a beautiful thing. There was snow. And it was falling down around us like a miracle.

5:00 a.m., Sunday, December 25

We woke up on Christmas at five o'clock in the morning, so that we could exchange gifts and then drive over to New Jersey to join Ray's family.

My mother was decked head to toe: Rudolph slippers with light-up red noses, snowflake pajamas, and a Frosty pin.

"She's so unfestive," Roger said. He was in a black sweat suit and mismatched socks with a hole at the left big toe.

"Oh, looks like Santa left you something in your stocking!" my mom said. "And Ray, too, and Roger, and someone named . . . Mom!" She lived for this, so we indulged.

"Who's Mom?" I asked.

"I never heard of her," Roger said.

"Was that the one on *Three's Company* after Chrissy left?" Ray joked.

"Yeah, yeah, I think I know who you mean." Roger pointed his finger, *bingo*, winked with a click of his tongue.

I turned my stocking upside down exactly the same way I always did, and out tumbled snowflake socks and cherry Chapstick and knee-highs in a plastic gumball machine globe, a package of Twizzlers, some chewing gum, and a tiny book about kittens no bigger than a cake of soap.

"How does Santa always know that I love Twizzlers?" I asked. "I must be a very good girl for him to notice something like that," I said, tearing open the cellophane, pulling off one of the sticky ropes.

"You are," my mom said. She grew somber for a second and said, "You always have been." Before the tear could come, she said, "Ray, go ahead!"

Ray seemed a little shy to open up gifts like that in front of my mother and Roger, which made me smile unexpectedly. I watched as he slowly pulled out one negligible item after another and reacted as if they'd bought him property in Malibu. "A new toothbrush!" he called out. "A pack of Double Mint gum!"

We were in stitches by the time he pulled the deck of cards out of the very bottom of his stocking. "Plastic coated!" he exclaimed.

Then came the big gifts. Roger had bought my mother a new computerized sewing machine that does all kinds of fancy quilting stitches on its own. My mother had bought Roger a fancy saw that does all kinds of notch cutting on its own. I had bought Roger a tiny television for the garage, where he's always working on something. And I got my mother a gift certificate for a spa day. Ray had bought them both a gift certificate to a little Italian restaurant they love, and I hadn't even known he had done that. They bought him a cozy green fleece with a zipper and a hood. I received a portable music device and a royal blue cashmere scarf.

They loaned us Roger's tan Taurus to drive to New Jersey. They were going to pick it up in Manhattan the following day. It was always unbelievable to me—their bottomless generosity, always giving. Roger had a Maroon 5 CD in the player, and we played it the whole way, over and over again without knowing most of the words, the hangovers starting to sink in, drying up our mouths and energy.

Ray's hand lay on mine, and I thought as we approached the

New Jersey Turnpike, that we looked quite beautiful that way—his one purple nail and my dried, peeling cuticles and all.

8:00 a.m., Sunday, December 25

Ray's family is loud. They speak very loud, and they clap loud, and they walk loud.

"ANNA, THAT PURSE IS PERFECT FOR YOU!" Mrs. Right exclaimed. We were all on the floor—around the tree, which was weighed down with ornaments of every color imaginable on every single branch. It was fake, but they sprayed it with "Christmas Tree Scent," so it smelled like a pine forest and the inside of a bottle of wine. It was very generous of them to buy me a pricey Captain purse. They really shouldn't have. But they did everything big—it was their way.

Ray smiled at me. He knew I could clam up in a situation like that.

After gifts, we moved over to the dining room for a huge lunch. There was turkey and sweet potatoes and stuffing, just like Thanksgiving all over again. We were all wearing our gifts—that's how they did it in the Right family. I had my purse over my shoulder. Ray's sister, Rita, had strung my arm through the strap. Rita had a fluffy, multicolor scarf with glittery bits around her neck, a cowboy hat on her head, and black stiletto boots on her feet. Her new lipgloss was slicked over her mouth. Mrs. Right brought the turkey out, wearing a brand-new purple silk robe and a diamond bracelet, which she showed off by rolling up her right sleeve to the elbow. And Mr. Right had reindeer boxer shorts pulled on right over his jeans. He spun around slowly so we could all laugh so hard we choked on our sodas. Ray got a flat-screen television, and since that was difficult to wear, he had the cord wrapped around his waist like a belt.

"So, you two are finally going out, huh?" Rita said, stuffing a potato roll into her mouth.

Ray shot her a look like she should shut the hell up. I kept quiet.

"We all had bets, you know," she said.

"Ha ha," Ray said. He grabbed for my hand under the table.

"No really. Mom had last May, Dad had two years ago New Year's, and I actually won with the closest—September of this year. I got three hundred bucks."

Mr. and Mrs. Right looked down into their plates. Rita had a big mouth and a sense of embitterment, with her divorce still fresh. We all knew that. Still there were certain things you didn't say to people's faces. The thing was, Rita didn't care to know it.

"Hey, don't worry, Mom and Dad, it's fine. We know it took us a long time to figure it out." Ray was trying to be extra understanding. Rita had suffered greatly. Holidays were the most difficult under those circumstances.

"And about three hundred girls," Rita mumbled into her fist and then cleared her throat.

My face burned. I knew this already. It was one of the things that had scared the shit out of me, one of the reasons I've been so afraid to throw myself into this. But I didn't want to think about it now. I just wanted to think about us, now. I knew Rita was just acting out. I could understand being mad at the world, but this was a bit much. I searched for words, but they all sounded condescending, simple, from where I sat.

"What the heck are you trying to do here, Rita? It's Christmas, in case you haven't noticed." Ray wasn't exactly yelling, but you could feel the anger in his voice. The whole mood changed. In between Mr. Right's underwear and my first bite of turkey, the ice age had come upon us. A fork dropped on the plate, and it was intolerably loud.

"Yeah, so? Christmas sucks when your husband left you and picked up a new wife the very next week at a speed-dating event! I tried to be festive, but . . . it's just not going to work. I'm sorry." She pushed her chair out. The screech of it echoed in the open format floor, seemed to cycle around through the living room and kitchen, and hit us again from behind. She thumped up the stairs and said, "This scarf is ugly." Then she slammed the door of her bedroom, the one she was living in again, and we all let out our breath.

Ray and I watched *It's a Wonderful Life* back to back, because we were too lazy to change the channel. During the second viewing, right after Henry Travers says, "Strange isn't it? Each man's life touches so many other lives. When he isn't around, he leaves an awful hole, doesn't he?" Rita came down to the TV room—the one unfinished room in the Right house, the one that still felt like it hadn't changed in about fifteen years, with its paneling and institutional ceiling tiles and faded-out corduroy sofa.

She plopped down right in the space between Ray and I, which was pretty small, so that she was half sitting on the both of us. She put both her arms out, behind our shoulders and pulled us in tightly. I thought of a time in college, when she'd gone to a keg party with us and done acrobatics on an open lawn. After each move, she arched her back severely and flung her hands up in the air until people cheered.

Now she started to cry. She cried and cried, her back heaving against my chest and Ray's, too, so that her misery shook us both.

"Welcome home, Mr. Bailey," Donna Reed said warmly.

In a quiet hour, I began a pitch letter about my advice column. If there was something I'd learned this holiday, it was that people needed help—lots of it.

10:30 p.m., December 25

Ray's friend Peter picked us up in front of the house in an old diesel Volvo station wagon. "Peter, this is Anna," Ray introduced us and opened the door for me to sit in front.

"Hi, Peter." I stuck my hand through the door, but insisted Ray take the front.

"No, you go," Ray said.

"No, you," I said.

"One of you get in the friggin' car! In case you haven't noticed, it's freezing out there!"

Ray climbed in finally. "I guess I *do* have long legs," he said.

"Geez," Peter said. "When did you become such a pansy?"

"He's always been a pansy," I offered. "He even watches Lifetime with me sometimes," I said, sticking my body through the space between the two front seats. I instantly liked Peter, his tone, his relaxed way.

"Nice!" Peter said, smiling wickedly at me in the rearview.

"So what's up?" Ray asked his friend.

"Ah, you know," he said. And it was, I could tell right off the bat, the "you know" of still living with your parents, of never having had anything work out quite the way you'd thought it would, and now seeing everyone for whom it had and acting like it didn't bother you. Not one bit.

The party was at the house of Ray's friend Linus. Linus was married and owned this brick, 1940s Cape-style house—with its curved entryways and thick plaster walls—with his wife, Francine. Francine had a bump the size of a seedless watermelon protruding from her red sweater. Her hair was swingy and very black, and she smiled like crazy. "Have some wine, lord knows I wish I could," she said, shuttling me off to the kitchen to select a wine and a glass from the huge lineup on the counter. We were all victims of the Pottery Barn culture.

"When are you due?" I asked, trying to make conversation, wanting too quickly to transform from the new person.

"Oh, in March," she said.

"Do you know the sex?" I asked, chose a nice-looking cabernet with a duck swimming by on the label, and poured it into the huge wine glass.

"It's a boy. Lord help us, the world is going to have another one," she said, sliding her hair back over her shoulder with her hand.

"Yeah, men," I said, for lack of anything more original.

"It's funny to see Ray in a relationship," she said, cocking her head and turning sober. "I just hope you don't take it all too seriously, because you never know with him. He's such a Don Juan." She turned around, and when she turned back, she had a tray of small cocktail franks in blankets. "Weenie?" she asked, as if she hadn't just hurled a stake at my heart.

"No thanks," I said and walked back to find Ray. There were too many people all of a sudden, and I wound up in the outer rim of a circle of guys talking about renting a beach house on Long Beach Island. I'd never been there and didn't recognize any of the guys. The one directly in front of me turned and craned his head to see who was breathing on his neck, probably. After a second he turned back around without acknowledging me. I took that as a signal and made my way outside. Though it was cold, I still had my coat. I hadn't bought any gloves yet, though I'd said I would. I held on to the wine with both hands, as if it were a portable heater.

All of a sudden I was overcome with the idea that maybe you were never "better." I loved the vision of Fenwick declaring, "You're all better. Now get the hell outta here, already." I'd see that too-happy ski portrait—the waving hands and the lift rising up the mountain, like it could have come with the frame—one last time and skedaddle.

I'd gone and done everything he'd told me to. I'd changed my life and fallen in love with my best friend and gone and seen my dead father's grave and told myself hundreds of times that I was just fine with having murdered him. But those were tears like raindrops, disturbing the surface of my red wine, all the same. Was I weak and doubtful, impotent as ever?

Someone else's girlfriend, a fellow outsider, came to sit near me. She wasn't horribly friendly. She lit a cigarette. Her long sheet of hair swung back and forth as she fanned the match flame out.

"Great party, huh?" She grimaced, sucked in a giant puff, let it go loudly—so different than Belinda, her refined smoking mannerisms, as if she'd invented it.

"Yeah," I mimicked her tone—sarcastic, condescending.

She looked at me strangely. "Hey, wait. Are you that Anna Walker chick?"

"I was, I guess," I said. No matter how un-fun this party might be, tomorrow I'd be back in New York City without a job—a failure, starting from scratch all over again. I'd have to take all this kindling thought and build it into a raging fire of activity. Could I?

"I'm sorry your column was pulled," she said. "I really enjoyed it."

"Yeah," I said, stupidly.

"But you can do anything. I'm sure you'll be fine. People like you always are."

Something about her tone intrigued me—"As opposed to people like you?" I asked, tenderly.

"Me? I'll never do anything. Believe me, I'd love to, but I'm not exactly what you'd call a go-getter."

Something about this girl was all too familiar. All those months ago, when everything looked so impossible. "Listen," I said. "I've got a story for you . . ."

When I finished speaking with Ingrid Swenson, when I saw that sparkle of hope, that bit of inspiration, I knew for sure that my advice column idea was the right one for me.

When we parted ways, I took a couple of deep breaths, shook my hair out, and went back in to find Ray. "You have to take the risk," Fenwick said in my head, "because there are no guarantees. Even if you stand still, you could still get hurt. That's the unknown we all have to live with in the background."

"Hey there, sexy," Ray said, kissing me—with a sweet-and-sour beer taste. I'd finally found him just where I'd left him. There were no guarantees, but there was this, wonderful this. "I missed you," he said.

"I know you did." My words were topped with hearts.

1:30 p.m., Thursday, December 29

It was odd at first, to enter Christmas, the bar, after we'd just had Christmas, the real thing. Maybe my Christmas hadn't been perfect, but it was real, and mine. This was my last bar. I felt like the *American Idol* loser of the week who had to muster up everything to sing her lungs out, though she knew she'd lost.

There was no publicist meeting me this time. He was away somewhere and didn't feel it was important to come back for me now—since I'd likely be a nobody in a week or two.

I sat with my hot cinnamon cider cocktail, twisting and twisting the warm glass.

"The holidays are hard," people say, and I thought of the significance of that to a place like this, where it's all holidays, all the time.

"Oh, it's so cute in there!"

I was surprised from my thoughts by my mother, returning from the bathroom. I knew she'd love a place named after her very favorite thing on earth. And that is why I called her to meet me there. "What's it look like?"

"Well, there are little angels everywhere, and they've got evergreen air freshener, and the toilet paper holder is a tiny wreath, and antique ornaments are hung all around the mirror."

"That does sound great," I said.

"So how do you feel, now that Christmas is over?" I asked her. She was retired, and her time was free for her to do what she liked.

"Well, Roger and I were talking about taking a vacation . . . to Bora Bora."

"You? Bora Bora!" My mother never went on vacation. Never. And here she was going straight around the world.

"It's just, you seem . . . well, you seem like you can handle things on your own now," she said, growing serious, squeezing my hand.

"You never went away all those years, because of me?" I said.

"You never stop being a mother," she said.

All my blessings, everything, under my nose all along. We went to Bloomingdales, tried on expensive clothing, didn't buy any of it, had a fancy tea at the Plaza, and when we parted, my mother and I didn't say good-bye. We said, "So long. I'll see you next week for outlet shopping."

I met Nina at Maryann's to pick out a bridesmaid dress. Maryann was again in taupe, and her glasses were pushed up on her head like a headband. She and Nina were fussing over rhinestone tiaras like a couple of teenagers.

"What have you got there?" I asked.

"Oh, you've got to try one," said Maryann. "Everyone goes nuts when they put one on." And she stuck one—with pink rhinestone flowers and golden twisted branches and emerald leaves on top of my head, my jacket and Captain bag still on, my face a strawberry patch. I looked like me . . . with a tiara. The pimple on my chin had faded to a faint dot.

"Anna! You are breathtaking," Nina said.

"Absolutely. Just breathtaking," Maryann said.

"She could be next!" Nina cheered, shrugging her shoulders, smiling wildly.

"Is that so?" Maryann had dollar signs in her eyes.

I pulled the tiara's teeth away slowly, said, "Who knows, right?"

and turned around to pull my jacket off, so they wouldn't realize that I wasn't convinced.

But these were women who knew things—Nina knew me, and Maryann knew weddings and the people who do and do not have them.

"What's wrong?!" Nina asked.

"It's just, well, how could it all work? There is so much baggage."

"Oh, that is normal!" Nina said.

"She's right," Maryann said. I guessed now that we'd officially spent money there, she took over this more casual identity. "This is what they call really falling in love—it's reality settling in after the infatuation stage dissipates. It's fitting all the pieces in, the more difficult ones you saved for last. The magical thing is that now you really get to know each other, the real true stuff down inside. And then you love each other even more."

"Remember when I said that thing to you about Bernard a while back?" Nina said.

I nodded. I hated to think of it.

"Well, that was my first encounter with it. And now . . . I don't know, it's like everything is new and refreshed, like a start . . . a more meaningful beginning." She must have meant it, because there were tears and contorted lips, and Maryann was blinking like she wanted to contain emotions, too.

"Here try this one," Maryann suggested of one rosy strapless dress. There'd been three before, and I liked them all. But ultimately it was Nina's choice. I was her doll, and she chose the outfits. Maryann zippered each one up, and if she couldn't, then she pinned it and straightened out the waistline and the hem with her palm. "Beautiful," she said each time. "Just beautiful."

"Yes, that's the one," Nina said. It was a chiffon dress with delicate little layers like rose petals that fluttered all the way down an A-line skirt . . . so beautiful it was almost like a bride's dress itself.

I'd never had something so beautiful on my body, and it was strange to see myself this way in the mirror—no spot on my blouse or undone hem or missing button, just everything as it should be.

She came right up to my face and said, "You are my best friend, Anna, and I love you dearly. Let me buy you this dress." I wasn't going to cry again. I wasn't going to think this was because I had no job and no income and this is what friends did for each other at a time like this. I just gulped loudly and whispered, "Okay."

11:30 a.m., Friday, December 30

"*Weight Watchers* magazine," the woman answered the phone.

"Can I speak with Trudy?" I asked. I'd known this particular editor since I first started working for *New York, New York*.

"Trudy, it's Anna Walker."

"Anna! My dear! I can't believe your column was cut! What can I do for you? Anything . . . you name it."

"Well, I'm going to try to start a new column over there, and I'm looking for a little help generating buzz."

"I like where you're going . . ."

"So, I'm looking to bombard Ed with calls from editors, producers, and advertisers who want to know about Anna's new advice column."

"Anna has a new advice column?"

"If this plan works out, she does."

"Sign me up. I think our readers would love to hear some great advice."

Over the next week, I called Channel 3 News, the local news channel, E! Entertainment, ten magazines, three of Judy's advertisers. I chose the best letters and offered sincere advice. I wrote my own troubles out and solicited advice in return. I set up a website so that I could receive letters instantly in the future. I was exhausted, broke, and nervous, but I felt I was working toward something important. And that kept me going.

THIRTEEN
A New Year

Have you ever gone to a bar alone? Sat there and not participated, but watched, as an observer? Eventually, if you keep yourself there long enough, you'll get pulled in.

— Velvet Rope Diaries, *New York, New York*

7:00 a.m., December 31

It was the last day of the year. I woke up early, jogged around the reservoir in Central Park. It was a "new thing" Ray and I were trying—something we started together—a shared experience that's ours alone. I left Ray, matted and sweaty in the shirt he'd picked up off his bedroom floor, at the subway station, and headed downtown to Nina's. The sun was just up, and I could hear the wind howling at the old wood frame windows alongside her kitchen table. A garbage truck backed up with a *beep, beep, beep,* and then I heard the empty clanging of its back end lowering to take in the trash. The thing is, all your trash has to go somewhere.

I knew where, too. Thomas worked at a garbage recycling plant after high school, and he'd once told me about a woman who'd come in frenzied, looking for her wedding ring, which she said she'd thrown in the trash accidentally. Thomas tried to tell her, "There's no way you're going to find it in all that trash." But she'd insisted he let her in the square-mile room, where they keep the trash until it was ready to be burned and converted into energy. When he took her there, he said, she just looked in at all of it—everyone's trash piled so wide and so high and mixed in like that—and said, "Oh."

The thing is, the pieces of yourself can seem meaningless among all that other stuff from everyone else. And the woman lost hope and turned around to try and forget about her ring.

I'd always thought that a very sad story, but now I realize there's a good side to it. It means there are so many people, with so much garbage, there's got to be someone's garbage you can learn from.

One of the garbage men yelled, "All done, Ronnie!" and I could hear the truck putt away.

"Morning, Glory," Nina said, her head poking around the door.

She was in a bathrobe, her hair wet, makeup on. Her mouth looked too bright like that—false or something.

"Morning," I said, sitting up.

"Bernard made some pancakes if you want breakfast."

"He's a real keeper, huh?" I asked.

"Yeah." She smiled.

"What's your plan for the day?" I asked. Later, we were going to a fancy formal party at The Four Seasons restaurant. I'd been personally invited by one of the owners. He'd called me and cooed in his Italian accent, "Please, darling, come and spend New Year's with us."

"Well, first thing, I'm handing in my letter of resignation," she said. "And then at lunch, Susan and I are choosing the sink fixtures."

10:30 a.m.

Afterward, I went to Bloomingdale's to buy some gloves and a hat. Right away the puff of warm air comforted me. This is the kind of place, with all its beautiful takes on life, that can make you feel good, no matter what. A pretty, neat woman in a white snap lab coat and black pants and heels sweetly asked, "Would you like to try some Love Yourself by Selvin Krein?" Her eyes were blinky and her mouth soft. She pulled my sleeve up just a bit and pressed the atomizer. Sweet lilac and currant came at me, through my senses and up, up toward the escalators where the clothing was. *You'd better not open that door,* David had said, at Fashionable, when I'd worn the Selvin Krein.

"Thank you," I said. This is a place that always amazes me. I passed by all the glass cases, with their potions, their colorful beads, back to the hat and scarf corner.

There were lots of sale signs over the chrome, T-shaped racks. There was a muzak version of *Hey Nineteen* playing as I pulled a brimmed green cashmere hat over my head. The matching gloves hung just beneath where the hat had been—in between a zebra print and a funny stripe. I pulled those on, too, and looked around for a mirror. There was a little girl looking in that mirror at herself in the very same hat I had on. Her hair was very thin, just a whisper of curls around the back of her head, and the ends slightly pecked out below the brim. Her father was to the side, looking in the mirror at her. The hat covered her face, and she sang precociously, "I can't see, I can't see, oh dear me, I cannot see." The father chuckled, snorted once. "I might be able to help you with that," he said and crouched down to her height. I watched them in the mirror and in real life, both, just three feet away.

He pulled the hat down in the back, folded the brim up, so that she could see him and we could see her. And she was semi-toothless with one dimple way up in the very middle of her left cheek. Her eyes were that shade of blue that might one day change to a brown or hazel, so that someone might feel compelled to claim, "Oh, she had the bluest eyes when she was a little girl. We thought they would never change."

She looked back, to me. "Dad, she's got the same hat. She's wearing the same hat as me." The dad looked at me, and I am not sure what happened, but I didn't want that hat any longer. I wanted to just remember it on that little girl, with her three fragile teeth popped a bit above her lower lip, and keep it at that. I finally went for a purple beret, which wasn't all that warm and kept flopping off to one side. The gloves had slight stripes of pink woven through.

On the way home, with the wind testing the limits of my poorly fit beret, I thought I might be someone new in this getup. And when people looked at me—once an older man in a belted coat and neat attaché case in his grasp, and later, a slender woman in a charcoal pantsuit waiting impatiently to cross the street—I felt they saw it, too. They, too, saw that I could go forward now, that I had let something go for good, and that my life would be very different . . . no matter what it might bring.

FOURTEEN

Survive

"The best and worst night of the year is New Year's Eve," said the owner of Cream and Sugar. Everyone's so excited to be there, but in the end, it's just a night like any other. People don't get that they bring the magic to us, not the other way around.

—Velvet Rope Diaries, New York, New York

8:00 p.m., New Year's Eve!

It was New Year's Eve, and I would probably have been more depressed about being unemployed if we hadn't started drinking champagne early. But I'm not so sure. Things seem to have a way of working out, I found—care of a lifetime fairy godmother or therapy, or working really hard, or something like that.

As soon as I approached the door of Susan and Nina's spa, I felt all tingly. This was something great. You could just tell. The sign was tiny—no bigger than five feet by two feet. But it was all hand painted, in a heavy gold frame. It said, "Susan and Nina's," in curly cursive. A mural was brushed in with sweeping strokes behind the words—an Italian looking landscape with those narrow, triangle trees and lots of orange and goldenrod. It was the kind of sign that made you want to rush right in, see what it was all about.

I rang the number three buzzer, which was clearly marked.

"Who *is* it?" Susan's voice rang out.

"It's your first customer," I sing-songed. "And she's freezing to death, so let her up!" My legs bounced up and down at the knee. I held a plastic dry cleaner bag containing my outfit—the dress given to me at Fashionable.

Bzzzzzzz! The two of them had me in either arm, and like that they walked me through the different areas of the spa. I had to use a lot of imagination, because it wasn't quite done yet. There was lots of dry wall and bare wood planks for floors, and wires twisted out of different areas of the ceiling and walls. But there was soft music, the boring string quartet kind that Nina was planning on for her wedding . . . but it worked in here, quite nicely, too.

"This is the first massage room," Nina said.

"There are going to be five like this one," Susan explained. "And we are having strictly male massage therapists. Hot ones," she said.

"That sounds like a good plan," I said.

She walked over to the wall to show me the scrap of wallpaper hanging there. It was a simple pale blue stripe. "We're only going to have it on the top half of the wall. Then there will be a strip of white molding and underneath that, the wall will be white bead board. And then all the upholstery will be this toile." She held up a swatch of fabric that looked like a farm scene—women holding eggs in their aprons, children playing in a nearby field, men toiling with crops.

"The beds are going to have seven hundred-thread-count Egyptian cotton coverings and featherbeds that heat up. You can control the heat with this remote," she said, shaking a long, technical-looking gadget with an infrared dot at the top. "It also vibrates." Susan winked at the both of us naughtily when she said that.

They walked me through the facial rooms and the wet treatment room with the Vichy shower. We toured where the private dressing room would be and looked at all the Chanel samples that would be used as amenities at the sinks and showers . . . as well as in the treatment rooms.

"Trick or treat," Nina said, dumping a handful into my palms. There must have been sixty bucks worth of creams and gels in there. It was all so high class. "Your friend Nina here's a genius," Susan said. "A freaking genius. She thought of everything."

Nina smiled, raised her glass, and replied, "No, you're the genius, Susan, truly."

"Yeah, you're right," she joked. Her hair was in rollers, big purple ones, strapped on with long silver duck clips—like a bunch of hollow grapes.

We had our hair done by Susan's personal stylist, Christopher. He swooped my perm into bigger, fuller waves, pulled the sides back with pretty combs. As I saw the combs catch the light, I tried not to feel downhearted, or think about things I didn't have with all of this amazing good fortune around me. "A beautiful look," he said.

"Tell me about it, Christopher . . . tell me about it," I said, though I didn't know why.

"Wow," I said, when I looked at myself in the mirror. It was unbelievable to me how I looked. Again, here, I was someone new. I looked like someone who knew things, who people might trust and respect and ask things like, "Now, how many cups are in two quarts?" I hoped the feeling would last, the confidence that I truly could help people, would last. I would make my column a reality, somehow. I knew that.

I couldn't help but think of the way I'd gotten dressed on that LYMJ night—everything in my closet strewn on the floor, my purse missing vital contents, the crazy jacket I'd put together. I'd been operating on half a brain, a quarter of a brain . . . and yet, somehow, amazingly, I'd gotten there and now here. I think I'd known all along that the whole thing couldn't last, wouldn't last. Sure, I could be titled and added to a list, but wasn't I just Anna? Despite how different I looked, how different I felt, without the title and the name on the list, who would I be now? I didn't know for sure, but I did know one thing . . . I wasn't going to spend my life looking for the magic clues to happiness, the mysterious symbols that would mean forgiveness. Instead, I would accept what I had and do with it what I could. Maybe it wasn't the rosiest outlook, but it was realistic and practical, and most importantly . . . it would work.

10:00 p.m.

The line at The Four Seasons was longer than a book by Herman Melville. Susan's driver pulled us out of the car gracefully, as if we were in a black-and-white film. Waiting for us like the rat pack were Bernard and Ray and one of Bernard's friends we were fixing Susan up with.

They were an imposing trio, standing there in tuxedos—all crisp black-and-white and shiny shoes and hair.

"My little meat lasagna," Ray teased when I snuggled into him, against the cold. It was impossible now to deny the things that tied us, always would. We were solid together. "Why don't we just skip this party and go right to the midnight kiss that leads to much, much more?"

When one of Ray's looks, when his words, the way the corners of his lips glided when he said them, got me, I tried not to let myself think how many other girls his words might have gotten this way. It wasn't important. What was important was us—this, now. Not that it all be perfect, but that it just be.

"Susan, this is Carl," Bernard made the introduction. "He works with me over at my day job at Goldman," he said. "He's from International Trading."

"Nice to meet you, Carl from International Trading," she cooed. And whether it was the champagne, or the plan to use men for sex, or interviewing all those sexy masseurs, we didn't know, but Susan leaned right in and kissed Carl like she meant it.

When they pulled apart, he said, "And it's *very* nice to meet you, Miss Susan, *very* nice." He was a little shorter than Ray, with lighter hair. He had puffy lips and a slightly off-kilter nose that worked well with his other features. His bow tie had a pattern of little champagne flutes klinking elegantly. Susan fingered it, looked him in the eye, and then turned to me. "So, you going to get us in or what?"

The funny thing was, now that I didn't have the column, I was more confident than I'd been when I had it. I had called earlier and spoke with Stephano Bertolini—the notoriously flirty co-owner of the landmark restaurant—to make sure we were still VIPs worthy of the New Year's Eve invitations, now that I didn't have my column.

"Anna Walker, darling beautiful thing, tortellini of my eye! What can Stephano do for you, my ricotta cannoli?" He'd nearly eaten me whole through the telephone.

I hate to admit this, but I am sort of taken by the way Stephano talks. He's older, but very persuasive and elegant. Though we were on the phone, I felt my cheeks flush. Finally, I said, "Well, I was just wondering if we were still invited to the party tonight . . . you know . . . with my column being canceled."

"Oh, *Madre Mia*! How could you even ask that horrid, horrid question, my little meat lasagna?"

I couldn't help but snigger. A *meat lasagna*?

"I just didn't know . . . it's well . . . it's such a transient thing, this kind of status."

"You see, that's just it. That's just what I like about you. It's called . . . humility. You see my dear espresso with lemon rind, I have been in this business a very, very long time—I held the arm of Miss Marylin Monroe, I dined with Jackie Kennedy and the Prince of Wales! And the columns! They have come and gone more times than a tray of marzipan cookies at Balducci's! It's the people, Anna. I stay loyal to the wonderful people with the instincts. Those are the people over time that you want to know."

And when my mind traveled that familiar path: "I'm not really wonderful; it's just that he doesn't know the truth," I didn't follow it there. Instead, I just stayed here, walked to the front of the line with my friends, past all the people waiting and wondering if they were good enough, if they'd worn the right shoes and chosen the right bag, freezing and pulling their pashminas and mink stoles in tightly—insecure as myself, as all of us really. We walked to the very origin, where the sinister clipboard was in custody of giant sausage fingers, just waiting to crush someone's evening.

As we came closer, I heard a familiar cry. It was a woman's voice, and it was burned and smoldering and desperate, yelling, "Do you know who I *am*?" I hated to hear such a thing, hated to see someone resort to such terrible, demeaning behavior.

I was coming closer now, and I heard a male voice say, "You'll have to step aside, miss, you'll just have to step aside." And then I heard the woman's voice again. I looked up to the face that went with the rejected woman, and I couldn't believe my eyes! Standing there in a sparkly dress, so skinny on the sideview she was nearly invisible, was . . . Nasty! And she was being manhandled by the clipboard wielder with the sausage fingers. I nearly fell right over at my opportunity to put us on even footing, to say well screw you right back!

And the best part about it was that sausage fingers was none other than Mr. LYMJ himself! The crazy thing was, he didn't recognize me. He didn't say one word, lift one eyebrow. He simply asked, "Name?"

"Anna Walker," I said, shocked, clutching Ray and my purse for dear life. I turned my head as I said it, and I looked long and hard at Nasty. She was as beautiful and miserable as she'd ever been, shivering—a white cashmere shawl around her shoulders, sequins poking out from beneath. I knew I couldn't do it. It wasn't me. And if I'd learned anything, it was that I might be the only thing I can count on.

"Ah yes, right here . . . party of six, by the fountain?" The Cararra marble tub is an awesome landmark, and to be invited there is an honor.

"Actually, we're seven," I said. Before she could say a word, I grabbed Nasty's hand, and held its frigid toothpick fingers tight, like I meant it, which I did—but honestly, only to kill her with kindness. I do realize that little good piece of her is not nearly as profound as I'd expected it to be before—because mostly, she chose not to use it. Maybe it had been larger, but from lack of use, it had atrophied. Or maybe she'd had it surgically removed. But I wasn't about to follow her example. I kissed her on the cheek and said, "Happy New Year's, Miss Jackson."

"Please," she said, shocking us all. "Call me Elizabeth."

Once we were inside, Elizabeth didn't stick around to ring in the New Year with us, to talk about my future plans and how pretty the lump crab looked wrapped in a palm leaf that way. Immediately, she ran to meet Christopher, who was supposed to be in there somewhere. Of course we all wondered why she hadn't been on the list if they were still together, but if there was news, I was sure I'd read about it tomorrow.

We settled ourselves in the most fabulous seats, right alongside the fountain, like a dream . . . a very glamorous dream, and drank wines from the Rhone Valley that must have cost a fortune or two, at least.

★ ★ ★

"Ten, nine, eight, seven, six, five, four, three, two, one...
Happy New Year!" I sang it loud, louder than I'd ever sung it before,
until my throat burned and bits of spittle formed at the corners of
my mouth. Ray held the kind of noisemaker you crank around and
around, and he twisted it and twisted it. I blew a horn directly in his
face. We were both somewhat drunk. We sat on the side of the pool,
and everyone else was close.

"Do you trust me?" Ray asked, that sparkle in his eye just that
much sparklier.

"I do," I said, unaware of what I was getting myself into, but
knowing this regardless: I had to trust him, or there was no point.

He smirked, scooped me up under my butt, and stepped over the
side into the pool.

"What? What are you doing?" I was yelling and waving my
arms as if I were guiding a plane in, trying to get away, though really it was fun, a thrill, something you can do and later say, "Yeah,
that was really living." He stood me up, and we were both soaked
from the thighs down. People cheered us on, yelling their heads off
and whistling, throwing confetti bits our way like Thanksgiving
Day Parade onlookers along Fifth Avenue. One guy screamed, "Get
naked!"

"Happy New Year, Anna," Ray said, ripples fanning out from
our bodies to the ends of the pool, splashing gently over the edge.
He said it seriously. And though the moment seemed anything but,
it was all very serious. It was a serious way of saying you're alive and
well, and you're going to start it out right from here on. It was a
wet, freezing, chic, oath to squeeze every last bit out of your life going forward.

"Happy New Year, Ray," I replied. And as we kissed, my back

dipped down so the ends of my hair got wet, weighed down.

There were pictures. I knew that from the flashes and clicks. But mainly, it felt good. Despite everything, it felt real good. We were alive, in the middle of life and living it, like two nut bags in a pool in the middle of the winter—we were alive and well.

"Tell them about the column, Anna!" Susan yelled, indicating the journalists.

"Yeah! What column, Anna?"

They asked, and I told. A very smart yogi once said you have to turn a negative into a positive, and that's exactly what I did.

7:00 a.m., January 1

My phone rang.

"Hello?" I droaned, dry as the Sahara.

"Anna, it's Ed."

"Ed? Ed who?" I said, confused and still half asleep.

"Ed, the Ed! Listen, I saw the pictures in the paper and all the publicity. Also there was Elizabeth's confession. And so I want to give you that column. Do whatever the hell you want. To tell you the truth all the damn numbers have gone down since you left anyhow. You're nuts, Anna, but you know how to put together a newspaper. And without Joseph we're going to need a new executive editor, too."

"What do you mean 'without Joseph?'"

"I fired him! And Elizabeth, too! What they did to all of us! Pathetic! From now on, I make all my decisions only after running them by Rima *and* you."

"Hey, Ed, I've got a great replacement for Elizabeth."

"Oh, yeah? You're quick! Who's that?"

"Belinda!"

"My secretary! She's too good!"

"I know. That's why she needs to be more than your secretary."

"Alright. I'll just run it by Rima."

"Great! One more thing . . ."

"What's that?"

"Can I finally get that raise now?"

"Not a chance."

"All righty, then! See you on Monday!"

Monday, January 16

"It's the anniversary of my father's death," I said to Fenwick. "Twenty-two years today," I said.

I loved that Fenwick never asked me, "How do you feel about that?" Instead he said, "A day like every other one . . . to get through and face the reality of, have lunch—"

I cut him off. "Stand in line at the bank, stock up on toilet paper."

He smiled. I'd learned things.

Today, I felt, was a milestone for me. I told Fenwick a story from a while ago, from when Ray and I had first come to live in Manhattan, and the subway seemed too loud and sinister—a tangle of lines and colors that could accidentally land you in Queens or Brooklyn if you weren't careful.

"I was just looking for a job, and I followed a lead—some friend of Nina's who knew of a job at a magazine. At the interview I'd blanked completely, couldn't remember what qualifications I'd had—none, really!—I couldn't remember the three positive things about myself that I should come back to when I had no other answers. At the end of the interview, the tall, thin man had said, 'Well, do you have any other questions?' and I'd shook my head, knowing, obviously I hadn't gotten the job."

I was surprised, that though I willed myself not to, I choked up and had to grab for a wad of tissues from the box at the side table.

"It's not surprising, Anna, that your worst anxieties came popping up when you needed them to go away most," Fenwick said. "Now, though, you'd know what to say to those anxieties." It was true, I knew just how to keep myself balanced between the two worlds, solder them together so that I could exist in the two places at once.

After the interview, I had to take the four train up to 86th, and I was so filled with embarrassment at how vacant I must have seemed at the meeting, I was so filled with guilt about my father, that I could barely see. I was listening to an old Hole CD that had a tough edge. The edge didn't rub off on me. *"Don't make me over. I'm all I wanna be."* I will stop thinking this, I thought. *"It's all so sugarless . . ."* I will stop thinking this at 34th Street. *"So glad you could make it nowwwww."* I will stop thinking it at 59th Street. At 77th. The CD had ended, and I hadn't even realized. "Next stop 125th Street," the conductor crackled over the P.A. system. I'd missed my stop! This was so stupid! And now I was in a neighborhood my mother would scream at me for coming to! It was just the kind of thing she'd said to dissuade me from moving here in the first place. She'd said, "Anna, knowing you, you'll wander off on the train and wind up lost!" It was true! I had! I'd done just that, though my mother had warned me.

The platform at 125th Street was empty. The downtown train came whooshing through on the opposite side, and I waited there with my hands in my sweater pockets. It was summer, and I had a light cardigan on, buttoned only at the top. Up the stairs, there was a scattering of footsteps, and then a woman who must have been fifteen months pregnant appeared, breathy, holding a little boy at her side. He looked about five and had a crew cut like a military boy, though the yellow chick on his T-shirt betrayed that this was probably not the case.

It was just the three of us there. We all sat on the bench eventually, and the boy's fleshy arm swung out in my direction, the exaggerated motions of his fingers like a scientist's, carefully curling and reaching.

"Chica! You have pretty hair!" The boy shouted each sentence, testing his voice, letting the sound echo through the tunnel and back at us, again, again. He pulled one of the longer sections of my hair away from my scalp. He was adorable, this boy. And I remember wishing that I would give anything to be him, to be filled with the possibility and not the regret, to not have this huge crate to carry around and around all day, so that every task was exhausting and impossible as a trip to the moon."

Fenwick uncrossed his legs and pulled his mouth, eyes, nose in tight. We'd been on a long journey, Fenwick and I, and here was real evidence of that—this going back and producing proof.

I continued on. "Chica!" he said it again, smiled—toothy—and finally sprang free and ran behind the bench to hide. His mother didn't yell, only smiled, as if helpless against his child cuteness, that potent drug.

The train arrived with a rumble and seemed too fast, like it wouldn't stop in time. But it did. It slowed suddenly, jerky, and the doors opened, and the boy and his mother didn't get on. They sat and waited, and the boy waved at me like mad through the window, his teeth like old tombstones—growing in this way and that."

That, finally, was the end of my story. It had no conclusion, really. And so I had to clarify. "I, well, I hopped like that—from wishing I was that boy and then a woman answering ten calls at a front desk, saying, 'Front desk, please hold,' like she meant it, and then a spunky salesgirl at Banana Republic, who could really get away with wearing colors, as if it meant the world to her."

Fenwick had a new photo displayed. In it, his two kids looked older. The daughter's hair was cut shorter, in layers, the way haircutters tend to do when a girl reaches a certain age, cutting in all kinds of maturity at this angle and that. She smiled more self-consciously, like she thought pictures were stupid, like she had better things to do and had just said, "Da—*ad*!"

I didn't have a picture like that with my dad, with him hugging me, and me kind of squirming away, because we hadn't been able to get that far. We were forever frozen in mutual idol worship. I saw that now. And if that was the only choice I had, then maybe it wasn't so bad.

Monday, February 13

Yesterday, my mother and I went to Saks Fifth Avenue for lunch, the way Nina and her mom normally did, but without the "magic number" mind trips. We had the best time sharing both the turkey club with extra mayo and the tuna salad with extra pickles and then a slice of apple pie with extra ice cream.

She slept over, and we made Ray stay in his old bedroom, and we stayed up all night watching *Terms of Endearment* over and over again. And I kept thinking, *Boy, I am glad I am not going to die*. I didn't tell my mother that, but she cried so much I thought she might have known. Right when it was over, we pressed "rewind," and then we went through it all over again.

"Is everything okay in there?" Ray kept asking and asking that so much that eventually we let him come in and sit with us on the bed, and then it was the three of us blubbering like infants. Only, when we went to pass Ray a tissue, he sobered up and said, "For what?"

Wednesday, February 22

Every single day new letters arrive. I can't even get to them all. The crazy thing is, although, of course, I miss the royal treatment I got during the bar reviews, I enjoy this so much more. I get these letters, and I connect with these people, and it's like something inside of *me* feels better. Of course I would never say that to Theresa. I'm afraid it's a little un-chic. For me crossing the velvet rope had been more of an emotional journey than a physical one; my journey into the high life served the purpose of helping me to understand the life I already had. Also, I got a lot of cool stuff and discovered I really like foie gras and look good in a perm.

10:00 a.m., Saturday, April 8

By the time her mom arrived at the bridal suite, Nina was more than two glasses of Chardonnay ready to handle the commentary. "Nina, you really should have had the wedding in the country. The traffic was ridiculous!" And "Nina, maybe you could have waited until May when it's warmer."

Nina just flashed a tight-lipped smile and said, "More wine please!"

The service was beautiful. The priest remembered both of their names perfectly—which greatly improves a wedding, just ask my cousin Meredith—and they lit the Unity candle without the flame going out or growing into a three-alarm fire.

When the choir sang that song, "When a man must leave his mother, and a woman leave her home," Ray looked up at me on the altar, silently delivering an operatic version with mouth open wide. I laughed out loud but turned it into a cough—I think discreetly enough. We always thought it was a funny, archaic song, but now that I think about it, it does hold a bold, big truth—a man must leave his mother and a woman leave her home. That is the way—stripped of all its terrors and confusion and false starts and near misses. It had been played at Ray's sister's wedding, but what did that mean now? Did it mean anything at all? Dare we try with all the track records heavy on our backs?

Nina's childhood dog, Trevor, trotted the ring up the aisle on a pillow saddled over his back, to thunderous applause, a "You go dog!" and a few fancy whistles.

And when they kissed, for that first time, as husband and wife, I saw so clearly, in the tiny sunlit bits of dust swirling up around them, something I hadn't seen in many, many years. Though I'm not a religious girl, I looked up to the stained glass windows and their desperate story that is supposed to depict—ultimately—our salvation. And I didn't have any great revelation or find any great truth. But I thought, wasn't it striking that all of that pain and suffering was right up there on those windows, lighting up the face of my lovely friend at the best moment of her life?

"I now pronounce you man and wife," the priest said.

And I saw the glimmer of hope in that.

And we all roared and hooted and streamed tears, because right there with all the pain, life can sometimes be quite beautiful.

Dear Anna,

I think I might be in love with my best friend, but I'm not sure if it is a good idea to risk our friendship by venturing into romantic territory. What do you think I should do?

Sincerely,

Cindy Roberts

Dear Cindy,

Life is all about risks. The most wonderful rewards are all waiting on the other side of the mountain. Somehow, we all have to find the courage to climb it.

Best,

Anna

Dear Anna,

I am writing from the National Syndication Company. We produce columns that are syndicated in hundreds of newspapers across the United States. We would like to speak with you about turning "Dear Anna" into a nationally syndicated column. We will outbid any competitors. Also, we have enclosed a letter about a small private matter "we'd" like to ask your advice on.
Sincerely,
Douglas Penningman
Executive Editor
National Syndication Company

Dear Anna,

It absolutely killed me when you of all people got me into the Four Seasons on New Year's Eve. But I've been doing some soul-searching since Christopher broke things off, and I wanted to apologize and ask if you had any advice for someone who's grown stagnant and can't seem to make things happen for herself.
Best,
Elizabeth Jackson

Dear Anna,

This is Ms. Jackson's former assistant. I am sorry I called you a bitch. It turns out I didn't need to stay there. That it would be no one's fault but mine if I did. I left and on a lark applied for a photographer's assistant job. I love it. Thanks.
Yours Truly,
Cynthia Johnson

Dear Cynthia,

That is wonderful news! It's always that first step that's the most difficult. After that, it's just the rest of your life you've got to get though.

Best,

Anna